HECTOR

Books by Elizabeth Reyes:

Moreno Brothers Series
    Forever Mine
    Forever Yours
    Always Been Mine
    Sweet Sophie
    Romero
    Making You Mine

5th Street Series
    Noah
    Gio
    Hector
    Abel

Fate Series
    Fate
    Breaking Brandon

Desert Heat Series
    Desert Heat

HECTOR

(5th Street #3)

Elizabeth Reyes

Hector

Elizabeth Reyes

Copyright © 2013

All Rights Reserved

This book is a work of fiction. Names, characters, places, and incidents are products of the author's imagination or are used fictitiously. Any resemblance to actual events or locales or persons, living or dead, is entirely coincidental.

The scanning, uploading and distribution of this book via the internet or any other means without the permission of the publisher is illegal and punishable by law Please purchase only authorized electronic editions, and do not participate in or encourage electronic piracy of copyrighted materials. Your support of the author's rights is appreciated.

Cover art by Ashley from The Bookish Brunette and Claudia from PhatPuppyArt

Editing by Theresa Wegand

To Mark II. Your extraordinary gift for the game of chess and funny stories about the chess club sparked another story plot. Thanks for the laughs! Love you.

PROLOGUE

As he approached his locker, Hector could see that the drama going on all week wasn't over. It was really starting to get old. Lisa, a girl whose locker was a few lockers down from Hector's, had been having *issues* with her boyfriend. Apparently that past weekend after an argument, her boyfriend, who was drunk and mad, posted something about her on his Facebook status, and it was the talk of the school.

Hector neither cared nor bothered to ask anyone what the idiot posted. All he knew was he was forced to be witness to their constant bickering all week because the dumb ass was trying to beg her back and she wasn't having it. What sucked is they did it right there by his locker, and usually they had small crowd listening in on their arguing. It was *so* stupid.

Today the crowd was bigger than the norm, and Hector could hear that the argument was a bit more escalated. Even hearing her boyfriend's angry accusatory tone when he spoke to her now, Hector had every intention of staying out of it as he had all week.

Ironically, Lisa had been someone he'd been interested in getting to know a little better the previous semester. He wasn't sure if it was because she was the new girl to his school or because she was quiet and shy, but she'd sparked an interest. Most of the girls he knew had been going to his school the entire four years and were loud and anything but shy about flirting with him. There'd been something refreshing about Lisa's timid smiles.

As usual, by the time Hector would so much as consider getting to know a girl for real, not just think about getting in her pants, she started seeing someone else. He was never one to move in on another guy's girl. His brother Abel said,

"There are too many girls out there to be fighting over one," so Hector left well enough alone.

Lisa had been seeing this guy now for months. Up until this week, as far as Hector knew, things between them had been peachy. For the most part all week, Hector would overhear their arguments while he got whatever he needed out of his locker but only because it was inevitable. Not so much Lisa but her boyfriend was one of those persons that didn't care who heard his business. He'd argue with her loudly no matter who was around. In fact, Hector got the feeling he enjoyed the attention. Today, he was louder than he'd been all week, and with his friends there laughing and egging him on, he got even louder.

From what Hector could see as he walked up to his locker, she wasn't even looking at him. She was staring into her locker as he stood behind her, demanding something. "Move," Hector said to the guys blocking his locker, and they did immediately.

As annoying as it was that she was obviously uncomfortable with the attention her idiot boyfriend was getting, Hector was still going to mind his own business and not say or do anything.

"Just admit it," her boyfriend said. "You were skyping with his ass all night, right? Why not just text if it was such a friendly conversation? Huh?"

Lisa was ignoring him. If she did respond, Hector hadn't heard it. The banging on the locker forced Hector to pay attention. Annoyed, he turned to see the guy's fist against the locker next to Lisa's. She'd finally looked up and was facing her boyfriend now, but that wasn't good enough for the punk. He got in her face all menacingly as if she were another guy. "Admit it. Did you show him your tits?" He got even closer to her now, and she tried to back up, but the guys behind her were too close. "Did you? You skank!"

Instantly on fire, Hector slammed his locker shut and pushed the few guys in his way aside. Without giving it so much as a thought, he grabbed the guy by the hair and slammed his face into the locker right next to Lisa's more than once. "You think you're a tough guy talking to your girl like that!"

Now, the crowd, which had closed in so much that Lisa hadn't been able to move, backed up real fast. Just as Hector suspected, there was absolutely no fighting back from her boyfriend. Hector lifted the guy's bloodied face away from the lockers and turned him to face his stunned friends. "He look like such a tough guy now?"

None of them said anything, and not one of them so much as stepped up to try and help her boyfriend either. Hector threw him against the locker, this time letting him go. "Get in *my* face, tough guy!" He took a step closer to the guy. Seeing the guy brace himself only pissed Hector off more. "Or is that something you only do to girls, you fucking pussy?"

Luckily for the guy, in the next instant, Hector himself was pushed up against the lockers by school security as was Lisa's boyfriend. They were both hauled into the dean's office.

As much as it sucked since he knew this was grounds for suspension, Hector had a feeling his brother Abel would go easy on him for this one. All Hector would have to do is defy his brother to stand there and watch a guy get in a girl's face the way this asshole had and not do anything about it.

Months Later

By the time Hector looked up, Vanessa was too close for him to tell his friend A.J. to be cool. The huge mole that covered half of her cheek had always been a draw for cruel jokes, and A.J. had one of the biggest mouths in school.

"Morning, Spot." A.J. waved at Vanessa, who after all these years had gotten pretty good about playing it off like she didn't care.

She ignored him and kept walking past them.

Hector shoved A.J as they reached the top of the stairs to their school entrance. "Why do you have to be such an asshole?"

A.J. laughed. "What? That's what everyone calls her."

Before Hector could respond, a commotion by the front entrance caught their attention. "Check out nerd boy's toy robot."

Two of Hector's other friends, Raymond and Theo, were playing keep-away from Walter, a heavyset awkward guy who was in a few of his A.P. classes and someone they'd been picking on forever. Walter tried in vain to get it back. Walter's eyes met Hector's for a moment.

In class, the guy was nice enough, even on the funny side, but Hector didn't talk to him outside of class, not that Hector wouldn't if Walter ever attempted to. He just seemed to disappear in between classes. This, no doubt, was probably the reason. The guy was overweight, hadn't a fashion clue, and was a social disaster. He may as well have a "kick me" note permanently posted on his back.

But Hector remembered hearing about the impressive chemical-smelling robot Walter had built for the science fair earlier that year, which not only won first prize in the district but had qualified to enter the national event in a few weeks.

Holding up his hands and laughing wickedly, A.J. caught the *toy robot* Theo tossed him. *Geez!* Hector's brother, Abel was right. Maybe Hector *did* need to get some new friends.

A.J. motioned to Hector, about to toss the robot his way, but Hector frowned, shaking his head. He was about to tell them to give it back to Walter when he felt a soft tug on his arm.

He turned to see Lisa standing there smiling at him. Her pretty brown eyes sparkled, making him forget all about Walter. "I wasn't even going to come today because I figured there was no need to." She bit her lip, glancing away for a second then looked back in his eyes. "But I couldn't leave without saying goodbye to you."

Surprised by the overwhelming disappointment he immediately felt, the fact that she'd come by just to say goodbye to *him* didn't even register. "Goodbye? Where you going?"

The sparkle in her eyes faded a little, and she cleared her throat but then smiled again and shook her head. "It's a long story. I'm gonna go live with my grandparents up north now."

"But you just moved here." He insisted.

After his suspension a few months ago, he'd come back to school to find out she and her boyfriend, who Hector now knew as Jairo, had broken up. But it was weeks before Hector's dumb ass began considering the possibility of getting to know her a bit better. There'd been something about those haunting dark eyes of hers that had made him put it off for too long.

Lisa lifted a shoulder. "Like I said, it's a long story. Maybe someday I can tell you about it in an email or something, but for now, I just wanted to say goodbye."

Loud cackles brought Hector's attention back to the guys heckling Walter. He turned just in time to see them all rush into the main building, and he hoped that maybe that meant a teacher would see them and put an end to their harassing Walter. At the moment, he couldn't tear himself away from Lisa.

"Well, that sucks." He shrugged. "I mean I don't know the details: maybe this *is* a good thing for you, but I think it sucks that you're leaving."

The sparkle was back in her eyes. Hector couldn't help but smile, wishing he could touch her, even if it was only for a second. She glanced away for a moment, giving him a chance to openly admire that dark, almost black, long hair he'd begun to have visions of running his fingers through and maybe putting his face against.

Before he could ask anything more, she took a step forward and hugged him. Taking advantage of the moment, he did the very thing he was hoping he could and pulled her to him, burying his face in the side of her neck. Her hair felt as soft and smelled as perfect as he thought it would.

"I'll miss you," she whispered in his ear.

Hector didn't want to let go. "I'll miss you too," he whispered back.

She began to pull away, forcing him to loosen his hold on her until they were facing each other. Damn. He wanted to kiss her now. Why the hell had he taken so long to get to know her? This sucked big time.

"When do you leave?"

"Tonight."

"How come," he paused, knowing he really didn't have any right to be upset. It was his own damn fault he'd been so slow to get things going with her and they'd barely gotten to the talking-often-and-texting stage. But damn it, he wanted to know now. "How come you hadn't mentioned this before?"

"I just found out a few days ago, and, even then, it was iffy. But it's a done deal now."

She stood on her tiptoes and kissed his cheek. To hell with it. Hector turned his face and pecked her on the lips. He knew he'd stunned her, but he'd at least get that much out of this. For weeks, he'd been taking it slow and was really beginning to think he wanted so much more with her. Now this may very well be his last chance. To his surprise, she pecked him back. It took him a second to get his thoughts together, but he brought his arm around her waist, pulling her in and really kissed her this time. It was soft and sweet but enough to warm his insides and begin to ignite other parts of his body, and then she pulled away a bit breathless.

"I'm," she looked away, licking her lips, "I'm sorry we didn't get more time together, Hector. I thought I regretted it before, but now I really do. Maybe someday we'll meet again."

Feeling an unexpected ache in his heart, he forced a smile. "Yeah, I'm sorry too, but never say never. It's a small world. We may just meet again someday."

She smiled and nodded. "You have my number. Text me or call me whenever you want."

"I will." He stood there, his jaw tightly clenched as she walked away, thinking back to the day he'd finally *really* noticed her—the day he'd gotten back to school after being suspended.

He thought he'd noticed her before she got a boyfriend, but that was the first day she'd actually spoken to him, and that was to thank him for what he'd done. Even though she didn't have to, she'd also explained about the skype chat Jairo had been so pissed about. After chatting with a friend from her old school, her friend thanked her for the chat by posting an image of a bouquet of flowers on her Facebook wall. When Jairo's stupid friends saw the post, it went viral.

Admittedly, though Hector dare not tell her, he probably would've been a little pissed himself had he been her boyfriend. But no way would he have acted the way Jairo did, and he certainly wouldn't have made a public stink out of it.

The warning bell rang, pulling Hector out of his Lisa thoughts, and he remembered Walter. Suddenly feeling a little worried, he hurried to the front doors of the school building they'd all gone into. There was no way those idiots realized they were messing with the science project that would be representing their school in the national contest.

With no sign of any of them as he entered the main building, he hoped that was a good thing. Hector got to his Advanced Stats class just in time but noticed immediately that Walter wasn't there yet. Not only was Walter never late but they had a final today. Feeling the smallest bit of guilt sink in that he'd lost all interest in helping Walter out when Lisa had showed up, he wondered now if something bad went down after he left.

By the time class was over and Walter never made it in, Hector was really feeling like crap about not having done anything to help him out. He ran into A.J. and Theo on his way to his next class. "Hey, what happened with Walt? He never made it to class."

A.J. brought his hands to his mouth, trying to stifle a laugh and pointed at Theo.

"Nah," Theo laughed, shaking his head. "That was *all* you!"

"What?" Hector asked, the concern weighing even heavier now.

A.J. lifted his arm to flex his muscle. "It's not my fault these guns can throw so hard." Then he turned to Theo. "And it's not my fault you can't catch for shit."

Theo busted out laughing heartedly now. "Man! That guy is probably still trying to put his toy together."

Feeling his insides go hollow, Hector looked at A.J. disgusted. "You broke the robot?" Without thinking, he grabbed his stupid friend by the shirt. "Why would you do that?"

A.J. laughed a little nervous now and brought his hand over Hector's. "Hey! I told him I was sorry. I didn't mean to." A.J's attempt to loosen Hector's grip on his shirt was a weak one, and it only made Hector grip it tighter. "What the hell, man?" A.J. asked his words a little shaky.

"You really are an asshole," Hector said, releasing him with a shove then turned to Theo who looked a little nervous himself now too. "You are too, Theo—assholes—both of you." He walked away, shaking his head, feeling like an asshole now himself for not having stepped in and taken the damn robot from them.

Hector was just glad he was almost done with high school. He only ever hung around these jerks at school. Outside of school, he hung out at 5th Street, the boxing gym he was now part owner of, with his brother and his older partners and much more mature friends.

HECTOR

He couldn't even believe now that he'd spent all this time with these guys and never stood up for Walter and all the other people they'd picked on and messed with over the years.

Just before getting to his next class, he saw Walter. Feeling the sting of guilt even deeper when he noticed Walter's red-rimmed eyes, he was almost afraid to ask, but he had to. "Hey, Walt, did you fix your robot?" Walter walked past him, the contempt in his eyes nearly burning a hole through Hector, but he didn't say a word.

"Listen, Walt, I'm sorry I didn't stop them. I got sidetracked, but if there is anything I can do to help you fix it—"

"Are you kidding me?" Walter snapped so loudly a few heads turned their way. "You or your sorry-ass friends wouldn't know the first thing about building something like that! Why don't you and those other jerks just go fuck yourselves!"

The moment his words were out, Hector saw something flick in Walter's eyes—fear. Fear that in a moment of anger he'd said something he would've never said before because under normal circumstances it might've gotten his ass kicked. Walter glanced around, a little pale-faced now at the other students standing around looking just as stunned.

Hector decided he'd let the guy off the hook this time. Walter had every right to be pissed. "I'm sorry, man. I hope you get it fixed."

Walter stared at him for a moment wide-eyed, apparently just as stunned as everyone around them that he hadn't gotten Hector's fist to his face. Without saying another word, Walter spun around and stalked away. Yep, Hector deserved that. He only hoped the outburst had made Walter feel a tiny bit better. Knowing Walter, and from what Hector had heard about the things that robot could do, it probably took him years to perfect it.

Hector walked away in the opposite direction, leaving a very confused audience standing around behind him whispering. He knew they were all wondering why he hadn't at the very least given Walter a fat lip. Today was different. He didn't think he could feel any worse after hearing Lisa's news, but now he did. He should've done something to stop his dumb-ass friends. But it wasn't like Hector always stood back and didn't say anything. Lisa's ex-boyfriend wasn't the only one who'd ever had to answer to him for threatening or trying to hurt someone weaker.

Besides, this was different, he tried to convince himself. The guys he hung out with might be jerks sometimes, but they never hurt anyone. Mostly they just messed around and poked fun at people. The only thing they ever bruised was maybe a few egos.

Hector tried to appease his guilty conscience by reasoning that, just like all the other times, Walter would get over it. And he insisted the guy was going to have to stand up for himself sooner or later or this kind of crap would keep happening to him.

The next day, Walter didn't show up to school, nor did he show up at all for the rest of the semester. Since he wasn't popular and didn't have many friends, no one really knew what happened to him. He just never came back. The only news they'd gotten was that his science project hadn't been entered in the national competition.

As much as Hector wanted to believe Walter not coming back had nothing to do with the robot incident, that maybe Walter had moved or something completely unrelated was the cause of his absence, his conscience kept reminding him of all the other times Walter had been the recipient of his friends' taunting. This may've been the last straw that just drove Walter over the brink.

Now standing here in the school's crowded football field while his mom and brother and the rest of the gang from 5th Street happily snapped pictures of him in his cap and gown, he still couldn't shake the guilt from not having done the right thing.

A weakling had been picked on in front of him, not just this one time but time after time, and for years, he'd watched and done nothing about it. His only hope now was that dropping out of school was the only thing his idiot friends had driven Walter to do.

CHAPTER 1

The laughter and loud screeching from other students happily making their way through the campus of East Side University was just another reminder of why Charlee was so out of place here. Her best friend, Drew, assured her that after a few weeks she'd begin to enjoy college life. That was easy for Drew to say. She'd attended public school her whole life. Charlee had been homeschooled after a disastrous two-month stint in the first grade that proved she had the social capacity of skunk.

Although she later attempted public school a few times, each time, she'd had the same basic outcome. Even what would've been her senior year in high school, when Drew had just about convinced her to her to enroll that one final year so they could do prom and all the other fun senior things together, had been a no can do.

For three weeks now, Charlee had managed to not make a single friend. She was just as much a friendless hermit as she'd been most of her young life. If it hadn't been because Drew lived next door to her since they were both babies and because Drew was a social butterfly, Charlee was sure she wouldn't have even attended the few parties and school dances her friend had dragged her to over the years. This, too, was Drew's idea. Charlee would've been perfectly happy attending online and keeping any need to actually be on campus to a minimum. But no, Drew insisted, and she somehow convinced Charlee that moving clear across the country to attend college full time would be *fun!*

Charlee glanced around, careful not to make any eye contact with the group of guys not too far from where she sat. The whole time she'd been sitting there waiting for her ride, they'd been teasing and taunting just about every girl that walked by them. They seemed harmless enough. Some girls even appeared to be flattered by their remarks, but there had been a few times they'd crossed the line and gotten a little rude. Charlee would die of embarrassment if they said anything to her, even if they kept it nice. As they'd inched closer in her direction, she'd actually considered getting up and moving to another spot. But they were already too close, and walking away might call more attention to her than if she just sat there and hoped she could remain as invisible as she usually felt.

She pretended to be immersed in her phone as so many other students seemed to be *all* the time. Only she wasn't using Facebook or Tweeting or even texting like she knew most were. She was reading—one of her favorite pastimes— although right now she was having a hard time concentrating on the latest steamy novel she'd downloaded and was supposed to be engrossed in. The guys' voices were getting closer, and she'd heard the dreaded phrase, "Check out red over there."

Charlee froze, her palms becoming instantly moist, and her heart began doing that pounding it always did when she got nervous. Shaking off the incredible urge to grab her things and run, she stared at her phone screen, praying Drew would miraculously drive up before they reached her bench.

Why the hell did her car have to break down? It was the one thing that she'd been counting on when she decided to take the plunge and move here. She bought the thing first thing when she got here so she could just drive herself to school, go straight to class, and leave as soon as classes were over. Now she was forced to hang around campus longer after classes until Drew or Drew's dad could pick her up. And Drew said this was a good thing?

"Hey, Red!" One of the guys called out to her.

Though there was no doubt he was talking to Charlee, she pretended not to realize and continued staring at her phone.

"Don't act like you didn't hear me, Ginger. Because I know you did."

Forced to, Charlee glanced up at him but couldn't help frowning. Of course, it would be the loudest, most obnoxious one of the group who'd taken an interest in her. It took all but a second to recognize the familiar and undeniable smell as they all got close enough. She knew the stench all too well since her own step-dad been smoking marijuana for years for his "glaucoma."

"What?" he smirked. "Why you looking at me like that? I just wanna say hello and find out what your name is."

The guy had that same sleepy, somewhat glossy-eyed look her father got when he smoked the stuff. She forced a faint smile. "It's Charlee."

Scrunching up his nose, he turned to his friends then laughed a little too loudly as he turned back to face her. "Charlie? Ain't that a guy's name?"

"Apparently not," she said as she began to gather her things.

His friends began laughing now too as if she'd just said something hilarious. "Okay, okay," he said a little too amused. "Don't go. I haven't introduced myself. I'm Ross and this must be your first year here, right? Because I know I would've noticed a beautiful thing like you before."

"Yep," she said, feeling her face warm from the compliment, "first year." She flung her bag over her shoulder just as he lifted his hand toward her.

"That hair, wow, it's . . . so bright."

Charlee cursed her *bright* head. Her entire life, all she wanted was to go unnoticed—blend in with everything, but this hair had and would always be the bane of her existence. Even after Drew's plan to make it less noticeable, she still may as well sit there screaming, "Look at me! My head's on fire!"

She smiled faintly and tried making her way around Ross.

"Wait, wait." He stepped in front of her and stared at her hair with an almost perverted expression. "Are you red *everywhere*, Charlee?" he whispered but loud enough for his friends to hear because they burst out laughing and were already falling all over each other.

Her face was instantly ablaze and she looked away.

"Can I touch it?" he asked.

With a jerk of her neck, she was facing him again. "What?" She stepped back away from him.

He took a step forward with a sardonic smile that made the hair on the back of her neck stand. "I meant the hair on your head, not on your . . ."

"No, you can't," she gasped, glancing around wishing to God she'd spot Drew's car in the parking lot somewhere. "I gotta go."

His friends laughed even more now. "Burn!" One of them said, covering his mouth, because her having to go was apparently side-splitting.

Ross didn't seem quite as amused as they were now, but he still managed to smirk. "C'mon, Red," he lifted his hand toward her again. "I just wanna see if it feels as soft as it looks."

"Sorry, I gotta go," she repeated.

She started to walk around him, beginning to feel a little nervous about how deserted the campus suddenly felt. This wasn't unusual for a late Friday afternoon, and normally she wouldn't care, but being alone here with these three obviously high guys was really starting to unnerve her.

His hand touching her made her gasp again. Ross held her arm as she tried going around him. "I'm asking nicely." His voice was low and deliberate now.

Charlee tried to shake his arm off her, but he held it firmly.

"Let her go."

They all looked up at once, and Ross immediately laughed. A heavyset boy she recognized quickly as Walter, a guy on both her chess teams, stood there looking a bit unsure of himself, but he cleared his throat and spoke even louder the second time. "I said let her go."

Ross dropped her arm and took a few steps toward Walter. "You're gonna tell *me* what to do, fat boy?"

The voice in Charlee's head screamed for her to get out of there. She was free to run now, but she couldn't. She couldn't just leave Walter there with these three pothead assholes.

"J-just let her be is all I'm saying." Walter looked about as scared as Charlee felt.

"Yeah? Or what?" Ross asked, taking a few more steps toward Walter. "What are you gonna do, fat ass?"

"Let's go, Walter." Charlee said, walking toward him, but Ross stopped her, grabbing her arm again.

"I said let her go!" Walter pushed Ross, making him tumble back off balance for a second, but he recovered quickly and swung, landing his fist solidly on Walter's nose.

In the next few seconds, while Walter brought his hands to his bloodied nose, Ross swung at him again. Charlee screamed at him to stop when she saw Walter lose his footing and tumble to the ground in pain. Ross began kicking him in the stomach and chest, and his friends joined him, kicking Walter mercilessly. Completely panic-stricken now and terrified that they were going to kill him, especially when she saw one of Ross's kicks go for Walter's head, Charlee begged them to stop. She thought for sure security or someone would've come by now, but unbelievably, there was no one around. That's when she saw him.

Out of nowhere, a guy ran up to Ross, and with one swift powerful punch to the face, he knocked Ross out cold.

Charlee was too stunned to move, even when Ross's body flopped lifelessly at her feet. He never even knew what hit him.

"You okay, Walter?" The deep resonate sound of his voice barely registered as she finally pulled her eyes away from the body lying at her feet. Looking up, she watched the mystery guy bend over at Walter's side. Ross's friends were long gone, running the moment they saw Ross drop like a sack of rocks. The guy hadn't bothered going after them, too concerned about Walter instead.

Mesmerized, she now couldn't take her eyes off *him* as he lifted Walter's big body effortlessly, helping him to his feet.

Charlee hadn't even noticed that Drew had driven up until she honked. Coming out of her daze, she turned to Drew, stepping away from Ross's body and lifted her hand at Drew to give her a second. "Are you okay, Walter?"

Walter nodded but looked away. He seemed upset or maybe just embarrassed. "Are you sure? I can ask my friend to take you to the emergency room if you want. We can also call the cops." She turned to Ross who was still lying on the floor but appeared to be coming to. "We can try and keep him here until the cops come."

"He ain't going anywhere." The guy assured her with a lift of an eyebrow.

Her eyes met with the guy's intensely serious eyes for a moment. She'd never seen such heavy lashes on a guy in her life, and she was having an awfully hard time keeping her eyes off his big arms. Looking at his face now, she could see he was probably her age, but he had the body of a man—a full-grown *amazingly* built man. With his toned arms and shoulders and his more than confident demeanor, he was a complete contrast to Walter, who stood there still spitting out blood.

"I'm good." Walter said after wiping the blood away from his nose again.

Drew honked again. Charlee knew Drew was in a hurry, but she felt terrible about just leaving Walter there.

"Go ahead." Walter said, already starting to walk away. "I'm fine, really."

She hurried to him before he could get too far and gave him a quick hug. "Thank you. I'm so sorry this happened."

Walter nodded and gave her a small smile. "It wasn't your fault. Don't worry about it."

Of course, Charlee felt entirely to blame, but she wouldn't argue with him. She glanced at the guy who'd really saved the day, suddenly incredibly grateful that he'd showed up when he did, but dared not attempt to even ask his name much less hug him. Instead, she smiled softly. "Thank you too."

He winked at her, the intensity suddenly gone, then flashed one of the most breathtaking smiles she'd ever seen. In an effort to not become completely mesmerized again and make a fool of herself, she glanced away from his lips and his nearly perfect teeth. Instead, she focused on the skin on his big arms. Being so pasty white her entire life, she'd envied people with skin like his: so perfectly tanned. She felt almost ashamed that any thoughts about Walter's well-being had been completely snuffed by visions of touching this incredible guy's skin.

Another honk from Drew yanked her out of said visions, and she turned to Drew then waved back at Walter one last time. "I'll see you next week."

She noticed Ross was attempting to sit up now, holding the side of his face in pain. Walter and his hero were already walking in the opposite direction.

"I'm sorry I had to pull you away from that delicious guy, but my dad's waiting, and I'm already running really late." Drew stared at her as she sat down and started putting on her seatbelt, the *delicious guy* still in her head. "So what happened? Why is that guy on the ground?"

Charlee glanced one last time at Ross who was now being helped up by his coward friends. They'd finally come back after they saw Walter and the other guy walk away, but they kept looking nervously in their direction. Then her eyes turned to where they really wanted to be. Even from behind and from this distance, the guy's body was unbelievable. She took a deep breath, looking back at Drew as they started out of the parking lot, not even sure where to begin.

~*~

"Is she gone?" Walter asked, staring straight ahead.

Hector turned to look back just as the car that picked up the redhead he assumed Walter was talking about drove out of the school's parking lot. "Yeah."

These were the first words they'd exchanged since they'd walked away from the scene silently. Other than that, Hector had asked him if he was sure he was okay to which Walter simply nodded.

Suddenly, Walter flung his backpack against the fence next to him with a loud grunt. "*Gadamn it!* For weeks, I've been trying to make a connection with Charlee and then this," he pointed forcefully in the direction they'd just come from. "*That* happens? Fuck!" He hunched over for a second, holding his side in obvious pain.

Hector was still stuck on what Walter had just said. *Charlie?* At a loss for words, he turned back to the direction they'd come from as Walter continued to pace, cussing and grunting under his breath, Hector tried to figure it out. He'd heard of stuff like this. Gay guys coming out to the guys they were into, and it turned out the guy they were into was not only not gay but homophobic. Was that really what had happened? Did that guy lose it because Walter tried making a *connection* with him?

Turning back to Walter, who was kicking his own backpack now, he stared at him for a moment, still not sure what to say. He had no idea Walter was gay. But it *did* explain a lot of stuff. Like why he'd been such a loner all those years.

"So he got mad?" Obviously the guy had been mad, but that's all Hector could think of to ask. This was so damn awkward.

Walter slowed his pacing to look at Hector, a little confused. "Well, yeah, that kind of jerk doesn't like being told what to do."

Almost afraid to ask, Hector *had* to. "What did you tell him to do?"

"To leave her alone," Walter said, wincing in pain as he bent over to pick up his backpack. He unzipped it, pulled out a t-shirt, wiped his bloody face with it, and started walking again.

"I'm not following, man," Hector admitted, walking alongside of Walter.

Walter winced as he dabbed his nose with the t-shirt. "I'd been watching her sit there for a while. Then these pricks start harassing her, being stupid and asking if she was red *everywhere*. I wasn't gonna say anything until he put his hands on her. So I told him to leave her alone, and when he didn't, I pushed him."

Hector smiled. "Good for you. Was Charlie the one I knocked out?"

Walter's face soured. "No! Charlee's the girl, and now she probably thinks I'm the biggest wuss ever—no thanks to you coming in with your one-punch knockout."

Charlie's a girl? Then it dawned on him. "Wait." He stopped in front of Walter, forcing him to stop. "You're mad at me for helping you out?"

Walter frowned. "I could've had that guy. I was getting ready to make my move."

Hector's eyes shot open. He wasn't sure if he should laugh or shove Walter. "Are you kidding me? You were on the ground in a fetal position."

"I had a plan!"

This time Hector did laugh. "And what was that? To play dead?"

Hector laughed even louder now. Walter shoved past him and started walking again. Hector followed him, continuing to laugh loudly. He was glad now that Walter's response had been so utterly ridiculous; otherwise, he might be pissed. Here he'd risked getting in trouble, very possibly arrested, and Walter's ungrateful ass was mad about it?

"Go ahead; laugh it up." Walter said, walking a little faster now. He turned to Hector with that same glare he remembered so vividly from the last time he'd seen Walter back in high school. "It's what you've always done, right? Why stop now?"

Okay, *now* Walter was pissing him off. "Look, don't be stupid. There was no way you were gonna make a move back there. You were already down, and there were three of them and one of you. If I hadn't showed up when I did, *you'd* be the one lying there unconscious right now, not him. I didn't have to get involved, but I did. You're welcome, asshole!"

Hector stopped then spun around. *Fuck this!* He stalked back in the direction of the parking lot. For the first time since he'd slugged the guy kicking Walter, he began to feel the tingling pain in his knuckles. Maybe he should've let them beat Walter's ass.

"Why did you?" He heard Walter ask.

Taking a few more steps before deciding to stop, he turned around. "Because it wasn't fair." He shrugged. "Three on one is how pussies fight. I hate that shit."

"You didn't in high school."

Walter's words stunned Hector for a second, and then he reacted to them. "That's bullshit!" Hector pointed at Walter, stalking back toward him with a purpose. "They never hurt you. Okay, so they teased you and messed with you, but they never ganged up on you to physically hurt you. If they had, I would've stepped in."

This was the very argument he'd had with himself for months now. For too damn long, he'd been plagued with the guilt that Walter very possibly had done something tragic because Hector and his friends had pushed him over the edge. As much as it was a relief to know that Walter was alive and well, he hated that Walter *did* see him as the same kind of piece of shit as the guys kicking him while he was down today. Because ever since that last day he'd seen Walter, it's exactly what Hector had felt like.

Walter shook his head and started walking away. Suddenly Hector was mad again. This wasn't fair. "What was I supposed to do, Walter? You were bigger than most of the guys back in high school. Why didn't *you* stop them? Why didn't *you* ever stand up for yourself?"

Walter turned around. "Like today? Against more than one bully? Because I got news for you: it was never just one. Oh no. You said it yourself, 'Pussies don't start shit one on one.' It was always at least two or more, and you saw today how that ends."

"Still, you fight!" Hector insisted. With Walter on the ground today, Hector had been outnumbered, too, but he never once thought about that when he went at them.

"I'm not a fighter like you, man." Walter said loudly. "I don't have a knockout punch. Hell, I don't have a punch period."

Hector was tired of this. All these months of beating himself up about Walter, was ending *now*. "And what?" His voice was so loud he practically yelled. "You think this happened overnight? You think this is just some gift I was given? It wasn't, okay? It took years of training and hard work at the gym. You should try it sometime. But let me tell you something: I am *not* like them." He pointed behind Walter with conviction. "I'm sorry, okay?" He lost a little of the conviction as the guilt inundated him once again. *This* is what he'd been hoping for months that he'd get a chance to say to Walter someday, and now here was his chance. He took a deep breath when he saw Walter's confused expression. "I'm sorry I didn't stop them from breaking your robot." He took another deep breath. "And I'm sorry for all those years I stood back and watched them bully you without saying anything. I really am, Walt. I'm sorry."

Walter stared at him for a moment and then glanced away. Obviously, he wasn't expecting to hear this from Hector, and that's what burned the most. As much as Hector didn't want to admit it, he *was* as bad as the guys beating on Walter today. Maybe he'd never physically beaten Walter, but he'd been a part of beating Walter's self-confidence to the ground for years. Any sense of self-worth Walter might have ever had, Hector had a hand in beating it lifeless. Hector knew he'd never join the jerks he hung out with in ganging up to beat on someone, but how were Walter and some of the other weaklings that got picked on regularly supposed to know that? Of course, they'd never fight back. Who would fight a group of overconfident bullies that included a trained fighter among them?

Hector waited for what seemed too long, but hell, he'd waited for months. He could give this guy a few more minutes. He understood how Walter could be so stunned. An apology from someone he considered to be one of his bullies for so many years was probably the last thing Walter thought he'd ever hear. Of course, he'd been stunned into silence.

They both looked up as the noise from a public bus that turned into the college campus parking lot distracted them momentarily. "I gotta go," Walter said. "That's my ride." He started toward the bus stop a few feet away from them but stopped just before he got to in and turned to Hector, still holding his side in obvious pain. "I always knew you weren't like them." The bus pulled up behind Walter, and he began to turn around to get on but stopped again one last time to face Hector. "Thanks, man." For the first time that day, Walter smirked and lifted his chin. "I really didn't have a plan back there."

Hector smiled, laughing softly. "Yeah, I didn't buy that shit for a minute."

Walter smiled and got on the bus. Hector walked back toward the main building, flexing his now-aching fist and feeling a bit bittersweet. He finally got to say he was sorry, and it was good to know Walter never thought Hector was like his jerk ex-friends. But Hector couldn't help shake the feeling that he had done Walter wrong and for way too long.

CHAPTER 2

More than a week after the whole Walter/Ross incident, Charlee still couldn't stop thinking about the guy that saved them. At first, she kept shuddering at the thought of what might've happened if he hadn't showed up when he had. Then, as the days went by, she stopped shuddering and started daydreaming.

The only information she had on him was what little Walter offered. His name was Hector, they'd gone to high school together, and he was an amateur boxer at a boxing gym over in East L.A. That explained how he'd knocked out Ross so easily. In her daydreams, Hector was now a superhero: a beautifully tanned, perfectly sculpted specimen of a hero.

What he said and did to her had become a little more elaborate with each daydream she had. She figured she'd never see him again, so it didn't matter how ridiculous or naughty the dreams became. As far as she or Walter knew, Hector didn't attend East Side U. Walter hadn't asked him, but neither had he seen him on campus ever since. His being there at all that day was a mystery to them both. Never in her life had she felt so distracted and all because of a guy she got the pleasure of being in the presence of for about five minutes.

"Hello!" Drew waved her hand in front of Charlee's face.

Charlee snapped out of it and smiled sheepishly at her friend, who held out a can of Red Bull for her. "What's with you this week, girl?" Drew smirked at first, and then a look of concern washed over her face. "Are you sure you're okay?

Ever since what happened with that jerk Ross and his friends, you've been a little weird."

Charlee shook her head, taking a sip of the much needed energy drink. "I'm fine. I've just had some stuff on my mind lately: midterms. You know that and the Jr. World Olympiad are coming up, soon." In an effort to avoid her inquisitive best friend asking more questions, she tried changing the subject. "They're having a knockout tournament this weekend to replace Vladimir." She then frowned, thinking about what she'd just said. "I don't think we're gonna find anyone as good as he was."

"How good could he have been, Charlee?" Drew rolled her eyes. "He got caught cheating."

Charlee was about to argue that he technically hadn't been caught *cheating*. He was just caught with a wireless device and headphones in his last tournament, something that was strictly against the rules, but it was never proven he'd actually used it to cheat. It was a bit unfair, Charlee thought. Whatever happened to innocent until proven guilty anyway? The punishment hadn't even fit the crime. Not only had he automatically been disqualified from the tournament but he was kicked off the US team *and* the school team, losing his free ride to ESU. But before she could start her argument, she noticed Drew had slowed down and was glaring at something straight ahead. No sooner had Charlee looked up to see who she was glaring at than she regretted doing so.

"Why is it that before last week I'd never even noticed this guy and now it seems I see his stupid ass everywhere?" Drew asked as they walked out the cafeteria.

Ross and his friends were sitting just outside the cafeteria. Thankfully, unlike for Drew, this was only the second time Charlee had seen him since the incident the week before. The first time she'd run into him, he stared her down, giving her a major case of the heebie-jeebies but hadn't said anything. His cheek still had some signs of the swelling Hector's blow had left but nothing like last week when his left cheek was about an inch higher than his right and the whites of his left eye were all red.

Charlee didn't look at him long enough now to take inventory of his injuries. But she may've looked too long because he smiled at her. It was early in the morning. Charlee and Drew were barely on their way to their first class of the day, but from the looks of it, Ross and his friends were already glossy-eyed. She turned away without smiling back.

"Just keep walking and stop looking their way," Charlee said, pulling on Drew's arm.

"Morning, Charlee."

Charlee nearly jumped out of her skin at the sight and sound of Ross right next to her now. She flinched but kept walking. "Morning." She responded, deciding ignoring him might elicit another rude reaction from him. Her heart was already racing.

"Can I talk to you?" He asked in a voice much nicer than last week's.

"No, I'm late already." She tugged at Drew's arm to warn her that she didn't need to her to come to her rescue. Charlee could already feel the anger radiating from her friend.

"Maybe later then?"

Charlee glanced at him for a second. "Maybe."

"What!" Drew nearly roared.

"I gotta go." Charlee said quickly and picked up her pace to a near sprint, pulling Drew along with her.

When they were far enough away and in the humanities building, Drew stopped in front of Charlee. "Maybe? You're not actually gonna talk to that creep are you?"

"No, of course not," Charlee assured her. "I just didn't know what else to say."

"How 'bout *no*?" Drew placed her fist on her hip.

"I just said the first thing I could think of so that I could get away from him as fast as possible. That's all." Drew gave her the stink eye. "It worked, didn't it?"

"Yeah, well, now he's gonna think he has the go-ahead to confront you the next time he sees you."

Charlee frowned. She hadn't thought that far ahead. Truth was he'd spooked the hell out of her. The only thing she could think of at the time, aside from wanting to run away like a crazy person, was to agree to anything and get away without making a scene.

"I'll cross that bridge when I come to it, *if* I ever have to."

She didn't even want to think about having to talk to Ross again. Unlike that first time, today she'd been in the middle of a crowded campus with her best friend at her side, and she was still terrified. There was something so ominous about him. If he ever confronted her alone again, she'd probably freak out.

They reached their class, and Charlee decided she'd not think about it until she absolutely had to. For now, she had the bottle of mace she'd bought the day after the first incident, and if she was forced to use it, she would. She sat down and thought of something much more pleasant: Hector, her dreamy hero.

~*~

It'd been weeks since Hector's texts and emails with Lisa had tapered off. When she first moved up north they'd spoken on the phone a few times late in the evening, and their conversations had begun to take an intimate feel. Hector actually thought he was really starting to feel something for her. She even said she was going to try to come back down to L.A. and visit as soon as she could. Normally something like that might've scared him a little. He'd never done the relationship thing. He wasn't sure if her making such a long trip meant she thought he was getting *that* serious. But the thought of it had begun to grow on him.

Then, he noticed a change. She'd say she was going to call him and wouldn't. The texts began to dwindle, and any talk of her visiting was suddenly never mentioned again. That's when he noticed a reoccurring dude in her Facebook photos. The captions only ever mentioned his name and where they were but not what relation he was to her. Never one to beat around the bush, Hector asked her flat out who the guy was. All she said was that he was a friend, but soon there were photos of them at college football games and at a fair. The kicker was the photo of them posing in front of a movie theater, holding hands. That's when Hector unfriended her and stopped responding to her texts. They were few and far between anyway. He'd already started to feel a bit creepy stalking her Facebook photos, but he still insisted she should've just been honest with him.

The most maddening thing of all, though he was more pissed at himself than he was with her, was that his dumb ass actually passed up hanging out with some of his regulars in the last couple of weeks. He'd never admit it out loud, but clearly he was secretly hoping she was doing the same thing.

He decided not to give it another thought. He'd already obsessed too much about her as it was, and all he'd ever done was kiss her one time. Instead, he decided to focus on his latest challenge.

Shaking his head, he finally admitted it. He'd screwed up. Hector had never actually discussed college in depth with his mom and his older brother, Abel, but apparently he was expected to go. He hadn't even bothered taking his SATs because he was sure that being part owner of 5th Street he'd go straight to working full time there after high school. It's what Abel had done when *he* graduated.

His mother, being old-school, had been fine when Abel went straight into fighting and working at 5th Street after high school. Of course, it had always been his brother's dream to be a heavyweight champ, and the way things were looking, Abel had a damn good chance of making it. There'd already been one alumnus from 5th Street to make it to the big time. Abel wasn't far behind.

Hector was a good enough fighter, but he did it for the same reason he'd done just about anything growing up: because of his big brother—his *hero*. He almost never admitted it aloud, especially now that he was older, but he had always been and still was his brother's biggest fan. Abel was the real fighter of the two and would someday be the heavyweight champ. Everyone said he had a real good chance at the title. Hector only really did it for the adrenaline rush fighting gave him, and he liked what the workouts did to his body, but he'd never really been interested in fighting professionally.

It wasn't just the fighting. There were a lot of other reasons why Abel was his hero, so hearing him say he was disappointed in Hector was all it took to get his ass scrambling. He needed to figure out a way to get into a good school, even if it meant waiting until the winter session since it was way too late for fall.

The day he'd gone down to East Side U, he did so for one reason—to see about trying out for their coveted chess team. He thought he could just go down there, show the instructors his skills, and just like that he'd be in. Unfortunately, that's not how it worked, and with the fall semester already well underway, there was no other way he could think of getting into that particular school. So it was back to the drawing board because Hector was determined to get in one way or another.

Then something came up. In high school, Hector had refused to join what he referred to as the "nerd fest"—the chess club. Chess was another thing Abel had gotten him into. Abel played for fun and was pretty good, but he quickly realized Hector wasn't just good but he had an exceptional gift for the game. Next thing he knew, they were on a bus to Santa Monica to play with the hard-core chess players at the chess park on the beach.

That's where he'd met Sam, a retired, cranky-as-shit Army vet and chess grandmaster with many championship titles under his belt. Abel had taught Hector the basics. Hector had tossed in his own spin on the game, stepping it up so much he impressed the hell out of Abel. But Sam, Sam was why he was here today, why he thought he had so much as a prayer at winning a knockout tournament that would get him on the US under-20 chess team—a team that would be playing for a spot in the Junior World Olympiad later this year. Sam had trained him and taught him everything he knew about mastering the game. Most importantly, Sam thought Hector had this.

Even with all the smaller events he'd won over the years and the online tournaments he'd taken first place in over and over, Hector never thought he'd be playing in major knockout event like this. But having played and won in the World Olympiad more than once himself, Sam recommended Hector be entered in a chance to make a team that would be trying out for it. A week later, Hector was invited.

At first, Hector was hesitant. Then Sam mentioned some of the team players for East Side University chess team were already on the US under-20 team and the trainers for the school team would be at today's event: trainers that Sam said would no doubt notice Hector even if he didn't win. Getting noticed by them this way might get him invited on the school team. This was his chance at early admission to the spring semester. Hector wanted nothing more than for Abel to take back how disappointed he'd been with him about not taking school more seriously. He hadn't even told Abel about today. He was hoping to surprise him.

Getting out of his truck in the quickly filling parking lot, Hector looked around for Sam. Sam was meeting Hector there and had told him to get there early. This was Hector's biggest tournament ever. Sam had been pushing him for years to enter some. When he was younger, he'd been in a few, but then puberty hit, and once Hector discovered girls, forget about it. He already knew from his brother and some of the other guys at the gym that girls had a thing for boxers. And did they *ever!* Somehow he knew saying he was a chess player and won lots of tournaments wouldn't have quite the same effect on girls as it did when he mentioned winning a bout.

Add to that, physically, because of all the training he did at the gym, he was bigger and had a lot more muscle to flaunt than most boys his age, starting very early on. So the attention he received from the female population at his school won out every time Sam mentioned a new tournament. Sitting and playing chess for hours on a Saturday was up there on his list of things he liked doing. But once the options were that or steaming up the windows of his truck for hours on a Saturday instead, the latter won hands down every time. He knew it annoyed the hell out of the old man, but certainly Sam had to understand that for any guy, but especially one like Hector in his prime, the choice was a no-brainer.

Hector didn't see Sam's old Volkswagen van anywhere. It was hard to miss. Although, ironically, Sam had it custom painted to look Army camouflage, it stood out like the eyesore that it was everywhere he went.

Doing a double take, Hector stared at the guy getting out of a beat-up car two spaces over. "Walter?"

Walter turned to him, at first expressionless, then he smiled. "Hey, we meet again."

"Yeah," Hector reached out for Walter's guy handshake, trying to push away that still-lingering guilt that hadn't completely disappeared even after making amends with Walter, "under better circumstances this time."

Walter chuckled. "I know. My face ain't being kicked into the ground this time."

Hector smiled and motioned to the beat-up car Walter had just gotten out of. "And I see you got some wheels now too."

"Yeah, well," Walter shrugged, "when it's running anyway."

Thoughts about Walter's car were pushed back by thoughts of the beating Walter took. "You all healed up now, though? Were your ribs okay? I remember you were hurting bad."

Walter pressed his lips together and shook his head. "Not broken but I did have hairline fracture. By the next day, it hurt to even breathe, and I ended up in the emergency room. One had the fracture; the others were just bruised real bad."

Hector winced. "Ouch, I've been punched in the ribs before but never bad enough to have anything fractured."

"Yeah," Walter nodded. "It was no fun, let me tell you. I was down for days."

It still pissed Hector off that those pussies had ganged up and beat on him like that, especially since he was already down. "So those guys ever bother you again?"

"Nah." Walter shook his head. "That school is so damn big. I don't know if they're avoiding me or I just haven't run into them again."

"Well, that's good." They moved off to the side of the crowds walking toward the auditorium. Walter seemed to be taking in the crowd or looking for someone as they stood there for a moment without saying anything. Hector remembered another thing he had always wondered about. Although he had an idea of what had happened, he still wanted to know. He may never get another chance to ask.

"So what happened to you, man? End of school year, you disappeared. Did you move?"

Walter's eyes met his for a moment, but then he shook his head and continued to glance around. After a few awkward silent moments, he finally spoke. "I just decided to get my GED and get out. I hated high school."

Knowing Walter was a top student the entire four years, Hector knew he didn't mean he hated the academics part of high school like most kids. Hector knew exactly what Walter hated about school. He hated what Hector and his friends had put him through all those years. Even though he had the incredible urge to apologize once more, he decided he wouldn't go there again, so he nodded and let it go.

"I was still able to get into East Side, and . . .," he turned his head, and Hector turned to see what had distracted Walter: a passing car that parked nearby. Two girls got out of the car—a blonde and a redhead.

Walter's shoulders went limp, and he backed up and leaned his elbow against a brand-new Mustang behind him that still had the dealership plates on. His demeanor went from awkwardly shy and quiet like he normally acted to this weird smug guy leaning on his own brand-new Mustang, almost as if he were trying to show off. As the girls got closer, he looked around with the goofiest expression on his face. "Yeah, I've been working out a few times a week."

Hector turned to the girls, wondering if maybe he was talking to them. When he realized he wasn't, because the girls weren't even looking at him, he turned back to Walter. "Huh?"

When the girls got even closer, Walter very obviously sucked in his big gut and lifted a flabby arm. In a somewhat strained voice, he spoke again. "Yeah, I bench about thirty pounds on a bad day, about fifty the rest of the time."

"Hey, Walter," the redhead in a ponytail said, "new car?"

Seeing the ridiculous expression go even stupider, Hector finally figured out what Walter was doing. It was obvious he was about to lie about the car being his when the alarm on the car went off, startling Walter, whose elbow slipped off the car, and he nearly fell.

The blond girl squealed as the sudden blaring alarm startled her as well, and then both girls laughed and continued walking but not before the redhead glanced in Hector's direction for just a split second. That's when he realized who she was—Charlie—the same girl that was there the day Hector saved Walter's ass, the one Walter had been so upset about not being able to make a *connection* with.

Never having been or even hung around with any girls but those with dark features, he was caught by her big deep blue eyes just as he had been that first day he saw her. But just like that day, it was only for a moment because she turned away too quickly. Hector turned to a now-back-to-awkward-and-frowning Walter. "What the hell was that about?"

Walter rolled his eyes, kicking a bottle cap on the floor. "Nothing you'd know about." He kicked the bottle cap even harder. "Crap on a stick! Just like last time and all the other times, it never fails. I always end up making an ass out of myself instead of impressing her."

Hector couldn't help laughing as they both started toward the doors of the auditorium where the event was taking place. "What exactly was supposed to impress her: you sucking your gut in or the fact that you could bench fifty pounds?" He laughed even more now. "Because let me tell you fifty pounds ain't shit. For a guy your size, you might want to up that to more than two hundred."

Walter turned to him, incredulous. "Over two hundred? Are you crazy!"

"Nope," Hector said, looking around again for Sam then back at Walter. "And it wouldn't kill you to actually get your ass in a gym if you really want to impress this girl." He reached over and patted Walter's soft middle. "Getting in shape would probably help your little dilemma, you know. Girls appreciate the effort we put into getting our bodies nice and hard." Hector lifted his arm and flexed with a smirk. "And they show their appreciation in real nice ways."

Walter rolled his eyes, flinging his backpack over his shoulder as they reached the auditorium doors and walked in ahead of Hector. "Yeah, that's easy for guys like you to say."

With Sam nowhere in sight, Hector decided he may as well go in also. "Wait up. Are you here for the tournament too?"

Walter stopped, turning to look at Hector wide-eyed. "You're in the tournament?" He shook his head, frowning when Hector nodded. "You play chess well enough to be invited to one of these things?"

Hector shrugged. "I'm here, right?"

Walter shrugged, imitating Hector. "Oh, yeah, of course, because it's not enough that you look like this." He lifted a finger up and down in front of Hector. "And that the girls in high school went crazy for the badass boxer from 5th Street, but you're smart too?" Walter dropped his head back, looking almost disgusted.

Hector laughed. "You've always known I wasn't stupid. We had a lot of the same AP classes together, remember?"

"Yeah, but to play chess at this level—" Walter stopped suddenly and raised a bushy eyebrow. "You do know this is a speed tournament, right? Thirty minute games and that there's players here that flew in from all over the world—places like the Soviet Union and Romania—just to get on this team?"

Sam had explained some of that vaguely to Hector, but being here now and having it spelled out for him was starting to make him nervous. Not wanting to let Walter in on his teetering nerves, he played it off by shrugging again. "Yeah, I know," he said as the self-doubt sunk in fast.

Charlie and her friend walked by them and Walter's shoulders went all limp again as the goofball smile once again made an appearance. He bobbed his head up and down then actually bit his bottom lip and held his teeth there as he continued bobbing his head. Charlie smiled at him while the blonde looked away, and Hector could only assume she was trying not to laugh. "The team is sitting over there," Charlie said, pointing toward a group by the back door.

She glanced at Hector again, giving him another glimpse of those dramatically blue eyes, but like all the other times, she quickly looked away, and she and her friend kept walking.

After a few seconds of staring at the back of her head and that intensely scarlet ponytail, Hector brought his attention back to Walter, who was still doing the slumped shoulder thing and bobbing his head. "*Why* are you doing that?"

Walter looked at him and stopped. "It's called muted confidence. Read about it. I'm giving her the impression that I'm cool, confident, and just, you know, chillin'." He started bobbing his head again.

Hector couldn't help laughing again. "You're giving her the impression that you're a moron. You look like an idiot. What's with the biting your lip shit?"

"It's sexy!"

"No, it isn't." Hector laughed even more but made an effort to not ridicule Walter. The guilt of having done that to him for years was something he was still dealing with. He cleared his throat and stopped laughing, especially since he saw Walter's expression go all serious as he gazed in her direction.

"So her name is really Charlie?"

"Yeah, but not like a guy. It's Charlee spelled with a double e at the end." Walter took a deep breath. "Charlee Brennan. Isn't she beautiful?"

Hector was still stuck on the odd name. *Charlee?* "She's cute," he said, following Walter's gaze.

More like okay, and he left out what else he was thinking, *if you're into white girls.* Hector wasn't, never had been, especially ones *this* snowy white. The neighborhood he grew up in and the schools he'd attended his whole life had maybe a handful of them. He had nothing against them; he just didn't think he could relate. Everyone he hung out with was Hispanic, and so he was attracted mainly to Hispanic girls. He liked his girls with a little color, and, by that, he didn't mean bright red on white. He was into dark hair, dark eyes, and the darker the better—like Lisa. He pushed away the annoying thoughts of Lisa blowing him off so easily.

"She's amazing," Walter was still gazing in her direction. "And she's always nice to me. Like today she always says hi and even made sure I knew where the team was sitting. Stuff like that."

Hector was about to comment on that: say something like maybe she liked Walter too. Though it was obvious she was *just* being nice. No way could she or *anyone* be into Walter. The guy was a mess. And his ridiculous muted confidence bullshit only made things worse, but then it hit him. "You're on the team? U.S. under 20?"

"Yeah," Walter turned back to Hector. "So is Charlee. We're on the team at East Side too." Walter looked around and lowered his voice. "Personally, I don't think a speed knockout tournament is the way to go about looking for a replacement on the team. But we'd made it into the Junior World Olympiad just before the whole cheating scandal broke, and we had to drop that player. Luckily, they didn't punish the whole team by disqualifying the team, but they did give us only so much time to fill that spot. With a regular tournament taking days, we had no choice but to do a one-day knockout tournament."

Hector tried not to stare at Walter's bushy eyebrows as Walter peered at him. Did the guy not realize a near unibrow was not an attractive quality to girls? "You really think you have a shot at this?"

Again, shrugging off any signs of nervousness, Hector glanced away at the crowd growing larger with every minute they stood there. "Sure, why not?"

He wouldn't tell Walter that speed chess was his specialty. He knew a lot of serious players looked down on speed chess as if it weren't as dignified as playing the six-hour games. Walter's lowered-voice comment about this not being the greatest way to pick up the best player to fill the open spot on the team, was all Hector needed to know—Walter was one of those chess snobs.

Looking around again for Sam and not seeing him anywhere, Hector knew he had to get on with it and get registered. Sam had said he'd be there to walk him through the whole thing, but it looked like he was on his own now. With a deep breath, he turned back to Walter. "Well, I better get going if I'm gonna do this. Right?"

Walter smiled. "Best of luck. If you're anywhere near as good at this as you are at knockout punches, you should do well."

With that, Hector nodded and started through the crowd, his heart already beginning to thump anxiously.

CHAPTER 3

From the moment Charlee had spotted Hector with Walter in the parking lot, her heart had gone wild and her entire body literally went warm everywhere. In the past week, her fantasies about this guy had crossed over to another level. The times she touched herself privately now had become more often with him being whom she pictured doing the touching. But she told herself it was only because she truly thought she'd never see him again. And when she Googled her fantasies, she was reassured that erotic fantasies like the ones she'd been having were perfectly normal. But now, seeing him again, she felt almost mortified as if he could read her filthy thoughts. It was irrational, she knew, and though she hadn't been able to resist looking at him, she'd barely been able to for very long because of those damn fantasies.

Charlee hadn't even told Drew about them, and she normally told her everything. She'd considered telling her this past weekend when she and Drew had drank a couple of wine coolers and Drew made a few confessions of her own. But even Drew's confession wasn't bad enough. Basically, Drew had been one of those dumb girls in high school and actually sent her ex-boyfriend a photo of her boobs when she'd always said she would never do such a thing. She said she'd felt so stupid after sending it, and that's why she never even told Charlee about it until now.

That still wasn't bad enough for Charlee to share what she'd always thought was a little freaky about herself. Even now, Charlee felt the heat creep up her spine at the very thought of sharing this with anyone. She'd been around the guy for all of five minutes, and already late at night with her door locked deep under her blankets and in her freaky mind, he was doing to her things she'd only read about and caught glimpses of when she accidently went into a porn site on her computer.

She reasoned that it was because he was quite possibly the most gorgeous guy she'd ever seen. Why not choose him if she was going to fantasize about anyone? As the days passed since she'd seen him last and the details of his looks were beginning to get fuzzy, she'd come to the conclusion that she was probably building him up to be more amazing than in reality. But seeing him again today only confirmed something she hadn't thought possible—he was even more perfect than she remembered.

Sitting there now, watching him from across the room, she felt almost starstruck. It was as if the star of one of her favorite shows, or in Charlee's case her scandalous fantasies, was right here just a few yards away, and he was even more beautiful in person. Her eyes gazed downward from his face to that body. As Drew had so eloquently put it earlier, "The guy was built like a brick shithouse." Apparently that was a good thing—a *very* good thing indeed. Just watching him even from this distance made her gulp.

Not only was she sitting here shamefully intrigued by a guy based on his looks alone but there was something new adding to her excitement. It was rare. No. It was *unheard of,* at least in her experience, to see a guy like him at a chess tournament, but not only was he here as a spectator it appeared he might actually be a contender. Her jaw had nearly hit her knees when she saw Walter walk back to a confused-looking Hector and walked with him over to the registration tables. Just as mystifying was the fact that someone like Hector would be hanging around the likes of Walter.

Walter was obviously not competing, so there was only one other explanation: Hector was a chess player—one good enough to be competing here. *Geez!* Why did that excite her so?

"Take a picture, why don't you?" Drew said, nudging her.

Charlee straightened out in her seat, immediately tearing her eyes away from Walter and Hector. "Hmm?" She glanced around casually, trying to appear completely unaware of what Drew meant.

"Oh, stop," Drew giggled. "You haven't taken your eyes off him since we got here." Drew turned her head to Walter and Hector's direction. "Can't say I blame you. Mr. *Muy Caliente* is quite the eye candy." Drew leaned in and whispered but not soft enough. "You know what they say about Latin lovers."

Charlee nudged her and glanced around, feeling a little alarmed. "Will you stop? O.M.G., someone's gonna hear you."

"So what?" Drew looked around at the people sitting near them with that feisty little glare of hers. "Who cares?" She turned her attention back to Mr. *Muy Caliente* and clucked her tongue. "You think he's here to compete?"

"Looks like it," Charlee said, glad that she had reason to gaze at him again. "That's where you register to get your badge and number."

They'd already established earlier that Hector was the same *delicious* guy that had knocked Ross out, but Charlee hadn't told Drew much else about him, not even what little Walter had told her about him, and especially not that he was a boxer. She hadn't even shared his name with Drew. It was silly, but she and Drew had always sort of shared and lusted over the same unattainable guys together. For that very reason—because they seemed so unattainable—it didn't matter if they both fantasized about the same guy. But this time she didn't want to share. No other guy had ever invoked such fantasies in her. And she just didn't think she'd be as giggly and enjoy hearing Drew's fantasies about Hector like she usually did about other guys. Just listening to Drew referring to him as Mr. *Muy Caliente* had her pressing her lips together tightly already.

Thankfully her BFF had the attention span of a tick. She was already checking her phone for texts or any Facebook updates, no doubt.

"You better respond to anything you need to, using that phone now, because once the tournament starts, all phones are to be shut off completely." Her dramatic friend looked up at her with the horrified expression. "Drew, you act like this is the first tournament you've been to."

"Yeah, but watching you is different I don't get so bored. And I almost always make sure I get there when I know it's nearly over. This is different. I don't even know these people." Drew looked at her with a suddenly content expression as if she just remembered something. "But you said this was a fast one right?"

Charlee shook her head, exhaling softly. "No, I said these are *speed* games. They are shorter. Thirty minutes versus four to six hours. But there will be lots of them until everyone is knocked out and there is only one player left standing: the winner."

Drew was nothing if not dramatic. Her shoulders slumped, but she didn't say what Charlee knew she was thinking. She knew she should've just come alone. Her car *was* working now, but Drew had insisted on accompanying her. "You don't have to stay, you know? You can take off if you want. Go get those boots you wanted at the mall, and just come back for me later."

"Or I can give you a ride home."

Both Charlee and Drew turned around to look at Walter. Charlee glanced at Drew, who was already beginning to smirk, but her smirk morphed instantly into a bigger smile. Charlee had seen her do that many times, and she knew what it meant. She was up to something. "So who's your friend, Walter?"

Charlee closed her eyes for a second, praying this wasn't Drew's way of calling dibs on Hector, not that Charlee thought either of them had a chance with him. Drew was cute enough, and her socializing skills were light-years ahead of Charlee's, but even Drew had never been with someone like Hector. The guy was way out of both their leagues. Well, at least Charlee thought so, but judging by Drew's comments and the way some of the other girls in the auditorium were ogling him as well, she wasn't the only one that couldn't keep her eyes off him.

Glancing around casually, Charlee did her best to appear uninterested in knowing any more about Hector than she already did, but it was almost impossible. She was already bracing herself for what else Walter might let her in on.

"Oh, that's Hector." He glanced back in Hector's direction then back at Drew before finally looking at Charlee. "You didn't tell her about him?"

Drew glanced back at Charlee then shrugged and responded before Charlee could. "Well, I know he's the guy that knocked Ross on his ass, but what's he doing here?"

"He's in the tournament." Walter informed them as if it weren't a big deal.

It was a *huge* deal. If he won and took Vladimir's place on the team, it meant Charlee would get to see him on a daily basis. She stopped mid thought to swallow hard. She might actually get to talk to him—maybe even become a friend or at the very least an acquaintance.

A little worried that Drew seemed too interested but incredibly grateful that she was the one doing all the asking, Charlee hung on Walter's every word now. Unfortunately, he didn't offer much else except that he didn't know how good Hector was, so he wasn't sure what his chances were. Drew got a text, so the interrogation about all things Hector was momentarily dropped.

Charlee took advantage of Drew's distraction to gaze at Hector again. She'd never felt so drawn to someone in her life. What was it about him? Obviously his looks had a lot to do with it, if not *everything,* since she didn't know much else about him, and she'd never even spoken to him other than to say thank you. But there had to be more. She couldn't be *that* shallow, could she?

"So what's his deal?"

Charlee brought her attention back to her best friend, who was now putting her phone away. Drew's eyebrows lifted as her gaze went from Hector to Walter. Apparently, she wasn't done with her inquiring about Hector. As much as Charlee wanted to know more about him, she almost wished Drew would stop. She didn't like that she was so damn interested in *her* fantasy guy.

"What do you mean?" Walter was doing that weird thing with his head again, moving it slowly up and down, and he was biting his lower lip.

Drew rolled her eyes. "Does he have a girlfriend?"

Great, Drew *was* interested in him. But Charlee had to admit she was glad Drew asked. A guy like Hector *had* to be spoken for. She could tell already, based on the looks he was getting here, he could easily walk out with any girl he wanted tonight. Sure it was a chess tournament, not a social event, but this guy could probably walk into a funeral and pick up. Maybe this would put to rest her insane fantasies once and for all.

"I dunno," Walter said, glancing back in Hector's direction and chuckled. "You might find this hard to believe, but the guy's always been pretty popular with the ladies."

Drew rolled her eyes again this time, smiling and exchanging glances with Charlee, who was now feeling completely uncomfortable about the subject. "Oh, yeah, that's real hard to believe."

Her best friend turned her still-lifted eyebrow over in Hector's direction. All three of them watched now as he took his seat at one of the tables set up for the tournament. He smiled at his opponent as he shook his hand. God, there had to be *something* wrong him; even that smile was incredible. Charlee actually hoped Walter would tell them he was a criminal of sorts or maybe he was a big conceited jerk. He certainly had every right to be conceited.

They all continued to watch the players set up silently, but Charlee made note of the fact that Drew watched only Hector. Although Charlee was shy to a fault and the thought of holding even a conversation with this guy scared the daylights out of her, it secretly excited her that for once when both she and Drew found a guy attractive, she might actually have more in common with him than her much more outgoing best friend. Maybe for once she would have the always unspoken dibs Drew automatically had on any attractive guys.

It wasn't that Drew would selfishly stake her claim on all guys they met. She wasn't like that. But it was common knowledge that Charlee was about as socially inept as Walter seemed to be. Drew was a good friend. She often tried to encourage Charlee to be more flirtatious, and Charlee knew that not only would Drew step aside and give her dibs if she asked for it but she'd be utterly excited about it. Aside from Charlee's mother, Drew was the only other person who knew why it was so hard for Charlee to ever consider something like that. That's why Drew encouraged but never pushed. So while Charlee did her best to go as unnoticed as possible, Drew with her unreserved personality was just the opposite. It was inevitable that if either of the two would grab the attention of any guy it was always Drew.

As the tournament began, Charlee found it impossible to keep her eyes off him. Something nervously strange, but at the same time exciting, stirred in her the entire time. Even after he'd won twice and was moved to the next table as the players were narrowed down to just eight, the chances of him actually winning the whole thing seemed slim. She'd heard at least a little of each of today's contestants, yet she'd never once heard of Hector.

Turning her phone away from Drew's view, she Googled his name. There had to be something about some of the tournaments he might've been in or won. Even she got a few hits when she typed it in her own name.

Almost everything that came up was about his boxing. Her heart sped up a little when she clicked on one of the hits and a few images of him in the boxing ring shirtless came up. His half-naked body was everything she'd imagined and more. He even had a tattoo on his very muscular upper chest.

After staring at the photos, she clicked on a few of the other hits. There was one from this past summer of a ribbon cutting for the grand reopening of 5th Street, the gym Walter had mentioned Hector boxed at. Tapping on one of the photos so her phone would zoom in on it, she swallowed hard at the sight of him and a few other handsome guys in suits, smiling big. Her eyes were glued to his image.

"He's part owner."

Charlee flinched at the sound of Walter's voice so near her. She knew he'd been sitting next to her, but he'd been so into observing the competition she didn't expect him to be watching what she was doing. She instinctively moved the phone out of Walter's curious eyes. "I uh," she looked back down at the phone and closed out the browser. "I was just trying to get some stats on his game." She stared ahead, refusing to look Walter in the eye. "I know a little about all the other contestants, but I've never heard anything about him."

"Did you find anything?"

She frowned, still staring straight ahead but made sure she didn't look in Hector's direction. She pretended to be overly interested in the only female still in the competition. "No nothing. Aside from his boxing, there were a few hits about the online tournaments he's played and won but nothing near this level of competition." In an attempt to sound almost snobby about her doubts in Hector's abilities as a chess player because it was less embarrassing than Walter picking up on her real reasons for her interest in Hector, she continued without looking at him. "Is he supposed to be good or something? Because I'm a little surprised he's still in it."

Walter shrugged. "If he was invited, I'm sure he's pretty good." Charlee finally turned to look at him. He froze for a split second, and in the next he was doing that thing with his head again, moving it up and down. "Probably not as good as me, but you know," he bit his bottom lip again and even closed his eyes without saying more.

"Are you okay?"

His eyes flew up and his head stopped moving. "Yeah, why?"

"I dunno. It's just that you were . . ." She waved the thought away with her hand. "So what's his forte? I'm thinking it's gotta be speed play, or he wouldn't be in this still."

Walter nodded. "I actually don't know too much about Hector's game, but I agree. Speed's gotta be his thing. My money is on Kowalewski taking the whole thing today." He pointed at a blond guy with glasses playing in the next table over to Hector's left. "That guy right there. If both he and Hector win this round, they're up against each other next. If Hector wins, then he'll likely take the whole thing because I don't think anyone else here is a stronger player than Kowalewski."

Charlee stared at Kowalewski, though she'd rather have been staring at Hector. But she'd already been caught Google-stalking him on her phone, so she needed to be even more discreet now or at least continue to reaffirm that her curiosity in him was merely in the best interest of her chess team. They needed the best player here to replace a player she thought was one of if not *the* strongest on the team.

To her surprise and somewhat annoyance, not only did Drew stick around for the entire tournament but she seemed just as interested in seeing if Hector would win. They all watched in anticipation as Hector took the seat in front of

Kowalewski and shook his hand over the chess board. If Walter's prediction was right, this could be it. It seemed Walter wasn't the only one thinking what he was thinking, because this time around, things got really quiet. All eyes were on the mysterious dark horse who had ridden in and taken down each of his opponents with ease. It seemed everyone knew this would be the real challenge.

Squirming in her seat as the game commenced, Charlee's eyes were fixed on their play. She didn't even care that she was now showing complete and blatant interest in Hector, because everyone else was too.

Thirty minutes later when Kowalewski reached over to shake Hector's hand, admitting defeat, Charlee nearly jumped out of her seat. She managed to remain seated, though her hand *did* fly to her mouth. Drew turned to her with a curious twinkle in her eye. Charlee withdrew the huge grin she knew was plastered on her face now and quickly pretended to be wiping something off her lips. She sat back in her chair, glancing away from Drew's inquiring stare.

Her best friend was too damn perceptive for her own good. Charlee wouldn't give her anything further to scrutinize. Doing so proved harder than expected. After Hector took down Kowalewski, Charlee could barely sit still. Visions of him sitting in the school's small chess lab flooded her mind. She knew that if he did make the team, she'd likely not only get to know him but she'd for sure get to play him eventually—sit for hours across from him close enough to touch him if she ever dared.

They announced the last two players standing: Hector Ayala and Morgan Bisbee. Walter seemed to think Hector had this, and for some reason, that appeared to bother him. "I would've rather had Kowalewski on the team," he whispered as the time on the last match began. "Obviously speed play is not his thing, but he's a force to be reckoned with in regular tournaments. He would've been a tremendous asset to the team."

Charlee shifted her weight from one leg to the other, chewing her pinky nail. Her heart hadn't stopped pounding since Hector had started his match with Kowalewski. They'd gotten up with everyone else and went and stood closer to the last table where Hector and Morgan sat battling it out.

From where she stood now, as much as she wanted to pay close attention to the moves being made on the chess board, she could barely keep her eyes from wandering to his face. He was one of those players that checked out once he started playing. As many people that surrounded the table, it was obvious he was deep in his own world. The intensity in his eyes, as he watched his opponents move and then made his quickly, was unrelenting.

Charlee swallowed hard, her eyes traveling from the crease between his eyes, as he studied the pieces on the board, to his heavily lashed eyes. This close she could see a small scar that ran across his left brow, splitting the brow just so. It was the perfect imperfection to an otherwise flawless face. She also noticed how tight his jaw would clench just before he made a move. As big as his hands were, his fingers moved about the board gracefully from one side to the other without dropping any of the pieces.

As the game came down to the last few minutes and they began to move at a much faster speed, the crowd's whispers became louder with excitement. Speed chess had never been Charlee's thing. She could barely keep up with their moves, so it was difficult to anticipate what Hector's next move might be. Yet as they moved at what seemed like a ridiculous speed now, her heart began to pound against her chest. Any minute now, they'd have a winner. Then she saw it. Hector could bring his knight to f6 and his queen could swing over to the H file. He was going to win. *He was going to win!*

In the next couple of moves, it was over. The crowd clapped, seemingly as impressed as Charlee was. Hector stood surrounded by the officials and team trainers. Cameras, including phone cameras, went off left and right. Many congratulated Hector, while others from the team walked up to shake his hand and introduce themselves.

Charlee wished she had it in her to at least take advantage of the flurry and take a few pictures of her own: photos she could keep on her phone and stare at forever, maybe even while she . . . At the moment, she stood frozen in place barely able to believe that he—the guy she'd been secretly obsessing about all week—was now on her chess team and very likely would soon be attending ESU.

For someone who wasn't too keen on Hector being the newest member of the team, Walter changed his tune real fast. Hector went from being the unknown last minute contender to the newest member of the team—a team that would soon be going to the Junior National Olympiad. Everyone wanted to know him now. As soon as things finally began to die down and Hector was done with all the unrehearsed interviews for the school paper and meeting with all the trainers, Walter grabbed him.

He stood a few feet away from Charlee and Drew, congratulating Hector, and then he glanced up in Charlee's direction. Suddenly terrified at the thought of Walter possibly bringing Hector over to introduce him to her, Charlee grabbed Drew's arm. It was one thing to fantasize about this guy and worship him from afar; it was quite another to actually speak with him. She wasn't ready for that. She hadn't given it much thought, but she'd come up with something soon enough—work up the nerve to even talk to him slowly in the coming weeks a little at a time, not all in one night.

"Let's go," she said. "You've been a good sport all this time. Let's go check out those boots you wanted to buy. We can grab some Taco Bell on the way. My treat."

Drew stopped dead in her tracks. "Oh, no, you don't."

Charlee turned to face her smirking friend. "What do you mean?"

"I don't know when you were planning on telling me, and I don't know who you think you're fooling, but you got a thing for this guy—a *major* thing."

Charlee glanced back at Walter and Hector who were already walking toward them then turned back to Drew wide-eyed. "What?" She tried pulling Drew along with her again, feeling instantly mortified. "Don't be ridiculous," she whispered loudly. "I don't know him. I've never even spoken to him."

"Well, now's your chance." This time Drew held Charlee's arm and turned her around just in time to see that breathtaking smile once again as Walter and Hector approached them.

CHAPTER 4

Annoyingly, Hector was still feeling an incredible amount of guilt every time he even looked at Walter's bloated face. The least he could do was agree to walk over and talk to the girl he was trying so hard to impress.

Just a few feet away from them, Hector spoke through his smile, "If you start doing that thing with your head and biting your lip, I'm out."

"But—"

Hector turned to him incredulous. "Are you seriously gonna do that again? I wasn't kidding, dude. I thought we talked about this earlier." Hector lowered his voice. "Trust me. You look like an idiot. *Do not* do that again, okay?" He discreetly placed his hand on Walter's arm then squeezed *hard* and whispered. "Okay?"

Walter flinched then rolled his eyes but finally agreed with a nod. They walked over to the girls. Unlike when he and Walter had first arrived, Charlee wasn't acting as friendly anymore. She was probably tired of being there. Hector could relate. He was like that too. During play, he'd get so lost in the game hours could fly and he wouldn't even know it. Watching a tournament was different. While he enjoyed it, he could only watch for so long before he was done.

Neither one of the girls said anything when they arrived. Charlee even seemed preoccupied, glancing in another direction. Walter's dumb ass, who was supposed to be bringing him over to meet another member of the team, said nothing either. Instead he stood there looking all nervous and fidgeting with his hands. Finally, the other girl with Charlee spoke. "Congrats!" She smiled, holding out her hand.

Hector shook her hand and smiled. "Thanks."

"We know who *you* are," she said, prodding Charlee with her arm. "I'm Drew and this is Charlee. Looks like you two are going to be on the team together now."

Charlee nodded, her smile was forced, and she didn't offer her hand like Drew had. Those sparkling blues eyes of hers darted away in another direction the moment they met his. "That's an unusual name," Hector said in an attempt to get her to look at him again. "I don't think I've ever met a girl named Charlee before."

She turned to him a bit wide-eyed but then smiled, making his own smile go even bigger. "It's Charlotte actually, but everyone calls me Charlee."

Hector nodded, taking in her deep blue eyes. "Ah, I see. Charlee. I like that. It's cute—suits you."

Their eyes locked for the tiniest of moments before she glanced away again, pulling a strand of that fiery red hair behind her ear.

Her friend cleared her throat, and Hector turned to see her grinning. "So, is this the first chess team you've been on, Hector?"

It was only when he saw Drew grin even bigger that he realized he wore the biggest goof-ass smile still. Had Charlee smiling at him actually done that to him? He felt almost as stupid as Walter bobbing his head looked and immediately toned the smile down to a smirk.

Walter nudged Hector before he could respond to Drew. "Since you made this team, then most likely they'll be inviting you to play on the school team as well." Walter's head started the damn bobbing thing again. These girls must think them the two biggest idiots. Hector slid his hand in his pocket, making sure to elbow Walter in the process. Walter picked up on it right away and stopped the head movement then continued. "You can't start school mid semester, but their inviting you to come and sit in with the chess team as soon as you want is a sure sign they want you on it. You gonna be there on Monday?"

Trying to regain some of his cool back, Hector glanced around, not showing much interest. "I'll have to check my schedule, but I think I'll be able to swing it."

Walter started to fill him in on the time and place they meet, but Drew interrupted him. "So are you doing anything to celebrate this win, Hector? This is a pretty big deal." She turned to Charlee with a smile. "Isn't it, Charlee?"

Immediately his eyes were on Charlee again. *Yeah, real smooth. What the hell was his problem?* She nodded but glanced away again, not looking the least bit impressed. Hector wondered if maybe she too was a chess snob. He stared at her probably a little too long, because when he turned back to Drew, she was looking at him a bit quizzically with that same grin she wore earlier. *Damn it.*

"I hadn't made any plans," he said, overcompensating with a flirtatious smile. "But I'm sure I'll find one way or another to celebrate."

He had plenty of open invitations he could head to straight from here. Weekend or not, his evenings were never dull. "Well, I think you should do *something*." Drew smirked, giving Hector the tiniest bit of hope. Maybe he'd confused her grinning earlier for having caught him gaping at Charlee with his goofy smile, and she'd actually been flirting with him. He really hoped so, because he felt pretty stupid now.

He sized Drew up very obviously to test his theory. She was a little on the skinny side, and he'd never been into blondes, but then he'd never been into redheads either, and here one smile from Charlee had turned him into a bumbling idiot. Blond or not, Drew was *doable*. Typically, he'd be all over what was beginning to sound like an invitation, but for some reason, he wasn't feeling it. Still, he decided to play along just to make up for having been so transparent about getting caught up with Charlee—the girl Walter was pining after. "You have any suggestions?"

Bingo! Her face lit up as he expected it would, and he felt the relief seep in. His theory was right. This was exactly what the sheepish grins had been about. She was flirting with him—not on to him. Just as she began to speak, two girls he'd never seen before walked up to them. "Hector Ayala?" The taller of the two turned to Drew and Charlee. "I'm sorry to interrupt, but I just *had* to ask." She turned back to Hector without giving Drew or Charlee a moment to respond. "Are you really the same Hector from 5th Street?"

Hector smiled, nodding but didn't get a chance to answer before Walter answered for him, "The one and only!"

Hector turned to Walter, who was starting the stupid head thing again, and shot him a look. Walter stopped immediately and to Hector's relief lost the unconvincing smug expression as well.

"I told you." The shorter girl said with a big smile then reached her hand out to Hector. "I'm Miriam and this is Leticia." Hector shook Miriam's hand then Leticia's as well.

"Finally, a Latino on the team," Leticia said. "I was cheering you on for that reason alone, but then Miriam said you were from 5th Street in East L.A., and I couldn't believe it. I used to live right by there."

"Really?" He smiled.

Out of habit because it's what he usually did when girls came up to him like this and because Leticia's body language was giving him the go-ahead to do so, Hector checked her out. *Very nice.* Miriam wasn't half bad either but nothing real eye catching—your typical Hispanic girl—long dark straight hair, big dark eyes and a little too much makeup. But Leticia had it going on and she knew it too. She was tall and slender but not too thin. The curves were in all the right places, just like he liked them, and she was showing just enough cleavage to tease at how nicely stacked she was.

"Yes, I did," Leticia smiled a little more seductively now that she saw she had his full attention. "Not for very long, but even after we moved, we used to go back a lot because my mom liked the grocery stores in that area."

Hector nodded as Leticia continued to talk. He glanced at Drew, who did nothing to hide the annoyance she was obviously feeling over this little interruption. Charlee didn't look too happy either, but she wasn't as blatant as Drew. He had a feeling what they were thinking, because he was sort of wondering himself. These two didn't look the chess tournament type at all. And they were dressed more like two girls out on the prowl for the night than they were for a chess tournament. "We play chess too," Miriam said as if he'd read his mind.

"Not good enough to enter a competition like this," Leticia added with another flirtatious smile.

For the first time since they'd arrived, Charlee suddenly spoke. "It's by invitation only."

"Yeah, you don't just *enter* to try out for the U.S. team," Drew explained.

The sarcasm didn't go unnoticed by Leticia because her eyebrow lifted. "I know that."

"Have you ever played in a speed tournament?" Walter asked.

Apparently he was the only one of them that failed to catch the snarky tone in Charlee and Drew's remarks, because he seemed genuinely curious.

Leticia must've mistaken Walter's question to be another jab at her level of chess skill, because her response was just as snappy. "No, but I *have* been in tournaments."

"Ever won any?" Charlee asked, those deep blue eyes of hers finally staying in one place long enough for Hector to *really* get a good look. He'd never seen lashes the color of hers. From this distance, he could see they were as bright red as her hair. From further away, they'd looked almost dark brown, but he saw now that was only because they were so thick. It made the blue in her eyes stand out even more. They were something else: way different than any eyes he'd ever admired up close. And he could easily get lost trying to count all of the delicate freckles sprinkled over her cute little nose and around her eyes.

He glanced back at Leticia now. She'd gone from looking pissed to smiling playfully again as she whipped her long hair back. "I've won a few actually. But I'm not here to talk about me. I just wanted to congratulate the newest member of the U.S. team." She actually let out a loud hoot and did a fist pump. "You make me so proud, Hector." She moved in closer, handing her phone to Miriam. "Will you take a picture with me?" Without giving him a chance to respond, she wrapped her arms around his torso and adjusted them both so they now stood directly in front of Drew and Charlee but with their backs to them.

Never one to miss an opportunity like this but more than anything feeling the need to make up for having come across like such a sap earlier, Hector pulled her close. He felt her ample cleavage press up against his chest, and he moved his hand up and down her back as they posed for the photos. Miriam then asked Walter if he could take one of the three of them together and he did. The girls got a little silly and loud, asking Walter to take more photos: one pose here, a different pose there, one after another. Leticia, who'd been touchy-feely from the very first photo, eventually slipped her hand into Hector's.

By the time the impromptu photo session was done and the playful but mostly flirtatious banter was over, both girls were making it all too clear that if he were up for hanging out with one or both of them tonight, so were they. This was more than enough distraction. He'd just about forgotten about Charlee and Drew until he saw Walter searching the room, looking a bit disconcerted. There weren't anywhere to be seen.

Hector pulled away from Leticia's hold for a moment and leaned closer to Walter. "What happened? Did they leave?"

"I don't see them." Walter shrugged with a frown. "I didn't even notice when they left."

"They left as soon as I took the first photo," Miriam informed them.

"Are they good friends of yours?" Leticia asked. "Because I'm sorry, but they were a little bitchy."

Hector smirked, feeling even more relieved now. He couldn't argue there. They had been on the bitchy side, especially Drew—further confirmation that she'd been flirting with him. Walter, on the other hand, seemed completely at a loss.

He looked at the girls blankly. "They hardly said anything."

Of course, Walter hadn't seen it. He was so into little Ms. Blue Eyes she could do no wrong. Hector knew from the moment Walter had informed him that she was also on the U.S. team she had to be good, but he was even more curious now. "On a scale from one to ten, how good would you say Charlee's game is?"

A big smile spread across Walter's face. "Oh, she's good. She's our resident tactician. I'd say at least a nine maybe even ten."

Maybe even ten? And a tactician? Of course, if long, thought-out play was her specialty, she was no doubt a chess snob herself. No wonder she hadn't seemed even remotely impressed by his win like everyone else. And here Hector had actually considered for a moment that maybe she too was being a bit catty with Leticia for the same reason as Drew. It was just the chess snob in her.

Leticia squeezed Hector's hand, and he squeezed back then patted Walter on the shoulder. "See you Monday, big guy. Thanks for walking me through this today. I owe you one."

Hector and both girls made their way through the crowd, being stopped several times by people wanting to congratulate him. As smug as he felt and as great as this had worked out, one thought still came to mind. Would everyone else on the team be thinking the same thing—that a knockout speed tournament was not the greatest way to go about acquiring the best player for the team?

As if tonight's win hadn't been enough, he'd still have to prove himself? The good thing about knowing Charlee was not impressed by him was he wouldn't have to worry about the thought that crossed his mind more than once tonight when he got such a close look at those blue eyes—that maybe *just maybe* he *could* be attracted to a cute little redhead with the most amazing blue eyes he'd ever seen.

She was Walter's to pine over—not his—not that he thought Walter stood a chance with Charlee. Still, he'd done enough to bring Walter down over the years. He wasn't about to add more to his already insufferable, guilty conscience.

As Hector reached his truck, Leticia, who'd already been rubbing up against him even as they walked through the parking lot, wasted no time. She leaned her body into his, pushing him up against the truck. Smiling, he looked down at her, and she kissed him long and deep, her very skillful tongue already awakening parts of him that had sat still for too long that day. She pulled away, licking her lips with a coy smile. "That's to congratulate you for your awesome accomplishment today."

Before he could thank her right back in the same way for her graciousness, Miriam tugged at his other hand. He turned to Miriam as she tilted her head and bit her bottom lip. "I wanna congratulate you too."

Hector smiled even bigger. He thought he'd picked up on where this night be heading earlier. Walking through the parking lot holding both their hands had been an even bigger indicator that this might happen, but now Miriam was confirming it.

Without saying a word, he licked his lips, pulling Miriam to him. Leticia scooted over a bit to make room for her against Hector's body. His lips were on Miriam's as soon as she was close enough. Bringing her hand behind his head and running her fingers through his hair, Miriam's equally skilled tongue and the fact that he'd have them both naked soon enough, made him practically growl against her lips. Thank God his mom was away for the weekend. It was times like this Hector knew he needed to get his own place soon.

Miriam finally pulled away from his lips and stared at him for a moment before looking around the darkened parking lot, saying exactly what he was thinking. "Maybe we should all go *celebrate* somewhere a little more private."

"Definitely," he agreed quickly, motioning them to get in his truck.

Yep, he was better off sticking to what he knew. Being with two girls like Leticia and Miriam at once was something he was more familiar with than being with just one like Charlee.

He was treated to another crotch-tightening kiss by both girls as he helped them each in one by one into the passenger-side door of his truck. As he walked around the truck, he turned on his phone. He'd turned it off when he registered and was instructed his phone was to remain completely turned off and out of sight for the duration of the tournament or he'd be disqualified.

Still not knowing why Sam never showed up, he felt a twinge of nervousness as the phone powered on and he heard it ping several times. He'd been completely out of reach to anyone for over four hours now.

The second he climbed into the truck and sat down, Leticia kissed him a bit more frantically than she had earlier. Pulling away as he heard his phone ping several more times, he held his phone up, "Let me check my phone real quick, sweetheart," he said against her lips.

She pulled away from him but only a few inches, and she ran her hand up his thigh, stopping just before his crotch. With the anticipation building, he checked his texts first. He had several, but he could deal with the ones from girls later. He clicked on the two from his brother Abel. The first one he'd sent hours ago, around the time the tournament started.

Dude where are you? Sam's been trying to get a hold of you. He was in a wreck, but he says he's okay and wanted me to tell you he'll be late but he'll be there. Where's there? He wouldn't tell me.

Leticia's hand had worked his way a little higher, and he glanced at her when she rubbed him over his pants. She smiled, leaning in to kiss him again, but he held his phone up again. The fact that Sam hadn't made it worried him now, even though Abel's text said he was okay, so he read the next text quickly, ignoring Leticia. The second one was sent hours later.

Sam's got a concussion. But don't worry. He sounds fine to me. He's giving them hell over at the Veterans' hospital. He wants to leave, but they're not letting him. Where the hell are you and how come you're not answering your phone? That old crank still won't tell me where you are!

Hector frowned. Being a boxer, he knew all too well that a concussion could be nothing but it could also feel like nothing and turn into something *bad*. He'd been telling Sam for years now that old VW van of his was a deathtrap. He'd seen them look like accordions after a wreck. No telling how bad the wreck had really been. Sam was too old to be dealing with that shit.

He listened to his voicemail next: the first from Sam telling him he'd be late and arguing with someone else in the background then two from Abel saying basically the same thing he'd said in the texts. The last one was from Abel again just a few minutes earlier. In it, he wasn't as calm as in the first two.

"Sam's pissing me off. Nobody's heard from you in hours, and he's the only one that knows where you are, but he ain't talking. Call me *now*, Hector, or I swear to God, concussion or not, I'll go down to that hospital and beat it out of that old man."

"Damn it." He hung up and hit speed dial.

"Something wrong?" Leticia asked, pulling away just slightly.

"Yeah, there is. Do you two have a car here?"

They both shook their heads. "No, we were dropped off and were gonna call and get a ride until . . ."

Abel answered just then. "Where the hell are you!"

Hector motioned to Leticia to give him a second. He explained quickly about the tournament and having to turn off his phone then asked about Sam.

"How's he doing?"

"Good enough. You know him. He's probably driving everyone crazy at that hospital. I guess he's got some hemorrhaging in his brain, but he ain't saying much more." Abel chuckled. "He says they're full of shit. He feels just fine."

Hector was still focused on the words that scared the hell out of him. *He's got some hemorrhaging in his brain.*

As soon as he was off the phone with Abel, he asked the girls where they wanted to be dropped off and apologized for having to postpone their night together. He skidded out of the parking lot, his heart racing in fear. He should've known something was wrong when Sam never showed up. The only thing that would've kept Sam from being here today was death itself or being held against his will. Hector was only grateful it was the latter.

CHAPTER 5

Between dealing with Sam who was released the day after the tournament and his training for the fight that Friday, Hector hadn't been able to make it to either of the chess teams meetings yet. To say his brother had been ecstatic about Hector making the U.S team was the understatement of the century. Abel said he'd always known Hector was good but he'd never imagined he was U.S. team good. The guy was telling everyone that would listen, and even though Hector would roll his eyes and pretend to be annoyed by Abel's bragging, he secretly loved how proud he'd made his big brother.

Sam had been adamantly warned that he needed to take it easy—no overexerting himself, just rest. But he was moving that week to Florida, and, of course, his stubborn ass wasn't putting that off for anything, no matter what the "quacks" said.

So Hector and Abel had done most of the work, helping Sam load up the huge moving truck for the last few days, and then Hector hit the gym every evening. Sam and his brother would be driving cross-country for the next week. Hector had already downloaded and setup the video message app on the old crank's phone so they could stay in touch about anything Hector needed to ask him about chess. The chess team would have to wait until the end of week at the earliest. But he was getting antsy, wondering if he'd have to prove himself still.

Luckily, he didn't have to wait until the end of the week to find out. To his surprise, Walter showed up on Wednesday at the gym. Hector spotted him just as he was finishing up his training with Abel in the ring. He walked over to the side of the ring and leaned on the ropes. "Hey, what are *you* doing here?"

Walter shrugged, looking a little uncomfortable. He glanced around the gym. "I've been, you know, thinking about joining a gym. You're right: I need to get in shape."

Hector laughed. "But I thought you were up to lifting thirty-five pounds." He climbed over the ropes and jumped off the ring, landing next to Walter. He jabbed the big guy against the arm to show him he was only messing with him. "Well, you've come to the right place, my friend. And I just finished my workout, so I can show you around and get you started if you want."

Walter smiled. "Yeah, that's what I was hoping for." His eyes went a little sheepish. "You did say you owed me one, so I thought maybe you could show me what the best workout for me is. Just this once," he added quickly. "After that, I'll just do whatever you showed me on my own."

Hector smiled as they both made their way to the locker room. Walter certainly hadn't wasted any time cashing in the favor. Hector hadn't even remembered saying it until Walter brought it up. Of course, he agreed, not so much because he owed him for his help at the tournament but because he was still feeling that annoying twinge of remorse.

"First thing," he said as he took a seat on a bench in the locker room. He started to work on taking the wrap off his hands but stopped and looked up. "What your wearing is not gonna fly. It will for today, but next time you need to wear shorts."

Walter looked down at his baggy sweats and ridiculous long-sleeved oversized Adidas shirt then looked up. "What's wrong with this?"

Hector looked back down at his hands. "You'll see just a few minutes after you start working out."

The guy would be sweating like a pig in no time. Had he *never* worked out in his life? That's the only way he couldn't know this.

"And next time?" Walter asked. Hector looked up just in time to see Walter rub his neck with his hand. "I don't wanna take up too much of your time because, uh . . ." his eyes met Hector's for a second then darted away again. "I was hoping maybe you could help me with something else too."

Hector refrained from frowning, but was this guy kidding? Instead of frowning, he stared at him without saying a word and waited. What could he possibly want now? After watching Walter rub his neck a few more times without saying anything, Hector lost his patience.

"Just spit it out already. What is it?"

Walter hesitated again until Hector stopped refraining and unleashed an all-out scowl.

"It has to do with Charlee," Walter finally said.

Curiosity replaced his irritation, but the irritation was quickly back when he remembered her total lack of enthusiasm about her newest teammate. "What about her?"

"Well," Walter started with the neck rubbing again, but Hector gave him a look again and he stopped. "I was thinking now that you're on the team maybe you could help me . . ." A few guys walked by and Walter shut up until they were far enough away. "You know, help me get her attention or something."

Hector looked up at him, surprised at just how irritated he felt, remembering Charlee's indifference and the impression he must've made on her, smiling all stupid like he had. Growing up in a neighborhood where it was predominantly Hispanic, Hector had always gotten the feeling that white people sort of looked down on them. It never bothered him, and it wasn't his reason for preferring Latina girls over white girls. He just thought he personally wasn't attracted to them—they weren't his type. Now he was beginning to think maybe that wasn't the case. So maybe his reasons for never even considering being with one ran deeper.

Walter must've mistaken Hector's irritation about Charlee for irritation about his request, because he sat down, looking very frustrated and started pleading his case. "I really like her, man, and I know I need to get in shape. That's why I'm here, but I'm no good at talking to girls. I get all choked up and nervous, and then something stupid always happens."

Hector scoffed, throwing the final piece of wrap from his hands in the trash and stood up. As if he would know the first thing about impressing white girls. Obviously, he didn't. Then he remembered her friend Drew. She was white and she'd flirted with him. Okay, maybe he *was* being stupid about judging girls by their race. He'd never had a racist thought in his life, and he wasn't going to start now.

"Yeah, I guess I can give you a few tips." He pulled his t-shirt off and pulled out a clean one from his locker. "First things first." He punched his own abs lightly. "You don't have to get this hard, but you *have* to work on that gut. No tip I give you is gonna work as long as you're hauling all that weight around." He pulled the clean t-shirt over his head and almost didn't say his next statement, but he had to. If Walter wanted his help, he was going to hear the truth even if it hurt. "And you gotta do something about the unibrow and that hair. C'mon." He threw a towel at Walter and started out the locker room.

Walter touched his unibrow and frowned but said nothing then touched his hair. "What's wrong with my hair?"

"Dude," Hector glanced back at him. "The shaggy look wasn't even cool when it was in, and that was like five years ago. Cut that shit off already."

Saying Walter was sporting the shag look was putting it nicely. The shag had actually been a style once upon a time. Hector didn't know *what* to call that curly mess on Walter's head. Hector had his work cut out for him. *Great*. All he'd wanted was to ease a little of the guilt he felt about Walter. Now the guy had become his project.

~*~

He was a pig. Charlee reminded herself again as her heart pounded faster with every step she got closer to her school's chess lab. She knew Hector was too good to be true Saturday—knew there had to be *something* wrong with him. Walter had already mentioned he was popular with the ladies. *That* had come as no surprise, but to behave the way he had in the parking lot with those two girls was just disgusting.

It was bad enough to see the one girl, Leticia, throw herself at him the way she had, especially since they knew perfectly well she'd just met him. But both Drew and Charlee's jaws had dropped when they saw him pull the second girl to him and proceed to make out with her as well. Drew had been that close to honking as they sat there in her car, watching the whole thing unfold just a few spaces away. But Charlee had begged her not to.

There was no question where the three of them were headed and what the rest of their night entailed. The way he'd skidded out of there in such a hurry just added to her disgust. Obviously, he could hardly wait to get to it. And although Charlee would never admit it, even to Drew, she'd been green with envy that those two *whores* got to do with him what she'd been fantasizing about doing for days. But she'd never stoop to the level of being with a guy who clearly had zero respect for women, no matter how beautiful he was.

Granted those two sluts didn't deserve any respect but still. Didn't he have any respect for himself? If those girls were so ready to jump in his truck just minutes after meeting him, surely this wasn't the first time they'd done something like this.

Reality kicked her in the gut as she walked in the room and the very first thing her eyes saw was Hector standing around with Walter and some of the other guys in the class. He glanced at her for a moment and smiled when their eyes met. The visual of him and those two girls in the parking lot thwarted what should've been all out bliss that he'd actually showed up and she'd be seeing him this close *every* day now.

Charlee smiled back but looked away quickly. Her only hope now was that, aside from being a pig, he was a conceited jerk, because, honestly, who would blame *any* guy for taking up girls offering a threesome?

Feeling the irritation overwhelm her, she took a seat at one of the tables furthest from where Hector and the other guys were standing. For the past three days when he didn't show up to the meetings and just a few minutes, ago she was so ready to mentally lynch him from her thoughts that she completely disallowed herself to have any more fantasies about him. Now here it was only the very first time she'd seen him since being witness to that shameless parking lot scene, and she was already making excuses for his behavior.

A few nights this past week, she actually wished she hadn't seen him that night with those girls so she could continue her harmless *fantasizing*. But seeing him now only reaffirmed that being around him every day might not make those fantasies seem so harmless anymore. It was also painfully obvious from the way he'd handled those girls that it hadn't been the first time he'd been in a situation like that.

This could be bad news. Her hopes that maybe he'd changed his mind about joining the school team had been crushed. Falling for someone like Hector would not only be hopeless but, in her case, it would be *bad*. She could feel it already, and she'd barely spoken to the guy.

Glancing up when she heard the group of guys laugh, their eyes met again. Even as he laughed, he'd been watching her from across the room. Turning away this time not returning the smile, she began to set up her chess pieces. She was really beginning to get a bad feeling about this.

She sunk in her seat a bit. Her assumption about him being a conceited jerk was also slowly flying out the window. This whole week when he hadn't showed up, she'd played out a few theories in her head: perhaps making the U.S. team was obviously commendable but joining a college chess team wasn't cool enough for him, or maybe he was so arrogant as to think he didn't *need* to show up to the meetings or labs for the school team. Maybe just like he had on Saturday, he could show up at just the tournaments and blow everyone out of the water. She'd even imagined him walking in, completely full of himself and unapproachable.

Now here he was not only socializing and looking as down to earth as the next guy but he genuinely seemed to be enjoying the company of these people—her people—people she would've never in a million years thought would be intermingling with someone like him. He'd taken two girls home Saturday night for crying out loud. Most of the guys here looked as if they'd never taken a girl home *period*. Still, for someone her mother would probably refer to as a lady-killer and who'd won the way he did Saturday to actually come in here and not act superior in *any* way, well, it was just infuriating!

It wasn't even just about looks. She and Walter were the only other two on the school team who were also on the U.S. team with him. Nobody else in here had even been invited to play in the tournament. Hector was superior to mostly everyone in here in more ways than one. She'd hoped to see that he was stuck-up, arrogant—at the very least a little smug. Instead, he was being mindful of everyone. He'd even smiled at her—*twice*.

She hadn't realized how lost she was in her thoughts until someone pulled the chair across from her out. "Hey," Walter said as she looked up.

"Hey," she smiled then went back to setting up her board.

In the last few days, Walter had been talking to her a little more often than before. It seemed his sitting with her and Drew at the tournament then bringing Hector over to meet them after had sort of made them friends, not that she hadn't been nice to him before. The Monday after the Ross incident, she'd gone right up to him first thing when she got to the chess lab and asked how he was. She'd even thanked him for what he'd done once again, although he didn't seem too thrilled to be talking about it. But he did mention having to go to the emergency room the day after. Of course, she felt terrible, but he'd changed the subject quickly. She got that he was evidently embarrassed. She didn't want to embarrass him further, so she'd stopped asking him anything related, except for the few times she'd asked about Hector.

This week, she'd made it a point *not* to ask about Hector at all until yesterday morning. More out of hope than anything, she'd asked if Hector had decided not to join the school team after all. Walter said he hadn't talked to him since.

Walter began arranging the chess pieces on his side of the board. "Kind of cool to have someone like Hector on the team, huh?"

She stopped arranging her pieces and looked up at him again. Hearing the man-crush in his voice only added to her already conflicting feelings about Hector. "What do you mean someone like Hector?"

Walter smiled a little bigger this time but still looked every bit as nervous as he always did when he talked to her. Charlee would never hold his weirdness against him. In a small way, he reminded her of herself. She, too, did dumb stuff to hide her embarrassment or feeling out of place. Only now, there was an added oddity to Walter's normal weirdness. "I told you he boxes, right?" She nodded, pushing away the visual of Hector shirtless and in the ring. "So he's fighting tomorrow night, and he said if we go, we can all get into the after party right there at 5th Street." He leaned in, wincing a little as if in pain. "His brother is Abel Ayala. Not sure if you know anything about boxing, but he's getting pretty famous around East L.A. and in the boxing world."

Charlee stared at him. She'd never heard of him, but she could hardly believe that on top of it all Hector had a brother who was *pretty famous*. No wonder those girls were all over him. With fame, there also came fortune. Wow. She didn't think he could be any more unattainable.

"Anyway," Walter said, clearing his throat, still wincing as he set up his last piece. "He said it hasn't been formally announced and probably won't be for months until everything is finalized, but it looks like Abel's going for the heavyweight title next year. That's what the party is for. And it's not open to anyone else but close friends and family, so it's cool that Hector said we can all go." Walter's eyes suddenly opened even wider. "He said Felix Sanchez might even be there."

Charlee caught herself as her mouth fell slightly open. Felix Sanchez—now there was a name she recognized. He'd become one of those household names now like Shaquille O'Neal or Tiger Woods. Even if you knew nothing about the sport they played, everyone's heard of them because they were all over television and tabloids either for good reason or bad.

In the case of Felix, there was a little from column A and a little from column B. While he did a lot for his charity to help troubled youth and he won quite a few big bouts, he was also in the tabloids a lot. Because of his famously boyish good looks, in spite of how many fights he'd been in, his many romantic escapades with Hollywood starlets and other famous female athletes had made the front pages of countless gossip magazines.

Charlee purged the incredible urge to roll her eyes. Of course, Hector would be closely acquainted with someone like Felix. In a way, she was happy to hear this. His inviting the guys in the chess club to such an exclusive party had only furthered the confirmation of one thing: her theory about Hector thinking himself to too good to hang with the chess club people was completely debunked. She needed something, *anything* that would remind her he wasn't perfect. Sure being friends with someone like Felix added to the already staggering mountain of cool Hector stood atop of, but it also helped further the other conclusion she'd come to about Hector Saturday night.

She wasn't at all sure how serious he was about boxing, but if his brother was going for a major title, Hector couldn't be far behind. Felix was the perfect example of what anyone even considering getting involved with Hector had to look forward to. She almost smiled smugly. This could very well kill the already weak temptation to continue to fantasize about the guy.

Catching Walter's pained expression one more time, she finally had to ask. "Are you okay?"

The pained expression morphed into an even weirder one, and he started doing that head-bobbing thing again. "Yeah, I'm just a little sore is all. Me and Hector had a long workout last night over at 5th Street."

Charlee lifted an eyebrow. "You work out with him?"

"Yep," the head bobbing got more severe until Hector's hand landed heavily on Walter's shoulder and Walter froze.

"I'll play the winner." He pulled out the chair next to Walter, spun it around then straddled it, resting his big arms on the back.

Charlee's mouth went dry in reaction to seeing him this close so suddenly, and her heart kicked into overdrive instantly. Not only had he interrupted the thoughts she'd been so lost in—thoughts of him once again, working out—he was now staring at her with that smile that made her insides liquid.

"But let's put a timer on this one," he added, still smiling and looking right at her. "I heard you're the resident tactician. I don't have all night," his eyelids went a little heavy and he smirked, "not tonight, anyway."

Panicking about feeling her face already heating, she was incredibly thankful that he turned his attention to Walter, patting him on the shoulder. "Let's say forty minutes tops, big guy? This way I still get to see enough of your game to get an idea what I'm in for, but we don't go too long." She was just getting over the flush from the last comment he made to her when he turned to her again with a smirk. "I know you like going at it long and taking it slow, Charlee." His playful smile made her breath catch. "But tonight you can indulge the new guy, right? We can do this nice and slow another time. I promise."

She had to clear her throat for fear her voice would be a croak since her mouth was still bone-dry. "Forty minutes is fine."

How in the world she'd concentrate on her game with him sitting there watching her and in that manner was beyond Charlee.

"Okay, forty minutes it is," Walter said, setting the timer on, "unless someone wins sooner."

That just might happen. Charlee was already contemplating letting Walter win—the sooner the better. She was already having a hard enough time staying composed and breathing steady. She couldn't imagine beating Walter, which she'd done several times in the past, and have to sit there directly across from Hector.

Walter's opening was the same as usual. She already knew what his next few moves would be. Damn Walter and his predictable play. How was she supposed to let him win without making it too obvious?

After the third uncharacteristically bonehead move on Walter's part, Charlee looked up at him. Was *he* trying to lose? Their eyes met but not for long, because he immediately went back to staring at the board. *Great.* Maybe he was nervous about playing Hector too.

"So did Walter tell you about tomorrow?"

Charlee glanced at Hector. Why was it so damn hard to even look at him for too long? She nodded, glancing back at the board, and made her next move, taking Walter's knight.

She was now officially ahead in the game. If Walter continued to make the bad moves he'd been making from the beginning, she was sure to win.

"So you coming?" Hector asked, his unyielding stare burning into her now.

CHAPTER 6

Glad that it was Walter's turn to move, Charlee glanced away, taking a quick moment to think about what Hector was asking her. He wanted to know if she was coming to see him fight Friday evening then hang out at a party where he'd be for the rest of the night. Just as the excitement began to build, Hector squashed the growing tingling sensation when he added with a smirk, "Bring your friend, Drew. She wanted to help me celebrate, remember? Tell her she'll get her chance tomorrow night."

Charlee didn't even know why this surprised her. Of course, he'd be interested in Drew and not her. Why would he? Drew was outgoing, playfully flirtatious and charmingly confident—everything Charlee wasn't. No wonder he'd been smiling at her from the moment she walked in. He probably planned on asking about Drew even before she got there.

"It's only a day away," she said, making a move immediately after Walter did and took his rook. "I'm sure she already has plans."

She didn't mean for that to sound as snippy as it had, but she couldn't help it. Her irritation had reached a new level now. She was irritated at Walter for obviously throwing the game. Was he really that afraid of playing Hector the Great?

She was irritated at Drew for being so damn likable—irritated at Hector for staring at her as he had earlier from across the room and giving her an inkling of hope that there might actually be more to that stare. But mostly, she was irritated at herself for even going there.

Why would she even consider getting caught up on a guy like Hector? Hadn't she learned her lesson already about getting her heart set on someone she knew was completely out of the question?

"Well, let her know, or you could come alone," Hector said then put his hand on Walter's shoulder. "*Or* you could come with Walter here. You're coming, right, Walt?"

Walter smiled at her sheepishly then glanced at Hector and nodded. "Yeah, sounds like fun." He turned back to Charlee. "You can ride with me if you want."

Wonderful. Drew had Hector's attention, and Hector had just lumped Charlee off on Walter. As if asking about her friend hadn't made it entirely clear he had zero interest in Charlee, he had to double stamp it with this.

"Felix Sanchez is supposed to drop by," Hector added.

Oh yeah, that made it better. If Walter bored her Friday night, she could drool over the famous man whore. Trying desperately not to frown but unable to even muster a smile, she glanced at him coldly. "Yes, Walter mentioned something about that." She looked quickly back at the board because even as irritated as she was, she couldn't look into those sinfully playful eyes without feeling drawn into them. "But thanks, I already have plans." She cornered Walter's queen, knowing exactly what he'd do next, and when he did, she took it with her next move. "Checkmate," she said, glaring at Walter.

If she had it in her, she'd call Walter out for such an obvious phony loss. Was he really *that* spineless? Had he no confidence in his game at all? He hadn't made the U.S. team for nothing. But she wouldn't embarrass him. She knew all too well what it was like to be spineless. Maybe if she weren't, she'd stare back at Hector like she'd caught him doing several times during this game alone. Instead, she'd looked away quickly every time. No wonder Drew was the one Hector and every other guy they met together, were ever interested in. Drew would've stared right back, maybe even smiled and done or said something witty.

"Wow, that was fast," Hector said, standing up. "What happened, big guy? Not your day?"

Walter shrugged. "I told you she was good."

Not *that* good. "Hmm, that felt a little too easy," Charlee said, trying not to sound too sarcastic as she reset her pieces on the board again.

Glancing up for a moment, her heart sped up as she watched Hector and Walter trade places. Hector spun the chair Walter had been sitting in around and straddled it just as he had the first one. Charlee gulped at the sight of him even closer to her now. Why couldn't he just sit like a normal person?

He quickly set up his pieces then leaned over a bit with *that* smile, "You ready?"

For once, she didn't look away. It took all the courage she could summon, and she ignored the shivers already racing throughout her entire body. Out of nowhere, she felt suddenly enlightened. Sitting so close to her now, he didn't seem so elusive—so bewildering. He was human just like her, albeit a very sexy, nearly perfect human, who made her tingle without the need to even touch her. Still, this guy didn't possess superpowers or walk on water—although she'd hardly be surprised if he did.

It wasn't fair. *She* was the one that had fantasized about this guy for almost two weeks now. Just because she wasn't as outgoing as Drew or as slutty as those girls Saturday night, that shouldn't make her invisible. She may not exude sensuality like some girls did, but she was no ugly duckling—not anymore anyway. At the very least, she'd be noticed. Chess, if anything, was the one thing she could be confident about. Charlee had done her homework. It was time to make herself noticed.

She almost chickened out, because it was something Drew would say, not Charlee. But she sat up straight, full of determination. Lifting an eyebrow and refusing to give into the urge to break the eye contact with him, she smiled. "I was born ready."

~*~

For the first time today, Hector was able to indulge in Charlee's deep blue eyes for more than just a few seconds. Okay, so maybe dark eyes were not the only kind that could take his breath away. Unlike the rest of the day when she'd pull away from his staring, this time *he* had been the one that looked away first. He had to before Walter noticed but mostly before he gave into the incredible urge he had to tell her just how amazing her eyes were.

Once again, Walter hadn't wasted any time getting right to his lame plan of action. The second Hector had walked into that chess lab, Walter was on him. It actually worked out that Hector had a fight that Friday and that they were having a party afterwards. He'd invite Walter and Charlee to both, even though he didn't think Walter would capitalize much on the opportunity. But regardless, not only would Hector be more than even with Walter but he was determined to slowly rid himself of the guilt that, annoyingly, even after the time he'd put into Walter's workout last night, *still* lingered.

This should've been a painless enough payback, but then Walter had to open his big mouth around the other guys. Now Hector would be stuck hanging out with this bunch of virgins tomorrow night. As if that weren't bad enough, Walter nearly blew the first part of the plan already. The plan was to let Charlee beat Walter so that Hector could play her and take extra-long between moves. This would give Walter a chance to make small talk with her, and if he got stuck, Hector would be there to help him out.

Walter was supposed to have brought up the fight so that Hector could be the one to invite her since Walter didn't have the *huevos* to do it himself. But so far, not only had Walter hardly said a word but he was so ridiculously obvious about letting her win Hector thought she'd catch on for sure.

Hector was now the one making all the small talk while Walter sat there like a damn mute. How the hell did he expect to impress this girl? Worst of all, it was happening again. In spite of her indifference toward him on Saturday night, Hector *thought* it might actually be possible for him to be attracted to a cute little redhead like Charlee. Now he *knew* it was. Not only was he having an exasperatingly hard time keeping his eyes off her but he found it impossible to not add a flirtatious undertone to everything he said to her.

His comment about her friend Drew was meant to tone it the hell down and throw her off a little. He was sure if she hadn't already, she would notice his eyes tracing every inch of her face: her eyes, her lips, and that porcelain skin. Then there were the freckles. She didn't have as many as you'd expect on a redhead, but he never thought freckles would be so damn distracting or that he'd be having visions of kissing them slowly, one by one. Even that sexy little red eyebrow she'd lifted at him when she said she was "born ready" had sucked the air out of him.

Well, he'd just have to suck it back in because there was no way he'd be doing anything to move in on a girl Walter was so hung up on, no matter how unlikely it was that she'd be reciprocating Walter's feelings. Hector was already going above and beyond anything he'd normally do for someone he didn't even know all that well. And it was all for the sake of shaking the guilt that had troubled him for too long. He wasn't about to blow all his efforts away for this. Nope, this wasn't happening.

With everything he had going on in his life anyway, he didn't have time for relationships. The most he could do right now was fun. And there were plenty of other girls out there he could have *fun* with. Saturday night had been further proof of that. Of course, Sam had thrown a wrench in that one, but Hector had no doubt he'd finish what he started with those two eventually. The girls had been just as disappointed as he was, and since he'd invited them also to Friday night's party, he'd make it up to them soon enough.

After taking his turn, Hector glanced at Walter, giving him a look as Charlee took her time studying the board. Walter stared at him blankly. Hector opened his eyes wide, willing Walter to come up with something—*anything*. But frustratingly, Walter remained silent.

"Your turn," Charlee said, sitting back in her chair.

Unlike most players who leaned in the whole time studying the board and focusing on their possible next move, Charlee would sit back during her opponent's turn. Hector had observed that about her even during her game with Walter. For some reason, it irritated him now. Maybe it was because that chip on his shoulder was growing by the minute from her continued unimpressed and indifferent attitude toward him. Her sitting back the way she was made it seem as if she were sending out a message loud and clear—she didn't have to put much effort into beating him.

He knew he was being paranoid, and most likely, as usual, he was over thinking things. She'd sat that same way during her game with Walter, but obviously, she really hadn't had to try in that case since he'd so easily let her take the game.

With the sudden urge to not just win but really show off, Hector thought of some of the moves Sam had used on him in the past: the maddening ones Hector never even saw coming.

Thoughts of Sam distracted him for a moment. Hector had been so relieved to find out Sam was going to be fine. Having lost the only father figure he'd ever had recently, Hector wouldn't be able to handle something happening to Sam.

Being so busy with Sam and training, Hector all but forgotten about Charlee's snobbish attitude until Walter had showed up last night. Even though Hector refused to ask outright, he did get a few things out of Walter about what the people on the school's chess team thought of him so far. They'd been thoroughly impressed. Of course, Walter didn't say who exactly, and Hector was not about to ask, but he seriously doubted Charlee had been one of the ones so impressed.

It wasn't until they were into the game a good ten moves that Hector picked up on Charlee's plan. He couldn't be sure yet, but if he weren't mistaken, she was imitating the opening moves from his game in Saturday's tournament, not the game in the final round against Bisbee either. This was the opening he'd used on Kowalewski—the player he'd knocked out before Bisbee, the one who was supposed to have been the biggest threat, the guy he'd specifically prepared his opening novelty for.

After a few more moves, there was no mistake about it. It was exactly the game he'd played.

Clenching his jaw, his mind raced now. What was she doing? She had chosen to play this for a reason. Why? Should he be flattered that she'd obviously took the time to examine his game and apparently memorized it, or should he be pissed that maybe she really was being snobbish—showing him up? What idea had she found that he hadn't when he prepared for Kowalewski?

Hector looked up at her after her latest move, meeting those deep baby blues once again. Nothing in her blank expression gave anything away. He decided not to let on that he knew what she was doing, because he still couldn't figure out why. Instead he would use the fact that he knew what moves she'd be making before she actually made them to his advantage.

He'd completely given up on helping Walter make small talk with her. If Walter couldn't even come up with a few comments about chess, the one thing these two had in common, then he couldn't be helped. More onlookers gathered around Hector and Charlee: onlookers who may very well be thinking the same thing he suspected both Walter and Charlee thought—that maybe he wasn't cut out for the U.S. team or even the school team. It'd been common knowledge that whoever made the U.S. team would be automatically invited to play for the ESU team.

Walter was on his own. Right now, Hector was on a mission. There was something more important he needed to focus on now. Obviously, Charlee was up to something. Hector was going to figure it out one way or another.

And then, she played her new move. It was bold, nothing like the quiet play that had led up to this position. Kowalewski's knight had passively retreated here, but this was a challenge, a pawn pushed up the last file on the board, like a bomb going Ka-boom on his king's pawn shield.

Hector couldn't help but smirk. Was she getting nervous? Sure she'd taken out the pawns in front of his king, but it was such a gamble. He could just fend off her attack and then slowly squeeze out a win in the endgame.

The next move proved she was panicking because she sacrificed her queen for a pawn. Hector smirked again as he took her queen and set it aside with a sympathetic shrug. She wouldn't even look at him now. Hector watched her serious expression, more than amused at how she made her next move so quickly.

"Check," she said in the most nonchalant manner possible, meeting his eyes with a smug smile.

Hector's eyes were instantly on the board. The pawns she'd gone after so aggressively had actually opened up a file for her rook to put his king in check. He moved his king to the only place he could, stunned that he hadn't caught that. She had him on the run now. Examining the board, he saw how she must've planned this in advance, because in the next couple of moves using her bishop and then her knight, she got him.

"Checkmate," she said then sat back in her seat again, looking a little too pleased with herself.

CHAPTER 7

It played out more beautifully than Charlee could have anticipated. The look on his face when she said check was priceless. Everything after that point was just icing on what should have been her ever loving smug cake.

Just like all the other fantasies about what she wanted to do with him, this had now been included in them. But like all the others, she didn't think it would actually happen. She was going to just play her best game and impress him that way. It wasn't until the last moment, and after remembering how he'd followed up his invitation to his party that weekend by suggesting she go with Walter, that she gave into the temptation to do this. Sure he'd been interested in those two sluts Saturday night and at the same time interested in Drew, but her? Oh no. Not Charlee. Apparently she wasn't even a consideration. Walter could have her.

When she'd gotten home Saturday night, knowing full well that by then someone had already uploaded the play by plays of the games it took Hector to win the tournament onto YouTube, she looked it up out of curiosity. Since Walter had been so sure Kowalewski was a sure win, she was curious to see exactly how Hector had defeated him. She'd seen some of the moves that day, but they moved much too fast for her to catch all of it.

As it turned out, Walter had been right. It was Hector's strength in speed play that had won the game. Charlee had been so thoroughly disgusted still about Hector and the two girls that night, she'd almost been happy about this revelation. Had the game been more drawn out and not quite as fast, Kowalewski more than likely would have defeated Hector. Not that Hector's game hadn't been impressive, it was. She'd give credit where credit was due, but Kowalewski did manage to make him flub a few moves that were obviously not part of Hector's plan.

She'd taken a look at the game play posted of his game against Bisbee also, but Bisbee was clearly the inferior player in that game. Watching Hector's game against Kowalewski was far more interesting. It was petty, she knew, but for some reason, she took great pleasure in knowing he wasn't so perfect after all.

Charlee would never admit to how much time she'd scrutinized that game over the weekend, but it was long enough to figure out what moves were made in haste not only by Hector but by Kowalewski as well. Feeling a little devious but not enough to stop her, she'd even outlined a plan of what it would take to beat Hector, using his own game against him. It was easy once she'd figured out what moves he hadn't meant to make. Add a few violent pawn moves to make him think her game was self-destructing then, just when he thought he had her, end it. He'd never even see it coming.

The fact that he'd played into it so easily wasn't so surprising. Like all the lines of attack she put together in chess, this one was as well thought out as her others—possibly more so because of the motivation behind it. What did surprise her was his reaction to it.

After staring at the board in silence for what seemed much too long, his expression went from completely stunned to confused and then downright hard. She squirmed in her seat now, feeling a little anxious. Maybe this hadn't been such a good idea after all. She'd meant to get his attention—impress him even. Okay, maybe she had wanted to show him up a little, annoy him as he'd annoyed her earlier, but he looked more than annoyed now.

"Really?" He stood up, still staring at the board. "You put this much effort into this?"

She gulped, staring at his face. Even at a moment like this, it was a struggle to not glance down at that hard body underneath the formfitting jeans and snug shirt. She'd never been this close to anyone so magnificently sculpted. But his eyes were so hard now—angry at her. There was no way she could look away now. This was not the impression she'd meant to make on him.

Surely he knew at this level it was standard to study other worthy players and opponents' games. Certain that she wasn't the only one who'd done so already, she shrugged, trying to play it down. "Anyone interested in this game has probably already gone over the game play of Saturday's tournament."

Glancing around, she was more than thankful to see almost everyone nod in agreement. It helped her argument, but she was sure none of them had studied his game as obsessively as she had.

Hector glanced around at the others, his hard expression becoming even more severe. "You all did? So was this the plan then? To prove Kowalewski should be the one here and not me?"

"No!" Charlee stood up and answered for everyone. "No one knew I was going to do this. I didn't even think of it until the last minute. And you won that tournament fair and square. No one's disputing that."

"Bruno and Dempsey are about to start," one of the bystanders alerted everyone in an obvious attempt to take the focus off Charlee and Hector—cut the tension in the room.

Hector didn't even flinch, his hard eyes still on her. Charlee wasn't sure she should be glad that most of them walked away to gather around Bruno and Dempsey, leaving her alone with him now, or be terrified about that.

Taking the few steps around the table to come face to face with Charlee, Hector stood but inches away from her. Her heart rate spiked instantly like she'd only ever felt it do the day she watched Ross and his friends attack Walter.

"No one's disputing it, huh?"

With his lips this close to her face and having them pretty much at her eye level, it felt impossible to string even a few words together while concentrating on not staring at those lips. But she had to. "Yes. I, uh . . ." She swallowed hard, struggling to not look away from his still brutal stare. "I just thought it'd be interesting to see if my spin on your game would work."

The stare softened just a bit, but he lifted an eyebrow then licked his lips, making her eyes immediately glance down at his mouth. "Well, bravo," he said, glancing back at the board. "I guess you showed me, right? You found every hole in my game and used it to take me down." He turned to face her again this time with an evil smirk, and he lowered his voice to a whisper. "Did you like that?"

Her lips literally trembled as she began to shake her head, fluttering her lashes in an effort to come up with a proper response. Taking a few steps back because being that close to him was just too overwhelming, she glanced around at the couple guys still studying the board. Though she was certain Hector's question hadn't been heard by anyone else, she still attempted to make light of it with a chuckle that fell flat. "What?"

Hector closed in again, his words a near murmur. "Did it feel good to take me down, Charlotte?" The fact that he remembered her full name would've been enough to excite her, but hearing him say it, in that tone, made her nearly gasp. Then he added a final blow by licking his lips again and leaned in even closer. "It's what you wanted, right?"

Her entire face was ablaze, including her ears, even though no one was paying attention to them anymore, not even Walter. He was now engaged in what sounded like a debate about the game she and Hector had just played.

Charlee cleared her throat—twice. He was still talking about the game, right? She couldn't even tell anymore if he was still angry. "I didn't mean anything personal by it if that's what you're suggesting."

Hector seemed hell bent on speaking unnervingly close up to her, because he took another step, closing off the space between them again. This time Charlee stood her ground and didn't back up, but having him that close put every single one of her senses on alert. Her nose took in the mixture of his masculine scent with what was probably aftershave—a soft but very alluring aftershave.

"You always take that much time studying someone else's game?" It was low and subtle, but her ears didn't miss the low chuckle that reverberated from deep within him. "Or am I just that special?"

Unable to take how deeply he gazed into her eyes anymore, Charlee glanced away, noticing how the muscle on his big lower arm flexed. Looking further down, she saw why. His hand was fisted, and he was squeezing it off and on. How something so trivial could actually arouse her to the point she felt flushed was beyond infuriating. Did he know he could do this to her? Was this whole line of questioning—this closely—his way of embarrassing her he obviously thought she'd set out to do to him?

Unbelievably needing to clear her throat once again, she did then glanced back at those eyes that seemed to get darker each time he addressed her. "Actually, I didn't study it for as long as you seem to think." She was only grateful that he didn't know her well enough or he would see right through her.

She was feeling a little perturbed about how the mixture of playfulness and intensity in his eyes practically burned a hole through her now. He'd made it categorically clear earlier that he had no interest in her, so she crossed her arms in front of her. Embarrassing her was obviously the goal here. "Haven't you ever studied other player's games? Maybe you're not aware, but it's pretty much a requirement at this level—"

"As opposed to my level?" He snapped back. The playfulness in his eyes was gone, the intensity now prevailing.

"That's not what I—"

"Let me tell you something, Charlee." She didn't think it was possible, but he moved even closer, forcing her to uncross her arms or feel his body heat against them. "I may be a casual player for the most part, but I am familiar with classical chess study." His eyes were darker now than they'd been that entire time.

"I didn't say you weren't. It's just that . . ." She stopped when he very noticeably moved his eyes down from hers and stopped at her lips then he licked his own again, slowly.

He moved in so close she could feel the warmth of his breath against her own mouth. Feeling his mouth so close to hers she could almost taste it, was so intoxicating she froze in place, staring at his lips. He got so close her heart nearly gave out on her, because there was no doubt what he was about to do next. *God!* Even knowing with every fiber of her being that she shouldn't, that this could only end in heartache if she went there with him, she knew she wouldn't stop him. She wanted him to—so bad. Then he stopped suddenly and smirked. "Don't worry about it. I know *exactly* what you meant."

With that, he pulled back and walked away, leaving her standing there, feeling flushed, breathless and completely mortified. She watched as he joined the others standing around watching the game between Bruno and Dempsey. He glanced back at her where she still stood frozen in place, trying desperately to compose herself, but he didn't smile anymore. He didn't even give her that stupid smug smirk she expected that said he knew just how willing and eager she was to have his lips on hers.

The tears stung her eyes now that she realized exactly what he'd done and why. She managed to finally move. Grabbing her bag and light jacket from where she'd been sitting, she glanced at the board on the table where Hector's king still stood in checkmate. With the tears beginning to blur her vision, she rushed past Walter toward the door. "Where you going?" he asked.

She didn't bother responding but couldn't fight the urge to glance in Hector's direction one last time. He was still staring at her but not hard like he had earlier. It was an almost remorseful stare, sort of how she'd felt when she realized how personally he'd taken her setting him up.

Walking even faster now because she felt like a complete idiot, Charlee hurried to the door. He may've walked right into her plan, but her victory had been short-lived. He'd managed to do to her in a matter of seconds what had taken her hours and hours—days of studying his game. And as far as she was concerned, he'd won hands down. Because while he probably thought her a pretentious bitch now, she'd never felt so captivated with anyone in her life.

***

"All I'm saying is if you're this upset about it," Drew paused, tilting her head and pouted at Charlee, "and clearly you are, there has to be more to this."

Charlee shook her head, blowing her nose then dabbing the corner of her eyes with another tissue.

"Charlotte?"

Charlee glanced at her friend. She knew Drew only called her that when she was being very serious, even though right now all it made her think of was how it felt to hear Hector call her that.

She glanced down, staring at her hands knowing exactly what Drew was thinking. "No, Drew, it's not about that. It's been over a year and I'm over it. Besides that was totally different. I really don't think Hector is like that."

"I don't either," Drew said softly. "Most people aren't, sweetie, but I get the feeling you don't truly believe that yet."

Drew reached out and squeezed Charlee's hand softly. "What Hector did was probably just out of pride. You got one up on him, and he reacted, but I'm telling you, Charlee, I have a sixth sense about these things. There's something more going on here not just on your side but his as well. I haven't seen you this upset about anything since . . ."

Glad that Drew didn't go on, Charlee took a deep breath. Admittedly, it had been the first thing that had come to mind yesterday when Hector left her standing there to drown in her own humiliation. But Drew was right. This was different. Charlee had brought this on herself. He just reacted. She shook her head. It wasn't about that at all. "I just hate that the one place where I feel most comfortable being," she squeezed her best friend's hand, "except here with you, of course, has now been contaminated by this guy. I could never walk in there again without feeling uneasy. Even today, I was certain, because of his fight tonight, he wouldn't be there, and I still skipped out on the lab just in case."

The compassionate expression on Drew's face was suddenly replaced with a mischievous smirk. "About that fight."

"No." Charlee sat up. "Absolutely not. He didn't say it, but after what happened yesterday, I'm sure the invitation has been revoked. He hates me now."

"Charlee, you said you were certain he was going to kiss you."

"But he didn't. He just meant to humiliate me, which he certainly succeeded in doing."

Drew sat up too, taking in another spoonful of the quart of ice cream they were sharing then waved the spoon at Charlee. "No, no, no, Charlee Brennan. Not so fast. You said he flirted with you even before any of this happened."

"He flirts with everyone!" Charlee countered quickly. "And he asked about you, remember?" She took the quart of ice cream from Drew and sunk her own spoon in. "He lumped me in with Walter."

Gawd, could this be anymore mortifying? But she blamed herself. To even think for a minute that he would actually want to kiss her, especially after what she'd done to him. The worst part about this whole thing was that he now knew that, just like all the other girls he'd ever encountered, she too wasn't immune to his charm as she so snootily thought she was. Okay, maybe she didn't think so before, but after seeing him with those girls Saturday night, she certainly thought she could be. And boy did he prove her wrong. Now every time she'd see him she'd know what he'd be thinking.

"Hear me out, okay?" Drew said as Charlee licked another spoonful of ice cream clean. She was well aware that, even if she didn't want to hear Drew out, there was nothing she could do or say to stop her friend from saying what was on her mind anyway. So her shoulders slumped and she waited grudgingly. "You said you caught him looking at you more than a few times even before you began to play him, right?" Charlee nodded. "And knowing you, just like the night of the tournament, you made absolutely sure you showed no interest in him whatsoever. Which, by the way, good girl. After what we saw Saturday night, you don't want him thinking you're like those girls."

"That's just the thing," Charlee said, letting her head fall back against the headboard of Drew's bed. "Now, he knows I am!"

"No, he doesn't," Drew insisted. "It didn't actually happen, and who's to say you would have done it."

"He—"

"No!" Drew was even firmer this time. "Okay, so you went a little goo-goo eyed on him and froze. You were nervous. A guy like him has got to know a girl like you is not used to that."

"A girl like me?" Charlee sat up straight again. She knew exactly what Drew meant, but she felt the need to at the very least protest. "What does that mean?"

Drew rolled her eyes then scooted over closer to Charlee and leaned her head on her shoulder. "You know what I mean, Charlee. You're shy and quiet but very sweet. I think anybody can see that about you from a mile away. You're nothing like those stupid girls on Saturday, and there is no way he would think you are. He knew you'd freeze up. But he doesn't know for sure that you wouldn't have snapped out of it and pushed him away if he actually did kiss you. Heck, you don't even know."

Oh, Charlee knew all right. As mortified as she'd been, she'd gotten back to her bed last night, and even as she cried, she kept imagining what it would've been like. How amazing it would've been to feel those sexy lips on hers. She'd been thankful that Drew had been on a date yesterday and gotten home late enough that Charlee could feign the sleep of death. Charlee had been in no mood to talk about it last night. She wasn't this morning either, but when she got home early after skipping out on her chess lab today, Drew knew something was up immediately. It didn't take much before Charlee was in tears again and Drew came to the rescue with tissue, two spoons, and a quart of chocolate chip mint—her favorite.

Charlee shrugged, feeling too drained to argue.

"I have a theory," Drew continued. "Now even though you don't believe it, I'm telling you, believe in my sixth sense, Charlee. He acted very strange Saturday night. He couldn't keep his eyes off you, and you're saying he was doing it again yesterday, right? How many times would you say you caught him staring?"

Charlee exhaled. "I don't know," she said, dumping her spoon into the container of ice cream. She'd had enough.

"C'mon, Charlee, think. Roughly how many times?"

Charlee knew exactly how many times: four before he'd even come over to sit with them then at least four more times during her game with Walter. Not to mention the way he'd looked at her every time he spoke to her. It was why she'd begun to think maybe there was some interest, especially remembering what Drew had told her about the way she'd caught him staring at her on Saturday. But if Charlee—the most pessimistic person in the world—could let herself become hopeful over a few stares, she knew Drew the hopeless romantic with her unnerving sixth sense that always seemed to be spot on, would go nuts if she told her just how many times, in turn, giving Charlee false hope as well. Something she did not need.

She lifted a shoulder as indifferently as possible. "I don't know three, four times maybe."

Drew was on her feet at once. "I knew it!" She punched her fist into her hand, smiling. "We're going to that fight tonight."

Charlee's mouth fell open just as her heart rate took off. She knew she shouldn't have said anything. Before she could protest, Drew was already talking fast as she paced back and forth as she always did when she was trying to convince Charlee of something, just like she had back home when she convinced her to move out to California with her. This was not good.

"If for no other reason, we'll do this so I can prove my point." Drew lifted her palm up in the air when Charlee began to respond: another telltale sign that she wouldn't be backing down. "This guy has a thing for you. Maybe it's just an ego thing. Guys like him are not used to girls not showing any interest. Charlee, you go overboard doing just that when you're nervous, and, obviously, Hector makes you very nervous." She stopped and smiled. "Besides, this could be fun. Imagine all the other hot boxers we could meet tonight? Not to mention an exclusive party. What else are we gonna do tonight? Sit around drinking wine coolers and talk about the kind of guys we wish we could meet?" Drew danced in place now. "We can't stay long anyway. We have Long Beach in the morning. We'll just go for a little while."

This was true. They both volunteered for the Special Olympics, and tomorrow morning there was a marathon in

Long Beach. They had to be there bright and early to help set up. Charlee couldn't come up with a good enough argument fast enough, and quite honestly it did sound more fun than staying home on a Friday night—again. But the thought of facing Hector so soon terrified her. She was hoping he'd cool off over the weekend. She did the only thing she could and gave Drew her best pleading look.

"Charlee, he's fighting tonight, and Walter said he was part owner of the gym too. You really think he's going to have time to hang out with anyone from the chess team?" Drew gave her that evil grin she wore so well. "No offendamundo, but he probably just invited you guys to be nice. I'm sure he won't be spending too much time around any of you." She reached out her hand to Charlee and tugged. "Let's go. We got a party to get ready for."

With a groan, Charlee stood to her feet. Why did she have to have such a persuasive best friend? If it weren't for the sudden visual she was having of seeing Hector up close and shirtless in the ring like she'd seen in all the images she Googled-stalked of him, she'd certainly fight this tooth and nail. That and the curiosity of seeing exactly what the tattoo on his chest was about, won out. She could only pray now this, too, didn't turn into a disaster like yesterday.

CHAPTER 8

Hector sat in the corner of the ring in between rounds, breathing heavily when they walked in. Charlee had said she wasn't coming to the fight tonight. Turned down the invitation flat—she had other plans. "Better plans" is probably what she really wanted to say. So for that reason alone, Hector hadn't expected her to show up, and then after what happened yesterday, he knew there was no way she'd be coming. But seeing Walter and some of the other guys from the chess team arrive together, minus Charlee, somehow still managed to further Hector's already irritable mood.

He didn't even understand why her snub bothered him so damn much. Sam thought what she'd done was hilarious. And the fact that Hector had taken it so personally had him laughing louder than Hector had ever heard the old man laugh. Hector didn't think it was funny at all, but the more he argued the more Sam laughed.

Sam said Hector was ripe for the target, that it was his own fault for not doing going there prepared. She probably saw the lack of significant effort Hector put into the actually study of chess. Hector was too laid back about the whole thing, and Sam said it emanated off him. A serious player would see that right away. When he was finally done laughing, Sam had once again reminded Hector how seriously these players take the game and told him he better learn to respect that.

If it had been Sam in that tournament, he said he would've gone over the game himself that night, working through all the variations until he was sure his play was accurate. Hector hadn't bothered to until last night. Even then, he still couldn't figure out how she'd come up with such a clever way to completely blindside him.

Sam also told Hector to get used to it. He was in a different league now. The old man was just too damn pleased that Charlee had done this to Hector. This, of course, only pissed Hector off even further. Get used it? Like hell he would. It was one thing if he thought this had only been some sort of hazing: Charlee's way of welcoming him into the team with a ribbing. But there was more to it. He'd seen it from that very first day. She'd been nice enough and even smiled at him just the same as before she'd known he was a contender.

Unless she was a total genius, what she'd done must've taken her hours to memorize—to perfect. But why? The more he thought about it, the more it pissed him off. What the fuck was her problem anyway?

Then he remembered how close he'd come to kissing her, how badly he'd wanted to, and how quickly his anger had dissipated the moment he'd gotten close enough to smell the sweet scent of her lip gloss on those soft pink lips and the subtle sweet scent of her hair. He'd instantly gone from fuming to fighting the urge to kiss her.

Hector would've given anything at that moment yesterday to be able to go back in time and slam A.J and Theo's faces into the lockers a few times in high school. If he had, he would've been able to live with the guilt of kissing Charlee in front of Walter. It was the only thing that had stopped him yesterday.

After he'd finally made some major progress in alleviating his damn guilty conscience, Hector wasn't about to take a giant leap backwards. Even feeling as bad as he'd felt all this time about not sticking up for Walter in high school, he was now certain if Walter hadn't shown up at the gym Wednesday night he would've gone for a taste of Charlee's lips anyway. Not only was the guilt still alive and well but Walter was beginning to feel like a real friend now.

He'd gotten to know Walter a little better, and as big a goofball as the guy was, he was actually a really nice guy with a giant heart.

On top of being a full-time student and all the time he put into both the school and the U.S chess teams, Walter also volunteered several days out of the week at the convalescent home where his grandfather lived. He said there were a couple of old guys down there he played chess with regularly; he even invited Hector to down there with him sometime. Walter told him he'd be surprised how good it would make him feel to make someone's day just by spending a little time with them. Hector didn't doubt it one bit because he'd felt good seeing the hope in Walter's face when Hector assured him he could help him get in shape. Remembering what a nice guy Walt was yesterday when Hector had been so close to kissing Charlee was bad enough.

But worst of all, Hector now knew just how bad Walter had it for Charlee. Walter had told him all about it as Hector worked him out. This was going to be tough, but the fact of the matter was Hector could have just about any girl he wanted. It was only fair. If he wanted to do the right thing by Walter, this time he'd have to stay away from the only girl that would mean betraying his new friend.

"What the hell are you doing?" Abel asked from the side of the ring.

"I got this," Gio said as he applied the Vaseline over Hector's brows.

"Yeah, he's okay." Noah said, squirting water into Hector's mouth. "He still has a few rounds left. He just has to win them."

"Are you kidding me?" Abel glared at Noah then turned back to Hector. "Listen to me, Hector. You need to get your head out of your ass and knock this guy out. If this thing goes to judges, you'd be lucky if they call it a draw. Guzman took those first three rounds, and if you keep fighting like that, you're gonna lose the whole damn thing."

Gio, who was his actual trainer, started in on him with what he'd done wrong in the last round and what he needed to do in the next. "Use your speed, man. What's wrong with you? You're way faster than this guy. Guzman ain't got shit on your speed."

Hector closed his eyes but only for a moment because in the next one the bell rang. "Drop him, Hector," Abel said even louder. "Stop wasting time."

Jumping in place now as he waited for the go-ahead from the ref, he eyed Guzman. Gio was right. Hector was way faster than this guy. He'd watched film of the guy's previous fights and was pretty sure he had his weaknesses down.

The ref gave the go-ahead, and both he and Guzman took a few steps toward each other.

"Pick 'em up, Hector!" Gio yelled.

Hector lifted his gloves a few inches to shield his face. Gio must not have watched as much film on this guy as Hector had. Guzman went for the body way more often than the face.

Even thinking about watching film on his opponent brought back thoughts of Charlee and how closely she must've studied his game. Her words came back to him just then. "I didn't mean anything personal by it." *Bullshit!*

Hector landed a hard hit to Guzman's eye, splitting the skin just under it and prompting to the crowd to jump to its feet going wild. As much as they all tried to assure the fighters that signed up for bouts here that they'd be on neutral ground, fighting in your own gym inevitably made you the favorite.

Just like Hector's weak spot, his right eyebrow that had been split enough times that now any good hit to it would have it split and bleeding, this was Guzman's weak spot. Every one of the fights the guy had been in, where it had been stopped because of an injury, it had been because of that gash.

Before Guzman could recover, Hector landed another fast one on that same eye. Maybe it did pay to study your opponent so closely.

Feeling his insides heat just as they had yesterday when he'd realized what Charlee had done, he landed another then an even faster and harder one. If it weren't for the ropes, Guzman would've gone down. The crowd was going wild, chanting and jumping up and down. Hector couldn't help thinking this was probably what the rest of his chess teammates must've been feeling inwardly as they watched Charlee take him down.

Clenching his teeth so hard he thought he might bite through his mouthpiece, Hector went in for the kill. Check-motherfucking-mate!

The last jab was so hard it sent Guzman crashing onto the floor. The ref jumped in between them, pushing Hector toward his corner, and started the countdown.

Guzman wasn't getting up. This was a done deal.

"Hell yeah, Hector! Now that's what I'm talking about!" Gio pulled the mouthpiece out of Hector's mouth and Noah began squirting water into it.

Hector gulped the water as he tried to catch his breath and glanced around the loud and crazed crowd. He nearly choked when he saw it. It stood out like a flame in the sea of dark hair and pumping fists—Charlee's red flowing hair. Hector coughed uncontrollably as the water Noah had squirted in his mouth went down the wrong pipe.

"You okay?" Noah asked, offering more water.

Hector pushed it away. What the hell was she doing here? Glancing back at Noah and pushing the water away, he continued to cough. Gio patted him on the back as his coughing slowly calmed and he began breathing easier.

He dare not look back in her direction. Not only had she shown up but that hair wasn't up in a ponytail like he'd only seen it up until now. She wore it down now. That ponytail she usually had it in was so damn high he never imagined her hair would be this long.

Swallowing hard as Noah wiped his face down, he turned around to face the ref. The ref, who stood next to a still very dazed looking Guzman with his eye nearly swollen shut, now motioned for him to come over. Hector hardly heard a word of what the ref said, but once everyone started cheering, he knew he'd been announced the winner by way of knockout.

Lifting his glove up at the cheering spectators and not looking her way was a challenge, but he managed to get through it. He was already out of the ring and making his way through the crowd. The real challenge would start now—staying away from her all night.

What a pisser. Here he thought he'd unwind tonight and let some of the tension out that had built over the past twenty-four hours. He'd looked forward to throwing a few beers back with the guys. Having any alcohol now was not a good idea. He might do something bad and tell her little condescending ass off or worse: he might just be tempted to finish what he started yesterday.

~*~

They'd been there over an hour now, and still the only glimpse she'd had of Hector was when he'd been in the ring. Charlee cursed herself for not having worn higher wedges. When he'd walked through the crowd, she'd barely been able to see him with all the people in front of her. She so badly wanted a closer look at that tattoo.

Drew had been so excited as they walked into the banquet room where the exclusive party was being held. She said she'd never felt so special when everyone else had to leave and they, along with an elite few others, were led into the back of the gym and down a hallway where the banquet room was located. Charlee, on the other hand, had never felt so nauseous.

When she thought of coming to a party where Hector would be, she pictured lots of people. Even though it was exclusive, she still thought there would be crowds like the one at the fight that she could hide behind and become invisible—be in her comfort zone. This crowd so far consisted of about forty people, not nearly enough for her to get lost in.

Unable to hide what she was feeling, Drew had noticed Charlee's discomfort and insisted she have a glass of wine to help her relax. She was on her second glass now, and while it did help, the knot in her stomach was still there.

"Where do you think he could be?" Drew leaned in and whispered.

Charlee shook her head with a shrug. Wherever he was, Charlee only wished he would get there already. He couldn't be far, and the anxiety was only building with every minute that passed. She wanted that first look—glare—whatever she may get from him tonight out of the way.

In the meantime, Charlee had obsessively watched his brother, Abel. Walter had pointed him out, though it hadn't really been necessary. The moment Charlee had spotted him before Walter said anything, she knew who he was. Not only had she already shamelessly Google-stalked him but she even watched some of his fights on YouTube, more for the possibility of seeing Hector in the audience than anything else. Even in a suit and tie, everything about Abel said heavyweight contender. He was big, built like a truck and annoyingly as good-looking as Hector, only in a manlier way. Not that Hector didn't have the manly thing going on, but, obviously, his brother had a few years on him.

Another thing they had in common was the women's reaction to them. They zeroed in, made their move, and then clung to them, just as those girls had Saturday night with Hector. The entire time Charlee had been standing there with the rest of the handful of people from her chess club, she'd watched as these scantily dressed women behaved outrageously eager and disposed.

Unlike Hector, Abel was far more discreet about his response to them. Although these women made it blatantly obvious that he had the go-ahead to fondle them if he so wished to by the way they rubbed up against him when they greeted him, other than the polite hug he responded with, he kept his hands to himself. Hector had been a much more willing participant with those two girls Saturday night.

"I guess now we know what kept him so long," Drew whispered.

Charlee turned her attention from Abel's group to the banquet room door where Drew's annoyed glare was focused. She only hoped Drew hadn't heard the tiny gasp that escaped her as she took in the sight of Hector. Even under what appeared to be layers of clothes, a dark suit complete with coat and vest over a dress shirt and tie, there was no hiding his impressive build.

Swallowing hard, she also took in the two girls on either side of him, walking in with him: the same two girls from Saturday night. Apparently, he hadn't had enough. Both girls looked just as pleased as they had Saturday. Charlee could only wonder if that look of content on their faces meant they'd kept him nice and busy all this time.

"Stop staring," Drew whispered.

Charlee quickly glanced away. She hadn't realized she'd been staring so hard. Her eyes were on his brother's group again. They had also seen Hector and were now smiling in his direction. Some of the guys' big smiles were no doubt an approval of Hector's grand entrance with two girls at his side. The only one that didn't smile as big was Abel. In fact, if she had to guess, he appeared a bit annoyed. Charlee had to wonder, after watching Abel's reserved interest in the women vying so hard for his undivided attention, if it was expected of Hector to behave this way too.

Though Hector didn't hold either of the girls' hands this time like he had in the parking lot last weekend, the two girls' body language spoke volumes. They were there with him and would undoubtedly leave with him too.

"Can he really be that outrageous?" Charlee asked, looking away from Abel and the others in his group as Hector and the two girls reached them. "Walking in here like that with both of them?"

Charlee welcomed the flames she felt ignite inside her and all the way up her neck as she sipped her wine. This was a good thing. It was better that she lose all respect for him—hate him. She had no business fantasizing about this guy, even before she knew anything about him, and she certainly didn't anymore, especially now. Watching him Saturday even as he made out with these girls, she'd been disgusted, but she hadn't felt what she felt now.

Doing what he'd done with them in a dimly lit parking lot was one thing. Everybody had skeletons in the closet—sordid little secret fantasies. Charlee knew this firsthand. Some people were just brave enough to act on them in real life. She'd already cut him some slack yesterday when she got to be so close to him and was back to feeling mesmerized. Certainly most guys at some point in their lives had fantasized about not only getting the opportunity to be with more than one girl at once but to actually be able to handle it. Not surprisingly, Hector was one of the fortunate few who got the opportunity but apparently seemed more than capable of handling it.

Still, these fantasies should remain just that—secret. Or at the very least keep them discreet. To walk in here flaunting what he was doing was just appalling to say the least. Obviously, he was one of those types of guys. And those girls were those types of sluts. Good. All this was good. Drew had nearly succeeded in making Charlee believe Hector might actually have a thing for her.

She felt her face flush suddenly. The very idea was embarrassing now. While she'd watched Abel with the women who flirted with him, she'd done it with a purpose. Feeling her face flush even more, she sipped some more of her wine. To think she actually thought she might pick up a few pointers. In no way did she want to be slutty or pathetic like those women, but they all seemed so self-confident. Charlee yearned to pick up on a little bit of that. She should've known after being around Drew for all these years that wasn't happening.

"You guys enjoying yourselves?" Charlee had been so busy doing her best to look in any direction but Hector and his girlfriends' that hearing his voice so close startled her.

He stood two people away from her without the girls he'd walked in with, looking and smelling amazing. She let the rest of them answer his question while she nodded. When their eyes met, she saw that hardened look he wore yesterday, and immediately she regretted having come. Then to her relief, it eased slowly into a smile. Letting out a measured breath, she smiled back and took another sip of her wine. It was nearly gone now.

Hector motioned to one of the passing waitresses, and in the next second, she was there. "Let's get another round of whatever everyone is having here," Hector said, smiling even bigger now.

With the same twinkle she'd seen in just about any girl's eyes that looked at Hector, the young waitress smiled, nodding, and pointed quickly at everyone to make sure she remembered what each of them had ordered previously. She did and she rushed off to get their drinks.

Charlee wasn't sure she should have a third glass. She was already feeling a little light-headed. That last drink, or maybe it was seeing him finally and the fact that he was being pleasant, had her feeling much better now.

"Did you guys see the fight?" Hector addressed the group in general, but Charlee had begun to notice what Drew had been talking about.

The guys commented on the fight and how awesome his win had been. Even as he answered their questions and continued talking to them about boxing, he kept doing it—his eyes would go full circle and pause on her every time. At first, Charlee thought maybe she was just imagining it, but it kept happening. The wine had given her the courage to not look away this time like she had last Saturday and all the times he'd looked at her yesterday.

Was this his thing? Was this how he seduced women by giving them that burning heavy lidded stare? Charlee stood up straight, lifting her chin. She wouldn't give him the upper hand, not tonight—not again. Her heart fluttered as their eyes met again for a moment. Okay, maybe this wasn't going be so easy, but she was determined to at least try.

The waitress arrived with all their drinks, and Charlee took hers but made it a point to take tiny sips now. The times her eyes and Hector's were meeting were becoming increasingly longer each time. She sensed something was off. Did he intend to do to her again what he had yesterday? Humiliating her once hadn't been enough?

All the more reason to slow down on the alcohol. She didn't think it possible that he'd look even better than all the times she'd seen him before. While he looked athletic and sexy before, she could now add sophisticated perfection to the list. And here she'd argued with Drew about being too dressed up. She was just glad her pushy best friend was the most persuasive person in the world now. If not, she might've worn jeans like she first intended to.

Drew had talked her into wearing a dress. She'd even used her power of persuasion to get Charlee to wear one of Drew's sexier dresses—something so unlike Charlee. Or maybe Charlee was just a pushover. Just like yesterday, she was so ready to condemn Hector before he'd walked over to them, and now here all he had to do was smile at her and lift his beer her way and she was ready to swoon.

"To an incredibly impressive win," she heard herself say and lifted her glass toward him.

Gulping hard and unable to believe what she'd just done, she put her glass to her lips after everyone else lifted their drinks as well.

"Mine?" he asked, flashing that amazing smile before taking a drink of his beer. "Or do you mean yours yesterday?"

The guys all chuckled, and suddenly she had what she'd always hated—everyone's attention. Even Drew was smiling, very pleased and looking at her.

Taking a bigger sip than she should have, she smiled back with a shrug. "I was talking about yours, but you have to admit mine was pretty impressive too."

She held her breath, waiting to see if that breathtaking smile went flat, but surprisingly, he smiled even bigger. Then after glancing at Walter, his smile waned a little. He did his own version of a shrug, lifting and dropping his big shoulder. "I can admit it. We were impressed. Right, Walter?"

Walter smiled. "That was a heck of a move. I didn't see it coming either. I thought he had you."

Some of the other guys agreed, saying they'd thought the same thing. Charlee did her best not to freak out about being the center of attention for a few minutes. Thankfully, it didn't last too long. The topic switched to talk about Abel.

"So your brother is really gonna fight Hammerhead McKinley?" Dempsey asked.

Hector nodded proudly. "Yep, it's official. He's gone pro and he signed earlier this week. Next year, Vegas baby."

Hector clinked his bottle against Dempsey's. Dempsey was still hesitant looking. "Isn't he afraid? McKinley's in his prime, man. His last seven fights in a row he's won by way of knockout."

Hector shook his head, his face souring a little. "But why? Look who he's fought. Nothing but bums. Why do you think they signed my brother so quick? He thinks Abel's a bum too."

His eyes were back on Charlee every few words, and she was done even pretending to drink her wine for fear just the smell would make her feel even braver than she already did. She couldn't look away now, and she'd stopped making an effort a long time ago.

"I'll tell you what," he continued. "This guy's in for a big surprise." Once again, even though he was talking to Dempsey, he kept glancing at Charlee. A smile escaped her after the third time. She couldn't help it. She was enjoying the attention. "Abel . . ." he stopped and smiled at her, too, then shook his head and glanced at Walter. He turned back to Dempsey, speaking a little faster. "The guys Abel's been fighting are just as much bums as the ones McKinley's knocked out, and you know what? Abel's been knocking 'em all out too. Bad. The last guy had to be taken out on a stretcher."

Seeing his big chest puff even bigger and his smile brighten made her smile bigger too. "You really think he has a chance then?" she asked.

Just like that, she had Hector's attention again. She was beginning to feel a little like the attention whores across the room standing with his brother. Already, she was getting so used to having his eyes on her, that the moment he turned them away from her, she mustered up the nerve to ask a question again so that she would have his attention again.

Breathing in deeply in reaction to his big smile, she waited for him to respond. "I don't just think he has a chance, Charlee. I know he's gonna win." His smile turned into that sexy smirk she'd witnessed so often yesterday when she'd been sure he was flirting with her. "It's what happens when you catch your opponent sleeping. You know all about that, right?"

Charlee gulped hard again. This was the second time he'd referenced yesterday's game, and both times he'd done so with a smile. Maybe he didn't hate her after all. But what the heck happened to *her* hating *him*?

CHAPTER 9

The timing couldn't have been better. Even though he managed to catch himself every time so far, Hector was beginning to lose control—stumbling off his train of thought time after time. So he couldn't have been more relieved when everyone's attention was called to the small podium at the front of the room.

Hector took advantage of the distraction to regroup and gather his thoughts. He had to get a hold of himself. Why couldn't he have stayed angry like he'd felt the entire time he showered and got ready? Even as he'd been interviewed by the local media and the Spanish radio broadcaster over the phone, he'd been tense. Dealing with that would've been easier than what he was dealing with now.

He'd wondered the whole time if she possibly could be here looking to confront him: tell him off about yesterday—a confrontation that couldn't wait until Monday. Then Miriam and Leticia had walked into the gym just as he was wrapping up his final interview. They'd been a slight diversion from his ongoing speculation about Charlee's unexpected presence here tonight, but the diversion from those thoughts had been fleeting. The moment he entered the party, he saw her. He'd hoped to be there for a few minutes before having to see her and have a few drinks to calm the irritation he'd begun to feel just thinking about what she might be up to this time.

After his fight when he'd spotted her in the crowd, it was her hair that stood out. His eyes had been drawn like a magnet to the almost-glowing crimson locks in the crowd. It was more than that now. He was sure his eyes weren't the only ones being drawn to her. She looked spectacular. When he'd walked in and gotten a closer look at just how different she looked tonight, he couldn't dump Leticia and Miriam off with his brother's group fast enough. He was getting this over with now—the sooner the better.

He'd walked over to where she and his other chess teammates stood with one purpose only—to face off with her. Then to his surprise, she'd been nice, more than nice. Even when she congratulated him on his incredibly impressive win, it came off genuinely sincere. To make matters worse, she'd been playful. And if he weren't mistaken, she was having just as hard a time of keeping her eyes off him as he was keeping his off her.

Hector knew he was treading dangerous waters here, and he could already feel it. If he got some time alone with her, even just a moment, he might do or say something he shouldn't.

Glancing at Walter, who was listening to the exclusive announcement of Abel's signing as the next contender for the heavyweight title, he was hit with reality again. Walter was making the first real effort in his entire life to get into shape, and he was doing it for Charlee. As hard and as embarrassing as Hector knew it had been for Walter, he bit the bullet and asked Hector for help.

The big guy had nearly collapsed yesterday from the workout Hector gave him. But he said he'd be back today to work out again alone before Hector's fight, since Hector wouldn't be able to join him. Surprisingly, Hector had seen him in there before his fight, pushing hard on the treadmill. Being a part-time trainer, Hector knew the enthusiasm a client has when they first start working out is what keeps the momentum going. Nothing would kill Walter's momentum faster now than to stomp on his motivation.

Who knew? Maybe if Walter did drop a lot of weight, he just might have a chance with Charlee. The two did have a lot in common. Both were brainy and very good at chess. And while Hector couldn't be sure, because he didn't know too much about her, Charlee seemed a bit shy like Walter. At the very least, she was far more reserved than any of the girls Hector usually hung out with.

Unable to help himself even after he'd pretty much mentally made a case for why he should put any further thoughts of pursuing anything with Charlee to rest, he casually glanced in her direction. Like everyone else, her attention was focused on the front of the room where Abel was now speaking about next year's bout for the title. Hector should really be paying attention to his brother. This was huge. But he already knew all about what Abel was letting everyone else in on, and at the moment he couldn't tear his eyes away from Charlee's dress.

It was a simple enough dark blue wrap around that came together at her small waist with a thick belt. It was similar to the one Leticia wore so boldly that same night. Only as he'd observed before, Charlee's was far more reserved. While Leticia's was shorter and tighter and boasted a plunging neckline, Charlee's was a bit longer, and though it was snug enough to show off her cute but breathtaking little figure, it wasn't quite as body hugging as Leticia's.

The neckline of Charlee's dress wasn't nearly as low as Leticia's, but it was low enough to indulge Hector's probing eyes with a nice tease of her milky white skin. Visions of the perky bare breasts just under the soft fabric of her dress inundated Hector. They'd be just as white and feel just as soft as he imagined the skin his eyes now traced from the open neckline up her delicate neck to that stubborn but sweet chin would be. His eyes stopped at her lips, the very lips he'd been so close to tasting yesterday, and he gulped. As his eyes traveled upward, they met hers. She was watching him size her up, and surprisingly, the corner of her lips curved ever so slightly.

Hector knew he should look away—at least try to save face. He had no idea how long she'd been watching him, but her tiny smirk was all too telling. She'd seen enough, and as cold as she'd been toward him up until tonight, she seemed amused. Was it possible that what he'd thought he picked up on earlier was actually happening? Was the ice princess actually coming around?

Noticing the tinge of pink that colored her cheeks, he broke their stare. He had to. Abel was done talking and the music was back on.

"I changed my mind," Walter whispered, leaning into him.

"About what?" Hector asked, turning full circle and away from Charlee.

Walter rubbed the back of his neck nervously. "About asking Charlee to dance tonight."

Hector had forgotten all about that. When they talked about the party yesterday and Hector mentioned ways of making the most of it, one of the things he mentioned was they'd have a D.J. and a dance floor. Hector had even demonstrated the simple two-step he could do to any tune. Now that the announcement was out of the way, the lights had been dimmed, and people were already making their way onto the dance floor.

Wondering if he should encourage Walter to what more than likely would be a letdown or embarrassment or both, Hector thought for a moment then felt a small but firm hand slip into his. "Did you forget about me?"

Turning to see Leticia's smiling face looking up at him, he forced a smile. It was a strange and unfamiliar feeling, but he suddenly worried that Miriam was close behind. Typically he had no qualms about being seen with one or more girls. Tonight, however, his take on this was oddly altered. Walter had already made it clear what he thought happened with Hector and the girls Saturday once they all left together. He'd ribbed Hector about it the day he showed up at the gym. Hector hadn't bothered explaining, letting him think whatever he wanted. What difference did it make?

Now he was glad Charlee hadn't stuck around to see him leave with them. She already hadn't been very discreet about her distaste for Leticia Saturday night. Hector was sure she wouldn't have approved of what almost happened that night, not that he needed her approval. He just preferred her friendly demeanor to the indifferent one, and he didn't want to go back to that.

"I told you I was going to be busy tonight, sweetheart. He glanced up just in time to see Noah and Gio wave him over.

Nodding, he glanced back at Leticia. "You remember Walter from Saturday, right?" Walter's alarmed expression made Hector almost laugh. "I gotta go, but he'll keep you company until I get back." Walter's eyes went wide and Leticia's didn't even try to hide the disappointed pout. Any other time, Hector might've leaned in and kissed her just to make up for having to leave her again, but he didn't. Instead, he just squeezed her hand before letting go of it. "I won't be long. I promise."

He started off toward Noah and Gio purposely not looking in Charlee's direction. He had to snuff that flame out before it went wild. Charlee was not someone he should be getting involved with, aside from the obvious most ponderous reason: Walter. There were even more reasons now.

For one, she was totally not his type, not that he really had one, but all he knew was she wasn't it. She was nothing like any of the girls he ever hung with, and besides chess, he doubted they'd have anything else in common. Two, if he thought she'd be like Leticia, willing to have some fun and then just leave it at that, maybe he could consider it. But he could already tell she wasn't. Walter mentioned she was quiet, shy, studious, and very sweet. Even though she hadn't been very sweet to Hector so far, he did see the shy. He'd seen it in her eyes yesterday when he'd nearly kissed her. That kind of heavy sexual tension was a first for her. He wasn't even sure how she would've reacted if he had kissed her, but he was certain it wouldn't have been like most girls he kissed.

Something about Charlee and those thick red lashes she'd fluttered so flustered over those deep blue eyes yesterday said . . . romantic. Hector didn't do romance. He didn't have time for it. He learned from past experiences that you don't get involved in any way with girls looking for the real deal without it getting messy, especially ones you'll have to be around often. Even considering doing something with Charlee was out of the question. It couldn't get any more cut and dry than this. But this was the first time he found himself having to build such a case against getting involved with any girl, and it was annoying as hell.

"Congrats," Roni said as he reached her and Noah. She held up her camera in one hand and hugged his neck with the other. "Umm, you smell good," she said as she pulled away.

"Yeah, yeah," Noah frowned, taking her hand. "So he showered."

Hector laughed. "You're just saying that because it's the cologne you two got me last Christmas."

Roni's eye's brightened. "Is it really? No wonder. I gave everyone Armani. I just don't remember who I gave which to. Gio's is the only one easy to remember since it's his own name. I love all his fragrances."

"Code something or other," Hector shrugged. "I've gotten enough compliments. I'll probably buy another when it's gone."

"Your birthday's coming up. Isn't it?" Roni winked. "I got you."

"Are we gonna do this or what?" Gio asked. "Because I'm ready to get B on the dance floor already."

Gio pulled his fiancée, Bianca, to him, pressing his body against hers, and swayed to the music playing. Bianca swayed with him, giggling as he kissed her.

Hector rolled his eyes. Those two were insatiable. "What are we gonna do?" Hector asked.

Abel joined them. "All right, I'm here. Let's get this over with. I still have lots of people I need to schmooze with."

Suddenly Hector knew what was happening and he nearly groaned. "More photos? Didn't we already take enough before the fight?"

"Just a few more." Roni smiled at him sweetly. "You guys all look so handsome in your suits now, and this is for my 5th Street Journey page on my blog."

Hector's shoulders slumped in defeat, but he smiled, putting his arm around Roni's shoulder then kissed her on the head. "You always get me with that. Anything for the journey page."

She smiled smugly, motioning in the direction she wanted them all to stand. Ever since the original 5th Street gym had burned down last winter, Roni had started up the blog about the gym's journey. Hector loved looking through all the pictures she posted on it, old and new. So even though he was an impatient model for all the photos she so loved taking, he was a sucker whenever she mentioned it was for the blog.

She lined them up against the back wall of the banquet room. It was a meeting room really and meant for press conferences that were taking place more often lately as more and more of the boxers training here were making their way up the ranks. It was big enough for parties, especially the exclusive ones like tonight's that were kept on a smaller scale.

Nellie, Roni's best friend and coordinator of tonight's events, laughed as Roni adjusted the guys to stand just so. "And you call me the perfectionist," she teased.

Roni smiled and continued to adjust them, moving Hector slightly to the right. He took the moment she continued to fuss over the other guys to allow himself to do what he'd been wanting to do for a while. Casually, he glanced back in the area where Charlee and the guys from the chess team had been standing. Walter was still there minus Leticia. She must have ditched him the moment she got a chance.

Also noticeably gone were Charlee and Drew. Scanning the room, he spotted them just as Roni's camera began to flash. They were both on the dance floor, dancing with a couple of guys he didn't recognize.

"Smile guys," Roni said as she began to take the photos.

The guy dancing with Charlee pulled her closer, whispering something in her ear.

"Hector, the fight's over now," Roni said. "You won, remember? Now can you please smile for me? And I need you to look this way." She lifted the camera to her face again.

Hector turned to the camera with a quick smile before turning back to Charlee on the dance floor. The guy was obviously taking advantage of the loud music to continue leaning into her neck area and speak closely into her ear. From her body language, Hector could tell she wasn't digging it. The more he leaned in, the more she pulled back.

"Hector!" Both Noah and Abel said loudly.

Hector snapped out of his murderous thoughts and turned back to them. "What?"

"Turn this way, *burro*!" Abel said with a frown. "She asked you three times. What's wrong with you?"

Noah and Gio shook their heads but laughed like they always did when Abel called him that. Roni winced, promising she was almost done. As soon as she was, Hector marched over to Abel's side and held him by the arm before he could walk away to schmooze. "You know everyone here, right?"

Abel turned to him then glanced around. "Just about, except for your friends."

"Who's that?" Hector started to point at the guy with Charlee but dropped his hand when she looked up in his direction and nearly caught him pointing. "Fuck," he said, turning in another direction.

"What?"

"Nothing, don't look over there." He tugged at Abel arms, attempting to turn him in a different direction.

"Over where?"

"Just shut up!" Hector squeezed his brother's arm before glancing in her direction again. She wasn't looking his way anymore, but the horny asshole she was dancing with was at it again, pulling her to him even as her hand lay flat on his chest, defensively keeping the distance between them. The song wasn't even a slow one.

Hector let go of Abel's arm and started toward them.

"Where you going?" Abel asked.

Ignoring his brother, Hector kept walking, already fisting his hand, slowing only when the song stopped. He stopped abruptly when they separated and watched them walk off the dance floor. Someone bumped into him from behind. Hector turned around ready to push whoever it was off him then frowned when he saw it was Abel. "What the hell?"

"You stopped all of sudden. What's your problem?" Abel said, frowning right back at him then glanced in Charlee's direction. "Who is she, and why do you look ready to kill that guy she's with?"

Hector attempted to tone his adrenaline-pumped mood down. "Not ready to kill him." He lied. "She's a friend, and she looked like she might need some help. That's all." He took his eyes off Charlee, Drew, and the two guys with them, who were all headed back to where Walter and the other guys were and turned back to Abel. "You know him?"

"Nope," Abel shook his head. "But I think I saw that other guy with him walk in with the D.J's crew."

Great. Hector turned back to Charlee and the guy. That's all the D.J's guests ever showed up for at these things. They could care less who or what the parties were for. They were just there for the free booze and to try to get laid. "Figures."

"What figures?" Abel asked.

Hector turned back to Abel again. His brother had his usual imposing expression going: the one he always wore when he was on to Hector. "Nothing," Hector tapped Abel on the arm, "I gotta get back to my friends."

He started to take a step away when Abel caught his arm. The music was so loud Abel had to lean in. "No trouble, right?"

Hector pinched his brows. "No." Then he smirked. "Did you see me in the ring today? No one's starting trouble with this guy."

Abel didn't even flinch nor return the smile. "I'm not worried about anyone starting trouble with you. You're the one I'm worried about."

Hector glanced back at Charlee just as both guys walked away from her and Drew then turned back and smiled at Abel. "Dude, I'm not like that anymore, remember? I'm all grown up now: mature, responsible, and all that shit." Finally he got a little smirk out of his uptight brother. "Relax, I'll be cool."

At last free to walk away, Hector grabbed a beer at the bar before heading back toward Walter, who stood just feet away from Charlee and Drew. The feeling of ease only lasted so long, because as soon as he got there, he spotted the two guys on their way back from the bar on the other side of the room double fisting drinks.

If Hector really wanted to be an asshole, he'd card them, even though he wasn't twenty-one yet either. This was his party, his damn gym. He could call the shots. But then Charlee and Drew weren't drinking age either. Walter had mentioned she was about their age—nineteen. It'd be too obvious if he carded the guys but not the girls they'd bought drinks for.

He eyed the guys as they walked by them and stopped where Charlee and Drew stood. Hector didn't miss it: Charlee's surprised expression when the guy tried to hand her the drink. "Oh, thank you, but I said I was okay. I've had enough."

The guy held it in front of her. "You'll be fine with one more. C'mon, you can sip it."

Charlee glanced at Drew before taking it with a strained smile. Hector turned to Walter, trying not to sound as irritated as he felt. "See what happens?" he whispered. "That should've been you out there dancing with her."

Walter frowned but said nothing. Instead, he glanced in Charlee's direction before taking a sip of the purple drink he was having. Hector had seen it earlier when the waitress brought it to him with a kiwi slice wedged on the rim and an umbrella. Even Walter's fruity looking drink was annoying him now. "What is that?"

Walter looked down at his drink and lifted it. "It's called a Fruit Tingle. You wanna try it? It's good."

"No, I don't wanna try it." Hector didn't even try to hide the disgust. "You couldn't just order a beer?"

"I don't like beer," Walter said, looking down at his drink again. "What's wrong with this?"

Hector lowered his voice, but even then couldn't hide the annoyance in his words. "Because you're here to try and impress her, not stand there hiding behind your girlie drink while someone else dances with her." Hector shook his head. "Fruit Tingle? Seriously? You hold your pinky out when you drink that too?"

Walter started whispering something back, but Hector didn't hear any of it. He was too busy trying catch what Horny Toad was saying to Charlee. With the music so damn loud, it was hard to catch every word. The good thing was she held her drink in front of her strategically so the guy couldn't lean in as close as he had on the dance floor, giving him no choice but to speak loudly.

"It's really cool. I have a sound system in my front room, and since we don't use the dining room, we have a pool table in there instead. My roommate's gone tonight.

We'd have the place to ourselves. I can show you how to play pool."

Charlee smiled but shook her head. She was further away and spoke softer than the guy, so Hector couldn't hear what she said, but based on what he was saying now, she'd obviously turned him down.

"That's too bad," the guy said. "Well, you at least have to dance a few more with me."

Charlee shook her head again, saying something that was inaudible to Hector, but she looked uncomfortable. "Go ask her to dance," Hector whispered at Walter, reaching for his drink.

"What? No!" Walter pulled back his drink before Hector could take it. "She's with that guy."

"Trust me." Hector whispered a little more urgently. "That guy's annoying as shit. She'll thank you." Walter shook his head again defiantly, the panic already all over his face as if Hector were going to force him.

"C'mon just one more dance," the guy said, reaching for Charlee, who seemed almost as alarmed as Walter.

No shit she looked alarmed. The guy was a pushy ass. Hector was glad she didn't seem willing at all to get back on the dance floor and have him pushing himself on her again. To make things worse, the song playing now was a slow one.

"Damn it, Walter," Hector whispered through his teeth. "If you don't ask her, I will."

Just looking at Walter's annoyingly terrified face, Hector knew Walter wasn't going to. Glancing back in Charlee's direction, he saw the guy had repositioned himself on the other side of her so he could now lean in again close to her ear. There was no way Hector could hear what he was saying now, but one thing was clear from the way she kept pulling back away from the guy's face, Charlee was as uncomfortable as she had been on the dance floor.

"Here," He handed his beer bottle to Walter roughly. "You're seriously gonna have to man up. You should be doing this."

Who was Hector kidding? There was no way Walter would do what he was about to. He took the few steps to reach Charlee and smiled at her, ignoring the guy. "Dance with me?" Without waiting for an answer, he took her drink and handed it to the asshole. "Hold this."

They both seemed stunned, but neither said a word, and to Hector's relief, she didn't say no or protest his taking her hand in his as he walked her onto the dance floor.

CHAPTER 10

Before Charlee could wrap her head around what just happened, she was on the dance floor, pressed up against Hector's hard body, taking in the glorious scent of his cologne. His big arms wrapped around her waist felt nothing like when Roger had held her earlier. Just as she'd imagined, her body trembled in reaction to him inhaling deeply against her ear.

"I didn't mean to startle you or disrespect your friend," he whispered against the side of her face. "But you looked uncomfortable. I didn't like seeing you like that."

Like magic, his words warmed her insides instantly. He'd been watching her with Roger, and he hadn't liked it. Drew had been right. It was practically an admission of interest. Why else would he be watching her? Why else would he have whisked her away the way he had.

"Thank you. He did make me a little uncomfortable," she admitted. "I didn't realize it was so obvious."

Hector pulled back to look her in the eyes. His brows pulled together with that same hardened expression he wore when he'd taken her hand and shoved her drink at Roger. "He was the obvious one," he said, sounding a little more than annoyed. "Your reaction to him was to be expected. You just met him, right?"

Charlee nodded, swallowing hard and trying to stay poised. Standing this close to him was a reminder of yesterday, and just like yesterday, she was suddenly at a loss for words. What he did to her was unreal. It rattled her yesterday, but it really scared her tonight, because after being held by another guy so recently, she knew now nothing compared to this. Just feeling Hector's warm hard body against hers did things to her she couldn't even begin to understand—explain. It felt as nerve-racking as it did amazing. Even though she could barely comprehend it, the feeling was everything she imagined it would be. Taking a deep breath, she hoped he didn't notice the trembling manner in which she slowly let it out. Her entire body felt as if it could go into spasms at any moment.

"I can say something to him if you want me to."

Charlee smiled, trying to hide the excitement his offer made her. "I think you already made a statement back there. I doubt he'll even be there when I get back."

His rigid stare softened a bit, and he smiled playfully. "Did you want him to be?"

Fighting the urge to run her finger over the scar on his brow, the only imperfection she'd noticed the first time she'd been close enough to see it on his otherwise flawless face, she shook her head.

The playful smile vanished, and he was suddenly serious again. "I don't think I've ever seen eyes as blue as yours. They're . . ." He looked so deeply into her eyes she had to remind herself to breathe. "They're beautiful."

"Thank you," she heard herself say but really had no idea how she managed.

It wasn't what he said but how he said it that made Charlee nearly quiver. Again it was something she couldn't begin to explain. What she was seeing in his eyes was the very thing she was feeling. *Impossible.*

Neither of them noticed the song had ended until the D.J. started talking about giving away prizes: 5th Street t-shirts, tickets to upcoming bouts, and more. Hector cleared his throat, and to Charlee's relief, he seemed as embarrassed as she felt about not having noticed they were the only two still dancing even after the music had stopped.

He stepped away from her, leaving her body yearning to be pressed against his again. He even dropped her hand, which he'd held from the moment he took it in his and led her onto the dance floor.

Everyone's attention was suddenly averted to the entryway of the banquet room. A group of people were arriving, and the D.J. announced that Felix Sanchez had entered the building. The people around them began talking and whispering all at once.

"You wanna meet him?" Hector asked. "I know Walter does."

Drew was suddenly at her side, smiling. Charlee didn't even get a chance to answer Hector's question. He informed her and Drew that he would bring Felix over to introduce him to them and the rest of the people from the chess club.

As soon as he was out of earshot, Drew began the inquisition. "What was that all about?"

Since Charlee didn't know what to make of it either and the pulse in her ears was still humming too loudly to try to make sense of it yet, she shrugged as they made their way back toward Walter and the rest of their group. "I'm not sure. He just said I looked uncomfortable with Roger and he didn't like it."

"Really?" Drew smiled. "Roger was kind of pissed."

"Was he?"

"Yeah," Drew nodded then laughed. "He said someone should've told him you were Hector's property." She rolled her eyes. "I told the idiot you were no one's property. Although it was kind of hard to say it with a whole lot of conviction, considering the way Hector held you on the dance floor," she lifted an eyebrow with a smirk, "even after the music was over. What *else* did he say to you?"

Charlee felt her face flush, lowering her voice as they reached Walter and the others, almost afraid to say it out loud. "He said I have beautiful eyes."

Seeing the instant excitement in Drew's face was enough. Charlee wouldn't even attempt to explain what that moment felt like.

"I knew I'd prove my point tonight. There's no denying he's feeling something for you. And by the way," Drew reached over and squeezed Charlee's arm softly, "I didn't get a chance to tell you, but you did really well when you were talking to him earlier. I know you were nervous about facing him so soon after yesterday, and when he brought that up, I thought for sure you were going to choke, but you handled it beautifully."

Charlee couldn't help rolling her eyes now. "That was the wine, I'm sure. I choked when we were dancing. I could barely breathe straight, let alone talk."

Drew waved her hand at Charlee. "I wouldn't worry about it. He seemed so lost in your little dance I'm sure he didn't even notice." She smiled wickedly. "I mean, geez, neither of you noticed the music had stopped." Drew laughed again. "That's when Roger said he was out of here."

"What about Maurice?" Charlee asked, still feeling a little warm in the face that Drew wasn't the only one who noticed the room and everyone in it had disappeared for Charlee when she'd been in Hector's arms. And unbelievably her heart had sped up even more ever since hearing Drew say there was no denying Hector was feeling something for her.

"Oh, he'll be back. He had to go help the D.J. out with the giveaways." Drew smiled sheepishly. "I told him we'd be leaving early, and he said he wanted to walk me out to my car. I think he wants to kiss me goodnight. He almost did on the dance floor."

Charlee smiled now too. "Are you gonna let him?"

Drew lifted and dropped her shoulders quickly. "I might. He is kind of cute. And I heard Roger and saw the way he kept getting so close to your face. No wonder Hector came to your rescue. Maurice isn't nearly as pushy." Something caught Drew's attention. "Oh, wow, here comes the megastar in the flesh."

Charlee turned to see Hector and Felix walking toward them. The crowd literally spread for them as they walked through it. There were a lot more people there now than there were earlier, and they all stared at both Felix and Hector as they walked by them.

Taking a deep breath like she had when she'd danced with Hector, Charlee tried to gather herself. Hector was already smiling big before he even reached them. She'd dream of that smile and that moment time had stood still for Charlee tonight no doubt—all night.

"So you guys might have heard of this little-known boxer named Felix Sanchez." Hector patted Felix on the shoulder.

Hector began introducing them one by one, and they all smiled and shook Felix's hand. Even though Charlee should have been feeling as starstruck as everyone else appeared to be, her insides were still going wild as the reality of what had happened earlier with Hector set in.

Felix was very nice and surprisingly down to earth, considering how famous and not to mention good-looking he was. He was actually better looking in person than in all the tabloids she'd seen him in.

As much as Charlee tried to focus on what Felix was saying to them and attempted to mimic Drew's excited smile, she couldn't help it. Her mind kept going back to Hector and what an about-face his behavior toward her had done.

Another huge distraction was that he was doing it again. Every time she glanced his way, she caught him looking at her. He didn't even try to hide it now. He'd smile every time. A few times she thought he might laugh because she'd caught him yet again. And he wasn't just looking at her face either. Several times, like earlier when she caught him taking her in completely, she noticed he was engrossed in her hair or her hands.

She knew her hair was eye-catching. It always had been, and she'd always hated that, but the way he looked at it was different, almost as if he were in awe. All her life, she'd had people comment on her hair—compliment it even. But no one had ever gazed at her quite the way he did. It made her insides warm but in a good way.

Felix finished answering a few more questions from the guys then excused himself. To Charlee's surprise, Hector didn't go with him. Felix walked away with his entourage to the next group of people waiting to talk to him.

"Is it weird having a friend that's so famous?" Drew asked Hector.

Even though it wasn't directed at her, his playful smile made Charlee breathe deeper. "People's reaction to seeing him will probably never get old. That's different but hanging out with him, not at all. He's the same guy he's always been."

"Oh man, I missed him," Maurice frowned as he came and stood next to Drew. "I was trying to hurry and get over here to meet him before he walked away."

Since Hector had been so eager about bringing Felix over as soon as he arrived, Charlee expected him to maybe offer to introduce Maurice to Felix, but he didn't. Instead he seemed a bit off put by Maurice joining them again. He didn't even acknowledge him, ignoring his comment and turning to Walter. "So you gonna stand here all night or you gonna actually do some dancing?"

Walter glanced at Charlee nervously then turned to the dance floor. "I'm not much for dancing."

Hector bringing up dancing again made Charlee's heart start thumping. Would he be asking her to dance again? The D.J. announced the appetizer trays had been refilled. Walter and one of the other guys exchanged smiles. "Let's go," Walter said, and they both took off.

The look of disgust on Hector's face was almost comical as he watched Walter rush off toward the appetizer trays. "What's wrong?" Charlee asked.

Shaking his head, Hector turned to Charlee. The way his disgusted expression morphed into that sexy smile did all kinds of funny things to her insides. "Nothing's wrong. He's just supposed to be watching what he eats," he said, motioning with his thumb in Walter's direction. "He asked me to help him drop some weight. I'm doing the best I can in the gym, but that," he pointed at Walter who was now making his way down the buffet of appetizers. "That's not gonna help."

Charlee smiled, knowing that if Walter were anything like her, food was comforting. She could tell she and Walter weren't too different in terms of being outgoing. He was just as shy as she was, and she'd seen that look on his face when Hector suggested he maybe try dancing. It was the same she was sure she'd made when Roger asked her to dance earlier. As usual, it was only after Drew said okay for both of them that she reluctantly followed her to the dance floor. When Hector had asked her, she'd been speechless.

Hoping to make up for choking during their dance and clamming up, she tried to shake off any feelings of awkwardness. "It's nice of you to help him out. You two been friends long?"

She saw a subtle but noticeable change wash over his face. He started to answer then stopped when something behind her caught his eye, and he frowned then held his palm up. "Give me a sec," he said, bringing his hand down, and touched her arm. "I'll be right back."

As he walked away, Charlee stood there, trying not to smile too silly. She felt a little ridiculous about how excited something as simple as his touching her arm could make her. "What happened?" Drew leaned into her. "Where'd he go?"

"I don't know. He got called away." Again she did her best to flatten the silly smile that threatened to burst when she added, "But he said he'd be right back."

Charlee glanced back in the direction he'd walked away. He was talking to his brother and Noah. She'd never admit it to anyone, even Drew, because it was too embarrassing, but she knew the names and recognized the two other owners of

5th Street from all the Google-stalking she'd done this past week.

Drew smiled just as big as Charlee wanted to. "I know we said we have to leave early." Her best friend sounded almost as excited as she felt. "But we can stay as long as you want to."

Just the thought of dancing with him again, being held against his body, and seeing that special something she'd seen in his eyes earlier had her insides going wild again. She had to get it together. Hector had walked in tonight with two girls for crying out loud: girls she was certain he'd already slept with and at the same time to make it worse. Now he was ignoring them to hang out with her. Next time, she could very well be the one being ignored. Those girls could deal with it, obviously, since they hadn't left immediately like Charlee would've.

She knew all too well that even going into this knowing the type of guy she was dealing with, she'd be crushed just the same—absolutely, positively crushed. There was no way she could be dumb enough to let herself get caught up in something like this again. Oh, but she was. She could feel it already. And this was completely different from last year. She never felt the kind of intensity she felt from Hector. There was no comparison, and there was no way to describe it, but she felt something with him she knew she'd never felt before. This was truly a first for her. So why was she still so scared.

Drew touched her arm, leaning in again and whispering so Maurice or anyone around wouldn't hear. "I see your brain working. Relax, okay? This is nothing like what you're thinking. You may be the same person on the inside, but you're completely different on the outside now." She shrugged, giving Charlee a little smile. "So you dance with him again if he asks, and you enjoy the party. It doesn't have to go any further than that. You can do this. It's been long enough, Charlee. And remember my sixth sense about these things? I'm telling you this is not the same."

Charlee nodded, smiling and feeling extremely grateful to have Drew. She's the only one who really knew all about her fears. Drew had been there and lived through her worst nightmare with her.

"You wanna another drink?"

"No." Charlee shook her head adamantly. "No more alcohol. I'd like at least a fighting chance of not doing or saying anything too stupid tonight. I'm already a wreck."

"Don't be." Her best friend smiled reassuringly. "You're doing fine."

Drew glanced up in the direction where Hector had been standing with Noah and Abel, and the immediate change in her demeanor was enough to alarm Charlee. She didn't want to be so obvious about it and jerk her head around like she was so tempted to. Whatever it was Drew had seen, had her feisty friend practically glaring now.

"What is it?" Charlee focused on the revolted look in Drew's eyes to keep from turning around. It wasn't that hard a temptation to fight anymore because she had a feeling what it could be.

"He's dancing."

Charlee swallowed hard, ignoring the plunging drop she just felt her stomach do. His dancing wasn't a big deal. It was partly his party. But that look on Drew's face said there was more to it. What did she expect? After everything she already knew, did she honestly think one dance with him was enough to get all stupidly excited about? She didn't have to ask. She already knew the answer just by the look on Drew's face, but she had to know, and she refused to look. "Is it Leticia, and can you please stop looking that way already?" The only consolation was the song playing was not a slow one.

Drew finally turned her glare away from him. "It's both of them."

Now Charlee couldn't help but look. She turned just as his eyes looked up and met hers. The song was not a fast one, but it may as well have been a slow sensual one the way the two shameless bitches worked their bodies up against his. Noah and Gio were also on the dance floor, though each danced respectfully with only one girl, and neither of their girls was behaving as vile as Hector's partners.

Unlike he had earlier, Hector didn't stare. Instead, he glanced away quickly. He wasn't dancing nearly as sensually as the girls were, but he did sway his hips to the music and was in no way protesting their bodies against his. Visions of that night in the parking lot came crashing down on her. How could she have been stupid enough to let a few gazes from him, one dance, and one moment, no matter how intense it was, block every fact she already knew about him? She could never deal with this. Ever. "Maybe we should get out of here early."

She turned to see her friend's repentant frown. "Whatever you want."

Charlee knew what Drew was thinking. Her sixth sense had been wrong, and now she felt guilty about adding to Charlee's premature excitement. But this wasn't Drew fault. Charlee should've known better. Thankfully, it was a quick slip and early on. She'd never let on just what a letdown this really was because she'd begun to think she, too, had some kind of sixth sense. Obviously, she'd been completely wrong—again.

Pouting but then quickly replacing it with a smile, she tried her damnedest to shake it off. "There's still ice cream at home, right?"

Drew's smile was equally forced too, but Charlee appreciated the effort. "And wine coolers."

"Ugh, I don't think I want any more alcohol tonight, but I'll take more ice cream."

Waving at the guys from the chess team, Charlee, Drew, and Maurice made their way to the exit. Knowing Drew had used the ladies' room not too long ago, Charlee took advantage when she saw the ladies' room outside the banquet room to tell Drew and Maurice to go on without her. She remembered Drew saying Maurice would probably want to kiss her goodnight, and she wanted to give them a little privacy.

Drew began to protest, saying they could wait for her, but Charlee insisted they go on ahead without her. Finally alone as she walked down the empty hallway toward the ladies' room, she let the disappointment set in. She didn't even need to use the restroom, but she went in anyway. Charlee was only thankful that the banquet rooms had restrooms so this one and the halls leading to it were completely abandoned now that the gym was closed off for anything more than the exclusive party.

She stood in front of the mirror, staring at the clueless girl in the mirror. Gawd, she was stupid or pathetic or both. Why didn't she ever just trust her first instincts? Sure she'd made a big change physically since last year. It might've even been big enough to attract a guy like Hector but certainly not enough to tame him. Guys like Hector obviously couldn't even be tamed by sex kittens like the ones he'd been dancing with tonight. And in all the photos she'd found of him online with girls, they were all Latinas—dark-haired, dark-eyed girls, who could probably all move on the dance floor as sensually as Leticia and Miriam had. There was never one as lily-white as Charlee with her ridiculously bright red hair that exuded about as much sensuality as a nun.

She leaned into the mirror to get a closer look at her face. At least makeup helped conceal most of her infuriating freckles. Surprised by how knotted up she was still feeling, she walked away from the mirror toward the door even more angry with herself. It was embarrassing how easily her made-up mind had been changed just by the few nice things he said to her and his flirtatious gazes. She walked out, determined to leave this behind her and stop thinking about him.

Wanting to give Drew and Maurice a little more alone time, Charlee took her time walking down the hallway, peering into the windows of the doors she passed. Each room was for some kind of specific training. The one with the trophies and photos on the wall caught her attention for a little longer. There was one light on in the corner, and it was hard to make out much. Standing on her tiptoes, she strained to see the photos furthest away. As if she hadn't gotten her fix of photos of Hector online already, she scanned the wall, looking for more of him.

"Looking for something?"

Charlee gasped at the sound of Hector's voice echoing off the walls. She spun around, feeling her face flush immediately. "I was just . . . I had to use the ladies' room and uh . . . the trophies," she pointed behind her. "I was just curious."

Hector smiled, easily making her heart flutter even after everything that had happened tonight alone. "It's okay," he said, walking toward her. "Is Drew in the ladies' room still?"

Charlee shook her head. "No, she's waiting in the car for me," she said, trying not to be too obvious, but her eyes seemed to have a mind of their own now.

They roamed his entire body up and down. No longer wearing his coat, his snug black vest over his long-sleeved white dress shirt accentuated his chest perfectly. For a moment, she wondered if he'd taken the coat off himself or if had been stripped off by his dance partners.

"There's actually some pretty cool stuff in there," he said as he got close enough for her senses to be once again overloaded by everything about him: his eyes, his lips, his scent, and even the heat from his body when he got close enough that she could almost touch it. This was the very body she'd fantasized about so many times and now knew for a fact just how hard and solid it really was. "I could show you quickly before you go."

Feeling glued to the spot where she stood, she managed to move so that he could get by her to open the door. "No, I couldn't," she said, still embarrassed about being caught snooping and not wanting to confirm just how nosey she could really be.

"Why not?" he turned back with a quizzical expression then chuckled. "This stuff isn't top secret. Come on in," he said, opening the door and walking into the room.

She followed him into the dimly lit room and stood in place, taking in the photos on the wall as he walked around turning on lights. With her heart already beating way too fast, she took deep slow breaths to try and calm herself. Not only could she do this but she would and with as much dignity and poise as she could muster. He was after all just a guy—a guy she would in no way be getting involved with.

She turned to see him loosening his tie and unbuttoning the top buttons of his shirt. Her eyes flew open, and she nearly stopped breathing when he began to unbutton the vest.

Hector stopped midway through taking the vest off and gave her that same bedroom-eyed gaze along with the sexy smile that had left her breathless earlier. "Don't worry. I'll stop at the vest. I just feel a little stuffy."

Gulping hard as he continued to remove the vest then pull off the tie altogether, she nodded, knowing full well if she attempted to talk, there likely be no sound. Good Lord, she'd have to dig deep for any poise if he dared remove even one more piece of clothing.

CHAPTER 11

What the hell was wrong with him? Hector should've just let her go when he saw her walk out of the party. Charlee was not the type of girl he should be messing with. He saw this in her eyes yesterday when he'd nearly kissed her—felt it earlier when he held her on the dance floor. Keeping her at a necessary distance was easier when he thought she was just another brainy girl with better, more important things to think about than the new guy on the chess team: the unimpressive winner of the speed tournament—speed chess something apparently beneath her. But he'd been wrong. She had taken time to think of him and his game—lots of time. And he saw it in her eyes yesterday then over and over again tonight that she had been impressed.

So what? This wouldn't be the first time Hector had impressed a pretty girl or even a highly skilled chess player. What was it about her? Why did he care so much? Why was he so damn fascinated with her? Fascinated enough to come chasing after her when he knew it was a bad idea.

She was an enigma, one he had no business trying to figure out. He knew this already. He'd gone through the list of whys so many times, and the conclusion was always the same. Forget about it. Yet he'd gone after her, and now here he was dangerously alone with her.

When he left the party to see if he might catch her, even though she'd been gone for a few minutes, he had no idea what he would do or say if he did. But he did know exactly what he shouldn't do—the very thing that was already clouding his senses. Seeing those big blue eyes go even bigger when he realized she'd been watching him strip the layers of stuffy clothes off had done it.

Pushing away the all too fresh memories of holding her soft warm body against his, how good it felt to hold her hand and wrap his arms around her, he smiled, tilting his head. "So why are you and Drew leaving so early?"

"We have somewhere to be early tomorrow morning."

"Early on a Saturday morning? Where you going?" he asked, trying to sound more curious than prying.

"A marathon in Long Beach."

Hector raised his brows a bit surprised. "Really? So you're a chess genius *and* a runner?"

She shook her head, smiling. Even though her face tinged a little with color, Hector was glad she seemed to be calming. He could tell after catching her off guard she seemed more than unnerved.

"I'd hardly call myself any kind of genius." She tucked a red strand of hair behind her ear with a timid smile. "And no, I'm not a runner. I volunteer for the Special Olympics. They're having a marathon tomorrow."

"Oh, yeah, yeah, my partner, Gio, was just talking about that. He runs the youth program here at the gym and a few of them are special needs. He mentioned a couple of them running in that this weekend." He peered at her as she looked around the room at the photos on the wall. "So you and Drew are giving up your Saturday morning for this, huh?"

She turned back to him and nodded with that little timid smile he was becoming so fond of now. "It's not a sacrifice at all. I've been doing it for years back home. Drew didn't start until just last year, but after volunteering just one time, she was hooked. She's been doing it with me ever since."

Hector liked hearing her talk. There was something so soothing about her sweet voice. He hadn't really noticed that about her until earlier in the party. "And where is back home?"

"Maryland."

"Really? Wow. You're a long way from home."

She walked around now, taking in the photos on the wall again. "Tell me about it."

Hector liked how the longer he was around her the more relaxed she became. He liked how fast and easily she went from all tensed up to relaxed. Just like earlier on the dance floor when he first put his arms around her, she'd frozen up. But within minutes, he felt her giving into the moment, and damn, what a moment that had been.

"So who do you stay with out here?"

He'd come in here a little worried that he might do something he'd regret, but all he could think about was he wanted to know more about her.

She turned to him with that tiny smile again. It was almost as if she were afraid to smile too big. Though she'd come around a little, the evidence of her shy demeanor was still very much there. "With Drew and her dad. Though her dad is rarely around. He's a commercial pilot, so we pretty much have the house to ourselves most of the time."

He nodded. Good to know, but he wanted more now. He took a few steps toward her, aware that he'd invited her in the room to show her the "cool stuff" in there and he was yet to show her any of it. Still, he knew his time alone with her would be brief, and he still had so many more questions.

"Why'd you decide to go to school so far from home?"

Her brows pinched for a second, and she glanced back at him again, only this time minus the smile. "It was Drew's idea actually. She had to coax me into the idea." Now she smiled. "She does that a lot." She bobbed her head a little, but it was nothing like when Walter's dumb ass did it. Charlee looked cute doing it. "If it weren't for Drew, there'd be a lot of things in my life I wouldn't have done."

"She must be pretty persuasive. Moving from Maryland to California, that's huge."

For the first time, he heard her laugh. And, of course, it had to be the sweetest laugh ever. "Oh, you'd be surprised. The girl could talk an atheist into believing with little effort.

But it wasn't just that. The chess scholarship I was offered to ESU was a big incentive. So when Drew said she'd apply to ESU and got in, that sealed the deal."

That reminded Hector of something. Getting back to her earlier comment about not being a genius, he felt almost stupid now about being so pissed over what she'd done yesterday. "A chess scholarship? Impressive. Not that I'm surprised. I'd say only a chess genius could come up with what you did to me yesterday." Her timid smile flatlined immediately. "I'm not mad, okay? I mean I'll admit I did feel a little stupid—"

"I wasn't trying to make you feel stupid," she said quickly then added in a lower voice, shaking her head softly, "I swear."

He smiled even bigger, hoping to reassure her. "I know that now, Charlotte." He saw it yesterday when he called her that: a flicker in her eyes he didn't know what to make of then and still didn't now. "Do you not like being called Charlotte?"

Those big blue eyes looked up at him as she shook her head. "No, I don't mind. I just . . . I'm just a little surprised you remember."

Going against everything he'd been telling himself since he walked into that party tonight, he took a step closer to her. "Yeah, I remember," he said, taking yet another step closer to her. "I also remember you having more freckles. You cover them up?"

She nodded, staring at him the same way she had yesterday, the very way she had on the dance floor. As if she wanted to say more but wouldn't—couldn't. "Why?" Unable to hold back anymore, he touched the soft flesh of her cheek with the back of his hand gently. It felt as soft as he'd imagined, and the fact that she didn't protest or even move away from him made his heart pound like it had when he held her earlier. "You don't like them?"

Clearing her throat but not looking away, she stared right at him. "No, I don't."

"I like them." Feeling intoxicated by the touch of her skin against his, he continued to caress the few freckles that weren't concealed around her lips with the tips of his knuckles.

He knew he should stop, but he couldn't now. The tips of his knuckles moved over her lips, and she closed her eyes, her lashes fluttering along with the very subtle but undeniable tremble of her body. She breathed in deeply and so did he. He had to. He was beginning to lose it. Staring at her lips for a moment, he tried one last time to convince himself he shouldn't. Nothing in him, not his pounding heart, not his hungry lips, not his aching, growing need—none of it was cooperating here.

Leaning in slowly, he brought his hand around the back of her neck, touching his lips to hers and waited. Waited—his breathing growing heavier with anticipation—the need to taste her mouth insatiable now. He kissed her once, waiting again for a reaction. Then she parted her lips, and it was all he needed. Cradling her head with both hands now, he kissed her deeply, toying with her tongue, stopping only to suck her bottom lip before ravenously going back in for more.

Feeling her arms come around his back now, he took a few steps until they were leaning against the wall. A bit surprised that not only did she not object but she kissed him back eagerly, he wondered how far he should let this go. Sliding his mouth off her lips, he traced kisses down her jaw line to her soft neck. She smelled so damn good it made him feel crazed, and he sucked a bit harder than he anticipated. Then hearing her moan in response only made him suck harder. Pulling away when he remembered just how fair her skin was, he examined the area. He'd already left a mark. Luckily it was far back enough her hair would cover it. But not wanting to make it any darker, he kissed the spot one last time and went back to her lips.

To hell with Walter. He'd had his chance more than once, and he chose grubbing over dancing with Charlee. The guy had to be out of his fucking mind.

Pressing his body onto hers, feeling her soft breasts push up against his chest, Hector pulled back. As much as that drove him crazy, something in him wanted to make this very clear to her. This wasn't just about sex. Sure he had the biggest throbbing painful erection he could remember ever having, but that's not what this was about. A part of him would love nothing more than to pull her dress up and fuck her right there if she'd let him. The way her body was responding to his, something told him she just might. There was a bigger part of him making him hold back: the same part of him that had him tossing and turning the whole damn night last night.

Finally there was a sign of restraint on Charlee's part. She brought her hand to his chest and placed her open palm against it, pulling her lips away from his for the first time since he'd begun kissing her. Breathing heavily, Hector searched her eyes.

"Those girls," she said, breathlessly then licked her lips. "The ones you were dancing with . . ."

Hector shook his head. He had a feeling that's why she'd left. "They're just friends."

"They came here with you."

Still trying to catch his breath, he shook his head again. "No, they walked in just as I was done my last interview, and we just so happened to walk in together."

"I'm not like them."

"I know," he agreed quickly. God, did he know. She was completely different in every way.

She frowned. "I know that must sound really stupid too because I'm here with you now, but—"

"Trust me, Charlotte," he said, gently lifting her chin with his finger. "I know you're different." He kissed the small crease that had formed between her eyes from her frowning then kissed her lips softly again. "So different," he whispered then kissed her again. "So sweet." He felt her exhale softly then smile against his lips.

Dropping her hand from his chest and then bringing it around his neck, she kissed him and gave into him completely again. Groaning, he kissed her as deeply as he had the very first time, feeling utterly crazed again. Every time they stopped for air, they were both panting now as if they'd both just had a very long drink of water—an incredibly delicious taste of water after days of going without. Coming up again, he had to laugh a little. This was insane. She laughed too, biting her lower lip.

"You're beautiful." The words flew out of his mouth before he could catch himself.

Her big blue eyes opened wide, confirming what he'd just said like they had when he said her eyes were beautiful earlier. She was beautiful.

"Thank you," she said with that same apprehensive smile that had caught his attention that very first day she thanked him for knocking out the asshole beating on Walter.

"You're welcome."

She stared at him for a moment, then her eyes lifted a bit and she touched his brow. Even something as simple as feeling her fingers caressing his brow felt incredible. Her touch was so gentle, so sweet. "Is this a boxing scar?"

He nodded, unable to take his eyes off her lips. "I got it last year."

"Will it ever go away?" she said, continuing to run her fingers over it gently.

"It might if I stop reopening the gash."

Now she focused on his eyes. "But you're so good. I don't think I saw that guy land even one punch on your face tonight."

"That's what scars are for. You learn from them. I don't let my guard down nearly as much as I used to before I got it. But it's not that. The wound has been reopened a few times since then." He shrugged. "I'm getting better. Eventually it'll heal completely."

Unable to go even another moment without tasting those lips again, he went in for another kiss. The door flew open just as his lips touched hers, and she pulled back immediately.

Miriam stared at them wide-eyed. "Oops."

"Did you find him?" Leticia was at the door now with Miriam staring at them as well. Though she was obviously surprised, she played it off with a smirk, "I guess you did."

Charlee moved away from the wall, understandably looking uncomfortable by the interruption. She walked around Hector and out of the compromising position they'd been found in. "I, uh . . ."

Hector touched her arm. He didn't want her fretting or worse leaving because of this. Before he could say anything to them, the door opened further and Drew walked in. Since Charlee no longer stood against the wall, and Hector wasn't pressed up against her anymore, she didn't appear as stunned as Leticia and Miriam, but there was no hiding the surprise. "I was getting worried. You weren't answering your phone."

"Yeah, she was a little busy for that." Leticia said with a clearly forced smirk before walking out of the room. Miriam sneered, following Leticia out.

"I'm sorry," Charlee said. "I turned it off when we got here and forgot all about it." She turned to Hector then back to Drew again. "He was showing me the trophies and stuff, and I forgot about the time. I have to go," she addressed Hector now. "I told you we gotta be up early tomorrow."

Hector nodded. The disappointment of knowing he wouldn't be kissing her goodbye weighed heavily. If it were up to him, he'd do it regardless of who was in the room, but her he-was-showing-me-the-trophies comment was an obvious indication that she didn't want her friend to know what they'd really been doing. He'd let that simmer for now. She was obviously a shy girl, and he wasn't even sure where this would go, if anywhere. He still didn't know a whole lot about her other than he couldn't get enough of kissing her, and he hadn't lied when he told her she was different. She was. He just couldn't put his finger on exactly what it was, or maybe it was just everything.

He walked them all the way to the door, Drew taking the initiative after they'd walked a few feet in silence. She began telling them about her encounter with the talkative older man she ran into while looking for Charlee. Hector tuned her out, opting instead to sneak smiles at Charlee the whole way. He'd been in such a cloud, still thinking about everything that had happened that night. It wasn't until he was on his way back to turn off the lights they'd left on in the trophy room that he realized he hadn't asked for her number. Now he wouldn't talk to her until Monday afternoon at the earliest. He didn't even know where she lived!

"Damn it," he muttered, shutting off the lights in the room.

Asking Walter, the only person that might have that information in the meantime, was out of the question. He was just going to have to wait until Monday. Feeling the smallest pang of guilt, he pushed it to the back of his head. Walter didn't deserve Charlee, not with the little effort he'd put into trying to even talk to her. Sure he was trying to lose weight, and he'd cut his hair and trimmed his brows as Hector had suggested, but that was hardly enough.

Hector wasn't sure if anything would become of this or if he even wanted it to. For now, he'd keep things on the down low and continue to help Walter get in shape.

Obviously, Hector wouldn't be helping him with his efforts to win Charlee's affection anymore. Even before tonight's turn of events, Hector wasn't sure how to help him there anyway. The guy was oblivious about how to even talk to a girl. There was only so much Hector could do or had time for. He'd help Walter get into shape because it's what

Hector did on a daily basis anyway, but he was on his own when it came to Charlee.

Unbelievably, Leticia and Miriam were in the lobby when he walked out of the hallway on his way back to the party. He thought for sure they'd left. They both smiled now. Apparently seeing him alone had changed their moods.

"Hey," he smiled back but not in the normal flirtatious way he would've. He didn't want to encourage anything. The sweet taste of Charlee's mouth was still on his lips, and he'd like to keep it like that as long as he could.

"Didn't mean to barge in on you like that," Leticia said as they walked toward him.

The second she was close enough to him, Leticia reached for his hand. "Are you free for the rest of the evening, or did she stake her claim for tonight?"

Both of their eyes were telling of how much they'd had to drink tonight. Before he could begin to even think of a good enough response, Miriam slid her hand into his other one. Thankfully the doors to the banquet room opened and out walked Walter and the other guys from the chess club. The guys did their best to not gawk, but Hector knew this was not something any of them could ever imagine doing, so he saw the reserved humor in their eyes. Walter all out smiled, waving. "Thanks for having us, Hector."

Seeing an opportunity, Hector took it to get away from Leticia and Miriam. "Hold on. I wanted to talk to you guys before you leave. I'll be out in a minute." Walter and the guys nodded and kept walking toward the door. He turned back to the girls, pulling his hands loose from their hold and lowered his voice. "Yeah, I'm kind of taken tonight, ladies."

Immediately their smiles faded, and Leticia lifted her brow. "I saw her leave."

Not wanting to be rude and remembering he did invite them there with the insinuation that they'd finish what they started last week, he took a deep breath. "I'm meeting her somewhere else. But you two are welcome to stay as long as you want."

He made a mental note to never insinuate anything to these two again.

"Will you be coming back in after you talk to your friends?" Miriam asked then smiled wickedly. "Or do we say goodbye to you now."

Hell no. Hector wouldn't even be having another beer until he savored the very last lingering hint of Charlee in his mouth. "No, I'll be back." This would be the ideal time to wink, but he dared not. Instead, he started walking away. "You two go on back in."

Visibly disappointed, the two girls walked back toward the banquet room. He never would've thought he'd be so thankful to see Walter in his life. Smothering the life out of the guilt that began to fester, he walked outside to talk to the guys for as long as possible.

CHAPTER 12

With the memory of Hector still so clear in her head, Charlee could very easily visualize Hector lying over her, touching her where her fingers touched now. He was sliding in and out of her wetness, not her secret toy she had to hide deep in the box with the other stuff she mailed herself from home.

The idea that this may not be the only pleasure she'd have of this nature ever was no longer an impossible one. It usually took longer than this for her to start trembling when Drew was home, because Charlee was terrified of turning it on for fear her friend would hear it and know just what a freak Charlee really was. But tonight was different. Just closing her eyes and remembering Hector's kisses so vividly, the way his tongue slid all around like silk in her mouth, her fingers and her toy, even without power, were all she needed.

Burying it deep inside herself just as her entire body began to quiver, Charlee felt the spasms shoot through more intensely than she'd ever had before and struggled to refrain from moaning as she squirmed under her blankets still sliding it in and out. As the spasms slowly calmed, her heart still pounded uncontrollably. She lay there for a moment breathing hard, still thinking about the possibility that one day maybe Hector would do this to her. For so long, she truly believed deep inside that she'd never open up her heart to anyone again. But her urges had always been so insatiable—so much so it was the one thing she never shared with anyone. Not even Drew. She really believed she was destined to only experience this kind of pleasure alone.

***

Even after one of the best damn orgasms she'd experienced to date, Charlee still had lain awake most of the night, thinking of Hector and everything he'd said to her. She should've been a zombie this morning. Instead, she felt strangely invigorated. She would've liked to say it was the excitement of getting to work with the kids today, something she enjoyed so much. But she knew it was for an altogether different reason.

She'd been almost embarrassed last night to admit to Drew that she'd let Hector kiss her, even after seeing him with those two girls. Of course, Drew not only hadn't passed judgment she helped reassure Charlee she hadn't made the biggest mistake of her life. Drew made her promise one thing: if nothing became of it, she wouldn't let this take her all the way back to that dark place she'd once been.

"People make out at parties all the time, and nothing comes of it, Charlee." Drew had said then dramatically gasped and added. "Many do *way* more than just make out too, you know. So please promise me that if this is all it was for him you don't freak out okay? If, and I'm not saying it will, but if this turns out to be just that, then we'll go out and celebrate. You got your first time out of the way."

Charlee agreed, not wanting to argue, but she wondered how many of the people that did stuff like this had to face their one night stands every day. The school chess labs weren't mandatory every day, but they had to do a lab at least twice a week. Then there was the U.S. team. They met less often, but they'd even be traveling together eventually. Things could get very awkward. She finally decided she wouldn't do what she normally did and worry about something that hadn't even happened yet.

Last night, Drew had watched her very closely as Charlee gave her the blow by blow of her make-out session with Hector. Well, Charlee's version of the blow by blow. She'd kept a few things to herself, like how incredibly aroused she'd been. She'd never felt anything like it. Finally she understood what the big deal about sex was, and she hadn't even had the real thing yet. Last night had been just a precursor, and it'd been amazing.

She really should slow down with the fantasies. Charlee should be happy that they were not so farfetched anymore. Even now, she could still easily close her eyes and vividly remember, not just imagine anymore what it felt like to be kissed by him, feel his tongue on her neck, making the most private of places tingle in reaction. But as much as she promised Drew she'd take it all in stride, things had already changed. Even after last night under her blankets, her fantasies had also gone now from the most sexual in nature to replaying his words and the look in his eyes when he'd said them to her over and over in her mind.

"Trust me, Charlotte. I know you're different. So different. So sweet."

Hearing the sound of her own name had never left her so breathless. But the most breathtaking of all, and she closed her eyes once again to relive it, was his telling her she was beautiful. Only one other guy had ever said that to her before, and she'd thought for sure he'd ruined that compliment forever. But she'd been so wrong. Hearing Hector say it had been completely different. She'd seen the sincerity in his eyes—felt it in his kisses.

"Charlee?"

"Um hmm?" She didn't open her eyes in response to Drew, simply continued to picture Hector's intense eyes looking deep into hers when he'd spoken to her.

"Please tell me you're just resting your eyes because you're tired and that lovesick smile on your face isn't what it looks like."

Charlee opened one eye and glanced at Drew who was driving. "It's not."

She closed her eye again, hating that she was cursed with a best friend who was so damn discerning. The girl never missed a thing. It was a wonder Drew hadn't foreseen last year's debacle before it happened.

The rest of the day, Charlee managed to keep her mind on her volunteer duties for the most part. It wasn't too hard. They kept her busy. But inevitably, she'd find herself daydreaming and even feeling her body quiver at times with thoughts of Hector's kisses and the mesmerizing way he gazed at her all night—that amazing smile.

Of course, each time she'd fall too deeply into it, Drew had caught her, and each time she seemed a little more concerned about Charlee getting her hopes up too high. Drew's subtle reminders that Hector hadn't asked for Charlee's number and that he'd shown up with two girls, began to get annoying.

Charlee didn't even bother trying to explain what he'd said about how the girls had just so happened to show up at the same time he'd been ready to walk in. She knew it would only further Drew's worrying because it would sound as if Charlee were making excuses for him already. The fact remained, whether he'd showed up with them or not, that it didn't take from what they'd seen him do with those same two girls last week: the very thing he'd done with Charlee last night at the gym, except he'd clearly done much more with them since those girls had gone home with him.

The whole day had been a roller coaster of emotions. Charlee would begin to scold herself for getting so carried away when it could very well have been just a onetime thing for him, something he probably did all the time. She was sure he wasn't obsessing about it today like she was. More than likely, he had plenty of plans with other girls this weekend already.

With that thought in mind, she'd move on to convincing herself that if that was the case she'd be fine and would not freak out. She'd be stupid to fall apart again when she should be thankful like Drew said to have gotten her first onetime make out with a guy out of the away. And of all guys to have gotten it out of the way with, it had been Hector. She'd be happy that she got to at least experience what it felt like to be kissed by him, especially after fantasizing about it for so long.

Remembering his kisses would only take her full circle again, replaying the way he'd stared at her all night, the possessive way he'd held her on the dance floor, how he'd held her face in his hands, and those kisses. How in the world could she just shrug away such an amazing experience? The most amazing experience she'd had with a guy *ever*. And she'd be back to square one, worrying that there'd be no way she'd get over this as easily as Drew thought she could or should.

As much as she tried to convince herself it was just an infatuation with him, that she didn't know him well enough or even remotely enough to be so hung up on him this soon, she knew better. She'd been in tears after what happened on Thursday at their chess meeting, and he hadn't even touched her.

By the end of the day, she was spent. She'd gone full circle with this whole thing more times than she cared to think about anymore. All she could do now is wait and hope that, worst case scenario, she'd be strong enough to deal with it and get over it faster than the last time she'd been crushed.

~*~

Friday night, Hector stayed out in front of the gym for as long as he could with Walter and the guys. He kept hoping he'd see Leticia and Miriam walk out and leave, preferably with guys so they might not be too pissed at him. Not that he cared one way or another if they were, he just didn't want to deal with any drama in case they'd gone in and kept drinking, which he knew was probably the case.

His new chess buddies busted his balls about being quite the ladies' man. Hector laughed mostly because he thought only people over fifty used that term anymore. They were all under the impression that Hector would be leaving with two girls that night, and for some reason, this delighted them. Apparently, Walter had filled them in on last weekend when he'd seen Hector actually leave with them.

Not wanting to disappoint them, he neither confirmed nor denied it would be happening again that night. Obviously, a topic of that nature was not one any of those guys had ever had the pleasure of discussing. Usually, he would've cut it short. He wasn't one to kiss and tell. But that night he stood out there and let them have their fun, bouncing their brows, making stupid faces, and coming to their own conclusions about what Hector would be doing with the two girls that night.

Hector cringed the few times Walter made reference to what a lucky guy he was to be able to have any girl he wanted.

By the time they finally left, he'd been out there with them for nearly an hour. His plan had worked. When he got back to the party, Leticia and Miriam were both on the dance floor with two different guys. And judging by the way they were dancing, they'd had plenty more to drink. Hector took advantage of their distraction and snuck out.

The next morning, he went into 5th Street to cover for Gio since he'd be at that marathon—just another thing that brought continual thoughts of Charlee. He'd actually been tempted to ask Abel to take over the youth-training class so that Hector might take a little drive to Long Beach. He was still kicking himself about forgetting to ask for her number. He'd been that close to doing it too, and he was sure Abel wouldn't have minded, but then Walter walked in. He was there to work out and all gung ho about it.

Walter hadn't actually discussed a schedule for his workouts. Hector just assumed they'd start out slow—a few days a week, especially after that brutal first workout Hector had given him. But apparently Walter was going to work out daily. He told Hector he'd be back again on Sunday, and he seemed pretty damned determined.

Another thing Walter let Hector know he was also more determined now to do was whatever it took to impress and get to know Charlee better. He said after seeing how beautiful she looked at the party Friday night he was even more motivated now.

Annoyed, Hector reminded him what a contradiction that statement was to how hard Walter actually tried at the party. With the most pathetic expression Hector had seen on Walter, and he'd seen quite a few on him already, he told Hector all about the insecurity issues he'd faced all his life. As if that weren't enough of a guilt grenade, he then added how being harassed all through school only made things worse.

Sunday, Hector had to once again hear about Charlee the whole time Walter worked out. She was the typical main topic of conversation for Walter, but after what happened Friday night, Hector could hardly stand it anymore. A few times he told Walter to shut up and concentrate on his workout. It was killing him. How the hell was Hector supposed to do anything more with Charlee when she was all Walter talked about? He felt like a total asshole all over again for not having been able to hold back kissing her.

It was still hands down totally worth it, even if he was drowning in guilt all over again. He just had no idea how this was going to work. Walter was going to hate him again and for good reason. He'd trusted Hector.

When Walter was finished with his workout, he approached Hector before he left. "You have a minute? I wanna show you something."

Hector looked at him curiously. "Sure. What is it?"

"It's in my car. I don't want to bring it in here."

They walked out into the parking lot where it was already getting dark. Beverly, a girl he'd hung out with in the past, walked in and smiled at Hector knowingly.

Walter smirked as she walked past them, shaking his head. When she was far enough away, Walter glanced back. "I can't even imagine what it must be like to be you."

Gritting his teeth because he already felt like a big enough dick, Hector pushed the thoughts of being with Charlee on Friday away. "It's not as glamorous as you may think."

"Shit!" Walter laughed. "Glamorous or not, I'd trade places with you any day." He stopped and pointed his finger in the air just as they reached his trunk. "But only for a day at most. I think I'm finally gonna start liking my life."

He opened the trunk, and Hector froze, feeling every hair on his body stand. Staring at it for a moment, he wasn't sure what to say or why Walter would bring it to him now. Could he possibly know about Friday? Had he maybe talked to Charlee?

Finally able to put a few words together, Hector began to speak. "Is that . . ."

Walter picked up the robot and held it with a smile. "Can you believe Charlee read about this thing before she even knew me? She had no idea it was me who built it but said she remembered reading about it online." Walter slugged Hector's arm with the biggest goofiest smile. "I fucking impressed her, man!" The laugh he let out next was too happy, too genuine for him to know anything about Friday night. "And get this; she said she'd love to see it. So I brought it down from my garage this week for the first time since . . ."

Walter paused, meeting Hector's eyes, his expression falling but only momentarily before he was smiling again. Hector tried to match Walter's enthusiasm, but all he felt was the same suffocating guilt he felt when he heard Walter's robot hadn't been entered in the national event, even though Mr. Sifuentes, their Science teacher, was certain Walter was a clear front-runner to win the whole thing. Hector remembered feeling horrified, his first thoughts being that Walter must've taken his own life.

The one thing that had given him hope was that when Hector had Googled Walter's name, the only things that ever came up were stories about his chemical-detecting robot.

"Anyway," Walter continued with his story, "I wanted to work on it a little before showing it to her, so I did. I'm thinking of asking her to come over this week." His uppity mood suddenly swayed and he looked nervous. "You think it would be too much if I order pizza or something then maybe ask if she wants to hang out and watch a movie?"

Hector stared at him, suddenly knowing all the bullshit mental lists he'd made up this whole weekend of reasons why it had been okay for him to move in on Charlee had just blown up in his face. It wasn't okay. It would never be okay, no matter how much he tried to justify it. No matter how unlikely it was that Charlee would ever be interested in anything more than a friendship with Walter, Hector owed him that much: the decency and respect of staying away from the one girl that could make Walter this excited.

I think I'm finally gonna start liking my life.

"Too much, huh?"

Hector didn't even realize he'd been shaking his head until Walter's question brought him back to earth. "What?"

"Asking her to hang out and watch a movie." Walter winced. "Maybe just the pizza?"

"Nah," Hector finally responded with a weak smile. "The pizza's cool, and it wouldn't hurt to ask if she wants to hang out. Worst thing she can say is no, right?"

Hector couldn't stand to even look at the robot anymore, so he was glad when Walter set it down in his trunk again and closed it. But he had to ask. He wasn't sure why. He just had to. "So how come you never entered it in the national event? Sifuentes said you were a front-runner."

Walter's cheerful expression went flat again, and he shrugged. "I just lost interest in it. That was a real bad time for me, and I stopped caring about everything."

Feeling like total shit because it's what he'd suspected all along, Hector did what he said he wouldn't do anymore. "Listen, Walter, I am so fucking sorry about—"

"Nah, nah!" Walter shook his head adamantly. "It wasn't just what happened that day, man. There was a lot of other stuff going on. My parents were talking about getting divorced. I pretty much knew it was coming, and it was hard and all, but I still had this stupid robot to keep my mind off things. Then my uncle, the one who helped me built it," he frowned now, looking more irritated than dejected like he had a moment ago, "he was a science teacher over at Union High. He got arrested for getting involved with one of his underage students. It was just one of those times when everything happened all at once, you know? So the day that happened at school, I just said screw everything."

Once again, Hector felt numb. Even with the shitty hand Walter had been dealt, especially in comparison to Hector's, here he was trying to make Hector feel better. But he'd done just the opposite. Hector didn't think it was possible, but, unbelievably, he felt even worse now.

CHAPTER 13

Most days Drew and Charlee tried to carpool to school together to save on gas. So on Monday mornings, Charlee either left later, taking her own car, or she rode with Drew and hung out on campus for an hour, killing time because Drew's first class was earlier than Charlee's first.

Unable to sleep much again with the anticipation of seeing Hector today, Charlee was up early, so she had ridden in with Drew. She'd been trying to concentrate on the novel she started weeks ago. It was actually pretty good, but her mind kept wandering off to the usual—Hector.

Startled by the sudden body that sat down way too close next to her, she jerked away and gasped when she saw it was Ross. Since the time he'd approached her the morning she was walking through campus with Drew, she hadn't run into him again. She'd seen him a few times from afar and made sure she steered clear from him. Now he sat here next to her, the faint smell of marijuana not as penetrating as her first few encounters with him but still there.

"Morning," he smiled.

Instinctively Charlee moved away, but she didn't want to be too dramatic about it, so she abstained from jumping up and away from him like she really wanted to.

"Morning," she said as calmly as she could.

"I've been hoping to run into you alone." That statement from anyone else wouldn't be so creepy, but coming from Ross, it was just that. He must've seen it in her questioning eyes because he added. "I mean so I can talk to you. I wanted to apologize and tell you how sorry I am that I made such a bad first impression."

Not sure how else to respond, she nodded, gathering her things but avoided direct eye contact. "It's okay."

"I was also wondering if you don't have a class anytime soon if we can go grab some coffee or something. You know a kind of peace offering."

This time she did meet his eyes. Unlike Hector's sexy, carefree and very bright eyes even when they got all intense, Ross's were a bit bloodshot and glossed over as they were the last few times she'd seen him, no doubt from all the pot he smoked. But there was something more cynical about them too.

She started to shake her head, and when he reached over and touched her leg, Charlee sprung to her feet immediately. "Whoa wait!" Ross lifted his hand up in the air to show her he meant no harm. "I'll behave. I promise. I just wanna talk to you a little more."

"I can't right now. I have to go." She lied, picking up her last book from the bench.

Her heart sped up when he stood up next to her. She was only glad she was in the middle of the campus with lots of other students still around, unlike that first time.

"You ready to go, Charlee?" She turned to see Walter standing there with his backpack over his shoulder, looking a little surer of himself than he had the first time he came to her rescue.

Immediately catching on, she nodded. "Yes, we're late." With a quick half smile, she glanced at Ross, who was now frowning, and hooked her arm into Walter's. "Let's go."

"I'll take a rain check then," Ross said as she and Walter walked away quickly.

"Rain check for what?" Walter asked in a low voice. "What did he want?"

"To have coffee with me and you saved me again. Thank you, Walter." Charlee pulled her arm out of Walter's when they turned the corner of a building and she was sure they were out of Ross's sight. "Sorry about latching on to you." She shrugged. "It was an impulse I guess—felt safer."

"It's okay," Walter smiled. "I didn't mind. So he's still bothering you, huh?"

"Actually, I hadn't seen him in a while, and I'm pretty sure he's not out to harm me, not here on campus in broad daylight, anyway. It's just . . ." She glanced at Walter a bit hesitant to go on but then did anyway. "He brings back old memories for me."

Walter's eyes opened a bit surprised. "You know him from way back?"

"No." Charlee shook her head before taking a seat on a bench. Walter sat next to her, and she turned to him with a frail smile. "But feeling spooked or maybe just harassed by someone like him brings back old memories of when I was a kid in school." She lifted a shoulder. "I've always been really shy. So I didn't do well fitting in. The kids were . . . Well they weren't very nice. It's why I ended up just being homeschooled."

Walter's eyes opened even wider. "You left school because you were bullied? So did I."

She tilted her head. This shouldn't surprise her, but he was so big. "Really?"

Walter frowned. "Well, I was practically done with school. Just a little over a month before I finished high school, I dropped out. It was kind of impulsive and stupid actually, but I'd just had it."

Charlee shook her head, taking a deep breath and glanced away. "I just don't understand what it is about people that make them enjoy being cruel to others. I don't think it's Ross's intention to be cruel."

"He's a jerk, Charlee."

"Oh, I know." Charlee glanced back at him, agreeing quickly. "I'm just saying I don't think he means to hassle me more than pursue me, but it's the way he goes about it—so aggressively and intimidating, like his just sitting down so close to me today, especially because our first encounter didn't go over well at all. *That's* what drudges up the ugly memories."

"Well, I wouldn't take my guard down about him not meaning any harm." Walter said with a somber expression. "I still remember that look in his eye the day you wouldn't give into him."

Charlee thought about the first time she ran into him after that day and how creepy it had felt. "I won't." She smiled and stood up. "I better get going. I was so busy just trying to get as far as away from Ross that I went the opposite direction. My next class is clear across campus."

Walter stood up. "I'll walk you."

"No, you don't have to, Walter. Being my bodyguard is not your job."

Walter shook his head. "My next class is that way too. And I want to." His smile was a shy one. "Who knows? Now that I'm working out so much, maybe I will look into doing some bodyguard work."

Charlee smiled maybe a little too big. Just like that, the butterflies in her belly started up again. Walter talking about working out was all it took to bring on the thoughts of Hector, his rock hard body, and the fact that she'd be seeing him again soon.

With her heart rate already taking a flying leap, she reminded herself of what she promised Drew. No matter what happened, she would remain composed. Charlee had also promised she wouldn't do what she tended to do when she was trying to cover up feeling hurt or uncomfortable—overcompensate by acting too much the opposite way or say something rash if she got angry. She shouldn't be angry, because in this day and age people did things like this all the time. Becoming angry or hurt would only make it obvious that Hector had been the first guy she'd done anything like this with. Charlee shouldn't give him the pleasure of knowing that, if he didn't deserve it. She was a modern woman living in a modern world. This was true. She agreed completely, even though this *was* huge for her.

Charlee smiled inwardly, chewing on the inside of her cheek. She remembered the way Hector gazed so tenderly into her eyes, kissed her so sweetly, and how sincere he was when he'd said the things he had. What she didn't dare tell Drew was that the more she thought about Friday night, the more she was convinced this hadn't been so insignificant for him either.

***

Monday . . . Tuesday . . . Wednesday . . . Thursday. . . Disappointment didn't even begin to describe what Charlee was feeling. Hector hadn't bothered to show up for chess lab all week. It was already Friday, and Charlee was certain he was avoiding her. Overhearing the guys and Walter talk about Hector with the two girls he'd apparently taken home again last Friday night didn't help either.

As devastated as she felt, she was madder at herself than anything. He'd shown up with two girls—two girls he *knew* she'd seen grinding up on him on the dance floor just prior to them ending up in that room. And though he'd referred to them as just friends, Charlee knew exactly what kind of friends they were and, therefore, what kind of guy that made him, and still she'd gone against her better judgment and allowed him to kiss her.

The worst part of it all was even though Drew insisted this wasn't a big deal, and it really shouldn't be because she hardly knew him, it *was*. It was a *very* big deal. Every day that week when she walked to the chess lab, her insides would knot up about the possibility of facing him again.

Even though she'd given up hope that he would show up this week at all, her insides were already knotting up as she took the walk of shame to the chess lab again. More than likely, he'd give it at least an entire week, if not more, then show up next week sometime and act as though nothing had happened.

As much as she dreaded facing him now, she almost wished he'd just show up already so she could get it over with. Just as she made it up the stairs of the physics building, she heard it.

"Charlee!"

Her heart was immediately at her throat when she turned and saw him hurrying toward her. *Wish granted.*

Trying desperately to push back the emotion that just seeing him brought on, she focused on trying to appear unfazed. His expression gave nothing away. She didn't know what to make of it. The fact that he was hurrying toward her, however, could be a good thing. Had he missed seeing her as much as she'd missed him?

Instead of rushing up the stairs and pulling her to him like she'd begun to envision, he stopped at the bottom when he got to it. The dark 5th Street t-shirt he wore was a little on the snug side, and she could make out those abs and strong chest—the chest she'd been pressed up again that amazing night. "Can I talk to you for a second before we go in there?" He motioned to the doorway of the physics building where the lab was at.

Nodding and beginning to feel a little numb, she made her way back down the few steps, ignoring her tangling insides. Unlike Friday and all the other recent times she'd been around him, he now avoided making eye contact for longer than a few seconds. Charlee already had a very bad feeling about this.

They moved off to the side to avoid blocking the stairway, and then he said what he'd been in such a hurry to get to her for. "Does, uh," he glanced back at the building. "Does anyone know about last Friday? Anyone from the chess team?"

She shook her head, staring at him, her stomach dropping because she knew now where this was going. "No."

His relieved expression both confirmed it and mortified her, but she dare not show it. "Can we keep it that way?" His eyes met hers, and for a moment, she saw that tenderness she'd seen Friday night, but he glanced away quickly. "I mean I just don't want things to get weird, you know?" He shrugged, looking back at her with a forced smirk, but his eyes were vacant now—cold. "Shit happens when you're drinking and not thinking straight. People do things they shouldn't. That's all it was. But if you're cool with it, we can pretend it never happened."

Not falling apart. Not falling apart.

Feeling the air sucked out of her, she took a moment to gather her wits. As the realization of what he'd just said sunk in, the knots in her stomach unraveled into angry flaying whips. Just like last year, she'd been completely off the mark. Hector was no better than the other jerk who'd humiliated her so callously. Feeling a sudden rebellion like none she'd ever felt, Charlee smiled and began to move because she couldn't stand there staring into those cold unfeeling eyes for even another second. "Not to worry, Hector. Your party wasn't the only one I went to last weekend. I'd already forgotten about that."

That sparked something in those unfeeling eyes, and the smirk he'd worn earlier was wiped clean. She could tell she'd stunned him into silence. *Yeah, take that.*

"Is that right?" He finally said as he walked alongside her.

She smiled as naturally as she could and fought the urge to stop right there and tell him off, but she didn't. Instead she glanced at his hardened stare. It was the same one she'd seen last week when she checkmated his ass. Only instead of intimidating her as it had last week, this time it made her feel a little better.

Good. He probably expected her to be mortified or react the way she really wanted to and confirm that she really *was* different, just like he'd told her that night: different from all the whores he was usually with—prove what he'd obviously figured out that night. That he was the first guy she'd made out with *ever*. He'd messed with a prissy little virgin who was probably expecting much more from him now than all those other girls. Well, she'd be damned if she'd give him the pleasure. "Yep, I had an exhausting weekend."

Charlee realized she was overcompensating—being rash. Drew could call it whatever the hell she wanted, but she was done being the martyr. From that moment on as she hurried up the stairs feeling the slow boil in her veins with a silent, brooding, Hector beside her, she vowed never to let heartless jerks bring her down again.

Hector opened the door for her, and she strutted by him, doing her best to ignore the scent of his cologne because the memory it induced nearly choked her. As soon as she entered the lab, she zeroed in on Damian, knowing from experience a game against him would take just as long as she intended on being there: long enough so that it wasn't too obvious she wanted nothing more than to run out of there and as far away from Hector as she could A.S.A.P., but not too lengthy, because she wasn't sure how much longer the indifferent act would hold up.

As expected, she played a crap game. It was impossible to concentrate while trying to disguise how she was feeling. Keeping her eyes off Hector hadn't been difficult. She'd been terrified the entire time to even glance his way. The moment that Damian won, she shook his hand with a smile. "Good game."

She gathered her things, relieved that she could finally get out of there, and made her way to the door.

"You're leaving already?" Walter asked curiously.

He was sitting at a table with Hector and two other guys. Charlee allowed herself a quick glance at Hector after smiling and nodding at Walter. The hardened expression from earlier was still plastered on his face and that perfectly defined jaw from his flexing. "Yep," she said, looking Hector directly in the eyes and continued to smile. "I'm going out, so I gotta go get ready. Have a good one, guys." She waved at them with her fingers in that playful way she'd seen other girls do and walked out.

As she walked down the stairs of the building, she almost expected him to come after her, but, of course, he didn't. Feeling the hot tears already burn in her eyes and the boulder-sized knot in her throat swell impossibly bigger, she began walking faster. "Fucking bastard. Fucking *bastard*!"

With her chest already heaving, even as she tried to hold it all in, Charlee was only grateful now that Fridays were the one day she and Drew always took separate cars. The second she got in the car, Charlee slammed the door shut, buried her face in her hands, and sobbed.

~*~

It took every ounce of self-restraint to not go after her. Hell, it took everything in him to keep his comments about her *exhausting* weekend to himself. That *had* to be a lie. Either that or he misunderstood. She could've been talking about the Special Olympics thing. She wasn't *that* type of girl. He knew this, even if she had very easily given into him that night. It was just kissing. She wouldn't have let him do more. Would she?

Your party wasn't the only I went to last weekend. I'd already forgotten about that. "Bullshit," Hector muttered, fisting his hand on the table. Not a day had gone by since that night that he hadn't thought about it—thought about her.

"What?" Walter asked, looking up from the chessboard. "That's a fair move."

Hector hadn't even been looking at the board in front of him. He glanced down now, glad to see that in just a few moves Walter would have him. He knew he wouldn't be in a mood to play before he'd even driven down there, and he certainly wasn't after talking to Charlee. He moved his rook ignoring Walter's comment. A few minutes later, the game was over.

"So she's coming over tomorrow afternoon to check out the robot." Walter smiled, sitting back in his seat. "I finally perfected it again, and I set up a few things I could do to demonstrate it to her. This should be good."

Hector stared at him, continuing to grind his teeth like he'd been doing ever since he'd talked to Charlee. She was the last thing he wanted to talk about right now, but he knew this wouldn't be the case with Walter. She was all he *ever* wanted to talk about. That's why all week after Sunday, he kept the workouts with Walter to just that. He'd set Walter up then walk away before he could start talking. Avoiding any talk of her had been fairly easy that week since the only time he'd see Walter was at the gym. All week he'd debated with himself whether to do the right thing or not. He'd hoped that giving it a few days before seeing her again would take the strain off, but he'd been wrong—so wrong.

He expected her to be pissed or even hurt, not that he'd looked forward to that. He just thought it was inevitable. If he'd known this would be the reaction he'd get, he might've told her the truth. Here he held back telling her that Walter was his only reason for holding back, that if it weren't for Walter, he'd for the first time since he discovered girls, felt the desire to delve into something deeper than just a physical relationship with one—a desire that up until now had completely eluded him.

If he'd told her the truth and she felt the same way, which he'd been certain she would, he was afraid she might take matters in her own hands and break Walter's heart. Hector had no doubt that the poor sap would be disappointed in the end anyway, but he'd be damned if he was going to play a part in it.

Her reaction however had baffled him. Though he didn't buy it completely, she'd basically told him she felt just the opposite. Not only had their time in that room together that night been *forgettable*, according to her "exhausting weekend" comment, he was also supposed to believe she'd gone out and done the same or more with someone else already. As much as he refused to believe that, it was fucking galling.

She'd stopped in the middle of what they were doing that night to specifically point out that she was different, damn it! And she didn't even have to. He already knew it. She wasn't the kind of girl who would do that with him then go out and do the same thing with someone else the next day.

Hector knew it was pointless to over analyze it now, because it didn't make a difference. Whether or not it was true, it's what she wanted him to believe for whatever reason: that she had no qualms about pretending that night never happened.

Curious and because he needed to stop grinding his teeth before he broke one, Hector asked Walter about something else that shouldn't matter. "Did you mention her hanging out for a movie after?"

It shouldn't matter, but Hector wanted to know now if Charlee was not only going out tonight but again tomorrow night like she'd apparently done last week.

Walter frowned. "No, not yet. I'll wait until tomorrow." With a frustrated shrug, he added. "I'll probably chicken out."

The irritation was more than Hector could bear. He knew it wasn't Walter's fault, but that's where he channeled his frustration. As ridiculous as it sounded, if Walter could grow a pair, he may just keep Charlee from going out tomorrow and stay there with him where Hector knew nothing would be happening. Walter couldn't even get the nerve up to ask her to watch a movie with him. There was no way the guy would be making any kind of move.

"Dude, when are you gonna man up already?" Hector sat up a little and pointed at him. "You blew chance after chance last week. Now tomorrow, she'll be there at your place, and your pansy ass is gonna blow that too?"

Immediately, Hector felt bad. Walter sat back in his chair, looking wounded, but before Hector could take it back or at least rephrase what he'd said, toning it down a little, Walter smiled brightly, sitting up again. "I hadn't had the chance to tell you. I saw that guy again, and I went right up to him and Charlee."

"What guy?"

Walter's smile waned a little. "You know the one you knocked out on campus? He and his friends—"

"Yeah, Yeah, I know." Now Hector did the sitting up a little. "When?"

Walter thought about it for a moment. "Monday, first thing in the morning, I saw Charlee sitting and talking with him right here on campus, and I walked right up to them," he said proudly.

Hector didn't think that he could feel any more irritated tonight than he already was, but he literally felt his body heat go up a few degrees. "She was sitting with him: the guy that nearly broke your ribs because you were defending her?"

Walter rolled his eyes a little. "Yeah, well, she said something about him not actually wanting to harm her or anything. That he's just," Walter lifted his fingers, air quoting Charlee, "'pursuing her,' but she did say he's intimidating."

"Intimidating? Like how?"

Hector had been called intimidating by girls before, but it was more of a compliment than anything negative. This guy wasn't intimidating; he was a disrespectful little bitch, who didn't fight fair.

"She didn't really say, but when it started to sound like she might be taking up for the guy or making excuses for him, I told her the guy was a jerk, and she agreed."

"Taking up for him?" There was no hiding Hector's exasperation now. Walter had told him about the guy completely disrespecting her. He tried to put his hands on her even after she made it clear she didn't want to be touched. "How'd she take up for him? What excuses did she make?"

Walter was beginning to seem frazzled. Hector got that he was trying to tell him about manning up and going right up to them even after the guy had beat on him once. They'd get back to that soon enough, but first Hector wanted to get this part straight.

"I don't know, man. She just . . ."

Walter paused as if to try and recall exactly what she said, and Hector gave him all the time he needed, because he couldn't imagine what excuses she could've been making for the idiot. Maybe Hector did have her all wrong. Maybe she was a stupid girl that made out with guys randomly and then flaunted it shamelessly.

"Oh, I remember now," Walter finally said. "She didn't exactly make excuses, but she said she didn't think he was so bad—cruel! That's the word she used. She said she didn't think he was being cruel or something." He shrugged, looking a little irritated himself now. "It just sounded almost as if she were saying that if the guy weren't so aggressive or intimidating, he wouldn't be so bad."

Unbelievable. Hector couldn't get past this. "So what? Now she's gonna sit and chat with him like they're buddies or something?"

"No, I don't think so. She said he asked her to have coffee with him, and she did thank me for saving her again."

Finally, Walter shed some relief on the situation. Hector didn't even know why he cared. If what she said to him was true, she wasn't anyone he'd ever take seriously, and maybe Walter shouldn't either. He thought about maybe telling Walter what she'd said—warn him. But then he'd have to tell him how the subject even came up.

He let Walter tell him the rest of the story about how he so bravely walked up to her and asked her if she was ready. Hector held back rolling his eyes. If it had been him, Hector would've asked straight out and in the guy's face if she needed him to kick his ass again, not walked up with some vague excuse to get her away from him without hurting the guy's feelings.

Unaware that today would have taken so much out of him, Hector lay in bed that night, feeling completely drained. It was his own fault. He should've just done it first thing that week, not wait and let the anxiety of getting it over with build all week. Somehow he thought doing this would bring closure to the angst he'd been feeling and he could go back to feeling like he did before he'd met her—held her—kissed those sweet lips. Instead, all he could do was lie there and wonder who the fuck she was with tonight and what exactly she was doing with him.

CHAPTER 14

This didn't prove shit. So it was a beautiful Sunday afternoon and Hector could be anywhere, with anyone, doing something fun. So what? Walter had invited him more than once to accompany him to his grandfather's assisted living facility to play some of the old guys there. Walt had told him he'd be surprised how good it felt to make their day.

"Just don't purposely let them win," Walter warned as they walked into the old folk's home. "They'll know and be mad. One guy called me an arrogant asshole for not only assuming he wouldn't be able to win but for thinking he wouldn't notice me going easy on him."

Hector laughed. "Got it."

Hector had never been to an old folk's home, and he hadn't exactly looked forward to it. Already just walking in, he noticed the smell wasn't the most pleasant. He frowned, still unwilling to admit why he was really here. Yesterday morning, Walter had come in to work out and let Hector know he wouldn't be coming in today because of his visit to see his grandpa and some other stuff he had to do.

After deciding he wouldn't be torturing himself by going into the chess lab more than he absolutely had to, Hector didn't plan on going in until at least Wednesday. The soonest he'd probably see Walter would be Monday night when he came into work out. He didn't want to wait that long to hear about Walter's afternoon with Charlee. Most importantly, he was anxious to hear if she'd hung out with Walter after or if she mentioned having more plans that evening. Hector had also offered up some tips on small-talk topics like asking her what she did on her free time or maybe asking how her night out Friday had gone.

All right, so it was a little underhanded, but Hector needed *something*. He thought maybe if he could confirm she really was that kind of girl it would make it easier for him to take her off that damn pedestal he'd placed her ass on the week before. It'd be easier to scrape her out from under his skin.

Hector didn't waste time. He started in on Walter as soon as they started walking down the depressing hallway of the place. "So how'd it go yesterday with Charlee?"

Walter smiled instantly. "Good. She seemed genuinely impressed and excited about the demonstrations I showed her."

They'd been asked to wait in a small waiting room while they finished changing his gramps, so Walter had gone on longer than Hector cared to hear about the robot. As soon as he got a chance, he asked about what he really wanted to hear.

"So did she stay and watch a movie with you?"

Walters's excited expression fell, and Hector was already beginning to frown, irritated because he had a feeling Walter would chicken out. "You didn't even ask her to. Did you?"

"I was going to. I really was," Walter insisted. "But before I could, she started talking about some play she was going to later that night. I figured it was pointless since she already had plans." Walter was smiling again. "But we did have pizza."

Hector was still focused on the first part of what Walter said. "Was it a date?" He pretended his interest was for Walter's sake. "The play thing. Did she say she was going with a dude?"

Walter shook his head. "No, she didn't."

"And you didn't ask?" *God* dealing with Walter was the most exasperating thing *ever*. That's the first thing Hector would've asked. When Walter frowned, shaking his head again, Hector let out a sharp breath. "Well, did you at least ask about what she did Friday night? You gotta ask these things, Walt. What if she's seeing someone else? All this effort to impress her could be a waste of time."

"I know," Walter said with a pathetic expression, "and, no, I didn't ask, but she did yawn a few times and said she was really tired because she'd had a long night."

Hector stared at Walter, the frustration reaching another level. She makes a comment like that and still the guy doesn't think to ask what or *who* kept her up so late? *Fuck!* Hector was going to break a tooth or two if he didn't stop grinding them as he did when he thought of someone wearing Charlee into exhaustion.

"Hi, Walter." A young girl in scrubs with little teddy bears on them walked into the small waiting room and smiled brightly at him. She glanced at Hector for a second then looked back at Walter. "You look different." She smiled. "Your hair is shorter," she studied his face a little longer, and then it seemed to dawn on her. "Your eyebrows . . . You cleaned them up."

Walter smiled, running his fingers across his brows. "Yeah," he glanced at Hector and laughed. "After a friend told me I should name it, I decided to do something about it."

She frowned at that, and Hector was glad now that Walter didn't mention it was Hector, who told him he should name his unibrow. "I didn't think it was so bad, but it does look much better."

Walter shrugged but didn't say anything, not even thank you. The guy was clueless.

"Your grandpa is excited about your visit today. He said he has a few new tricks for you. Says he just might even beat you this time."

Walter smiled, standing up. Hector stood with him. "We'll see about that." He turned to Hector. "Hector, this is Natalie. She's the nurse assigned exclusively to my grandpa." Hector smiled, nodding at her. "This is Hector. He plays chess too."

Natalie smiled at Hector now. "You on the U.S. team too?"

Hector nodded with a smile. "Yep, just made the team actually."

"Wow. You must be really good. And smart." She turned to Walter, smiling timidly. "I know Walter is super smart. He's tried teaching me how to play." She shook her head, waving her hand in front of her. "Forget about it. I'm hopeless."

They started walking out the waiting room. "Nah, you're getting better every time we play." Walter said as they walked behind her. "You'll get it. You just have to practice."

They walked into a room where an elderly frail-looking man sat in a wheelchair, wearing a robe by the window. He was reading the paper and didn't notice them immediately. "Roberto," Natalie's cheery voice called out, "look who's here."

The old man looked up, his dreary eyes cheered up at the sight of them.

"Hey, Grandpa," Walter walked over and hugged him.

After the introductions, Natalie excused herself, saying she had to go get started on Roberto's lunch. She offered to bring Walter and Hector sandwiches, said she'd make them herself. While Hector passed, Walter said he'd take one. She was short and a little on the chunky side, but she was full of energy with a smile that seemed to brighten even that depressing place.

"Isn't she a little young to be a nurse?" Hector asked once she was gone.

"She's not actually a nurse yet," Walter explained. "She just got her L.V.N.'s certification. And as soon as she did, this guy," Walter waved his in his gramps' direction. "He insisted my dad hire her as his exclusive nurse. She's been working here for what seems like forever now. Did her high school R.O.P. program here and was assigned to my gramps a lot."

"She's better than any nurse I've had so far," Roberto said with conviction. "She's got spunk too. That girl; as young as she is, she don't take shit from the other older nurses. She's always on time; she's never in a bad mood."

"Yeah, yeah," Walter teased. "She's perfect. I've heard that a million times."

"She is. I tell her all the time, and," his grandpa lifted a finger, "she's the only one that makes my soup the way I like it—with extra *Tapatio*. None of the other nurses do that."

Walter smiled, shaking his head. "That's 'cause you're not supposed to have any, Grandpa. It's not good for you."

His grandpa waved his hand at him. "There are few things in this life left for me to enjoy. That's one of them and she knows it. Another one is playing you, boy. I just might get you this time."

They wheeled him out into the community room where there were a lot of other old folks hanging out as well. Walter introduced Hector to a few of them, and the day of playing chess with the oldies started.

Hector had to admit it did feel good to be able to provide these guys with some much-needed entertainment, though he felt bad about beating them. After a few quick games, Natalie came over and started setting up Roberto's lunch. Hector took advantage of the distraction to try and get a little more info on Charlee.

"So did you at least try to talk to Charlee about something other than the robot?" He tried to sound as casual as possible. "I mean she stayed over at your place long enough to eat. I'm sure you guys had time to talk about something else."

If he had to go by Walter's expression, as usual, it didn't look too promising. But Hector waited, making an effort to not show his exasperation again. "She asked about some of the photos in my room."

Hector smirked. "At least you got her to go to your room."

"It's where I'd set up the demonstrations," Walter said with a small smile. "But we did stay in my room the whole time. And we ate on my bed."

"Nice move," Hector pretended to be impressed and winked. "Setting up the demos in your bedroom."

"*Mija*, that's too much." Walter's grandpa held his hand out, waving it above his soup.

From where Hector sat, he could see that there was more red in the bowl from the *Tapatio* than there was soup. Walter glanced over and laughed. "You trying to kill my grandpa, Natalie?"

Her face was bright red as she hurried to put the top back on the small bottle of chili sauce. "No. I just . . ." She picked up the bowl. "I just got distracted. I'll bring you another one."

She hurried away, glancing back at Walter with a regretful smile. Walter laughed. "Don't worry about it, Nat. You can't *always* be perfect."

"You leave her alone," his grandpa said.

She eventually came back with another bowl of soup for the old guy, this time getting it right as Walter continued to tease her.

Hector hung around and played a few more games with the old guys, including one against Walter's grandpa. As expected, none were able to beat Hector or Walter. Hector might've gotten out of there earlier, but he agreed to play Walter, and they had quite the audience by the time Hector beat him more than an hour after they started.

Spending the afternoon with Walter at the old folk's home had served as somewhat of a distraction. But by the time he got back home, he was back to thinking about Charlee nonstop again. It was irritating as hell. Spending the day with Walter and watching the way he genuinely enjoyed spending time with his gramps and the other old guys only served to demonstrate further evidence of one thing: Walter was a real good guy, too good for Hector to even consider backstabbing.

~*~

It had been impossible. After sobbing in her car for as long as she had Friday night, Charlee had finally sucked it up, wiped her face clean, and insisted she was done crying. No guy was worth this amount of grieving, not this time and certainly not the first time.

She'd been fine up until she got home and tried smiling cheerfully for Drew. Her friend had seen right through her. All it took was one pout and the million dollar question. "You saw him, didn't you?"

Charlee had fallen apart all over again, and Drew dove right in with her best friend duties of holding her, consoling her, breaking out the ice cream, and then staying up with her into the late hours of the night talking. Drew was able to finally convince her of one thing, and as jagged a pill it was to swallow, it made sense. This was a good thing.

"You'll get over it, and you'll be stronger for it."

Drew hadn't been aware of just how sweet Hector had been to Charlee that night at the party—how convincing, without even having to say it, he'd been about making her feel as if she weren't just another one-night stand—how deeply he'd looked in her eyes and melted her completely. It hadn't been just a hot and heavy moment between them.

She knew none of that mattered now, but she wanted Drew to understand she wasn't being such a crybaby over nothing. After what she'd already been through, she knew better than to trust some fake, kind words from a guy. She'd been completely naïve the first time. This time she *felt* what Hector was saying to her. There was no way to explain it, but Drew got it. That's why she loved her so much. She totally understood.

"I believe you, Charlee." Drew said with that sympathetic smile. "I saw it too. There's something about the way he looks at you. I saw it at the party again. But maybe he's just *that* good. Even though, with his looks, he doesn't have to be."

"I know! That's what I keep thinking. Even if his act had been as obviously bogus like Danny's . . ." Charlee stopped and Drew stared at her silently. Charlee hadn't said that name in over a year. "I probably still would've fallen for it," she whispered, glancing down at her hands.

Drew reached over and took Charlee's hand in hers. "No you wouldn't have. You were younger and completely inexperienced when Danny got a hold of you. Plus that was totally different. There was no way you could've ever imagined what he was up to. But just like that experience, Charlee, you grew from it. I've watched you be overly cautious about these things, and trust me, even with my sixth sense I'm always going on about, I didn't see this coming from Hector. Sure, I was nervous this would be the case, but I truly believed I saw something else in the way he acted with you. So if you say you even *felt* it, then I believe you." Drew sighed. "I guess the jerk is just really *that* good." She smiled weakly at Charlee. "That's why this is a good thing. We were both duped by one of the smoothest, if not *the* best at being smooth. Anyone else who comes along now will have nothing on our reinforced asshole radars."

Surprisingly, her words made Charlee laugh out loud. Ironically, they made her think about Hector explaining his scar. He'd learned from it, and ever since, he hadn't let his guard down as much. Charlee had another scar to *reinforce her asshole radar*. She only hoped she'd be strong enough to not let her guard down again.

By Saturday she was over it. At least she told herself that, and she did her best to enjoy her time at Walter's and then at the play Drew's dad had gotten them tickets for that night.

Since then, she'd seen Hector one time. He decided to grace the team with his presence Wednesday afternoon. She and Drew had gone over the game plan. She wouldn't give him the pleasure of letting him see he'd affected her life in any way. Instead, she'd keep up the "I'd already forgotten about that" attitude. Drew had been especially proud of Charlee for making that comment. She'd even high-fived her.

So when he showed up Wednesday, she did just that—smiled sweetly at him, showing absolutely no resentment whatsoever. A few times she couldn't help feeling annoyed that their eyes would meet and she thought she saw what she had the night he kissed her. That's when it was hardest to *not* feel aggravated. He already knew he had the power to make her melt, and he made it clear it wasn't something he wanted to continue, so why was he torturing her now? It was the sickest kind of cruelty, and she'd walked out of the lab, cursing him under her breath again.

Day two, Thursday, hadn't been much better. She'd caught him looking at her more than once in that way that did crazy things to her insides. Charlee was trying so hard to remain composed and to act indifferent about the entire thing. It didn't even hurt as much as it made her angry now. How could anyone be that mean? Did he enjoy stroking his ego again and again each time he managed to get her caught in one of his intense gazes?

Once again, she walked out of the lab, feeling thoroughly nettled. Drew met her by the waterfall in the middle of campus, where she always did Thursday afternoons. "How was it? Was he there today?"

"Yes," Charlee huffed.

"That bad, huh?"

"I suppose it's my fault for giving him opportunity after opportunity to get me caught in a trance with him because I can't stop looking at him. But why does he have to keep doing that?"

"That just seems so weird," Drew pondered, holding her books to her chest and staring straight ahead as they began walking. "If he's really that attracted to you that he can't stop looking, why cut things off? Even players like him have to eventually get bitten by the love bug."

"Drew," Charlee warned. She wasn't about to get pulled into that again.

"Okay, okay." Drew turned to her. "Maybe not love. You two don't know each other well enough, but it seems to me there's more than meets the eye here. Maybe he's fighting it because he's just never been that type of guy."

"No, please don't start with this."

"No, no, I'm serious, Charlee. You hear about these types of guys all the time. There are guys who are seriously afraid of commitment." She squeezed Charlee's arm. "He fits the profile perfectly. These guys are usually the very good-looking ones who are used to having tons of girls at their beck and call but never have to commit to any one of them. That's him!"

Drew's excitement about her newfound revelation only irked Charlee further. "And how in the world is that a good thing?"

"Because, at some point, they meet their match." Drew was getting more and more excited with each word that came out of her mouth. "They have to fall for someone eventually, right? Maybe Hector's finally met his match, and you're it! And why wouldn't you be, Charlee?" Drew's excitement finally calmed. She stopped walking, making Charlee stop too then faced her tilting her head and looking very thoughtful. "I know you don't believe this, but you're beautiful, not just on the outside but the inside as well."

This, coupled with all the emotion she was still holding in, instantly choked Charlee up. She pressed her lips together, trying desperately to keep them from quivering. "Stop, Drew. You're gonna make me cry."

Drew smiled big. "Don't cry. And, no, I won't stop because it's true. This is good. I really think I'm onto something here. We should go have dinner and brainstorm—somewhere a bit fancier than Taco Bell." Drew snapped her fingers suddenly and her face scrunched. "Crap! That reminds me. I forgot something."

"What?"

"My check. It's ready." She took a few steps backwards. "They called this morning to tell me I could pick it up. I'll be right back."

Charlee watched as her friend hurried away toward the humanities building. Drew worked part-time in the office, even though she didn't have to. Her dad gave her all the money she needed.

Smiling now after having gotten all emotional just earlier, Charlee wondered what exactly Drew had in mind as far as brainstorming. She'd just as soon move on and leave this behind. Trying to figure out why Hector had no interest in doing anything more with Charlee would only make things worse. As soon as Drew came back, Charlee would tell her she was done analyzing this.

"So, is it possible to cash that rain check in now?"

With a flinch, she turned to face Ross. For once, he looked bright-eyed and fresh with no lingering smell of marijuana. Her eyes were immediately on his newsboy type brown cap that somehow made him look even more cleaned up. His smile was even a bit humbled, unlike all the other times when there was something so smug and cynical about it. Still, she knew she must've looked as alarmed as she always did when he'd approached her because he put both hands behind his back.

"I promise I'll keep my hands to myself. In fact, they'll remain this way the whole time."

Relieved to see Drew walking toward them, she smiled softly, gulping back the inevitable apprehension she felt about even holding a conversation with Ross. "I'm waiting for my friend. She's right there actually," Charlee pointed in Drew's direction, and he turned to see her as she got closer to them. "We've got somewhere to be."

Ross's smile dimmed a bit, but he shrugged. "I'll get my chance eventually, right?"

A bit curious suddenly and because he didn't appear so menacing this time, Charlee had to ask. "A chance for what exactly?"

Seeing Ross smile so big, especially about something she just said, felt wrong somehow. She didn't mean to get friendly with him. She'd just been curious and in a cautionary way, not in the way she knew he was thinking.

"Everything okay, Charlotte?" Hector walked up to them out of nowhere and stood right next to her, his presence even bigger now than normal. "Is this guy bothering you again?"

CHAPTER 15

With his hand fisted and ready to go, Hector stared into the guy's anxious eyes. He didn't even care that they were in the middle of campus and this could get him in trouble. All Charlee had to say was anything remotely negative about what this guy had just said or done to her, and he'd make sure it was lights out for him again.

The guy spoke first. "I was just telling Charlee—"

"No! You don't get to call her that," Hector got in his face now, feeling the real need to punch something, and this guy's face would do just fine. "You don't get to call her anything, you disrespectful asshole!"

Charlee attempted to get in between them, but Hector wouldn't budge. "I'm fine actually," she said, sounding almost annoyed.

Hector turned to face her. Drew was there now too. Looking almost as irritated as Hector felt, Drew asked the very thing he was thinking, "Are you sure?"

"Yes, I'm sure." Charlee said to Drew then turned to Hector. "We were just talking."

The guy had backed up away from Hector the second he'd turned to face Charlee. She then turned to the guy and actually smiled. "I gotta go, but we can talk another time."

"I look forward to it." Ross said, attempting to sound cheery, but there was no masking the dread in his eyes. "And I'll answer your question then." He tipped his stupid hat at her, glancing at Hector just before turning around and walking away.

Hector's mouth nearly fell open. "You're seriously talking to this guy now?"

Charlee started walking, but Hector kept up walking alongside her. "What's wrong with me talking to him? He's apologized for what he did already—more than once. He wants to make things right. That's all."

Unfuckingbelievable! "That's all? Really? Has he apologized to Walter too? Your friend—you know that one that ended up in the emergency room because he came to *your* rescue from *this* asshole and his friends?" His insides were on fire now. Was she really this stupid? Then it hit him, and he got in front of her, making her stop. "And exactly what question do *you* have for *him*?"

Her expression had changed from annoyed to a bit regretful when he mentioned Walter ending up in the emergency room. He hoped that meant she got how chicken shit this was of her to be hanging out with the dude now. But her expression went back to annoyed again. "That's none of your business, now, is it?"

Suddenly this wasn't about Walter anymore. Suddenly what he felt was more than just anger, and he didn't even care how clear he was making that. "You into this guy, Charlee? Is that it? You'd actually consider something with that piece of shit?"

Her pink lips parted, but she said nothing. He was done. If he stood there for even another second, he might just spill his guts—tell her why he was really so ready to beat the shit out of this guy. Because seeing her standing there with him, having an obviously enjoyable conversation, had set him on fire, and he was ready to blow now. From what Walter had told him already about Charlee making excuses for the guy, he had a feeling what that might mean.

He started walking away before he could explode but then stopped and turned to her again. "You might wanna let Walter in on this shit; otherwise, he may still think you need saving from this prick." She stared at him wide-eyed now. "You wouldn't want him to end up in the emergency room again in case he sees you and your fucking little boyfriend snuggling up somewhere."

Just the thought made him want to roar. He glanced at her friend Drew for a second, taking in the strange expression. She'd seemed just as irritated by Charlee moments ago. He wondered what the near smirk she wore now meant.

Without giving it another thought, he walked away before he spit out any more venom. He'd said enough. If she hadn't figured it out already, she would if he stayed there and continued to let it all out.

Stalking through the parking lot now, he tried to make sense of everything. Charlee was *not* a stupid girl. He'd heard of people being book smart but dumb as rocks when it came to street smarts. That could very well be the case, but he still didn't buy it. Shy girls that had the brains to get a full ride in college and did volunteer work for charity would have more respect for themselves.

So she let Hector kiss her at the party. That was different. They had a connection. He *felt* it. She certainly hadn't been so keen about that other guy she'd been dancing with. He may've been a douche, but he wasn't necessarily bad-looking. If she was really the type of girl she now wanted him to believe she was, then she would've just gotten friendly with *that* guy.

As much as she appeared to be at ease with pretending nothing ever happened between them, Hector was beginning to think maybe that wasn't the case—not entirely anyway. Since it'd been impossible to not stare at her like he did so often, there was no denying that she was having just as hard a time not looking his way. At first he thought he'd imagined it, but he was sure of it now. The irritation he thought he'd picked up on was loud and clear when she told him she was fine talking to the guy, even though she thanked Walter for *saving* her again just days ago. He picked up on it again when she'd told Hector it was none of his business. At the moment he'd been on fire—too wound up to put it together.

This actually calmed him now as he climbed into his truck. If that were the case, if she was, in fact, upset about him telling her to forget anything ever happened between them, then maybe that explained why she'd want him to believe she was really the kind of girl she made herself out to be. She didn't want him to know she actually was upset about his dismissing the very special time they spent together that night. It was special, damn it. He'd go with that for now. It was easier to accept that than the alternative.

By the time he got home, he'd calmed down some. His theory made total sense. The only hole in it was one nagging thing: *I'll answer your question then.* What the hell could she have asked him that she was so quick to say was none of Hector's business? Was it possible she could actually have some interest in the dirtbag? The guy who'd made her scream so loudly that if she hadn't, Hector never would've gone out of his way to see what was going on? No way.

"*Mijito*," his mom called out when he walked in. "Come look!"

Hector walked through the small living room into the kitchen where his mother stood over the kitchen table, holding some papers. Abel sat at the table with a plate full of food, looking through the papers also.

"This one!" she said excitedly, holding a paper out to him. "This is the one I like."

Hector took the paper from her. Now that Abel had signed such a huge deal, he was using the advance he got from it to buy their mom a house. Of course, she insisted they still live with her, and, for now, Hector wouldn't have it any other way, only he couldn't see himself bringing home girls to spend the night at his mom's house. She was old-school and considered it disrespectful unless he was married, and Hector knew *that* wasn't happening for years.

He smiled when he saw the pictures of the luxurious-looking home. "*Damn*, Abel! All this?"

Abel nodded then smiled at their mom. "Why not? Mom deserves it."

"*Ay, mi rey.*" His mom got teary eyed, leaned over, hugging Abel by the shoulder, and kissed his head. "I told him, Hector. I don't need all that. I've lived in this little house for years, and we've been fine, but he insists. You know I'm not asking for all that."

"I know that, Ma." Hector laughed.

Of course, his mom would never ask for something this lavish. He and Abel had been telling her for years she could buy the more expensive stuff from the supermarket to make life easier on her since she still insisted on cooking them home-cooked meals almost daily. But, no, she still bought the whole chicken, skin and all, instead of the more expensive boneless chicken breasts.

"*Estan locos!*" she'd say. "Pay over three dollars a pound when I could pay thirty-nine cents!" Abel and Hector had taken over the grocery shopping for the most part in the past year or so.

"Is that what I think it is?" Hector looked at Abel with a hopeful smile.

Abel looked up at what Hector was pointing at on the paper. "Yeah, but don't get any ideas. That place would be for me."

Well, shit. For a moment there, Hector thought he'd figured out a way around his mother's not-having-girls-overnight-at-*her*-house rule. The house his mother liked had a separate pool house way behind the main house, a house Abel would be making the most of.

"But don't worry. The place has two master bedrooms on either end of the house, and the house is *huge*. Each master has its own separate entrance."

"*Cochinos!*" Their mom said, frowning as she walked around the table to check the food on the stove. "Is that all you two are worried about?"

She turned around and waved a spatula at them, and it was on. She was going into one of her rants. Abel gave Hector a look. They should've known better than to talk about this in front of her.

"Even if are paying for it, Abel, if you want me living there with you two, you will not be parading a different girl in and out of there every day. I won't have it. You need to be respectful to me and yourselves. Besides," she turned to stir the food in the pan then turned back to them, "any girl who is okay with knowing she is not the only girl that's been in your bedroom that week or even month for that matter is not the kind of girl you want to be bringing home."

Hector wondered what his mom would have to say about Leticia and Miriam and smirked. *Try the same night, Mom.*

"*De que te ries?*" His mother glared at him.

Hector opened his mouth wide in protest. "I'm not laughing!"

That only made his mother's glare even more severe since he laughed while saying it. Abel laughed now too. Hector was sure Abel could only imagine what he'd been thinking.

She turned on Abel now. "Don't encourage him. You should be setting an example. You're no spring chicken. When are you going to start looking for a nice little Mexican girl?"

Hector muffled a laugh into his fist as soon as his mom turned her back on them. Abel's head was already hanging back defeated. It was the same song and dance with his mother. Abel wasn't even twenty-two yet, but by that age, she and all her siblings had been married with kids for years. So to her, Abel should be looking to settle down—with a nice little Mexican girl, of course.

"And the younger the better," she added.

"Oh, good. We're getting the long version tonight." Abel said, standing up with his plate in his hand.

"*No seas grosero,*" his mom snapped.

"I'm sorry. I'm sorry," Abel kissed his mom's forehead as he passed her to get to the sink. "I'm not trying to be rude. Go on."

"Did you get full?" she asked, immediately losing the angry tone and sounding concerned, as she if *ever* served them too little

"Stuffed actually. But it was good."

His mother smiled, satisfied, then continued with her rant. "I'm just saying. The girls these days are so different from back in my day. The days of innocence and saving yourself for your husband are long dead." She huffed. "So it's best to get them younger when they're still a little bit more innocent. You know, less experienced."

"I'll keep that in mind, *Madre.*" Abel kissed her forehead as he walked past her again. "I gotta go. Don't wait up."

"Where are you going?"

"I gotta go take care of some business," Abel turned back with a wink, "respectfully, outside of your house."

Hector's mom placed her hand on her hip, pressing her lips together with a frown but didn't say a word, watching him until he was out of sight. She turned back to Hector who was now sitting at the table, and he wiped the smirk right off his face, shaking his head in disapproval.

She rolled her eyes and went on about the age thing. Hector knew that argument was a bust. Younger wasn't always better. Noah was proof of that. Roni was eight years older than he was, and those two were insanely happy. But he'd never bothered to argue the whole Mexican girl part. It'd never crossed his mind that he'd ever have to. Now he was curious. He had a feeling the answer would be based on some of the stuff his mom had said in the past. Still he decided to bite.

A little annoyed that Charlee was back front and center on his mind again, he waited for his mom to stop and take a breath before interrupting.

"So why only Mexican girls?"

His mom turned to look at him, raising an eyebrow as she piled the food onto his plate. "They don't *have* to be Mexican. But it's just better if you stick with your own culture. At least stick with Latinas." She set the plate in front of him. "And hopefully to the ones whose parents were born in their country, not the second generation Latinas. They're just as bad as non-Latinas—too Americanized—too modern for their own good."

Hector rolled his eyes now, ready to chuck this theory in the fire pit along with the "the younger the better" theory. "And what does that mean? Too modern for their own good?"

He grabbed a *tortilla* and started rolling it up already, doubtful that his mom would have a valid argument for this one either.

After setting a glass of milk down for him, his mother sat across from him and picked up the home profile papers. "Well, you mean aside from the obvious? They don't cook."

She said that with so much conviction Hector laughed. Figures his mom would think *that* would be a deal breaker.

"And?" he looked up from dipping his tortilla in his *chili verde*.

His mom frowned. "*Mijo,* they're just too liberal about everything. You wanna nice girl that still has some of the same good old-fashioned values you grew up with. You stray away from what you're used to, and you'll be treading into unknown waters. They are brought up believing and being told things Latinas are not told. Like that it's okay to jump from one man's bed to another's just like that because men do it all the time. This equality stuff is constantly shoved into their modern-day heads. Some things are still sacred, and behaving that way is still frowned upon in our culture. Well, my era. And while I don't have any daughters, just as I harp to you and Abel, I would like to think women like me from my era in *my* culture are also passing their beliefs and morals down to their girls."

And there you had it. Another one of his mother's theories completely deflated. Although he'd met enough of the sweet Latinas his mother spoke of, he'd also met plenty like Leticia and Miriam. His mother's suggestion that only the Latin world still held morals was ridiculous.

Even he and Abel were perfect arguments against that. While his mother had managed to instill most of the morals and values she harped on about so often, neither Hector nor Abel had any qualms about engaging in a few acts his mother would certainly protest, so long as the girls were all for it.

Charlee was another contradiction to his mother's belief. He frowned, realizing that once again he was thinking about her, even as infuriating as that afternoon had been for him. It didn't make sense.

Uncontrollable desire was something even the most innocent would have a hard time masking. Hector had felt it in her kisses. It was exactly what he was feeling with every stroke of her tongue in his mouth. But the depth he'd felt in her kisses wasn't because of the level of skill she possessed. It was just the opposite. If he had to guess, that might've been her first time doing something that arousing, and except for that heavenly moment his mouth veered downward to her neck, it'd only gone as far as kissing. Even then, her entire body had come alive, but not as he was used to. There was something so chaste about her body's reaction to what he did to her, and he hadn't even done much.

That's why he'd been so stunned about her *forgettable* comment. What he felt when he kissed her was hands down new to him, and almost two weeks later it was still so fresh in his head. All he had to do was close his eyes and *feel* it all over again.

He stood up, once he'd polished off his food. His mother asked the same thing she asked both him and Abel every single time they finished eating. "Did you get full?" Hector nodded, placing the plate in the sink. "You got real quiet there all of a sudden." Hector glanced back at his mom's inquiring eyes. "Is there a reason why you were asking about girls that were not Mexican? Are you seeing one?"

His mom was a sly one. Too bad she was wrong. "Nope," he said, rubbing her shoulders as he came up behind her. "I was just curious." He kissed her on the head. "I'm gonna go to the gym for a while."

"I thought you were there all morning?"

"Yeah, I was, but I still have some paperwork to do in the office."

It was partly true. He did have some work to do but nothing that couldn't wait until the next morning. He just didn't feel up to sitting around watching T.V. because he knew he'd be plagued with thoughts of the inevitable. He only hoped Walter had already worked out and left. It's why he'd come home first and taken his time eating. The last thing he needed tonight was to hear the guy go on and on about Charlee.

CHAPTER 16

For as long as Charlee could remember, Drew had done the very thing she was now doing—tried to turn a negative into a positive. Ever since lasts weeks' outburst from Hector at school about her talking to Ross, Drew was trying to convince Charlee that, once again, this was a good thing. That it only confirmed even further the very thing that Drew had been talking about just prior to going back for her paycheck: Hector had a serious thing for Charlee but didn't do commitment.

Only after seeing how crazy it made Hector to see Charlee with Ross, Drew now had a plan—a plan Charlee refused to take part in.

"I don't understand why you're being so difficult, Charlee. You agreed there was no doubt about it. He was jealous."

"I never agreed that he was jealous." Charlee said as she took a seat outside of Starbucks. "I agreed he was angry and rightfully so. Here I was being all friendly to the guy he'd saved me from and who put his good friend in the emergency room just weeks ago."

Drew sipped her latte, shaking her head. "Difficult."

"I *am not* being difficult," Charlee insisted. "I just think playing head games is going make him think even less of me than he already does. I've made the most awful impressions on him already—each one worse than the last. First, I come off as a total bitch trying to show him up in front of the chess team on his very day there. Then, I easily give into making out with him at his party the very next day, after showing him up no less. And then," she squeezed her eyes shut at the very thought, "then I make myself sound like a total slut just to cover up the fact that I care that that night didn't mean *everything* to him like it did to me!"

"I don't think you made yourself sound like a slut—"

"Oh, yes, I did. You weren't there. You didn't see the look on his face. Oh, but the absolute worst part is that now he not only thinks I'm a slut but he thinks I'm the dumbest slut on the planet, because now even creepy guy Ross is someone I'd consider doing . . . whatever it is he thinks I'm considering doing with him." She peered at Drew. "Did you not see the look in his eye when he asked me if I was considering *doing* something with Ross?"

"Yes, yes," Drew said. "I saw and heard everything. He was jealous, Charlee. I'm telling you the guy's got it bad. And it wouldn't be head games we are playing. It's not like you're seeing him or anything and then trying to make him jealous. You're free to do what you want with whomever you want. Though I forbid you spend any more time being friendly with Ross. He *is* creepy."

Charlee sipped her coffee but nodded in agreement. The only reason she'd been pleasant to Ross at all and agreed to talk to him later was because standing so close to Hector had brought back all the pain, the pain she was trying so desperately to rid herself of. At that moment, she didn't want anything from Hector, not even his help, and she wanted to show him she had things under control. That she didn't need him. "Well, I don't flirt. You know that. Even if I did, I'm not flirting with anyone in the chess club. It would be too awkward. And since it's the only place I get to be around Hector, then this little plan of yours is not going to work."

Drew pulled her lips to one side. Good. Charlee had her. They could just forget about this once and for all and accept that anything between her and Hector was impossible.

She didn't know why she'd ever allowed herself to even think it a possibility. For starters, Charlee was so pathetically inexperienced when it came to romantic relationships even getting involved with a less assuming guy would be a challenge. But to think she could work something out with a guy like Hector was almost laughable, not to mention daunting as heck. Though she had to admit, after being alone with him for a while in that room that night, talking to him had surprisingly become easier and easier.

"So how long do you think we'll be at that old peeps home with Walter?"

"Just a few hours," Charlee said. "You don't have to go if you don't want to, Drew. It just sounded like something neat to do. He said they were really excited when Hector played them. So when he told them about the *girl* from U.S. team that also lived in town, they asked him to try to get me in there."

"No." Drew smiled as they stood up, putting her arm around Charlee's shoulder. "I don't mind going with you at all. You're too sweet."

Charlee smiled. "You know better than anyone this isn't so selfless. I have a hunch this is going to feel as good as it does when we do the Special Olympics. And you know how addictive that is."

Drew's face lit up. "I can play checkers or Yahtzi."

That made Charlee laugh, and she leaned into Drew. "I'm sure you'll find an opponent there."

Glad that they'd at last canned this idea, Charlee could only hope it was the very end of this. She really needed to move on. The main reason she agreed to move out here in the first place was to get away and leave the nightmare behind. The last thing she should be trying to do now is create a new one.

✳✳✳

"I got it!" Drew burst into Charlee's bedroom.

Charlee looked up from her laptop with her pencil still in her mouth. Her friend dropped her purse on the floor with a huge smile on her face. *Uh oh.*

Removing the pencil slowly from her mouth, Charlee watched as Drew made herself comfortable on the other end of the bed. "I didn't know you were home."

"I just got here," Drew said quickly. "Okay, remember that guy Miguel I told you about? The one I went out with a few times a couple of weeks ago?"

Charlee frowned. "The one you said was nice but you didn't like the way he laughed so you stopped going out with him just because of that?"

Drew's huge smile disappeared. "Charlee, you have to hear it. It's *awful*. Like a horse spazzing out or something." The huge smile was back instantly, and she waved her hands in front of her. "Anyway, I ran into him the other day. When we'd gone out, I talked about my dad collecting old records but how hard they are to get these days. He'd told me about some place in East L.A. that still sells all that. Long story short, he took me there today. Sounds of Music in the heart of East L.A, totally retro record store, something out of Pretty in Pink. So I go up to the register and pay, and there are all these flyers and stuff on the counter. Then I notice the pictures under the Plexiglas. Photos of what looked like the guy behind the counter with some rappers and singers, and then there it was—a photo of the guy and Hector standing by a boxing ring."

Charlee rolled her eyes. She knew it. They were back to this.

Drew placed her fist on her hip. "Charlee, you promised you wouldn't be difficult."

Scrunching up her nose, Charlee thought about it for a second. "I never promised that."

"Well, you should." Drew jumped off the bed and reached for her purse. "Just listen to me. This gets better." She pulled a small flyer-like card out of her purse. "I asked the guy if he knew Hector, and he said Hector and some of the other guys from 5th Street used to go in there often since it's right up the street. Then he handed me this."

Charlee glanced down at the card Drew was holding out cautiously. "What is it?"

"Read it," Drew shook it in front of her.

Charlee took it and read the header.

FRIDAY NIGHT FIGHTS @ 5TH STREET

THIS FRIDAY -- QUINTANILLA VS MACHADO

"The guy said Quintanilla is one of the other owners of 5th Street."

Drew didn't have to tell her. Charlee already knew all about Noah Quintanilla—one of Hector and his brother's partners and childhood friends. She had, after all, become the queen of Google-stalking. She lifted her eyebrow at Drew almost afraid to ask.

"You said the guys in the chess team have talked about having gone back to watch more fights since Hector's, right?"

Charlee nodded, looking back down at the card, continuing to read the rest of the details as she chewed on the inside of her cheek. She wouldn't tell Drew, but she already knew about Friday Night Fights at 5th Street. The internet knew *everything*. But she hadn't mentioned it before for this very reason.

"So I didn't know it was like this weekly thing, and it's not only open to the public but they actually promote it on the radio and everything. They *want* people coming."

Oh no. Charlee could already feel the uneasiness creep up her spine. As much as she'd try to fight this, she knew that Drew was always so damn convincing *and* unwavering.

"The best part is the guy down at Sounds of Music said it's this big thing in the area on Friday Nights and there are always all these backyard parties after the fights. A lot of the trainers and even *boxers* show up to them." Drew's eyes were as bright as Charlee had ever seen them. "Of course, I asked if Hector goes, and he said, 'yes'!" She weaved her head a little from side to side then admitted. "Not always, of course, but the guy said he's been known to show up. That doesn't even matter though. What matters is *you* may not have noticed, because you were so preoccupied watching Hector the whole time, but there were a bunch of hot guys there watching the fight last time. I'm sure they're there every week."

Charlee began to protest, but Drew was quick to stop her, holding up her hand. The girl had obviously come here prepared for an argument. She knew Charlee too well. "If nothing else, maybe you'll meet someone else. *Hell,* maybe I'll meet someone there." Drew made a pouty face. "You wouldn't deprive me of the opportunity to possibly meet a hottie boxer or trainer?"

Exhaling and feeling defeated, Charlee countered with the only thing she could think of. "What about Maurice? I thought you said you liked him."

Drew shook her head, tsking. "I was beginning to, but he blew it."

Charlee pinched her brows. This was the first she'd heard of this. "What did he do?"

Drew explained about the odd text she'd received from him just that morning, telling her his body was still recovering from the night they'd had last night. Problem was Drew hadn't seen him in days. She didn't seem too broken up about it, but it was enough that she said she was done with him. That only reminded Charlee how Hector had never even bothered asking her for her number.

"It's not like we'd agreed to be exclusive or anything, but the lengths he went to try to cover it up were such a turn off." She made a gagging noise. "I would've had more respect for him if he'd just fessed up from the beginning as he tried to do later when he finally figured out I wasn't buying it. Then he tried to act as if he was being all noble about coming clean and he'd sent the text to the wrong girl." She shrugged. "Whatever! He was a good kisser, but I never felt anything like what you said you felt when Hector kissed you." She went all dreamy eyed and sighed. "I think I'll hold off until I find someone that makes me feel that way too."

Not wanting to look at Drew anymore, Charlee glanced back down at her laptop. She knew her friend meant well, but she hated when Drew brought up Hector's kisses. And she did it a lot—each time with that same wistful expression she wore now. Charlee didn't need constant reminding of those kisses—kisses she may never get to experience again.

"So," Drew stood up off the bed. "You and me. Friday night. 5th Street." She lifted her hand before Charlee could even begin to protest. "I won't take no for an answer, Charlotte Brennan. The last time you went out was the night of Hector's fight. I won't let you do what you did back home and sink into your lonely little cave."

Charlee's shoulders slouched in defeat. "I wouldn't dream of arguing with you, Drew."

"Good," Drew smiled proudly, "because you'd never win. Now I'm off to brainstorm in the shower."

Charlee fell back on her pillow dramatically. "I wish you'd left that last part out."

"Okay," Drew winked at her. "Forget I said that then. I'm off to enjoy the vibrating handheld shower."

Charlee's jaw dropped, and then she burst out laughing. "T.M.I!"

"But I'll do it while thinking of Hector," Drew added as she walked out the door.

That immediately shut Charlee up.

"You know what I meant!" Drew yelled from the hallway.

Charlee thought about it for a moment then smiled. She had no idea what Drew had in mind exactly for Friday night, but her insides were already beginning to bubble.

~*~

> Hey stranger! I'll be in town for a while. I know we sort of lost touch, but I really would like to get together if anything maybe just to grab a burger or something. Let me know if you're up for it.

Hector sat in the gym's office and read the text from Lisa, tempted to ignore it as he had most of the other ones she'd sent him, ever since he'd figured out she was seeing someone else. The only ones he ever did respond to were the ones that had no flirtatious undertones whatsoever. He didn't want her to think he was all bitter and shit, so he could still be friendly, but he kept his responses short. He stared at his reply for a few seconds before he responded

> How long will you be in town?

Typically, he wouldn't be so uptight about knowing if the girls he hooked up with were doing so with him exclusively. Since he never made any promises himself, he didn't expect any in return. He actually preferred it that way, but Lisa had been different. Even though he didn't feel even the tiniest bit of what he once thought he felt for her, she wasn't the kind of girl you hooked up with and then just dropped. He already knew firsthand what it felt like to do that to a nice girl. Even though Charlee pretended not to mind, actions spoke louder than words. They were hardly speaking anymore, and Hector didn't think that had much to do with what he'd said about her and that guy. He saw it in her face now. She was hurt, and it was a real shitty feeling.

His phone vibrated on the desk, and he picked it up again.

> A few weeks maybe longer. I haven't decided.

That could only mean one thing. If she was texting him, wanting to get together and she wasn't sure how long she'd be around *and* she didn't sound anxious to get back, she must not be with the guy anymore. Hector wasn't sure how he felt about that. She *had* been a consideration before she started seeing someone else.

Before he put too much thought into this, he'd get one thing straight. The conversations they'd had even back when she was seeing the guy but called him "just a friend" had been flirtatious in nature. For all Hector knew she might still be seeing the guy.

After verifying that she was, in fact, broken up with her boyfriend now and that she was out here alone staying with a friend who was *not* a dude, Hector agreed to meet up with her, but not in an intimate one-on-one setting. He'd even told her to bring her friend. Lisa had been a serious consideration before her boyfriend came into the picture, but that was before Charlee. As frustrating as it was to admit and as nice as it had been to kiss Lisa, it didn't even come close to what he'd felt when he kissed Charlee.

He'd learned his lesson already. The way he was still feeling about Charlee there was no way he'd be considering anything serious with anyone for a while. At least not with anyone like Lisa anyway—someone he knew that like Charlee would not appreciate the one-night fling thing. And he wasn't about to add another thing to his already guilt-ridden conscience.

✳✳✳

So far anything to do with the U.S. chess team had consisted of conversations on Skype with the coaches and downloading tons of apps they wanted Hector to use for training. With an impending trip coming up in a few weeks to D.C. for one of their first meetings before the Jr. World Olympiad, Hector was hoping to make things a little more amicable with Charlee.

They would be spending an entire weekend traveling together, and since Hector, Walter, and Charlee were the only team members coming from Los Angeles, they'd be on the same plane and sharing the same transportation to and from the airports they arrived at. Not to mention they'd be put up in the same hotels. And this would be happening with every event the U.S. team attended. It'd be awkward at best if things between them continued the way they were now. He didn't want a repeat of the day before when they hadn't spoken a word to each other in the lab, so Thursday, Hector made it a point to sit next to her in between games.

He'd planned on just making small talk—something simple and safe about chess. But the second he took the seat next to her and she turned to him with those big startled baby blues, the last thing he anticipated saying to her flew out.

"I'm sorry."

She stared at him, looking almost as stunned as he felt. "About what?"

"About everything," the vomit of the mouth began, but he now very consciously wanted to finish, only he lowered his voice. Walter was a few tables over, and he wanted to be absolutely sure he didn't hear him. "About that day I went off on you the way I did for talking to that guy."

She shook her head. "No, I get why you were mad. And I only said what I said that day because I wanted to avoid any violence. I figured if I seemed agreeable he'd leave faster. But I don't plan on being his friend or anything."

Hector gulped, staring into her eyes like he hadn't been able to in so long. He noticed how she didn't conceal her freckles the way she had tried to that night of the party, not even a little bit.

"And I'm sorry about being such an asshole about what happened between us the night of my fight." Her eyes widened at that. "I know you said you'd forgotten about it, but—"

"I hadn't."

Her admission silenced them both momentarily. Then she spoke again.

"I just . . ." she shrugged. "I just didn't want you to think that . . ."

"It hasn't been my week all week." Walter said, plopping across from them.

Hector turned and glared at Walter. The guy couldn't possibly know what he'd just interrupted, but Hector felt like killing him anyway.

"First Dempsey beats me the other day, and then Samir pulls a Charlee stunt on me just now, playing my own game against me." He turned to Hector, who was grinding his teeth already. "Like you, I never even saw what hit me until he had me cornered." Walter shook his head. "I've been slacking. With all the time I've put into working out lately, I haven't been doing much research or even playing online. I'm getting rusty."

Charlee sat up, smiling. "Well, you can't do that, Walter. Our first meeting with the U.S. team before the Jr. Olympiad is in a few weeks." She stood up and grabbed her sweater from the chair it hung on. "You need to start training again." She pulled her purse over her shoulder.

"You're leaving already?" Both Walter and Hector asked at the same time.

Walter and Hector glanced at each other, and for an instant, Hector regretted sounding as desperate as Walter always did when she left early. But he *did* feel desperate.

"Yeah, I'm going shopping with Drew tonight." She smiled, holding Hector's gaze a little longer than she had since he told her to pretend nothing ever happened then said goodbye and started for the door.

She couldn't leave now. He had to know what it was she didn't want him to think. He wouldn't be back in here until next week. Tomorrow he'd be busy all day helping Noah prepare for his fight. Damn Walter for having the worst timing in the world.

Walter started to tell him exactly what Samir had done to stump him. It was all Hector could to do not jump out of his seat and go after Charlee. A few minutes later and unable to stand it anymore, he pulled his phone out of his pocket and stood up. "I gotta make a phone call. I'll be back."

He bolted out of there, his heart already pounding. Not at all sure what to expect, he just had to know now or it'd drive him nuts all weekend.

For a moment, he felt the huge disappointment of not seeing her immediately, but then he saw her headed toward the waterfall in the middle of the campus where Drew waited for her.

"Charlee!" He called out, hoping to stop her before she reached Drew. He had a feeling she might hold back if anyone else were around. She stopped and turned with that same startled expression she had when he sat next to her.

He rushed to her. "You didn't want me to think what?" he asked as soon as he reached her, stopping right in front of her and staring right into those beautiful blue eyes. She shook her head, her expression a puzzled one. "Back there," he motioned his thumb over his shoulder, "just before Walter got there, you started to say you didn't want me to think something after that night. What was that?"

Her eyes widened as they had when he apologized for acting like an asshole about the whole thing. "I uh," she chewed the corner of her lower lip. "I just didn't want you to think I had any expectations of anything else happening between us." She glanced away for a moment then back at him. "I figured since you were asking me to pretend it never happened you didn't want things getting weird and neither did I." She sounded as if she were trying to reassure him then added in a lowered voice. "I didn't want you thinking it was such a big thing for me, so I said I'd forgotten." She crinkled her nose and smiled in the most adorable way it made him smile despite the angst he'd begun to feel. "Maybe saying I'd forgotten pushed it a little too far."

A small but very relieved laugh escaped him. "Yeah, that was kind of messed up."

Her mouth fell open, but she recovered fast enough. "*You're* the one who told me to pretend it never happened. *That* was kind of messed up—embarrassing."

"I know. I know." He said, bringing both hands to his chest and holding them there. "And I'm so sorry about that. I didn't mean to embarrass you. I handled it totally wrong. I just really, *really* didn't want things getting weird between us." He held back saying what he really wanted to ask. Was it as big a thing for her as it had been for him? With the thought of Walter still hanging over his head, he couldn't, but he did say the one thing clearly—he needed to. "I meant it when I said you were different, Charlee." The blue in her eyes had never been bluer. Hector had to concentrate on not getting lost in them, or he'd lose his train of thought like he'd done so often the night of the party. "I don't want you to think that what happened that night was forgettable or insignificant to me *at all*."

She smiled that timid little smile that should be *anything* but arousing because it was so sweet and pure. But it made him want to take her in his arms and kiss her like he could only close his eyes now and remember doing to her.

Something behind her caught his attention, and he tore his eyes away from hers to see her friend Drew holding her books to her chest, swaying side to side with her eyes closed, and he smiled. "I think your friend is getting restless."

Charlee turned to see what he was talking about then laughed softly. "Yeah, she hasn't been feeling too hot this week, but she swears the flu is *all* in your head." She turned back to him with that timid smile that was slowly bringing Hector to his knees. "She says meditating works better than medicine." She lifted a shoulder and smiled. "She might be on to something, because she says she is feeling better now than she did a few days ago, and she's refused to take any meds."

There was a short silent pause where they stared at each other, and Hector knew neither of them was thinking about

Drew's flu. Finally, she smiled a little bigger this time, breaking their moment. "Thank you," she said simply then added. "I better get going. There's a reason I left the lab early. We don't want to be out there too late."

"Okay, I'll see you next week." Hector said, feeling a little disappointed that he couldn't say more—tell her how he really felt.

Something flashed in her eyes, and for a moment, he thought she might say something, but then it was gone and she nodded. "Next week," she said before walking off toward Drew.

CHAPTER 17

"Okay, tell me again why we're still going to do this? Because he was nice enough to apologize and it's pretty much cut and dry, Drew—"

"That he's definitely feeling something for you, but he's holding back." Drew interrupted her then blew her nose. "We're getting closer and closer to proving the very thing I've been saying all along."

Charlee had to admit it. Hector had practically said it to her yesterday. Yes, their time together that night, those beautiful kisses, had meant more to him than he initially admitted to. But he also said he really, *really* didn't want things getting weird between them.

"So we prove it. Then what? He's practically spelled it out already." Charlee stared at Drew through the mirror. As usual, they were sharing the same mirror in the hall restroom to get ready. "Maybe he did feel something that night, but he thinks anything more would be too *weird*. It's the very word he used."

Her insides still warmed at the thought that even if that were the case he'd still wanted her to know that the kisses she thought about on a daily basis now hadn't been forgettable or insignificant to him either—*at all*.

"And let's just admit it." Drew grabbed some more toilet paper and blew her nose again. "Things *did* get weird. I mean that blowup he had about Ross. *Geez,* I know Walter's his friend and all, and it made him mad that you'd be friendly to Ross," Drew turned away to sneeze then wiped her nose, "but there was *way* more to it than that. I don't care what you or Hector say. He was jealous, plain and simple, and now he wants to make sure you know that night meant more to him than he first let on?" Drew lifted an eyebrow with an evil little grin. "I'm even more certain my plan is going to work now."

Trying not to get too caught up or show just how excited the very idea that Hector might actually have real feelings for her made her, Charlee lowered her eyes down to Drew's red nose. "You're not even feeling well, Drew. We really should just stay home tonight."

Drew shook her head then closed her eyes and hummed loudly, swaying her head side to side.

Charlee smiled. Her friend was nuts. "You say you're feeling better, and while I'm all for the power of thought and everything, your body knows what it needs, and that's rest, Drew."

"I'll rest tomorrow," Drew said, opening her eyes.

"But—"

"If . . ." Drew pointed her finger at Charlee. "*If* I'm wrong and something happens tonight that totally proves I'm way off here, then I'll back off. I will totally drop this. I promise. But I think someone is forgetting the power of my sixth sense."

Charlee pinched her lips to the side but bit her tongue. She was not about to get into the last time Drew's sixth sense had been totally off, especially on a night like tonight. One thing was for sure whether Drew kept her promise or not: if, in fact, Hector was simply attracted to Charlee but in no way interested in anything more as he'd made clear enough yesterday, this would be the last time Charlee gave into Drew. As persuasive as her friend could be, Charlee had to stand her ground at some point.

If she thought she might be asking for it by letting herself get caught up on a guy like Hector before, it was an even bigger gamble to allow it now. Because after staring so profoundly deep into his eyes yesterday and hearing the words he said with such sincerity, Charlee was beginning to fear the worst. She just may be falling in love with the guy.

~*~

The place was a madhouse. The last few fights they'd had here as part of their fall lineup for Friday Night Fights had been pretty packed, including Hector's fight a few weeks ago, but tonight was a third-time rematch. Noah had almost lost to this guy the first time, but it was called a draw. Then the second time, Noah knocked the guy out. Now the guy had requested another rematch. Noah had agreed, even though he'd been distracted from his usual training because of his new baby this entire past year.

Hector knew Abel was worried that Noah might not be as ready as he'd been the last time he fought him. Hector reminded Abel that the last time Noah had fought this guy he had a lot going on too. He had been trying to get it together with his then roommate Roni. Things hadn't been exactly going his way, and he'd still knocked the guy out.

Since then, Noah had fought a few bouts but not with anyone they considered might actually be a threat. This guy was not only a threat he was hungry to beat Noah.

With Abel giving it a rest finally and letting Gio do his job of warming up Noah, Hector sat on a stool watching quietly. He was glad some of the other 5th Street trainers were in there lightening up the mood a little.ABEL Gus, Nestor, and Santos stood off to the side, cracking jokes and talking about the girls they'd seen there tonight.

Usually these fights didn't bring in too many girls, but tonight's fight was a big draw. There were also a lot of parties going on after around the local neighborhood, parties Abel told Hector he should stay away from. The neighborhood had never been the greatest, but having grown up in the area their whole lives, they were more than comfortable attending the parties in the area. Still they could get a little rowdy.

The guys were talking about hitting some of the parties tonight. "I need to get laid," Santos announced.

"Then find out where the keg parties are," Nestor said with a sly smile. "Those are usually a sure thing because the girls always overdo it with the free beer, and next thing you know they're all over you."

Hector turned to Nestor and gave them a look.

"What?" Nestor asked, laughing. "I know no means no, but usually after so many beers they're not only saying yes they're begging for it. "He brought his hand in front of him and waved it down. "Who am I to deprive any girl of all this? Especially when they're *begging* for it?"

It didn't surprise Hector that Nestor was one of those guys that would take advantage of a drunken girl. The world was full of douche bags like him, and 5th Street wasn't immune to them.

Distracted by his phone vibrating in his pocket, Hector didn't bother responding. He pulled out the phone and read the text from Lisa.

> I know you're probably really busy, but I just wanted to let you know we're here. In case you look for me, we're WAY in the back. If we had known it was going to be so packed, we would've gotten here earlier. THANKS, HECTOR! ;)

Hector stood up immediately and began texting back.

> I'll get you better seats. Don't worry.

He started to the door then turned back to Abel. "I'll probably just stay out there until the fight starts. It's almost time anyway, right?"

Abel nodded then went back to watching Noah warm up. Hector's phone went off again as he continued to walk toward the door.

No! I was kidding. We're fine where we are. You don't have to go to any trouble.

Hector smiled, feeling a bit bittersweet. Normally, he appreciated the perks of being part owner of a boxing gym. Things like this went a long way in impressing chicks. Too bad Lisa was no longer the girl he wanted to impress. He wondered how long it would be until he felt the urge to impress *anyone,* but the only girl he was interested in, he couldn't even consider.

Trouble? Did you forget I got connections around here?

Her only response to that was a big smiley face. He took in the crowd as he walked into the loud swarming gym. Lisa hadn't been kidding. Hector thought the place had been packed earlier. As he walked slowly through the crowd, he made a mental note to talk to the guys about upping the price of tickets to the bigger fights so they could add more security.

Lisa and her friend stood way in the back. Hector was glad he spotted them before Lisa saw him. He curiously checked her out, but he didn't want her to see that. She might get the idea he was still interested in something with her. She was just as cute as he remembered. Her dark thick hair seemed a little longer now, but he'd only ever seen her at school. This was a whole new side of her he'd yet to experience. Her short black skirt was bordering on too short, and her very high heels were all kinds of sexy.

She looked up from whatever it was she was reading and smiled when she saw him. As he got closer, memories of that last day he saw her came to him. Her eyes were still just as big and dark. He knew he was being biased, but they had nothing on Charlee's big baby blues. Maybe at one point they might've been—back when he thought only a dark-haired Hispanic girl could do it for him—not anymore. He'd been so wrong about that it wasn't even funny.

Lisa hugged him hard, and he hugged her right back, admitting to himself she *did* smell really nice. She then introduced him to her friend Estella. Estella smiled and shook his hand.

"Wow. Did you get bigger or what?" Lisa exclaimed, her eyes all over his chest and upper arms.

Hector smiled. "Maybe a little."

When Lisa gave him a knowing look then reached up and touched his arm again, he glanced away, not wanting to encourage the flirting. If it were anyone else, he'd just as soon go along with it, but not Lisa. "C'mon," he said, taking in just how crowded the place really was.

They were going to have to make their way back through that mess to get to the front row. "Stay close," he said, turning back to her, and reached out his hand.

Lisa took it immediately, but he didn't mind, even though she quickly laced her fingers through his. She *had* to know why he'd done it. There was no way she'd be able to stay close in this crowd if he hadn't. Glancing around trying to decide which would be the fastest way to get there, he froze when his eyes met Charlee's. Her hair was down again like the day of his fight. Only she didn't wear a dress this time. She wore skintight jeans with a turquoise sweater that made the blue in her eyes even more striking. She'd done something else tonight too. Her lips were so red it made the color of her fair skin that much more brilliant at the same time enhancing the red in her hair, brows, and freckles. She practically glowed.

Yanking him out of the hypnotic trance he'd gone into from just seeing Charlee, it finally dawned on him. She and Drew were standing near the entrance, staring at him—with Lisa.

He smiled, but neither of them smiled back. Charlee looked away altogether. *Well fuck.* What were they doing here anyway? He considered maybe going their way and saying hello, but then they began walking in the opposite direction. Hector didn't miss the way she turned heads. How couldn't she? Once again, she stood out like a bright flame in a sea of gloomy hues of gray. Involuntarily, his teeth began to grind as he pushed his way through the tight crowd.

When they finally made it to the front row where a very impressed Lisa and Estella sat next to him, the thought of going back to find Charlee seemed impossible. What would he say to her anyway? The fights were open to everyone. It was something to do on a Friday night then follow it up after with a neighborhood party—also open to anyone. But the nagging question of why she'd chosen tonight to come plagued him. Was it because of what he'd said to her yesterday? Was it that obvious how crazy she drove him now? Is that why she was so incredibly done up tonight? Even as casual as her outfit was tonight compared to the night of his fight, she looked just as *amazing*.

As pleasant as the thought was that maybe she had come here tonight looking to possibly continue where they left off last time, Hector knew it was out of the question. *Gadamnit!* Life was a fucking bitch!

Distracted most of the fight with thoughts of Charlee, he glanced around hoping, although he wasn't quite sure why, to spot her. He finally got into Noah's bout toward the end. It'd been a pretty close matchup until then, and then Machado came alive. Noah's legs began to look like rubber. *No, no, no!*

They both fired away punches until one landed on Noah's chin and he went down. Hector was already on his feet and staring at him, stunned. He'd never seen Noah go down, but within seconds, Noah was back up. Machado tried taking advantage of the momentum and Noah's still-dazed state and came at him again. Thankfully, Noah was saved by the bell.

Hector rushed over to Noah's corner. Abel was there now too. Everyone was talking to Noah at once, so Hector didn't say anything until it was almost time for Noah to go back in. "Noah!" Noah turned to look at him. "You got 'em with your left hook last time. It's still his weak side."

Noah nodded then turned to Gio who was talking to him again. Hector returned to his seat. When the next round started, Noah came in like a tornado, firing away hard. The place got so loud Lisa and Estella brought their hands to their ears but continued to cheer for Noah to stay in it, even as Machado landed another hard one on Noah. Hector had filled them in on Noah and his history with Machado.

They were all on their feet now. Hector cupped his hands around his mouth, "Use that left hook, Noah! C'mon! Do it and you got this!"

With both fighters firing away, the place went wild. Then it happened: Noah came up with a massive left hook, landing it solidly on Machado's temple, and Machado hit the canvas *hard*. Hector jumped up and down, fist pumping like a crazy person. He turned and hugged Lisa then hugged her friend too. Just like when Hector's opponent went down a few weeks ago, Hector knew this was over.

Seeing Noah go down had scared the shit out of Hector. For a few minutes there, he'd begun to wonder if Noah was going to be able to pull this off, even if he made it through the final round. The scorecard more than likely would've been in Machado's favor. Abel, Noah, Gio, and Hector had had many wins, but this was by far one of the sweetest.

It was such a rush that it wasn't until everything had calmed and they were all in the training room again that Hector thought of Charlee again. Even then, he'd still been busy listening to Noah's take on the fight when something Santos said hit him like an electric current.

"Did you see Nestor trying to talk to the redhead?" Santos laughed then said something in a lowered voice.

"What was that?" Hector asked, moving away from Noah, Abel, and Gio and toward Santos. Santos looked at him confused. "What did you just say?"

Santos smiled again. "About Nestor?"

"Yeah," Hector already felt irritated, and he didn't even hear the second part, but whatever it was, Santos found it amusing as shit.

"He's out there hitting on some redhead."

"Right now?"

Santos nodded. "Last I saw—"

"Is she with another girl?" Hector started walking before Santos even answered. "A blonde?" The odds of there being more than one redhead out there were slim, but they did have a big crowd tonight.

"Yeah, they're like the only two white chicks out there. Why? You know them?"

Ignoring Santos, Hector rushed around some more guys coming into the training room. He needed to warn Charlee about Nestor. Just then Nestor walked into the training room, smiling big. This was even better. He'd warn Nestor about Charlee.

Nestor smiled at Hector. "Looks like I'll be getting laid tonight."

"You think so?" Hector asked ready to slam Nestor against the wall.

"Oh yeah," Nestor continued, smiling big.

Nestor almost walked past him, but Hector stepped in front of him. "And what makes you think that?"

Nestor backed up a step, pinching his brows. "Because I just invited some chicks to a keg party tonight, and they said they'd be there." What had turned into a somewhat defensive expression eased into a smirk and Nestor added. "Hell, I may even have me a twofer."

"Really?" Hector did his best to sound as calm as he could. "The redhead you were talking to out there?"

Nestor's smiled. "Yeah, Charlee."

Just hearing him say her name made Hector want to punch him in the throat. "*Charlee* is my friend which means she's off limits to you." He turned to the other guys who were listening also and raised his voice a notch. "To all of you." Nestor began to frown, pushing Hector's agitation to another level. Speaking louder and more demanding, he took a step closer to Nestor. "You have a problem with that, Nestor?"

Abel, Noah, and Gio were now looking at them too, and the training room got quiet.

"Nah, man," Nestor said, glancing around as if he'd just realized who he was talking to. "I just didn't know—"

"Well, now you do. And stay away from her friend while you're at it." Hector wasn't even sure why he added that last part, but Drew was Charlee's friend, and for that reason alone, he didn't want this asshole taking advantage of her either.

Nestor stared at him for a little too long without saying anything. The tension in the room was so thick it was a living thing, and at the moment, it held its breath. Hector saw Abel making a move. No one knew Hector better than Abel. If Nestor so much as said the wrong thing right now, shit was going down because Hector's patience was spent. This guy either agreed right now or Hector would make him.

Nestor gave him a very stiff nod before turning to Santos then back to Hector. "You got it."

Hector stared at him hard. He didn't trust Nestor as far as he could throw him, and the way Hector felt right then he could probably heave Nestor clear across the room. Without saying another word to Nestor, he continued on his way out. He needed to find Charlee and Drew now and warn them about this party Nestor had invited them to.

CHAPTER 18

"You don't have to do this, you know?" Drew said as they pulled up to the stop light.

"I want to." Charlee looked up from her phone's navigation screen. "According to this, we're a block away."

"Do you even know what a keg party is?"

"Hello!" Charlee tried desperately to sound chipper. "A party involving many or one keg of beer. Everyone pays at the door per cup or for a bracelet."

Drew smirked. "You had to look it up, didn't you?"

Charlee couldn't help but smirk. Damn. Did she have to memorize verbatim? "It was pretty self-explanatory, but, okay, I looked it up just to confirm."

"You don't even like beer, Charlee."

"I never said I didn't like it. I prefer wine coolers, but I can do beer just fine."

"I was wrong, okay. I admit it. He's a sweet-talking jerk, who obviously can't get his fill of girls." Drew said as they slowed because of all the cars cruising by the party. "But you don't have to go to one of these stupid parties if you're not feeling it. You have nothing to prove."

Suddenly Charlee felt bad. If anyone wasn't feeling it, it was Drew. She sounded just awful. "I'm not trying to prove anything." She reached over and touched Drew's leg. "But if you're not feeling well, let's just go home."

Drew turned to her. "I'm fine, Charlee. I just want to make sure you are too." Drew pulled into a parking space at the end of the block, several homes away from the one where the party was. "I would like nothing more than for you to go into that party and enjoy yourself. Dance a little. Maybe even exchange numbers with someone, but I know you. You're holding it all in. It's okay to be disappointed."

Charlee frowned, glancing out her window at some of the people walking toward the party. As much as she'd been playing it off that she didn't buy Drew's sixth-sense crap about Hector, *of course,* she was secretly hoping Drew had been right. *Of course,* she was once again completely disheartened when she'd seen him with yet another pair of girls. But she was really done this time. She was only happy that Drew had witnessed the whole thing with her: his eyeballing the girl before he reached her then hugging her before escorting her and her friend to sit with him in the front row.

There was no way Drew could argue with her now. The guy's wasn't changing his colors for any one girl, not even Charlee, who Drew seemed convinced Hector looked at so differently than all the others. As mad as she wanted to be at herself for beginning to believe it too, she wouldn't be. It was true Hector was a sweet talker. It wasn't just what he said but how he went about it. He didn't have to apologize yesterday. What had happened between them was water under the bridge now—or should've been anyway. Yet he'd gone out of his way to tell her that he really meant it when he'd told her she was different. There was such sweetness about the way he spoke to her—looked at her—when he said it too not just yesterday but the first time he'd told her that. Obviously she wasn't different *enough.*

Now she was determined to wash her mind of him. This would be a good start. She could go to this party, let her hair down, maybe meet someone, and possibly even let someone new kiss her so she could finally stop obsessing about the only guy who ever had. Maybe that's why she couldn't stop. She'd come to that conclusion earlier. Maybe that's why it was so easy for people like Hector, who had so many experiences to compare, to easily move on to their next conquest.

It was so not like her, but she was certain a little alcohol could do the trick. Truth was she wanted nothing more than to go straight home, get into her jammies, and crawl in bed. But she knew what would happen then. The tears would inevitably start, and she refused to do that again.

She sat up, turning back to Drew. "If you're feeling well enough, I'm up for this." No, she'd be honest and admit it. "I *need* to do this."

The familiar bright smile Charlee was so used to seeing on Drew was back. Red nose and all, she actually looked excited. "Good! But I won't be doing any drinking just so you know. I finally caved and took medicine for this damn cold." Drew sniffled and reached for a tissue from the glove compartment then blew her nose.

"Are you sure you're feeling well enough, Drew? I can always do this another time."

Drew shook her head adamantly, opening her door. "I'm fine, and you are not putting this off even one more day. We're doing this tonight. I'm just doing it minus the booze." Charlee got out of her side nervously then looked over at Drew across her car's roof. "But you, my dear," Drew lifted her brow with a smirk, "will hang loose and enjoy yourself tonight. This night will not be a waste if I have anything to do with it."

Refusing to give into her natural instinct to tell Drew that just being out of the car and hearing the music coming from the party she was already having second thoughts, Charlee remained calm. She continued walking alongside of her best friend ready to do this. Even though she wasn't quite sure what *this* would consist of exactly.

Once inside the packed backyard, Drew wasted no time filling both their cups with beer. She said it would save them the time having to stand back in line to get Charlee's next cupful. She also reminded Charlee to not sip so slowly because the beer in the cup Drew would be holding for her would get warm.

"I don't care what you say, Charlee. You don't like beer, and there is nothing worse than warm beer. So drink fast."

"I'll give you that warm beer is bad, but I'm telling you I don't have a problem with beer," Charlee sipped from her cup, wiping the foam from her top lip. "See?" She smiled.

It really wasn't bad at all. She actually liked the taste. She sipped an even bigger drink for good measure then placed her hand over her mouth and burped. *Now* she remembered what she didn't like about beer. Drew laughed, making Charlee laugh too.

They began their stroll around the backyard. Charlee couldn't get over how blatant the guys were about checking her and Drew out as they walked past them. Their leering smiles as their elevator eyes took them in before stopping at their faces were almost comical. *Almost.* As ridiculous as they looked doing it, Charlee couldn't help feeling a bit unnerved by it all. She was so not used to any of this.

Drew leaned into Charlee after one good-looking and well-built guy in particular stopped talking to the group he was in and stared at them. "He's not bad," Drew whispered. "Not bad at all. Even looks a little like someone we're not talking about tonight."

Charlee finished the last of her beer as she glanced in the guy's direction. He smiled as soon as their eyes met. No, he wasn't bad at all. The vest over a t-shirt with jeans look was sexy and he wore it well. And, yes, he did look a little like Hector because he was tall with dark hair and somewhat of a buff guy, but that's where the resemblance ended. Still, Charlee wasn't here looking for someone just like Hector. In fact, she should be looking for someone totally different. She reminded herself the whole point of being here tonight was to get over the guy already.

One thing was for sure. Charlee would need more beer if she was going to get the nerve to *hang loose* like she'd come here to do. Already she felt like spinning around, bolting through the crowd, and running back to the safety of Drew's car.

Absentmindedly, because she needed any reason to look away from the guy staring at her, she glanced around for a trash can and found one. She started toward it, but she felt Drew's hand her arm. "Where you going?"

"Trash can," Charlee responded.

"No! We paid for these cups, remember? It's what we're going to use to refill all night." Drew traded cups with Charlee. "Here you go. Drink up, buttercup. We'll go refill when you're done."

The second cup went down a little smoother than the first, but then Charlee remembered the other reason why she didn't like beer. "Maybe I should've thought this out a little better."

Drew looked at her a bit exasperated. "What? Don't tell my you're changing your mind already."

"Sort of," Charlee admitted, but seeing the beginning of a reprimanding glare from Drew, she added quickly. "Not the having fun part, but I forgot beer makes me pee like crazy."

Ironically, the only other time Charlee had drank enough beer to have her running to and from the ladies' room was last summer at a party similar to this one where Danny first approached her. She hoped this wasn't an omen.

"Not a problem," Drew said, taking her by the hand. "The guy we paid to get the cups said only girls get to go inside to use the restroom."

Charlee followed her through the crowd to the backdoor of the house. Not surprising, there was a line for the restroom, but it wasn't as long as she expected. After getting her turn to use it but before she left the small room, she reflected on tonight's turn of events: the smile Hector had given her and how the stupid lump in her throat hadn't allowed her to so much as lift a corner of her lips in response. This was the first time she'd had a moment *alone* since seeing him with that girl.

She hated to even think about it, but she couldn't help wondering exactly what he was doing at that very moment. Was he kissing that girl the way he'd kissed her? Were they somewhere very possibly doing more? Was he telling that girl that she was different too? She shook her head roughly, willing the tears that were beginning to well in her eyes away.

Standing in line before she'd gotten into the restroom, she'd overheard some of the other girls in line talking about their ex-boyfriends, guys they'd gone on vacations with even. One of them even talked about her baby's father who apparently was seeing someone new now. They all spoke so casually of these guys whom they'd clearly had much longer and deeper connections with than Charlee had with Hector. There was no hurt in their words, no mention of not being able to move on, no stupid tears. Here Charlee had shared a few kisses with this guy who had said few nice things to her, and she'd already been a mess over the guy more than once.

These girls would not only think her a wimp but a total joke that here she was at a party, trying to get over something that never even was. So what if he looked deep in her eyes and made her heart stand still. Hector obviously knew what and how to say things to girls. And, of course, she'd fallen for every bit of it instantly because that sort of interaction with guys, especially a guy like Hector, was so foreign to her.

Even more determined now to snap the hell out of it, she made sure when they got back to the party to *not* look away from any guy she found attractive; in fact, she would smile. Within minutes of smiling at that same tall guy Drew had mentioned resembled Hector earlier, he and a friend began walking toward them.

"Here we go," Drew said through her smile as she glanced at the guys coming toward them.

Charlee took an extra-long drink of her beer. She needed liquid courage right now if she was going to do this. She wasn't sure if it was maybe too big of a drink or her nerves, but for a quick moment there, she felt completely nauseous. Thankfully, it was fleeting, and by the time the guys made it to them, she was just absolutely nervous but no longer nauseous.

"Hello," the tall guy said as soon as he reached them. "I'm Raul." He motioned to his friend who was just a few inches shorter than he was with wavy hair and a small piercing on his lip. "This is Joseph." Raul smiled at Drew but then turned to Charlee and smiled even bigger. "I apologize for staring, but it's not often someone catches my eye the way you did tonight. You're breathtaking, and that's not a line, I promise."

Joseph laughed. "Yeah, Raul doesn't do lines." He assured Charlee.

Charlee felt her face warm instantly but smiled despite the discomfort she felt about being the center of attention even in this small group. "Thank you," she smiled but for the life of her couldn't think of a single thing else to say.

"So let me guess," he said. "I've been trying to figure out what your name could be." He put his fist against his lips and stared at her for a moment, and, of course, Charlee made a note of how it felt nothing like when Hector stared at her. "Scarlet?"

Drew laughed and Charlee knew exactly why. Charlee had lost count of all the times people had told Charlee she looked like any name that remotely suggested the color red.

"Am I right?" Raul asked, bright-eyed.

"Nope," Charlee said, taking another big swig of her beer. "Not even close."

"Cherry?" Joseph offered.

"Ooh, close." Charlee said, lifting her cup at him and sipping again, glad that she was starting to feel a little more relaxed.

"Sherry," Raul said quickly.

"No, you're getting cold now," Charlee smiled, glancing at Drew, who winked at her. She knew that meant she was doing well, and for the first time that evening, she felt somewhat at ease. Maybe coming here had been a good idea after all.

Both Raul and Joseph looked stumped. "I'll give you a hint," Charlee said, feeling silly. "It starts with C H and it rhymes with Bob Marley."

Of course, the line about her name rhyming with Bob Marley was compliments of her pot smoking stepdad.

"Charlie?" Joseph asked, looking at her weirdly.

She knew he was thinking what everyone always thought. That's a boy's name. So she clarified. "Actually, it's Charlotte, but everyone calls me Charlee, and I spell it with a double *e* not an *ie* at the end like the male version."

Annoyingly, thoughts of Hector were instantly in her head again. The thought of him calling her Charlotte and the look in those intense eyes of his when he said it were enough to make her down the rest of her beer.

A few beers later and a couple of more trips to the restroom where the line seemed to get longer every time, Charlee decided she'd had enough beer. She was already feeling very tipsy though she assured Drew she was still fine enough to hang out as long as she stopped drinking.

Charlee and Drew had already danced with Joseph and Raul a few times, and Charlee was glad the guys had stuck with them the whole time. She didn't have to go through the whole introduction thing again with any new guys. All she wanted to do now is dance and have a good time, and Raul would do just fine for that.

The area where everyone was dancing was so crowded Charlee kept losing Drew. She glanced around and spotted her dancing with Joseph a few yards away. Charlee and Raul were supposed to be dancing apart, but because it was so crowded, even though they didn't have their arms around each other, their bodies kept touching. At some point, Charlee began to notice he purposely rubbed his body up against hers. She tried, but because of the tight space, she couldn't back up much.

"Where's your cup?" Raul asked, leaning in against her ear.

"I'm done." She responded, stretching her neck to speak against his ear.

"Really? Why?" She felt his lips graze her ear, so she took advantage of needing to stretch to speak in his ear to pull away from his lips.

"I've had enough. Plus, it makes me have to keep going to the bathroom, and the lines are ginormous now."

Feeling his hand against her lower back, Raul leaned into her ear again. "Try some of this then."

She pulled away to see him pointing at his own cup, and she stared at it quizzically. That whole time she'd assumed he was drinking beer like everyone else. He pointed toward the area where the kegs were. "They also have soda over there for the non-drinkers and for those of us who prefer the hard stuff." He lifted the flap of his vest open to reveal a flask. "Meet Jack."

Charlee's drinking experiences were few and far between: the party last year where she drank some beer, but not nearly as much as she drank tonight; wine coolers with Drew every now and then; and a handful of other times Drew had dragged her to parties, but she never actually drank *hard stuff*.

"Try it," Raul said, handing her the cup. She took the cup, smelling the contents, and he laughed. "It's just Jack and Coke." She took a sip. It wasn't bad, so she nodded, handing it back. "Drink more than that." He said, refusing the cup. Charlee took it back and took a longer drink. It tasted mostly like soda, but it did have a slight aftertaste. Otherwise, it wasn't half bad. "Best thing about it is," he said, his lip grazing her ear again, but she didn't pull away this time letting him finish, "you won't be running to and from the bathroom."

She handed the cup back, nodding. "Good to know," she began to say against his ear but froze when she felt his lips on her neck. She jerked her head back when she felt his tongue on her neck.

"I'm sorry," he smiled. "But after the second or third time of having your neck this close, I couldn't hold back anymore." He pulled her closer to him and whispered. "It tastes as sweet as I thought it would."

Charlee gulped, staring at him. Nothing. It felt *nothing* like when Hector's lips had been on her neck. Hector working his mouth down her neck had made her warm and ache in places she never imagined would have any connection with that part of her body. Feeling Raul's on it had made her shiver, but not in a good way. *Stop comparing!*

"Thank you," was once again the only two words she could think of, but she did think of something else that would help her get through this instead of running for her life.

She reached her hand out for his cup, and his satisfied smile made her smile too. Already, she could feel the difference in the buzz this was giving her compared to the beer. It was faster, but it was also numbing, and she liked that. Tonight she needed numb.

CHAPTER 19

It took a while for Hector to find Nestor when he went back to the training room. Gus and Santos told Hector that Nestor had taken off almost as soon as Hector had. Since he hadn't been able to find Charlee, Hector thought maybe Nestor had pulled a fast one and found her first.

Luckily for his own sake, Nestor wasn't that stupid. Hector found him working the girls still lingering around in the crowd again. Once Nestor told him what party he'd told Charlee and Drew to meet him at, Hector rushed out of there. He'd already told Lisa that something had come up tonight and they'd have to grab a burger another time.

As he crawled through the traffic near the house party where Nestor said the keg party was, Hector was already grinding his teeth. He had time to think of what exactly he'd say to her when he got there, but what he wanted to say versus what he could were so far apart that just coming after her almost felt wrong. Then he remembered the real urgency in getting to her, and that pushed any and all hesitation aside. All he could think of was all the other Nestors that would be there, counting on the girls getting too drunk and losing their inhibitions.

It was pathetic really. The only reason Hector went to keg parties was for the booze because they didn't card you, not to get laid. First of all, Abel had always put the ultimate fear in him that too many things could go wrong if you fucked a drunk girl: One: she could later claim it was date rape, and in a way, it sort of was. Two: typically if you're partying with someone who's that drunk, it means you're pretty hammered yourself, which would then lead to sloppy sex, and sloppy sex could mean forgetting to use protection or putting it on wrong. If that happened, you had STD's and pregnancies to think about. No fucking thanks.

But aside from all that, Hector completely agreed with Abel that it was a douche thing to do. Besides, sloppy, drunk girls were not his thing.

Hector finally found a parking spot around the corner from the party. He jumped out of his truck in a hurry. As he stalked down the sidewalk and into the driveway of the house, he realized this was insane. He couldn't possibly protect her from every asshole at every party she ever went to. But he had a feeling she'd showed up at 5th Street for him tonight. He still didn't know what her intentions could've been exactly. But he didn't think that it was something she'd done on a whim. So now he felt responsible for anything that happened to her tonight, especially in his neighborhood. He knew for a fact she wasn't from around here.

He spotted Drew first. Her platinum-blond hair was hard to miss in the crowd of all brunettes and a few bottle blondes. She was dancing, but the place was so crowded she and the guy she danced with were off to the side. Walking toward Drew, he still wasn't sure what he'd say to Charlee, but alarms were going off already because, even as he glanced around, he didn't see her anywhere.

Drew's back was to him, so she didn't see him when he stopped right next to her. The second her dance turn brought her around to face him, she stopped. Glad to see that Drew didn't appear drunk at all and wasn't even holding a cup, he felt relief set in. Maybe they'd decided not to drink tonight. It would be the smart thing to do since Charlee said she stayed at Drew's house and Walter mentioned that was all the way in Burbank. That was another reason why Hector suspected they hadn't driven all this way just to watch a fight and then party in East L.A.

She put her fist at her waist. "Don't tell me you're here looking for Charlee."

Hector had barely been able to hear, so with that in mind, he took a few steps to get closer so he wouldn't have to yell and leaned forward a little. "I came here looking for both of you, actually."

Her jaw dropped and she backed up. "You have *got* to be kidding me. What is it with you? Is one girl at a time not good enough for the boxing stud?"

It took a second for the implication to sink in, and when he realized how she would come to that conclusion, he almost laughed. "No. That's not what I meant at all." She glared at him still but waited for him to explain further. "I was just checking up to make sure you girls were okay." He pointed at her empty hands. "But you're not drinking. You two should be all right then." He leaned in again because he could tell she was straining to catch everything he was saying. "I said if you two aren't drinking you should be okay. There are a lot of guys counting on girls overdoing it with the bottomless keg."

There was a noticeable flicker in her eyes, and she glanced around. "Well, I'm not, but Charlee was."

Immediately, Hector looked around too, and then he looked back at Drew. "Where is she?"

Drew stood on her tiptoes now, stretching her neck. "She was dancing, but she stopped drinking a while ago. We got rid of our cups."

Hector stopped stretching his own neck to glance back at Drew. "We? I thought you said you weren't drinking."

"I wasn't. She was drinking both cups." She stopped talking then turned to Hector again, the alarm in her eyes an obvious sign she was as anxious as Hector now felt. Charlee had been drinking enough for two? "She said she was fine," Drew said, but even she didn't sound as if she believed that now.

"So where is she?"

"I don't know!" She turned to the guy she'd been dancing with who now stood there checking his phone. "Do you see them, Joseph?"

Them? The guy looked around but shook his head. Drew pulled her own phone out now from her pocket and started dialing. "She was over there the last time I saw them—dancing."

"Who's them? Who is she with?" Hector already had a feeling he knew, but even though it was unlikely, he wanted to rule out it wasn't someone she already knew.

"Raul," Drew said, frowning as she hung up the phone. "She's not answering."

"Who's Raul?" Hector asked without even looking back at Drew. He was busy still scanning the party, but there were too many dark corners.

"He's a guy we met tonight who asked her to dance—his friend."

Hector stopped searching and turned back to see Drew pointing at Joseph. His eyes zoomed in on Joseph, who for some reason looked nervous. "Raul's your friend?" Hector asked him. Joseph nodded. "Call him. Get him on the phone *now*."

It wasn't a request, and Joseph got that loud and clear, because he was already doing something on his phone.

"There she is!" Drew said, pointing. "Oh, shit."

"What?" Hector asked, looking in the direction Drew had pointed.

"She wasn't that drunk earlier." Drew was already moving through the crowd.

Hector followed her and then he saw Charlee. She was dancing and sort of hanging on some guy who also looked drunk but not nearly as drunk as Charlee. Hector practically pushed his way through the crowd now to get to her, and the way he was feeling, if anyone had a problem with it, he'd gladly unload some of what he could feel building inside him already.

As they got closer, Hector could see Charlee still held a red cup in her hand. The guy took Charlee by the other hand and started walking toward the side of the house just as Drew reached them. "Where are you going, Charlee?"

Charlee spun around, nearly losing her balance, but she held on to the guy's hand for support. She laughed, bringing her cup up to cover her mouth. When she was done giggling, she waved the cup at Raul. "Raul here is going to show me his van," she slurred. "He said it's just outside."

"No, he's not." Both Drew and Hector said at the same time.

Almost in slow motion, Charlee brought her attention to Hector. She hadn't even noticed him standing next to Drew. She stared at him for a moment, confused, as if she were trying to figure out or remember who he was.

Drew took the cup from Charlee's hand. "And why are you still drinking? I thought you'd said you had enough?" She smelled the contents of the cup and looked back at Raul accusingly. "What is this?"

"Jack and Coke." Raul said, opening his vest to show off the flask in the inside pocket.

Charlee was still staring at Hector curiously then shook her head and turned back to Drew with a big smile. "Yes, and Raul said it wouldn't make me wanna have to run to the restroom so much." She stopped then looked back at Hector again and lowered her voice. "Is that really him, or am I seeing things?"

Drew's entire body slumped. "Oh my God, Charlee, how much of this crap did you drink? Yes, it's really him."

Charlee tilted her head then pouted. "You make me sad." She said it so simply Hector wasn't so sure what to make of it.

"All right, don't say anything else, Charlee, or you'll be regretting it tomorrow," Drew warned then turned to Hector. "You just ignore anything she says right now. Obviously she's drunk as shit." She then turned and glared at Raul.

"Was that the plan? To get her wasted so you could take her back to your van?"

Raul lifted his free hand in the air. "Whoa! No, no, no. Back up. It's not even like that." Suddenly, the guy didn't seem nearly as drunk as he appeared to be moments earlier. That flask wasn't very big at all, and if Hector had to bet on it, based on how drunk each was, Raul had made sure Charlee drank most of it. "I told her about the sound system in my van," the guy continued with fervor. "*She* said she wanted to hear it."

"Yeah!" Charlee did a little dance, grabbing Drew's hand. "I wanna hear it."

"No!" Drew was firm.

"She's a big girl," Raul said. "If she wants to—"

"She's not going with you, dude." Hector said as calmly as he could, but he'd had just about enough of this guy. It wouldn't take much now to make Hector blow. The fact alone that the douche was still holding her hand was enough to drive Hector nuts. If this guy thought Hector was about to let him take Charlee to his van, he was out of his mind.

Since Raul was a pretty big guy himself, it didn't surprise Hector that he immediately took a defensive stance. "And who are you?"

"I'm her friend," Hector said, still speaking in as calm a voice as he could. "And I'm gonna say this one last time. She's *not* going with you."

That caught Raul off guard because he cocked his head back then laughed. He swung Charlee's hand in his and smiled at her then blew a kiss. "I say if she wants to then—"

In the same second, Hector grabbed Raul's neck with one hand squeezing hard and the front of his shirt with the other. He got about an inch away from Raul's reddening face and looked him square in the eyes. "Look at me, asshole. Does it look as if you're gonna take her back to your fucking van?" Raul clawed at Hector's hand desperately, which only made Hector squeeze harder. "You really think I'm gonna let this shit happen?" Hector squeezed even harder now making Raul's eyes bulge now. "Do you!"

"Okay, okay!" Drew said, anxiously pulling at Hector's arms. "He's not! You can let go of him now. He's turning purple!"

"Get the fuck out of here." Hector said, finally releasing him with a shove.

Raul keeled over, coughing for a few seconds before walking back toward the party. Wisely, he didn't bother to even look in Charlee's direction again. Only then did Hector notice the crowd that had gathered around and Charlee, who seemed frozen in place staring at him wide-eyed. A guy with a flashlight came by, flashing it at everyone.

"All right, move it along before someone calls the cops and gets us shut down." Everyone started moving, including Hector and both girls.

As much as he was dying to, Hector didn't dare ask Charlee what she'd meant about him making her sad. She probably didn't even remember saying it anymore, much less why. Plus Drew was right. Charlee was drunk. Nothing she said now should count. Although his mother always said that drunks don't lie.

Drew had begun to scold Charlee about almost walking out with Raul but then put her arm around her shoulder and leaned her head against hers. "It was my fault actually. I should've never left you alone with him."

For a drunk, Charlee was surprisingly quiet, and whatever she did say, she said it too low for Hector to hear. He walked next to them as they whispered some things louder than others. "Are you sure you're not feeling like you're gonna be sick?" Drew asked as they reached a car they stopped next to.

Charlee shook her head then whispered something again inaudible to Hector.

"Yeah," Drew said, opening the passenger door to her car and then leaning in and opening the glove compartment.

She pulled something out then came up and handed Charlee a stick of gum. She turned to Hector and offered him one.

Hector took it then watched as Charlee stuck the gum in her mouth then patted her pockets. "Oh my God, Drew. My phone." She started to take a few steps and quickly tripped.

Hector reached out and held her up. "Careful."

Charlee glanced at him then back at Drew. "I gotta go get my phone. I think I left it in the restroom."

"You're not going back in that party, Charlee." Drew took Charlee by the arm. "C'mere. Sit down." She held the car door open for her.

"But my phone." Charlee protested.

"I'll go get it for her." Hector offered.

Drew looked up at him and shook her head. "Oh, no, you won't. Raul and all his friends are still in there."

"So what?" Hector said, feeling that familiar heat again that he'd felt when he saw Charlee with him.

Drew rolled her eyes. "*I'll* go get it, but you'll need to stay here and keep an eye on her."

She hurried off before Hector could protest. Hector watched her until she disappeared into the backyard. When he glanced back at Charlee, she was leaning over with her elbows on her knees and her face in her hands. Her "you make me sad" comment was the first thing that came to mind as his heart sped up.

"Hey," he walked over and squatted next to the open door. "You okay?" She nodded but didn't lift her face away from her hands. "Are . . . Are you crying?"

She didn't respond at all to that. Almost afraid to, he touched her leg with his fingers but couldn't think of anything else to say.

"Why are you here?" She finally asked but still didn't lift her face away from her hands.

"Because I was worried about you."

She turned her face, removing one hand to look at him but still cradled her head in the other. Hector couldn't tell if she'd been crying or if her makeup was just smeared. Somehow even the dark smeared makeup around her eyes made her eyes bluer. "Worried about me?"

"Yeah, you're my friend, and I didn't want anyone taking advantage of you. I know what happens at these parties. You do things when you're drinking that you might not otherwise. Guys like Raul are banking on that."

She stared at him for a moment, a little too thoughtful. "Were you . . ." she began but then seemed hesitant.

"What?" She'd already said something tonight he'd be wondering about all weekend. He didn't want her adding more to that. "Was I what?"

"Were *you* drunk that night?"

She stared at him as his stomach took a dive because he knew exactly what she was asking and why. "No, I wasn't, not at all."

"Then why?"

Now he wasn't sure what she was asking, but he took a guess anyway. "Why did I kiss you?"

"No." Her eyes welled up fast, and she shook her head, burying her face back in her hands. "Never mind."

Oh, hell no! "No, tell me," he said, squeezing her leg now. "Why what?"

She reached into the glove compartment and pulled out a tissue, still shaking her head. Dabbing her eyes, she sniffled a little.

Hector slipped his hand into hers. "Charlee, please don't cry." He'd seen plenty of drunk girls crying over silliness, but instinct and her expression told him this wasn't the case. This wasn't something she was feeling just because of the alcohol. He thought he'd suspected resentment from her before, and now he knew he'd been spot on, but this was more than resentment. She was hurt. *Shit.*

She still wouldn't look at him. "Forget it, Hector. You've already told me why anyway." She reached for the glove and grabbed the tissue. "You don't need to say it again. In fact, I don't want you to, so please don't."

Hector pushed up on his back leg so he could get closer to her inside the car. "Okay, I won't," he said so close to her face he could smell the gum in her mouth, feel the warmth of her skin. He knew he shouldn't ask, but he had to. It would drive him crazy if he didn't. "Why did you say I make you sad?" She closed her eyes and her entire face scrunched in what looked like pain. He grazed the side of her face with the backs of his fingers. "What's wrong, baby?" her eyes flew open at the sound of that last word, and those beautiful but too sad eyes searched his.

If she asked why he called her that, he wouldn't have an answer because he had no idea why either. It just came out—felt right. Slowly she sat up a little and touched his face with the tips of her fingers as her eyes traveled down to his lips. A single tear traveled down the side of her cheek, and he caught it with his finger. "Tell me," he whispered. "Why are you sad?"

"You," she said then pressed her lips together. Before he could urge her to finish, because he sure as hell wasn't leaving her this way tonight without finding out what she meant, she went on. "You don't feel what I do."

"What do you feel?" The words flew out instantaneously, but before she could say anything, he took them back. "No, don't tell me."

"*Why?*" Her expression was a frustrated one now.

"Because, Charlee, you've been drinking and it's not fair. You probably wouldn't be saying any of this if you weren't, even the part about me making you sad. So it was wrong of me to ask you why you had. I'm sorry."

Charlee dropped her hand away from his face and fell back into the seat. "You're sorry?" She laughed, but it was hardly a happy laugh.

"Yes, and I'm sorry that I make you sad, whatever the reason."

He looked away from her when he saw someone walking toward them from the corner of his eye. Drew was already on her way back to them. He leaned in quickly and kissed Charlee on the cheek, making her close her eyes for a moment. He wasn't *that* dense. If she was hurt—sad—he knew why. "But you're wrong about one thing. I won't let you tell me what you're feeling, but I'm pretty sure I'm feeling it too."

She sat up, getting dangerously close to him again. "If that were true, you wouldn't have asked me to pretend what happened between us never did."

"It is true, but it's better if nothing like that ever happens again."

Her wounded expression made him want to take her face in his hands and kiss her despite what he'd just said. "Because you're afraid I'll want more?"

Staring into those beautiful eyes—eyes that could own him with one single request—he frowned. "Something like that."

It was partly true. If she did want more, as much as he'd be willing to give it her, he couldn't, but it wasn't for the reasons she was thinking. She stared at him for a moment before sitting back in her seat and sighing. "You're right. I *would* want more."

He wanted nothing more than to tell her that if she wanted it then she had it. It's all he could think about now anyway.

"Okay delete, delete, delete!" Drew said as she reached them. Hector stood up, still lost in Charlee's last statement. "Remember," Drew continued, "whatever she said tonight doesn't count. This is probably the drunkest I've ever seen her. In fact," as soon as Hector had moved away, Drew closed the passenger door, "let me just make sure she doesn't say anything else that she'll be killing me tomorrow for letting her say." Drew turned to him and smiled. "Thank you for, once again, coming to her rescue. It's like you're becoming her personal guardian angel."

Hector managed a smile. "You two are going straight home, right?"

"Yes. Well I'll probably go through a drive-thru and get her something to eat before taking her home and putting her in bed."

For the first time since the night he won the tournament, he really looked at Drew. She was a little on the spunky side, and he liked that, but she obviously had a good heart and really cared about Charlee. That made him like her even more. He was glad now he'd told Nestor to stay away from her too. "You're a good friend, Drew. Charlee's lucky to have you."

Strangely that made her smile nearly flatline. "Thanks," she said simply before walking around the car and got in.

Hector waited until the car was out of sight before making his way back to his truck.

~*~

Bits and pieces were all Charlee remembered of what happened last night after she started drinking the Jack and Coke. Some parts were clearer than others, like chunks of her conversation with Hector, while she sat in Drew's car. Though parts were still choppy, and she couldn't remember when he got there exactly or how she got to Drew's car.

Drew assured her she'd walked on her own and no one had to carry her. She didn't even remember Hector grabbing what's his face by the neck until Drew jarred her memory. Another thing she sat there thinking about now was what Hector said last night. Thankfully she'd told Drew last night what he said; otherwise, she wouldn't actually remember him saying it.

"You were right, but you were also wrong. He *is* feeling for me what I'm feeling for him. He told me so. But you're wrong about him finding his match in me. He's afraid if we ever do what we did before I'll want more, and apparently, he's not willing to give any more than that to even me."

Drew said after that Charlee had cried most of the way home until she passed out. Her best friend set the cup of chamomile tea in front of Charlee a little too loudly. Even though Charlee knew her head was just sensitive to any noises right now, she caught the added force in which she set the cup down. "You seem angry."

"I *am* angry," Drew said, pouring the pancake batter onto the skillet.

"I'm sorry, Drew." She laid her head against her arm on the table. "I swear to you I will never get that drunk again. I doubt I'll ever drink again period."

Drew flipped the pancake and then turned to Charlee. "Not at *you*, silly. The whole point of last night was for you to get a little juiced and hang loose, just not as juiced *as* you did, and even that wasn't your fault."

Ah. Charlee closed her eyes. She should've known Drew would never be mad at her for trying to have a good time at a party. She was mad at Raul for getting her *that* drunk.

"I still can't believe what a jerk Hector really is."

Charlee lifted her head a little too fast and paid the price. "Ouch!" She held her fingers at her throbbing temples. "Hector? But he saved me from getting in the van with that guy."

"Yes, and that's exactly my point. Charlee, he went above and beyond last night to go there and find you because he was worried about you. You should've seen the look on his face when he realized I didn't know where you were. I swear to you he seemed almost as freaked out as I was."

That almost made Charlee smile, but her head was still pounding too much.

"You don't remember," Drew continued. "But, God, I wish you did, because that rage in his eyes, when he wanted to strangle Raul to death for simply insisting you were leaving with him, was like none I'd ever seen." Drew flipped her pancake again and then turned to Charlee. "No, I take that back. I have seen it. It was the same look on his face the day he saw you with Ross and he called him your *fucking little boyfriend*. Remember that look?"

Charlee closed her eyes, pretending to be trying to remember, but how could she forget? She'd played that scene in her head over and over. But she just nodded without saying a word.

"Okay, picture that only ten times worse. He looked ready to kill Raul. There is no denying he's got it bad for you. Then he actually admits he does have feelings for you?" Drew shook her head, looking back at the skillet. "The concern was written all over his face when I reached the car and saw your teary eyes, Charlee. I knew whatever it was you two had been talking about was something that weighed heavily on him. And he's still going to fight everything he's feeling because he can't commit to just one girl?" She flipped her final pancake onto her plate and shook her head again. "I'm sorry, but that just makes him such a pig. Someone outta call him on it."

"Don't you dare," Charlee said as her friend took a seat in front of her. "At least he admits it and doesn't do what some guys do—promise to be true and then not follow through. We at least have to give him credit for that."

Charlee hated to admit it, but it was actually noble of him to do be doing this. She was sure no matter how many times he tried to kiss her without the promise of anything more she'd probably let him and he probably sensed that she would. He could take advantage of that and he hadn't. It just hurt that she obviously wasn't enough for him.

Taking a deep breath, she glanced up at Drew, who looked a little too pensive for Charlee's comfort. She knew that look. Drew was up to something again.

"Drew?"

"Hmm?"

"We're dropping this now, okay? No more games. No more trying to prove your theories. No more of anything. There's nothing to prove anymore. He's admitted it now. It is what it is. We can't change who he is, and I'm done getting emotionally beat up over this. In fact, I'm considering going back home for a week or so. Maybe that would help me stop thinking about this so much and move on already."

"Go home? You can't go home in the middle of the semester."

"I can if I'm way ahead and make sure I do it on a week like next week when I know I have no tests or anything important do."

Making the most pathetic begging face, Drew placed her hands in front of her as if she were praying. "No, Charlee. Please! I don't want you to go."

"Then promise me we're done with all this."

The pathetic expression was gone, and Drew chewed her food now with a little smile but didn't say anything.

"You haven't promised."

Reaching for a napkin, Drew was able to cover her nose and mouth just before sneezing. "Bless you," Charlee waited through three more sneezes, and still Drew promised nothing. "Drew?"

"Yes, yes," Drew finally conceded. "No more games. No more theories."

"No more *anything*." Charlee repeated. "I'm done with all this." She stood up from the table, taking her cup with her. "Say it, Drew."

"*You're* done with all of this."

Charlee turned to look at her too-smug-sounding friend and peered at her. If her head weren't pounding so much, she might put more effort into trying to figure out what that grin on her face was about. Instead she gave in to the pain. "Good. I'm going back to bed now."

Charlee was glad that the pain was all she could think of right that minute, so she headed for her bed and would worry about having to face Hector again after last night's disaster later.

CHAPTER 20

Walter hadn't talked about Charlee nearly as much as he normally did, and still the workout with him that morning had been grueling. After hearing Charlee say she wanted more last night, it made it that much more torturous to have to hold back from giving it to her. To think, if it weren't for his loyalty to Walter, a guy whose only move so far was to invite her over to see his robot and play chess with his grandpa, Hector could be holding Charlee every day now.

She wanted more, damn it. He'd suspected she might but couldn't be sure. Now he was one-hundred percent sure that if he asked her to be his, *all* his, she'd be willing to at least give it a go. And if they gave it a go, he'd make sure it'd work out, because after having just a tiny taste of what it'd be like, he was sure if things ever went further between them there would be no turning back for him.

Hector still didn't know too much about her, but he knew enough. He knew she was sweet, smart, and when he looked into those eyes, he felt things he couldn't understand but felt damn good. To be able to feel that all the time would be heaven.

Grabbing a handful of clipboards, he threw them in the box under the counter, and they crashed loudly. Continuing to mutter under his breath, he cleared off the counter of the greeting station in front of 5th Street. Someone behind him sneezed, and he didn't bother doing the polite thing and saying, "Bless you." He was too fucking irritated again to talk to anyone. The sneezing went on again a few more times before he finally glanced back, not bothering to hide his annoyance, and to his surprise, he saw Drew staring back at him. She didn't look nearly as friendly as she had last night.

Wiping her nose with a tissue, she glared at him. "Oh, I'm sorry. I must be allergic to assholes."

If he weren't in such a bad mood, he might've laughed at that. "What?"

"I just called you an asshole," she said, lifting an eyebrow.

"Yeah, I got that. You mind telling me why?"

She leaned against the counter and glared at him. "I don't even know where to start. Maybe because you made my best friend feel special and kissed her like she's never been kissed before then avoided her for days only to finally tell her to just forget it ever happened."

"I explained why and even apologized for that. And she *is* special." Hector's words got a little louder now. "I never took *that* part back."

Drew lifted an eyebrow. "Maybe because she cried all the way home last night because the guy she's crazy about told her he's crazy about her too—only not enough."

"She cried all the way home?" Drew had just told him Charlee was crazy about him, and all he could focus on was this part. He slammed his fist on the counter. This was the last thing he needed to hear this morning. "I never meant to make her cry."

"Yeah, well, you did. And F.Y.I., it's not the first time she's shed a few tears for you." Feeling his stomach drop like a brick, he stared at her as she continued. "You can't tell her I told you though."

Hector peered at her. "But last night she'd been drinking. What other time did I make her cry?"

Drew rolled her eyes. "First of all, you're delusional if you think the only reason she cried last night was because she was drunk. Second, I know what kind of girls you're used to. We saw the little show you put on with those girls in the parking lot after the tournament."

She paused for a moment, letting that sink in, and it did. Hector felt sick. Charlee had seen that? As if reading his mind, Drew nodded. "Yep, we were just a few cars down, and saw the whole thing and how eagerly you drove out of there. And let me assure you Charlee is nothing like that."

"I know that." Hector said quickly. "I've told her that more than once. I know she's different. That's why I was worried last night. She's not like the girls that guys go to these parties to meet. I knew she'd be vulnerable."

Drew tilted her head, looking very unimpressed. "So she's different—special even, just not special enough?"

The receptionist that usually worked the greeting station arrived, making Hector free to leave. He didn't like that anyone within earshot could hear their conversation. He walked around the counter. "Let's talk outside."

He walked out into the parking lot, and Drew followed him. "Can you just be honest here? Do you really care about Charlee? She said you told her you do last night. Was that just a lie because you saw a few tears and freaked—"

"Hell no! I wouldn't do that."

Drew put her hand on her hip and wiped her nose with the tissue in her other one. "So, it's true then. You do have feelings for her, but you're incapable of being with just one girl at a time."

"It has nothing to do with that, Drew. I *can't* be with her."

She gave him the hairiest of any eyeball he'd ever seen. "What do you mean you *can't* be with her?"

He shook his head. Visions of Charlee's pained expression last night battered him. "It's a long story, and I can't tell you anyway because . . ."

"Because what?" Drew crossed her arms in front of her, the hairy eyeball replaced with curiosity.

"Because I just can't. It involves someone else." He crossed his arms in front of him now, leaning against the block planter wall in front of the gym.

The hairy eyeball was back. "You're already seeing someone? Or several someones?"

"No," he shook his head. "It's nothing like that."

"And whatever or *whoever* this is, is worth it? Worth passing up on Charlee—making her cry?"

"Look," Hector said, annoyed that she kept reminding him about Charlee crying. "I should've never kissed her, and I should've never told her how I feel about her. And the only thing I ever lied about was when I insinuated that the kiss we shared meant nothing to me. But there's nothing I can do about that now."

"Okay," Drew said, looking even more annoyed than when she got there. "I didn't drive all the way down here to leave even more confused than when I got here. So you're telling me you do have feelings for her and that kiss *did* mean something, even though you wish you hadn't now."

"I never said I wished I hadn't. I said I shouldn't have. It just makes things even harder now."

Drew ran her fingers through her hair, looking completely flustered now. "Are you *trying* to be so annoyingly cryptic, because this is confusing as hell."

Hector let his head drop back. She didn't appear to be going anywhere anytime soon, and he doubted she was going to let this go now. "Walter is in love with her, okay? Or at least he thinks he is." Hector pointed his finger at Drew. "But you can't tell her. I don't want him finding out about what happened between Charlee and me. When that happened, I already knew he was in love with her or whatever. He and I go way back, and I owe him this much—probably more. To at least stay away from the one girl he's ever felt like this about."

Drew's mouth had dropped open and closed several times throughout his explanation. "But she doesn't like him that way. And I've been around them. He can hardly speak to her without stuttering or acting really weird."

Hector shook his head. "It doesn't matter. Either way she's all he ever talks about, and he's working on the weird thing." Hector frowned, remembering the stupid muted confidence bobbing-head thing. "He's a shy guy, is all."

Drew stared at the ground, shaking her head then glanced up at him looking completely bewildered. "I *knew* I saw something in the way you looked at Charlee. I saw it that very first time at the tournament. I saw it last night. What if she's the one, Hector? Are you really willing to take the chance of missing out on that for Walter? He's never going to get her anyway. Why should all three of you be miserable?"

Hector took a deep breath and glanced at his watch. "Have you eaten?"

Her brows pinched. "Not since breakfast, why?"

"I mentioned it was a long story." It was a gamble, and it wasn't a story he was proud of or cared to relive, but he knew she'd never understand otherwise. Maybe someday she could explain it to Charlee. "You wanna grab something to eat, and I can tell you all about it. Might make it easier to understand."

With a lift of her eyebrow, Drew nodded, and they made their way to his truck.

***

Since Drew wasn't from around the area, Hector chose where they ate, keeping it simple: a deli near 5th Street where many of the boxers and trainers ate. Even though it was lunchtime and they'd be busy, there'd be plenty of room to sit and still have some privacy because the place was huge.

Drew ate silently, listening to Hector tell her all about his bully friends in high school. He tried to read her, make out what she might be thinking as he told her everything: the continual harassment of Walter, the robot, and Walter dropping out of school.

It wasn't until he told her about all the times he spent searching for anything about Walter on the internet, even after he'd graduated, that he realized just how obsessed he'd been about the whole thing. Looking back now, seeing three guys beat up on one guy was enough to make Hector jump to try and help out. But realizing who it was on the ground was what really made Hector deliver that knockout punch the way he had. Not only had it been an enormous relief to know Walter wasn't dead but not having punched A.J or Theo out the day they took his robot or at least forced them to give it back was now one of his biggest regrets. That punch had a lot of weight on it. It had months and months of Hector lying awake late at night, wondering if he could've possibly played a part in Walter's demise.

He'd even begun to wonder, since he hadn't found anything on the web about Walter's suicide, if maybe one day Walter would turn into one of those crazy dudes. Because of all the shit he'd been put through in high school, maybe one day he'd snap the way they did and do something crazy like shoot up a mall or school or something. Hector heard these stories on the news all the time. These guys were fucked up in the head to do stuff like that.

Hector remembered how, for a second, Walter had snapped and gone off on him then suddenly came back to reality and appeared stunned that he'd told Hector off. So many times when Hector had watched the news of these kinds of tragedies, he wondered what had driven them to it. Where had the anger all begun? And every single time, he had the nagging reminder in his head that maybe one day he'd be responsible or partially anyway for another bitter and tortured soul doing something similar.

As often as Hector had gotten lost in his thoughts while he explained to Drew just why he felt so strongly about not betraying Walter yet again, he noticed she'd repeatedly looked as if she were lost in her own thoughts.

By the time he was done, she was chewing on the corner of her lip and appeared to be trying to put it all together.

"So if Walter were out of the picture, you'd have no reservations about giving up all your little girlfriends to try something *different* with Charlee?"

Hector wiped his mouth with his napkin and sat back in his seat. Of all the things Drew could've said about everything he'd just laid on her, this was the only thing she got from it? From her expression, he could tell she had an idea, but he didn't like it already. He'd gone over all the possibilities, and the main reason he couldn't tell Charlee his real grounds for not being able to offer her more was this: the last thing he needed was for Charlee or Drew to tell Walter that Hector was the reason he didn't have a chance with Charlee.

If either of them thought that's how easy it would be, they were wrong on so many levels. There was no way Hector would chance Walter dropping out of the chess team or even school again to spare himself having to see Hector and Charlee together. Hector had enough on his conscience already. And keeping his relationship with Charlee a secret was out of the question too. If Charlee were ever to become his girl, Hector would make sure everybody, including that asshole on campus that was still trying to talk to her, knew it.

"What do you mean if Walter were out of the picture? How do you propose that would happen?"

She lifted her chin. "You answer the question first. Would you be willing to depart from your swinging bachelor life to try something a little more profound with Charlee?"

Hector stared at Drew now. She also had blue eyes, and while he supposed some might think them pretty, they were nowhere near as breathtaking as Charlee's. Most importantly, with what he felt when he looked into Charlee's eyes, they may as well be transparent. It wasn't even about the color or how big her eyes were anymore. It was about what they did to him. He had to close his eyes for a moment. Hell, yeah, he'd be willing to give it all up for a chance with her, but . . . He opened his eyes and frowned.

"It's impossible, but," he shrugged, "sure, I'd be willing. I just don't see how—"

She waved her hand in the air before he could finish. "Where there's a will there's a way. I have an idea already," she leaned forward, lifting her brow and gave him a heavy dose of that hairy eyeball she'd brought out earlier, "if you promise me that you're serious about this and you won't dare break her heart or toy with her, Hector. I mean it. So help me you'll have me to deal with, and trust me you don't want that." Drew paused, apparently waiting for him to respond to that before going on.

Hector almost smiled at the determination in her eyes. As delicate and small as this little girl was compared to him, he had no doubt she'd come after him with a vengeance if he ever hurt her friend—*again*. "I need to hear what this idea is before I agree to anything."

He couldn't even imagine what it could be. He'd had weeks to ponder this, and there was no way, not without Walter feeling betrayed again.

Drew suddenly stood up, and for a moment, he thought she might leave. So he sat up ready to go after her in case she misunderstood and thought he wasn't willing to agree to not breaking Charlee's heart. Instead, she began to pace, tapping her finger against her mouth. He watched for a moment then had to ask. "What are you doing?"

"I'm thinking. Give me a sec."

Okay?

She stopped pacing then sat down. "So Walter thinks he's in love with Charlee, but the guy can hardly talk to her. I'm thinking this is more of an infatuation thing with him. She told me about how awkward it was when she went over to see his science project. The only time he'd been comfortable was when he'd been demonstrating it to her. The rest of the time he was his usual nervous self and barely talked." Drew rolled her eyes. "The guy had time to prepare for her coming over, and the only thing he prepared for was his demonstrations."

Hector shook his head, feeling a little annoyed. "Nah, he did prepare. I helped him actually. He just choked like he always does. But that's just who he is. That doesn't mean he's not really into her."

"Well, I thought so too," Drew quickly countered, "until I went with him and Charlee to his grandpa's assisted living facility." She smiled big. "You've been there with him too, right?" She gave him a knowing look.

Hector stared at her blankly. "Yeah?"

"He's not so awkwardly shy around *everyone,* now, is he?"

Still drawing a blank, he thought about it harder, feeling a little stupid because he had no clue what she was talking about.

She frowned now and sat up. "How many times have you been down to the old folk's home with him?"

"A few." So Walter wasn't shy around his grandpa or the other oldies he played. Big deal. Hector didn't see how that was going to help.

"And did you meet Natalie?"

Hector had to think about it for a moment. "His gramps' nurse? Yeah, I met her. She's been there every time."

"*And?*" Drew pressed.

When he thought about it a bit too long for Drew's liking, she plopped her hands down on the table, and her eyes flew wide open. "Oh my God, I've only been there once with Charlee, and we were there for all of five minutes before we picked up on it. Charlee even thought it was cute, but at the time, I was too annoyed to give it much thought because I didn't like how rude Natalie was to Charlee."

Hector lifted an eyebrow unbelievably. "Natalie was rude to Charlee?" Natalie was a sweetheart. He had to wonder if Drew was exaggerating or if this was a chick thing.

"Yes, she was rude to her. She obviously has a thing for Walter and wasn't thrilled about him bringing Charlee with him. The girl wasn't exactly sweet to me, but she must've picked up on Walter crushing on Charlee because she really laid on the rude with her." Drew dug into her chip bag and shook her head. "Though, the big lug is as oblivious about it as you are. Charlee and I actually considered getting involved and maybe giving him a clue, but after the way she treated Charlee, we both said, 'screw her.'"

This was total news to Hector. He'd been there a handful of times with Walter now, and while he noticed Walter seemed comfortable enough with Natalie, Hector hadn't caught any interest *she* might have in him. Still, he liked where Drew was going with this. It wasn't as simple as he'd been thinking. "So what's your plan?"

"We get Walter and Natalie together! Charlee even says they're perfect for each other. His grandpa's in love with the girl. This will be a piece of cake." Drew smiled wickedly. "Once they're together, trust me, he'll need to get over Charlee real fast because that cute little nurse with the big attitude won't be having it."

Hector thought about it. Funny, he hadn't picked up on any discourteous behavior from Natalie. But then he wasn't another girl vying for Natalie's love interest.

"And here's the beauty of it." Drew had Hector hanging on her every word now. "Walter's going to be traveling with Charlee a lot, right? Spending time on the road, staying in the same hotels. Natalie already doesn't like Charlee."

Hector didn't even realize he was frowning until Drew laughed. "Relax. This is where you come in. I can guarantee you she'll have issues with it that may lead to arguments and fights and ultimately her not being able to deal with it. I know *I'd* have a hard time dealing with my man going on the road with someone I knew he had a thing for, especially someone as adorable as Charlee. So you'll actually be helping him out. If she knows Charlee will have her hot boyfriend with her along on said trips, she won't be so freaked out about it." Drew reached for her straw and took a sip of her soda. "You'll be Walter's hero, not someone who betrayed him."

"Did you just call me hot?" Hector smirked.

With a laugh, she rolled her eyes. "Get over yourself." She reached for her purse. "But I will need your number. We gotta collaborate here. Charlee *cannot* know about this. She'll kill me. As a matter of fact, I have to get going, or she might get suspicious. I'm never gone this long without her knowing where I am, and she sort of already caught on this morning that I might be up to something. Only today, I knew she'd be out of it for most of the day, so I figured I could pull this off. Let's have it." She held her phone up, ready to enter his number in her phone. He gave it to her, and when she was done, she stood up.

"I'll be in touch with you to let you know what I come up with. I'll have to think fast. Charlee was already talking about going back home."

"What?" Hector stopped in his tracks. "Why?"

She continued to walk, making him walk with her. "It's what she does. That's how she deals with being upset. She runs into her little Charlee hole and wants to hide from the world. I talked her out of it for now. But if this goes on much longer, I don't know that she won't change her mind." She must've seen the worry in his face because she added. "Don't worry. If you knew how my mind works, you'd know I'll probably have a plan before I even get home. I'm all over this."

Hector smiled now as they walked out the restaurant. Drew seemed as genuinely excited as he was beginning to feel. And she wasn't kidding about how fast her mind worked. By the time they got back to 5th Street, Drew had already gone over several possibilities about how they could go about this. The more excited she got, the faster she talked.

"Catch your breath," Hector said as they got out of his truck.

Drew laughed, but she did take a very long dramatic deep breath. "I needed that." She laughed.

Hector stared at her for a moment then smiled. "So you'd do all this for Charlee, even though there's a possibility she could kill you if she found out?"

Her smile didn't flatline like last night when he told her she was a good friend, but it did lose some of its glow. "I just wanna see her happy. She deserves to be."

With his insides already stirring, Hector could hardly wait to get on with this. The excitement of knowing this might actually work made him smile. He was glad now that he'd decided to tell Drew everything. This day could've gone in a completely different direction, and now he felt over the moon. "I know I said it already, but Charlee really is lucky to have you as a friend."

That really snuffed what was left of her smile. "You did that yesterday when I said that. Why is that a bad thing?"

She was quiet for a moment then shrugged. "Let's just say this is not an entirely selfless act on my part. You're not the only one whose conscience is dragging him down. I need to do this for me as much as I do for Charlee." Hector waited for her to elaborate, but she didn't. "I gotta go, but I'll text you."

That last revelation didn't sit well with him. Did Drew mean she'd done something to Charlee she felt guilty about? *No way.* The girl had protective best friend written all over her. She'd even marched in and called him an asshole for making her friend cry.

He made a mental note to bring it up again if he ever got the chance.

CHAPTER 21

If there were any rhyme or reason to the days Hector showed up to the chess lab, Charlee could prepare herself accordingly. Monday she was fairly confident he wouldn't be there because the last two weeks he'd been consistent and only showed up toward the end of the week. She'd been right and thankfully so because she still hadn't felt up to facing him yet.

It was Tuesday now, and as Charlee walked to the chess lab, her heart sped up. As unlikely as it was that he'd be there this early in the week, the rattled nerves she felt from the possibility of seeing him again were out of control.

Since Friday, more and more had come to her about their conversation that night. She hadn't just cried on her way home. She cried when she spoke with him. She just couldn't remember why—or rather what explanation she'd given him for her tears.

Glancing up, she quickly lost her train of thought. Ross stood by the stairway she needed to take to get to the chess lab. He was leaning against the rail with both hands in his pockets, smiling—waiting for her. This was the first time she'd seen him since Hector had blown up at her for talking to him last.

"You promised you wouldn't be talking to him anymore." Completely startled by Hector's voice, Charlee nearly jumped.

With her hand on her chest, she glanced up at Hector, who was now walking alongside her, staring Ross down, and she gathered her thoughts. Was this something she'd promised Friday night? "I did?"

"Something like that." He took a step in front of her and stopped. "Last week you said you wouldn't be talking to him anymore. Is he waiting for you?"

Charlee looked up behind Hector. Ross wasn't leaning against the rail anymore, but he was still there, only the smile was gone, and he seemed to be contemplating whether he should still wait or leave. "I don't know."

"He's a bad guy, Charlee." his words urged. "Trust me on this. Like the guy Friday night, you don't want to associate with him. I can get rid of him for you. Just say the word and I will."

She shook her head. "No." His already hardened eyes seemed to almost darken with that, so she touched his tense arm and added, "I won't associate with him anymore, but I don't need you to say anything or do anything to him."

"How 'bout I do it to you?"

"What?"

Before she could try to figure out what he meant, he leaned in and kissed her softly. As expected, her lips gave into him without even the slightest resistance. When he pulled away, he smiled, licking his lips. "In case he didn't see that," Hector said with a smirk then brought his arm around her waist, pulling her against his hard body, and kissed her again this time deeper.

Push him away. Tell him he can't do this. It's not fair!

But her brain was no match for her heart. It pounded soundly and happily in her chest as Hector's delicious mouth continued to devour hers. Even after Hector pulled away, she stood there breathless and feeling completely enchanted. This was the last thing she expected to happen the very next time she saw him.

Hector turned around then brought his smiling face back to face her. She glanced back in Ross's direction too. He was gone.

"You see," Hector smiled even bigger. "That was a *much* more pleasant way to handle that. I didn't even have to touch the douche."

The second she could manage to move her wobbly legs, Charlee began walking. She wasn't sure what she should be feeling, but at the moment she was feeling it all: excited, confused, a little angry, but not sure if she should be angry with herself or Hector. Mostly though, she felt embarrassed—embarrassed about how easily she'd given into his amazing kisses. Frustration was also peaking in her lineup of emotions. She'd been having a hard enough time getting over something that never was, and now she had more to add to it.

Hector stopped her again just as they reached the stairs, placing his hand on her arm. "Okay, maybe I shouldn't have done that. I'm sorry. But I couldn't help myself. It was either that, or I might've done something to him. No," he stopped and thought about it for a second, "I would've definitely done something to him."

"You can't do that again, Hector." It almost hurt to say the words, but she had to. "It's not fair," she added with a whisper and began up the stairs.

"I know," he agreed with a regretful frown. Then his eyes brightened a bit. "But if he even thinks of still trying to talk to you after that, you have to admit I'll have good reason to react *any* way I see fit."

This time she stopped and looked at him. "No, you don't."

His face went all serious again. "What do you mean? The guy thinks you and I are—"

"But *I* know we're not. And if he decides to talk to me again and you happen to see it, you will not react *any* way you see fit. *I'll* handle it."

Hector shook his head. "Charlee, if I see that scumbag anywhere near—"

"Let me ask you something," she said, crossing her arms in front of her and tilting her head. "Who were those girls you sat in the front row with Friday night?"

Oh, yeah, if he was going to act as if a kiss somehow gave him any liberties to do and say what he pleased, then she'd be taking a few liberties of her own. She almost smiled at the way he so desperately tried to hide how her question stunned him.

He recovered quickly and answered. "They were friends. One was actually. She's someone I knew from high school, and she brought her friend along to watch the fight."

She lifted her eyebrow. Was he trying to insinuate that, because he'd only met her friend that night, it *had* to be completely innocent? "Did you have fun with them too in the parking lot like you did with the two other girls you met the night of the tournament?"

The fact that she knew about that didn't stagger him quite as much as she would've thought. Still he pressed his lips together before responding. "No. We were supposed to grab a burger after, but when I overheard someone talking about inviting you to that keg party, I cancelled so I could go look for you instead." This time she was the one stunned and obviously he noticed. He took a step closer to her. "The decision was a no-brainer, Charlee. *You* were my priority."

She gulped, feeling something strange happening, but she dared not even think it. It was hard not to the way he stared at her now. His eyes looked deep into hers like they had on the dance floor that night and then later that same night when he'd kissed her so profoundly. That same stare made her insides feel all kinds so of craziness.

Still, she reminded herself that while his eyes and kisses may be saying one thing, he'd made it clear more than once now that anything deeper with him was out of the question. And as much as she'd love to give into having the pleasure of being in his arms, experiencing those amazing kisses of his, even if it was only temporarily, she knew she couldn't. She didn't have it in her to do that. Inevitably, she'd be in tears and drowning in despair, knowing someone else was enjoying those arms and amazing kisses too. There was no way she could do that. But what was fair was fair.

"Well, thank you for making me your priority *that* night. And given the circumstances Friday, I'm glad you reacted the way you did with that jerk at the party. Even today, I know you meant well, but this needs to stop." She hated to admit the next part, but she'd since decided she had to be honest from here on. No more games of *any* kind. No more wondering what he might be thinking nor making it unclear what she was thinking or feeling. He already knew anyway. She'd use her big drunken declaration in some way to her advantage. "You said it yourself, Hector. I'm not like those girls you hang out with so casually."

He nodded, still staring at her in that way that was going to be the end of her. "I can't do this and pretend it doesn't affect me, and I won't anymore." She glanced away, unable to take his penetrating eyes anymore.

"I agree," he said. "And just so you know," his fingers grazed her arm. That alone was enough to send shivers swarming through every part of her body, and just like that he had her locked in his hypnotic stare again. "I can't do it either without feeling more. And while I'll do my best to let *you* handle this guy, I can't make any promises. I'm just being honest. I don't think he deserves so much as a nod from you, but I will promise that if I do decide to do something it won't be what I did today."

Smiling at him as if that were a good thing, Charlee took a deep breath. Maybe the fact that Hector had just promised never to kiss her again was the last thing she thought she'd ever ask him to do, but deep inside, she knew it was the smart thing. The tingly feeling she got just from being around him and knowing that he felt something for her too made it feel all the more impossible that she'd ever give up hope for more. Any more kisses from him would certainly have her clinging to something that he already said wasn't happening.

Hector's own forced smile suddenly disappeared, and he looked at her suspiciously. "Since we're in agreement now that this guy's a douche you shouldn't be associating with, can you tell me now what question he was gonna answer for you later? Maybe that's why his dumb ass is still creeping around trying to run into you so he can answer it for you."

Charlee had to think about it. She wasn't sure what he was talking about and then it came to her. "He mentioned wanting me to give him another chance."

Hector's entire face went rigid and his brows pinched. "A chance for what?"

Shrugging, she responded. "That's exactly what my question was just before you got there. He never got a chance to tell me."

"And he never will," Hector said very seriously.

She stared at him for a moment but decided not to argue. Clearly after seeing the way Hector kissed her today and judging from his reaction to Ross around her in the past, there was no way Ross could still think there was any chance of anything with her. Charlee didn't think she'd have to worry about Ross still wanting to answer that question.

Finally able to tear herself away from his those eyes, Charlee made her way up the stairs, feeling drained. Going back home for a few days—weeks maybe—to regain a little of the willpower she now felt completely devoid of, was beginning to sound like a really good idea because even after her little speech to him, if he so much as asked to kiss her one last time, she'd be in his arms in a heartbeat.

~*~

Drew was a fucking genius. This plan of hers was not only working out, it was happening a lot faster than Hector had expected. He'd gotten the text from Drew Saturday night.

She told him to plant the seed as soon as possible. Get it in Walter's head that Natalie was interested in him.

In hindsight, Hector felt a little stupid now that he hadn't noticed what Drew said was so pathetically obvious, and she couldn't believe he'd never noticed how lovesick Natalie was. Drew even gave him specifics he could point out that even Hector couldn't believe he'd missed. Like how when Natalie made Walter a sandwich, she was very meticulous about making it just the way he liked it right down to the extra pepperoncinis and choice of bread—seven grain.

Hector had noticed but didn't think anything of it, even when Walter mentioned she always got it right. Drew pointed out that Walter hadn't asked for his sandwich made in any particular way but apparently Natalie had made note of his preferences. She also mentioned how Natalie would laugh at all of Walter's jokes, no matter how lame they were. But most notably, Drew said there was no hiding how impressed Natalie seemed with Walter's level of intelligence. *That* she'd said was the clincher. Drew said she wasn't being mean, but Walter had little else to impress this girl with, so it was huge that Natalie was already so taken by his intellect.

It amazed Hector that Drew had picked up on all this in one visit while he'd been there several times and never made anything out of any it. To his credit, he *did* think it odd that a young girl like Natalie would choose to work at an old folk's home instead of a hospital or clinic with young staff like her. All the other nurses there were old and crabby-looking. They looked like they belonged there, but not Natalie; although, Hector never would've attributed it to having anything to do with wanting to be around Walter. He just thought it had something to do with the amount of money she might be getting paid being someone's exclusive nurse.

Of course, Walter had been just as clueless as Hector when he told him. Sunday morning, when Walter had come in for his workout, Hector got right to it. The workout that morning was pretty much a wash because Walter had stopped so often to listen to Hector tell him everything he'd picked up on from Natalie in the past few weeks. Hector could kick himself now for not thinking of setting Walter up with *anyone* else sooner. The poor sap had been instantly excited about the prospect that someone was actually interested in him. Right there laid the real reason why Hector hadn't thought of setting Walter up with anyone else. If he had to be honest, the idea that anyone would be interested in Walter had never crossed his mind. But Walter *was* making progress with his weight loss now. And the haircut and brow trimming had been huge improvements. The best thing about this was that none of that mattered with Natalie. Her attraction to him was obviously for what was on the inside, not the outside.

By Monday evening, Walter was already talking about going to the movies in a few days with Natalie. It didn't surprise Hector that Walter said it had been *her* idea after Walter brought up wanting to see a new movie coming out that week. But it didn't matter. The most important thing was he'd talked about Natalie the whole time and only once brought up Charlee. That was only to mention that she seemed a bit down at chess lab that day, prompting Hector to make an early visit to the lab that week.

He knew it was way too soon for it, but he hadn't been able to restrain himself from kissing her, especially after seeing that shithead smiling and waiting for her. Already, he was marking what was *his,* and they weren't even there yet. But after a week of Walter talking non-stop about his new love interest and the successful date to the movies with her, Hector was ready to go for it. He could hardly stand to be around Charlee anymore and hold back.

Drew worried it was too soon and thought he should wait at least until Walter kissed Natalie. She said as awkwardly shy of a guy as Walter was this would likely be his first kiss so that would certainly seal the deal. After getting his first taste of that and especially if things went any further between him and Natalie, Walter would be saying, "Charlee who?"

Only a week after springing the plan into action, Hector got a call from Drew. This whole time she'd done nothing but text him, so he had a feeling this was bad. Normally he didn't answer his calls while he was in the middle of training someone, not even Walter. Abel said it was in bad form. You were supposed to give your trainees your undivided attention at all times. But Walter wasn't exactly a paying customer. Hector had agreed to train him for his own reasons. So he told Walter he had to take the call and rushed out.

"Hello?"

"We need to move this along a little faster." The urgency in Drew voice only worried him further.

"Why? What happened?"

"She's talking about going back home again. She says she needs to get away. I'm doing my best to talk her out of it, but she's saying things like maybe she can finish up the semester via the internet. Because of her status on the chess team, she thinks they might give her special privileges if she lies and says someone is sick at home."

Hector brought his hand to his head, his stomach dropping instantly. "You mean leave for good?"

"Yes! Either you take your chances that Walter will still be upset with you and just tell her how you feel or you get that boy to first base with Natalie already!"

"How long do you think you can hold her off?"

"I don't know. She's in her room now, looking into the online school stuff. I'm not sure if it's even possible, but if it is, it'll probably take at least a few weeks for her to get it all together."

"A few weeks? I think I can pull something off in that amount of time." He thought he heard Drew groan. "What?"

"Nothing," she said sounding frustrated. "You just need to think of something *fast*."

Hector's mind raced. Walter had just finished telling him he and Natalie would be going to the aquarium later that day. Maybe he could give him some *more* tips on how to make the first move. Ever since Drew mentioned that once Walter got that first kiss down Hector should be golden, he'd been laying it on thick that Walter should just go for it. From what Walter had told Hector, he was certain Natalie would be more than willing.

"Okay, in the meantime, I'm setting her up with a friend of mine."

"*What?*" he didn't even realize he's been pacing until he stopped cold.

"It's just a double-date thing. This guy I went out with a few times has a friend who thinks Charlee is cute. So I figured—"

"Are you fucking kidding me?" Hector gripped his phone tightly, already regretting that he'd cussed at Charlee's best friend but feeling like his choice of words just may get worse. "You're gonna have her go out with someone else? Someone who's *already* interested in her?"

"It's just one date, and—"

"I don't care if it's just coffee!" *Fuck Walter.* "Did you already set this up?"

"I'm waiting for him to return my call, but I'm sure if they don't have plans tonight, they'll be up for it."

"Tonight?" He started pacing again. "You're gonna do this tonight?"

"I was desperate, Hector." She lowered her voice. "I needed to distract her so she could stop talking about going back home."

"Call the guy back." Hector said almost through his teeth. "Tell him to forget about tonight then text me Charlee's number. *I'll* distract her." He stalked back toward the front door of the gym. He couldn't believe this shit. All week long, Drew had been spot on with all her ideas and now she comes up with *this?* "And do me a favor, will you? The next time there's an emergency like this, call me before you go setting her up with anyone else. I can guarantee you I'll come up with something better."

Drew was quiet for a moment. "Are you sure? What about Walter?"

"I'll worry about Walter. Just cancel that double date."

"Hector," she whispered.

He stopped just before entering the gym. "Yeah?"

"Who are you gonna tell her gave you her number? She can't know I did this. I promised I'd stay out of it."

"I'll think of something. And don't worry. I won't mention you," he said then just before going inside he added, "Drew?"

"Yes?"

"Thanks for doing this. I owe you big time."

She was quiet for a moment before speaking again. "Anything for Charlee."

There was a noticeable change in her tone, and Hector remembered her I-need-to-do-this-as-much-for-myself-as-I-do-for-Charlee comment. He considered asking her to clarify, but he didn't have time. He needed to talk to Walter, and then he had a very important phone call to make.

***

Hector was unbelievably thankful that Walter had Natalie to distract him now, because having this discussion with him before would've been even harder. This was way sooner than he anticipated having to have this conversation, but Hector's mind was made up. He wouldn't deprive himself of Charlee for even another day. He could already feel the blend of excitement and anxiousness building.

Walter would just have to appreciate the fact that Hector did think to come to him first before he did anything. He wouldn't have to find out any other way. Hector was manning up and telling him before anyone else did.

"You done?" Hector asked as he walked up to him in the locker room.

"Yeah," Walter wiped off his sweaty face with a towel. "It's definitely getting easier, and I actually like the way I feel when I leave here now, not like before when I'd be dragging my ass out of here in total pain."

Hector patted Walter on the shoulder. "That means you're getting there. Eventually, you'll be doing this just for *that* feeling, not because you need it." Hector straddled the bench and leaned against the wall. "I gotta talk to you."

Walter turned to him and stopped mopping his face, letting the towel drop on his shoulder. "What's up?"

"The way you've been talking about Natalie this week, I get the feeling that trying to get Charlee is a thing of the past."

Hector kept a close eye on Walter. He was doing the honorable thing here, asking for Walter's blessings to go ahead and do what he'd wanted to for what seemed like forever now. But he also needed to get one thing straight. Once he did, he didn't want Walter so much as daydreaming about her, because after today, Hector wouldn't be taking any steps back. He'd be going forward with this full throttle, and if she was all for it, Charlee would be *his*.

Walter was pensive for a moment before responding to Hector's statement. "All this time, even after you told me you thought maybe Natalie was interested in me, I thought Charlee would still be the ultimate goal, if I could ever get there." He shrugged. "I almost feel guilty now that I saw Natalie as a consolation prize, someone I'd be settling for. To tell the truth, this whole week talking to Charlee was just as nerve-racking as always but nowhere near as exciting and as easy as when I talk to Nat." Walter seemed almost embarrassed by that. "I was nervous at first, thinking that knowing Natalie might be looking at me in a way I would've never imagined would change things—that I wouldn't feel at ease as I always have talking to her. But we've had our moments this week, and things are still the same."

"That's a good thing." Hector smiled. Walter had no idea how good that was for Hector too.

"I see it now, Hector." Walter smiled a smile Hector had only seen the day he brought out the robot from his trunk and told Hector Charlee had been impressed. "What you said you saw and I had such a hard time believing. Every time Nat looks at me now, I see it." He shook his head, but the smile was still there. "It's no different than how she looked at me before. Now I have to wonder how long she's been feeling this and I was too blind to see it."

"Which means," Hector reminded him with a smile, "that what you were thinking, that she only noticed you because you started making this transformation isn't true."

Walter laughed full on now, and Hector was relieved to see him so damn happy. "That's the best part about it. I mean I still wanna lose weight and all. And I'm gonna keep coming to the gym no matter what, but it's nice to know that, unlike with Charlee, that's not the only thing Nat will appreciate about me." He stopped laughing and got a little serious. "That's not to say I think Charlee is shallow or anything, but you know what I mean. Charlee's never been anything but nice to me, but obviously my personality alone is not gonna cut it for her. And it's just as well, because after spending so much time with Nat this week and then trying again to feel comfortable with Charlee, I think maybe she and I are just too different." He scrunched up his nose. "Plus her head is always somewhere else. I always get the feeling she's not really listening to me." He laughed again. "I guess in a way that's a good thing because I always manage to say something stupid around her."

Hector laughed now too, and he'd like to think he knew just where Charlee's head had been when Walter had been trying to make a connection with her. "So you're done with Charlee then, right?"

Walter nodded then slipped a dry t-shirt on. "Good," Hector said, standing up but lost the courage to look Walter straight in the face when he said it, so he smiled at one of the trainers walking out of the locker room and waved, "because I think I'm gonna ask her out."

Hector held his breath, still not looking in Walter's direction, but after the silence went on for too long, he had no choice. To his surprise, Walter was smirking. "Funny, it never even dawned on me that Nat might be looking at me as more than just her only patient's grandson, who she had no choice but to be nice to. It's not surprising really since I'm usually pretty lame about picking up on those kinds of things. But I've seen the way you look at Charlee. I was beginning to think I was just paranoid since, obviously, you weren't doing anything about it. I thought maybe you just liked what you saw but she wasn't really your type."

"I don't have a type, Walter." Hector smiled, feeling a little stupid that here he thought all this time Walter hadn't noticed his fascination with Charlee. "I only recently found this out. And the only reason I hadn't done anything," he crossed his fingers behind his back. Walter seemed happy enough now. Hector didn't have to tell him just how weak he'd been about staying completely away from Charlee, "was because I knew you had a thing for her. But you're cool with this now."

Hector purposely made his last comment a statement not a question. He didn't want to give Walter any room to say no because regardless of what Walter said now, Hector was not about to chance Charlee leaving.

Walter nodded. "We're cool. Just don't ever tell her I was pining for her all this time. That's embarrassing."

Not sure how he'd explain to Charlee why he fought this thing all this time without mentioning that, Hector agreed. At this point, he'd agree to anything.

"Well, I got a date to the aquarium I need to go get ready for." Walter said, grabbing his gym bag.

And Hector had a phone call to make. As much as he knew Charlee wanted this—she'd told him she did and so had Drew—Hector wanted this too. So why the hell was he suddenly scared out of his mind?

CHAPTER 22

Flipping back to what she was supposed to have been doing, Charlee chewed the inside of her cheek and pretended to be looking up show times on her laptop. Drew had suggested they go catch a movie tonight. She was leaving to meet with her dad and his new girlfriend in Seattle the next morning and needed to get her mind off it. Drew had actually wanted Charlee to come with her, but Charlee had a presentation she had to make that Monday in school. Even though Charlee hadn't brought it up in a while, she was still considering going back home. She had to keep up with the big stuff in her classes like this presentation to make up for whatever she might miss while she was gone.

Drew would be gone overnight and wouldn't be back until Monday afternoon. As much as Charlee wasn't looking forward to being alone, she just couldn't miss class Monday. All this time while Drew had been on the phone finalizing her arrangements for her trip then jumped in the shower, Charlee should've been deciding what movie they would see, but as usual she'd veered off to read a website she'd recently come across.

Of course it had everything to do with 5th Street, but it wasn't just the stuff about Hector that had drawn her back to the site time and time again. The wife of Hector's partner Noah had put a blog together chronicling the history of the gym. Charlee was sure Drew would find it hard to believe, but she really was visiting the website for the articles and story about the gym. The photos of Hector that went back to when he was much younger until now were just an added bonus. Charlee really found the story behind the making of

5th Street by one man alone to what it had now become, extraordinary.

Drew walked in with a towel on her head. By now, Charlee should've had the show times memorized for her, but she hadn't even looked them up yet.

"Anything good playing?"

"Umm," Charlee said, typing quickly. "There's that baseball one with DiCaprio."

It was the first thing that popped up. She started reading off the others as soon as the list came up.

Drew made a face, plopping down on Charlee's bed. "Don't they make any good movies anymore?"

Actually, a few of the ones Charlee read off did sound good. She had a feeling this might be Drew's way of starting up on her talk of going to a club again tonight—something Charlee refused to do. After last week, she'd just as soon lay low for the next *forever* weekends.

Charlee's phone buzzed next to her laptop. She picked up the phone, frowning when she didn't recognize the number. With one tap she sent it to voicemail. She was in no mood for student surveys or telemarketers.

"Who was that?" Drew asked.

"I dunno," Charlee said, staring at her laptop screen. "Maybe we can just go grab some grilled-cheese sandwiches instead."

"*Again?*" Drew asked.

"But it's so good!" Charlee turned to her with a pleading smile.

Her phone buzzed again. Glancing at it, she saw the same number she hadn't recognized the first time. Because of the area code, she knew it was a local number. So she knew it wasn't anybody from back home. It had to be one of those never ending surveys she'd been suckered into before. She hit the ignore button once again and looked up at Drew who was staring at her wide-eyed. "What?"

"Nothing," Drew cleared her throat. "I was just wondering why you're not answering your phone."

"Because it's no one I know." Charlee shrugged, bringing her attention back to her laptop screen. "Or we can go to Hollywood." Charlee glanced up at Drew whose expression was a strange one. "But not to any clubs. I mean we can go sightsee. We can check the Mann's Chinese Theater, or I know . . ."

She started typing when her phone buzzed again. This time it was a text from that same number that had called twice. Curiously, she clicked on the envelope.

> Are you busy?

Certain whoever it was had the wrong person, she almost put the phone down, ready to just ignore it, but then it buzzed again.

> This is Hector by the way.

Feeling her eyes widen as her heart started thumping, she read it again then looked up at Drew who was chewing on her pinky fingernail and staring at her. Her stomach immediately did that funny thing it did every time she was around him, and for whatever reason, Charlee felt the need to whisper. "It's Hector, and it's the same number that called twice."

"Really?" Drew smiled. "What does he want?"

"He's asking if I'm busy."

Her initial reaction was to respond to ask him how he'd gotten her number. Her pessimistic side wanted to be sure it was actually him. But he wouldn't have called her first if it were anyone else. She'd know immediately by his voice that it wasn't him. Plus he might think it rude or that maybe she was mad that he had her number.

"Well, respond!" Drew urged.

Her insides were already doing all kinds of crazy things as she typed in her response.

> Chess Hector from 5th Street, right?

Okay, so she couldn't help giving into her pessimistic side. Before she got too worked up over this, she *had* to make sure. But this was less rude sounding. His response was immediate.

> How many Hectors do you know?

That made her smile silly.
"What?" Drew scooted closer to her. "What did he say?" Charlee showed her then wrote back.

> Only one, but I wasn't aware he had my number.

Drew wiggled next to her, seemingly as excited as Charlee felt. She hit send. "Where do you think he got it?" Charlee asked, turning to Drew.

Drew stopped smiling and the wiggling ceased. She shook her head. "I don't know, but it's pretty easy nowadays to get anyone's number."

Charlee was just beginning to think about that when her phone buzzed in her hand again. She and Drew read it together.

> He does. And he wants to talk to you. If he calls you again, will you answer this time?

Charlee brought her hand to her mouth. She and Drew stared at each other. "What do you think he wants?" she was whispering again.

"I don't know," Drew whispered back then giggled. "But say yes and find out."

Charlee did, and less than a minute later, her phone buzzed with Hector's call. She stood up, not sure what to do with herself. For a second, she thought of going and sitting in her closet to take the call then had a flashback of doing the same thing when Danny had called her last year a few times. So she decided she'd just answer right there in the middle of the room. To her surprise, Drew smiled, waved, and then walked out of the room, giving Charlee the privacy she didn't even realize until that moment she wanted.

With a deep breath, she answered. "Hello?"

"Hey." The tone alone in that one word gave her visions of the beautiful smile he must've been wearing. "It's Saturday night. What are you up to?"

She blinked a couple of times, her head soaking in that deep resonate voice until she recovered enough to realize he'd just asked her something. "Oh . . . I'm not sure yet. Drew and I were supposed to go out."

"Really? Where to?"

Just then Drew stuck her head in her bedroom and shook her head. Charlie covered the phone mic with her finger. "What?" she mouthed.

"I'm not feeling so hot after all." Drew whispered loudly. "I think I might take some meds and hit the hay early. I've got a long day tomorrow."

Charlee stared at her then heard Hector's voice again in her ear. "*Hello?*"

Nodding quickly at Drew, she focused on Hector again. "I'm sorry. Drew was just saying something to me."

"That she's cancelling whatever plans you two had?"

Charlee was quiet for a second then sat on the bed. "Actually, yes, how'd you know that?"

She heard him laugh softly. "Wishful thinking, I guess. So now that your plans are shot, can I pick you up?"

Charlee glanced back up to her doorway, feeling a familiar stir deep inside her. Drew was gone now, and she was free to say what she wanted to say so badly. Yes, yes, *yes!* But she hesitated, gulping instead. "Pick me up?"

"Yeah," he said in the most casual tone. "I was hoping we could talk. I'll behave. I promise."

She smiled and wished she were brave enough to tell him he didn't have to. His voice alone had her envisioning his amazing kisses already. But that was her heart and her raging hormones talking. Her brain annoyingly reminded her to be careful. She was having a hard enough time moving forward. This could be a *major* setback. What could he possibly want to talk to her about? "I live all the way in Burbank."

"That's okay. You're worth the drive."

Again she could almost envision him smiling, and it was enough to set the swarm of butterflies she'd been trying to keep calm loose in her belly. She glanced at the clock on her nightstand. "What time?"

"Now," he said immediately. "I can hardly wait."

That set cannons off inside her now. What did he mean? Wait for what? "Oh." The single-syllable word escaped her lips without thought. This was so unexpected and bizarre, and exciting and frightening all at the same time.

"So you're good with that?" he asked. "'Cause I'll leave right now if you are."

His voice was so deep—so perfect. She was almost afraid to speak again, but she had to. Shaking her head, she tried to snap out of the trance he so easily put her in and gathered her thoughts. What exactly did he have in mind and should she be excited or worried? She'd just admitted what little plans she had this Saturday night were cancelled, and as nervous as this made her, she had to admit she was more than curious to know what he wanted to talk about. "Um . . . okay. So we're just going somewhere to talk? I can wear what I'm wearing now—jeans?"

"Yes. Whatever you're comfortable in is fine. Text me your address, and, Charlee?"

"Yes?"

"Did I mention I can hardly wait?"

Surprised by the laugh that escaped her, she brought her hand to her mouth. Okay, she didn't care anymore if he were anxious about talking to her or stealing another few meaningless kisses. Suddenly she couldn't wait either. "The curiosity is killing me now."

"It won't be for too long. I promise."

After hanging up, she didn't even have to go fetch Drew. Her best friend was obviously doing what Charlee suspected she'd been doing ever since she'd stuck her nose in the door at the most opportune moment to tell her that she was cancelling tonight. She was standing somewhere very nearby, listening in, and as soon as Charlee said goodbye, she rushed in the room.

"So what happened?"

Charlee smiled at her suspiciously. "I think you already know."

Drew's smile flattened. "Why? What did he say?"

"Oh, that's right. You couldn't hear *him*." Charlee smiled big, patting the bedspread right next to her for Drew to have a seat. "I don't know what to think, so I'm not going to. He wants to talk to me, and I have no idea what about, except he said he can hardly wait."

Drew's smile slowly resurfaced. "So why didn't you just ask him?"

Charlee thought about that for a moment. That seemed so simple. Why hadn't she? "I don't know. I guess I was just too stunned. I didn't even think to ask him how he got my number. But he's on his way now."

Drew jumped to her feet instantly. "Then what are we waiting for? Let's get you ready!" She grabbed Charlee's hand, tugging her to her feet too.

"He said to dress casually. We're just going somewhere to talk." Charlee might as well have been talking to the wall because Drew was already hauling her down the hallway toward the bathroom. "And I thought you weren't feeling well. You were going to take meds and go to bed."

Drew turned to her with a telling smirk. Her best friend hadn't been sick for days. "First things first. It's time to get you looking casually gorgeous. I can sleep later."

Charlee decided for once to kill the stubborn pessimist in her and just go with it. He could be making excuses to get together with her because he was just looking to have some fun on a Saturday night, and while her head reminded her what a bad idea that was, her heart kept saying, "How bad can that be really?"

They got to the restroom, and she stared at the self-conscious girl in the mirror while Drew searched the cabinets for the straightener and box of combs and brushes—her "weapons." The corner of her lips twitched into a smile. To hell with it! Whatever happened today, she'd enjoy it for what it was worth. She'd likely regret it later, but for now she could *hardly wait* either.

~*~

It was almost funny how hearing his phone announcing that he'd arrived at his destination made his stomach turn. Hector parked in front of the house and turned off the engine, taking a deep breath. As certain as he'd been earlier that this would be easy, he wasn't so sure now. What the hell was he supposed to do? Ask her to be his girlfriend? Did people even do that anymore? That seemed so high school.

He got out of the truck, muttering under his breath, but as annoyed as he was with himself for not thinking this through a little further, it didn't take from the excitement of knowing Charlee just might be in his arms very soon. Seeing her at the door took away any misgivings he was beginning to have about this. She was beautiful, and soon she'd be all his—he hoped.

"Hey," she said, opening the door and stepping out.

The outfit she wore looked comfortable enough. Like she'd said, she wore jeans, but they rode low on her hips, and the short, tight, baby-blue hoodie made the outfit sexier than anything he'd ever seen her in. The shirt she wore underneath was a tiny bit longer but just barely. If she lifted her arm even just a little, Hector would get a glimpse of her bare midriff for sure.

Hector smiled, trying not to swallow up every inch of her with his eyes, but it was difficult. "You look very nice."

She glanced down at her clothes and shrugged, obviously not getting what was so nice about it. "You said comfortable."

"Yeah, I did." He smiled, tearing his eyes away from the sliver of milky white skin showing just between her shirt and jeans. "You ready?"

She nodded and walked to the edge of the porch stairs before he could walk up them. He reached his hand out and she took it. Just like that, they were holding hands already, and they hadn't even begun to talk. This might be easier than he thought. "You hungry?" He asked.

To his surprise, she turned to him, eyes wide open, and smiled. "You like grilled cheese?"

This excited her? He laughed. "I guess. We don't eat too much of that at my place, but I had it in high school a lot when they served it for breakfast."

"Oh no, this doesn't even compare to high-school grilled cheese. And Drew doesn't care for it much, so I don't get to go there as often as I want."

"What is it, a grilled cheese restaurant?" He opened the door for her.

"No. A food truck."

He stared at her bright blue eyes for a moment before closing the door. Walking around the truck, the reality of how different this girl was from any of the ones he was used to beginning to set in. Taco trucks in East L.A. were more than abundant. Hell, there was one parked on every corner.

And while the idea of them making grilled cheese wasn't unheard of, he'd never once seen anyone order one, much less get this excited about a food-truck grilled cheese.

"So it's a truck," he said as he climbed in and turned the ignition on.

"Yes, well, it's sort of a specialty truck All they serve is grilled cheese—a bunch of different kinds. When Drew and I first got here, we went to see a game show being aired at NBC studios. Her dad gets all kinds of tickets from his friend. We heard people talking about the food trucks just outside the studio, so we tried the grilled-cheese truck, and I've been hooked ever since."

Hector nodded, pulling out into the street. "All right, that makes more sense."

"Why? What were you thinking?"

"Never mind," he said, laughing inwardly.

He wouldn't tell her he was back to thinking of her as a bit of a snob who walked up to a taco truck with all kinds of greasy Mexican food on the menu and ordered a grilled cheese.

When they got there, he was surprised to see the amount of people standing around the big yellow truck. Obviously he'd been way off. This wasn't just any grilled cheese. Once they got to the small park just around the corner from the truck where Charlee told him she and Drew ate every time they came here, Hector discovered just *how* off he'd been. Since he'd never been, he asked Charlee to order for him. Charlee watched him intently as he took the first bite of his grilled cheese. She looked so damn cute. If his mouth weren't full, he'd just go for it and kiss her.

His thoughts were suddenly on the party going on in his mouth, and he chewed slowly, savoring all the incredible flavors. Looking down at the grilled sandwich he'd barely paid any attention to as he bit into it because he was so into Charlee's excited eyes, he had to know now. "What's in this?"

"That's by far my favorite of theirs," she said with a very satisfied smile. "It's mac and cheese and pulled pork with caramelized onions. Isn't it to die for?"

Hector nodded, taking another bite. It really was incredible. If he weren't so anxious to talk to her, he would've gone back for another when they were done. He gathered up their trash and walked it over to the nearby trash can. On his way back to the picnic table, he saw Charlee spray something in her mouth, and then she turned bright red when she realized he'd seen her. He couldn't help laughing. "Why does that embarrass you?"

She shook her head and began putting it back in her purse, but he reached out her hand. "Let me have some of that."

Without making eye contact, she handed it to him. He read the bottle, "Cinnamon Binaca. I didn't know people still used breath spray." He sprayed some in his mouth then smacked his lips, sitting down next to her. "Damn that's strong."

He handed it to her, and even though the color was gone from her face, he asked her again. "So why did that embarrass you?"

Her cheeks tinged but not nearly as much as the first time, and she shrugged, focusing on the things in her purse. "I just didn't want you thinking that . . ."

From the moment he'd seen her at the door of her place, the smile had been a permanent fixture on his face. With her getting so excited over a damn grilled cheese and now this, his face was going to start hurting soon. He touched her hair, leaning in closer to her, and she turned to him. With her lips inches away from his now, he couldn't help himself. "You didn't want me to think you were getting ready for this?"

Leaning in slowly, wondering if she'd pull away since she *had* said this couldn't happen anymore, he was relieved when she didn't. He pecked her softly, and he was supposed to stop there, but unlike with other girls, with Charlee he had no self-restraint. His greedy lips and tongue couldn't get enough of her, so he parted her lips with his tongue and went in for more. She allowed him to indulge for a bit longer before pulling away a bit breathless.

"Hector," she began then stopped. She seemed almost upset.

"I'm sorry," he said quickly.

"No. Don't be." She frowned, shaking her head. "I just wish I wasn't so damn..."

She stopped, and he waited for her to continue, but she didn't. Instead, she looked away.

"So what?" he asked confused.

Turning back to him, she licked her lips, and that's all it took to distract him. Then she spoke again. She glanced away, clearly not wanting to make eye contact when she spoke. "I was going to just go along and enjoy today and not think about the consequences, but it's impossible. I can't."

Beginning to understand what she was saying, he slipped his hand in hers. The nerves he felt as he drove to her house today were back in full swing. "That's exactly what I wanted to talk to you about."

Now her big baby blues were staring at him, and if he thought she'd let him, he'd kiss her again and again. Instead, he focused on what he'd come here to say to her. "You said it before, and I think it's what you're saying now. You can't do this because you need more than *just* this." He squeezed her hand. "I can't stop thinking about you, Charlee. I've never done anything more than just this. I never needed to, but now I . . ." He kissed her hand because his lips needed to be on hers, and he didn't want to kiss her lips again until he knew she was okay with it. "Now I need it. I need *you,* and I'll probably suck at the relationship thing at first, but if you give me a shot—if more is what you want and it's what I need to give you in order to have this, then you got it—I promise I'll try real hard to get this right."

She looked almost alarmed now as what he was saying seemed to sink in but said nothing. He waited for her to respond, because he wasn't sure if he'd said enough or worse said too much. Apparently, he'd stunned her into silence, and he wasn't sure if that was a good or bad thing.

"I don't know what to say," she finally said.

"Say yes!" He laughed nervously.

She began to nod, relieving for an instant the knot that formed in his stomach halfway through his declaration, and then she stopped. "I need to know what I'm agreeing to exactly first. You say you'll probably suck at it. I don't want you to mistake me needing more to mean more often. At the risk of sounding greedy, I have to be completely honest. I've never done the relationship thing either, but I *know* now I can't do the open kind."

"Open?"

She nodded, clearing her throat. "I'm not sure what you're proposing exactly, but you have a lot of girl . . . friends. I can't do a relationship where we're seeing each other but will still see others on the side."

What she was saying—thinking he might be *proposing*—hit him suddenly. "Hell no! I don't want that either." He leaned his forehead against hers, taking her face in his hands. "Have you not seen my reaction to you with someone else already? I think I've made it pretty clear that I'd definitely have a problem with an *open* relationship. And, of course, that would go both ways." He kissed her softly. "I meant I might suck at the formalities: remembering anniversaries, being romantic and saying the right things when I'm supposed to—that kind of stuff. But if I'm doing this with you, then it's *only* you."

Finally, the hesitant expression gave way to a smile. "Okay," she said softly.

The smile was once again plastered on his face. He'd never felt so relieved in his life. He kissed her again a little longer this time then brought his leg over the bench to straddle it. He then pulled her leg over too then over his thigh and pulled her closer to him. To his surprise, she lifted her other leg over his other thigh also and brought her arms around his neck. *She* was now straddling *him,* and he was only glad her behind was still on the bench or she might feel just how turned on this made him.

"So how does this work?" he asked, leaning against her forehead. "Do we like wear matching outfits and give each other nicknames?" She laughed so heartily and sweetly he had to laugh too. "Well, I don't know." He feigned feeling slighted by her laughing at him. "I've never done this."

"I've never done it either," she said, still laughing.

"Really? That surprises me. Never? Not even come close like seeing someone or something?"

She wasn't laughing anymore and even looked away for the first time since they tangled up the way they were now. He rubbed her back. "All right, this is good," he said, feeling his muscles getting a little tense already. "I may've never been in a relationship before, but I've been around people who have and have a couple of close friends who are in them. This is a huge thing for them and will be for me too, okay? Honesty. *Complete* honesty."

He lifted her chin because she was looking down again, avoiding his eyes. When he had her full attention, he spoke again. "The closest I've ever had to a relationship was with a girl I thought I was falling for, but she moved away, and even then we kept it up via texts and phone calls. Turned out she wasn't nearly as serious as I was, because she started seeing someone else." He'd take this honesty thing a little further to make a point about how serious he was. "It was the same girl you saw me with at the fight, the one that sat with me in the front row. But we're just friends now, and she was just out here visiting." Charlee lifted an eyebrow and he kissed it. "I sent her packing that night to go look for you, remember?" That reminder seemed to ease her a bit. "Now." He pulled her even closer to him so her legs were practically around his waist. "Your turn."

Staring at her, he tried to understand why she seemed so uncomfortable suddenly when she'd been laughing so happily just moments ago. What difference did it make if she had been in a relationship in the past? As long as it was just that—in the past.

She was sitting so close to him with her arms and legs around him that he could feel how tense this conversation was making her. Whatever it was, he was getting it out of her now because he didn't like how whatever it was had changed the mood so abruptly. This could be someone she wasn't over yet, and he braced himself, his muscles going even tauter as that thought sunk in.

CHAPTER 23

It was so unfair, and Charlee cursed Danny that even after all this time thoughts of him could almost ruin what should be one of the best days of her life. She hated that Hector's playfulness was gone and he was now staring at her with that same intensity she'd seen in him before. It wasn't that she had anything to hide from him. It was just so humiliating. Not even Drew brought it up much because she knew that Charlee had been so mortified by the whole thing that she hated talking about it.

She took a deep breath, trying to come up with a short and sweet version of the truth. "I've never had a boyfriend, nor have I ever been in a relationship where I was seeing someone. But like you, I thought I'd started seeing someone last year. That's what he made it feel like anyway, and it turned out I wasn't even close." She smiled, leaning in and kissing him in the hopes that they'd drop it.

"That's it?" He asked, not looking the least bit satisfied.

Trying to appear as happy as she'd been moments before the thought of Danny had come barreling into her wonderful day, she nodded. "In a nutshell."

To her surprise, the corner of his lip went up, but he lifted a brow, taking the lightheartedness out of what might've been a playful smile. "Do you realize you blink really fast when you're lying?"

She pulled back, but with his arms around her waist, she didn't get very far. "I'm not lying." She was very aware that her eyes blinked like crazy when she lied. Drew had pointed that out years ago. She was just surprised Hector had picked up on it so quickly.

The half-smile was gone, and he stared at her hard now. "You're doing it again. Why are you lying, Charlee?"

"How do you know—" she caught herself and rephrased that. "Why do you think I'm lying?"

"Because the only time I've ever seen you do that was the night I asked you to pretend what happened between us never did. You said you already had and that," his jaw clenched for a second, "that you'd had an exhausting weekend, and I know now that it was all a lie. So why are you lying now? Just give it to me straight. I can take it. You've had boyfriends before, so what?"

"I haven't." He was so focused on her eyes now it completely unnerved her.

"Okay, that's the truth," he said smugly. She tried pulling away from him now, annoyed that he really thought he had her pegged so quickly, but he held her tight. Staring at her more concerned now, he asked, "What's wrong with you? What's upsetting you this much?"

"I'd had a crush on him for years, okay? Then suddenly last year, he pretended to really be into me. I fell for it completely. Even Drew, who claims to have a sixth sense about these things, thought he genuinely liked me, and it turned out he did it all for some kind of stupid football team dare." She couldn't even look at Hector anymore. "It's incredibly embarrassing to talk about, so can we not anymore, please?"

That hardened look was back, but she knew it wasn't because of or directed at her. He was thinking about what she'd just told him. He pulled her closer, and she leaned her face against his chest. It felt so perfect to be held by him like this that she never wanted to let go, and she took a deep satisfied breath.

"What an asshole," was the only thing Hector said and the only thing either of them said for a long while. When he spoke again, his tone had changed. There was a strangeness in his voice. "I won't ask you anything more about what he did, but I do need to know something."

She lifted her head away from his chest and looked at him. He searched her eyes immediately. "You said you had a crush on him for *years*. This happened a year ago?" She nodded. "And it still upsets you this much? You *are* over him, right?"

"Yes," she said without hesitation. *Gawd,* he must think her the most pathetic thing on the planet. "I was over him the moment I found out the truth." That wasn't exactly true, but she was over him *now* and had been for quite a while. "It's just the thought of telling anyone about it," she lowered her voice, "especially you, is so . . . embarrassing."

"Don't be embarrassed, Charlee." He rubbed her back. "Only idiots actually give into stupid peer pressure like that. I remember hearing about that kind of dumb shit in school all the time. It was always the assholes who went along with it. And what was so daring about pretending to like a sweet, pretty girl like you anyway? What a schmuck."

What she'd told him was mortifying enough. She didn't have to tell him *everything*. It was just ironic that of all words he could've chosen he chose schmuck in this instance. She concentrated on not going into a blinking spasm and shrugged. "So you know now. Can we talk about something else?"

He leaned in, kissing her softly, and then slowly his tongue became more ravenous. She held both hands to his face, kissing him back equally insatiably until she tingled *everywhere,* but he cut it short, breathing heavily as he pulled away. Rubbing the tops of her thighs, he smiled that breathtaking smile. "You wanna go see something? It's close by here. I didn't realize how close you lived to it."

She nodded, staring at him all dreamily, and she didn't even care. There was no hiding how she felt about him now, and she didn't have to anymore.

He leaned in against her forehead again. "Or we can stay here if you'd prefer." His fingers grazed the bare small of her back now. In this position, Drew's ridiculously short hoodie had ridden halfway up her back, exposing her entire lower back. The touch of his fingers sent a tingling sensation up her spine, making her shiver against him. "I am *not* about to ask you to get off me."

"Oh." She sat up, realizing she had to move off him in order for him to stand. Okay, maybe she would have to try a little harder to not get so mesmerized by him. It *was* a little embarrassing.

She scooted back and pulled her legs off his big thighs. Feeling her face warm a little, she wondered what he'd think of her fantasies in which she'd sat on him that very same way many times minus their clothes. The heat moved down from her face to her neck and warmed every part of her body as the reality began to set in. If this were really happening, if she weren't really going to wake up from this soon and find out all this was just another fantasy of hers, the possibility of her fantasies happening now was very real.

They got in his truck and set out to the mystery place Hector said he'd rather just show her than tell her about.

His truck was an old classic one, something he said his brother had passed down to him. As soon as she got in, he made sure the seatbelt in the middle seat was accessible to her, and Charlee chewed her bottom lip, loving the fact that he wanted her sitting right next to him.

"He's got a badass Gran Torino now," Hector said as he continued to explain about the old cars he and his brother drove. "He's always been into classics, and," he shrugged, "so have I."

Charlee smiled, pondering whether or not she should mention she already knew that. She wondered if he'd think her creepy for knowing so much about him, his brother, and his friends already. For the time being, she decided she'd just let him talk and keep that tidbit to herself.

"If you're not familiar with Gran Torinos," he continued, "it's the car they used in Starsky and Hutch. Maybe you saw the movie with Ben Stiller. That's a lot more current than the TV show. Anyway, now Abel's looking into getting a fifty-eight Chevy Impala." She loved watching how excited he got when he spoke about his brother, like the night of his fight when he talked about Abel going for the title. "We're gonna restore it together."

"So it's just you and your brother, no other siblings?" She already knew the answer to this as well, but it seemed like something she should ask.

"Yep, just me, him, and my mom." He turned to her with a questioning expression. "I've never done this, but I get the feeling this isn't typical."

"What is?"

"You and me. I don't know a whole lot about you yet. All I know is that you do something to my heart I don't quite understand, and ever since I kissed you . . ." He paused and seemed to think about that for a moment. "No, I'm thinking now it started way before that. I haven't been able to think about much else but you. And even though I don't know much about you, here we are—officially together. Normally, there's a courting process to get to know each other before things become official, right?"

She hadn't even looked at it that way. Now she *really* debated on whether she should just admit she knew so much about him, like how, according to the Roni's blog, even though he was the youngest of the four partners who owned 5th Street, he handled the books. Roni called him a mathematics genius—another thing he and Charlee had in common. Math had always been her strongest subject. But then most chess enthusiasts were good at math, so that wasn't too surprising.

Another big thing she knew about him was that it was his idea to start the Children's Burn Foundation in honor of Jack, the late 5th Street founder who'd passed the gym down to him and his friends. Hector had been a victim himself and suffered some minor burns in the fire there at 5th Street. Being a minor himself at the time, he'd been in the children's burn ward of the hospital and saw firsthand what those kids have to go through, so that's when he came up with the idea.

Feeling guilty now that he didn't know much about her and yet she'd already fallen in love with everything she'd read about him, she decided to fess up. "Actually, I know a little more about you than you think."

They came to a stop light, and he turned to look at her confused. "You do?"

She nodded, hoping he wouldn't think her too weird. "I came across something called 'The 5th Street Journey' online." Immediately she saw the discernment come over him, and thankfully he didn't seem bothered by it at all. "It's really interesting," she added as he slipped his big hand in hers. "But there is a lot about you, and, well, I couldn't help reading most of it."

She leaned her head against his shoulder. It amazed her how comfortable she felt with him now that she knew she didn't have to fear the inevitable heartache. *He* initiated this. She would've never even considered suggesting it. There was no way what he was saying could be insincere like with Danny. He wouldn't have done all this for nothing. In fact, he'd been thoroughly disgusted when she told him about Danny.

"So it looks like I have a lot of catching up to do then," he said, turning onto a street with huge homes on it. "Let's start off with the most important." He glanced at her lifting his brow. "You're out here, but your home is on the other side of the country. You're not planning on moving back there anytime soon, are you?"

"No," Charlee said, looking out the window at the massive homes they were passing. "But I was actually contemplating it a few weeks ago."

Hector turned to look at her but didn't say anything for a moment. "Really? A few weeks ago?"

She nodded, a little embarrassed to admit it, but Hector had such an easy going demeanor—when he was in a good mood as he was now—telling him the truth felt like the most natural thing to do. "The day after that keg party, I had myself a little pity party. I thought I needed to get away for a few days, maybe weeks, but I happened to mention it to Drew, and she begged me not to."

They were stopped at a stop sign, and there were no other cars around, but Hector didn't move. Instead, he stared at her before finally letting out a strange, "Hmm."

"What?"

"Nothing," he turned his attention back on the road and started through the intersection. "Good to know what it takes to get your mind off moving back." He smiled playfully, glancing back at her. "If I have to beg, I will—totally worth it."

This time *she* squeezed *his* hand. Pushing her pessimistic this-is-too-good-to-be-true thoughts away, she allowed herself to accept that this was really happening.

Hector drove into the driveway of one of the huge homes in the next block, but instead of backing out and turning around, which is what she thought he might do, he drove all the way up until the truck was parked on the side of the house.

"Whose house is this?" Charlee asked curiously as she admired the kind of house she'd only ever seen on television or magazines.

"My mom's soon and where I'll be moving to as soon as the sale is final," Hector said, opening the door. "Abel bought it for her. We're just waiting for escrow to close. C'mon out. I'll show you around."

Charlee got out and walked around the truck, meeting Hector by the walkway that went from the driveway to the front door. He reached his hand out, and she took it, gasping when he pulled her to him then wrapped his arms around her waist. She brought her own arms up around his shoulders, fully expecting to be kissed again, but he didn't. Instead he buried his face in her neck, and she let her head fall to the side, giving him better access. He squeezed her tight, taking a deep breath followed by a sated groan then made her gasp again and laugh when he lifted her off the ground. "*God,* I'm gonna get used to this so fast."

His lips were suddenly on her neck, raining soft, gentle kisses across it, making her entire body quiver until he pulled away to look at her. Those expressive eyes that penetrated deeply into hers nearly choked her now. He eased her down slowly, never breaking the eye contact. "What are you thinking of right now?" he asked in one of the most gentle tones she'd heard from him.

"What?" her mind was in such a daze she could barely put any thoughts together.

"That," he said, his brows coming together in what appeared to be bewilderment or intensely piqued curiosity, "I saw that same glimmer in your eyes way back on the night of the tournament. I didn't know what to make of it, and it's haunted me ever since. It's what's crawled into my mind, and since then, I haven't been able think straight. What is it? What are you thinking?"

Charlee shook her head, not sure if she should tell him exactly what she was thinking. He might think her crazy—too soon. She could very well chase him off and make him change his mind about this whole thing. There was no way she could've been feeling the same way back on the night of the tournament. She barely knew anything about him then, except that he'd already made one of the most unforgettable first impressions on her, he was incredible to look at, and she actually had something in common with him. Maybe she *had* been thinking the same thing she was thinking now.

Running a finger across his imperfect brow, she smiled. Now that he was promising she would be the only one for him, this was the only thing imperfect about him, and somehow what he'd said about learning from your scars made him even more perfect. "How easily I could fall in love with you."

Staring at her for a moment with that same profoundness that had her holding her breath, he said nothing for a moment. Then the corner of his lips twitched into a smile. "And you were thinking that back then too?"

"I don't remember exactly. All I know is I'd been impressed with you from the moment I first laid eyes on you." She tilted her head and smiled, feeling more relaxed now that he tightened his hold on her instead of letting go and running for the hills like she was afraid he might. "Knocking a guy out cold at my feet was a hell of a first impression, and then everything you've done after that only added to my growing admiration of you."

Hector smiled then suddenly laughed. "I'm not laughing at you," he said quickly. "I'm laughing because I'm an idiot. I would've never guessed that's what you were thinking, not even close. I thought you were completely *un*impressed by me. And then you went and beat my ass in chess in front of the whole team—"

"Oh God! Please don't remind me about that," she covered her eyes with her hand then moved it aside to look at him again, "because if we're being honest here, that was actually *my* way of trying to impress *you*. Talk about being an idiot. It completely backfired on me."

He shook his head. "That's the thing, Charlee. That was pure genius. I was even more intrigued after that. And maybe it was that I saw something else in your eyes. I kept flip-flopping from thinking you hated me to maybe you were feeling something. I just couldn't figure it out. As confused as I was about how I felt about you, I know now looking back after that day I was hooked."

His smile was so sweet she didn't even bother hiding the deep breath she needed to take because of it. "You're obviously better at this than I am," he said as he continued running his finger gently down the side of her face. For as big, rugged, and tough-as-nails a fighter as he was, it amazed her how very gentle his touch was. "But I promise I'll work on it. Just promise me this much, because clearly I'm not very good at picking up on subtle stuff: if there is ever *any* doubt about anything on my part from here on, I can guarantee I will not be holding back about it. I want you to do the same. I may not be an expert on relationships, but it's pretty universally known that trust and communication are key. Let's try to get this right."

How easily she'd begun to get used to the way he looked at her now—too easily. It was almost frightening. Already she could feel herself becoming addicted to it.

"Okay," she whispered simply. She'd be crazy not to agree to that. What more could she ask for?

Kissing her nose, he slipped his hand in hers. "Let me show you the house."

She walked alongside him now, trying very hard to not feel so awestruck. He was, after all, her boyfriend now. The very thought made her gasp.

"What's wrong?"

"Nothing," she said, shaking it off.

Pretending to be distracted by the huge entrance, she glanced away so that he wouldn't see her, once again, flushing face. *Get a grip!* Just as they stepped onto the first steps of the grand entrance, there was a honk behind them, and they both turned.

"Well, shit," Hector smirked.

Charlee didn't remember exactly what the Starsky and Hutch car looked like, but the car coming up the driveway was close enough. Seeing Abel behind the wheel only confirmed it—Gran Torino. He held his hand out the window, dangling something.

Hector started down the walk, bringing Charlee with him hand in hand. "What is that?"

"The keys!" Abel yelled out. "It's a done deal. Escrow closed today."

Now that Abel was closer, Charlee could see he wasn't alone. And as she and Hector walked toward the car, she could see who was with him. Even though she'd seen them all at the party a few weeks earlier, she hadn't since, and after spending so much time reading about them on 'The 5th Street Journey' blog, she almost felt as if they were minor celebs.

Though she hadn't quite got past the way Hector made her feel so captivated, and she honestly didn't think she ever would, she *had* begun to feel more at ease around him. At least she could talk to him now without feeling so tongue-tied, but suddenly, as the guys all stepped out of the car, her stomach was in knots again.

"What are *you* doing here?" Abel asked, glancing at Charlee with a smirk.

Her face warmed, knowing what they all must be thinking, because secretly she'd begun to not only wonder but hope that maybe Hector had brought here for a little more privacy.

"I was gonna show her the place. She lives close by here." Hector turned to her and smiled. "Charlee, this is my brother, Abel. These other two clowns are my partners, Noah and Gio." He pointed at each respectively. "Guys, this is Charlee," he paused with a smirk and to her surprise added, "my girlfriend."

They all seemed momentarily stunned just as Charlee was, but then each one nodded greeting her. Abel was the only one who actually commented. "Girlfriend, huh? Well, this is news."

"Fresh off the press," Hector said, squeezing her hand.

Like in all his pictures and even the night of the party, Abel's expression was deadpan now. She got that in most of his promotional pictures for his fight he *had* to have that hard look that fighters purposely put on to stay in their tough fighter character. But even in all the other ones he was always the most serious of the four. He started toward the house and they all followed. "Mom know about this?" Abel asked without turning back at Hector.

"Not yet," Hector said, nudging Gio, who walked next to him and laughed.

"That'll be interesting," Abel said then glanced back as he walked up the stairs of the entrance. "She doesn't know about this yet either. She thinks it's still gonna be weeks before escrow closes." He pushed the buttons on the keyless lock and opened the front door then stopped and turned back to face Hector. "She's going to see *abuelita* in a few days. She'll be gone for at least a week. I want to surprise her when she gets back and have everything moved in here by then."

"I probably won't be here for the surprise," Hector informed Abel as they walked into the luxurious lobby of the house. "But I'll be here to help with the move."

"Where you gonna be?" Abel stopped walking and faced Hector.

"D.C., remember? U.S. team meeting?"

Abel nodded and continued walking. "That's right. Don't worry about it then. Just do what you have to do."

Charlee tried focusing on their conversation and not obsess about Abel's "that'll be interesting" comment. But it was nearly impossible. Why would it be so interesting?

The house, however, did make for a good distraction. It was incredible as they all walked through the front lobby, taking in all the impressive granite fixtures and enormous chandelier. Hector leaned into Charlee, taking advantage of his friends' distraction. "That's over a week away," he whispered in her ear. "Maybe we can let whoever is making the traveling arrangements know we'll only need one room."

She froze as he nibbled on her ear before kissing her neck just below it and sucking just hard enough to start up the tingles.

They continued to walk through the enormous house as the reality of it all sunk in even more rapidly now. She wouldn't just be traveling all over soon with her *boyfriend*, Hector. He was now making it clear they'd be staying in the same room when they did. Sleeping with this incredible guy would no longer be a farfetched fantasy. It was happening soon and then on a regular basis. He'd had no qualms about introducing her to his brother and closest friends as his girlfriend, and he was obviously planning on introducing him to his mother.

This was really happening, and while a part of her wanted to squeal like a schoolgirl in delight, another part of her, the one she needed to kill and bury already, was setting off warning sirens that screamed this was just too good to be true.

CHAPTER 24

Since introducing Charlee to Abel and the guys the day before, Hector felt even more certain that taking this leap was the right thing to do. He hadn't expected to be telling any of them about Charlee so soon. He figured he'd mention her slowly, letting the idea that he was actually taking someone serious simmer with them for a while. He was certain none of them would buy into it. One thing he'd always made sure of in the past and they all knew was he'd never call a girl his girlfriend unless she really was. This was the first time any of them had ever heard him say it, not like some of the guys at the gym who, for the sake of making the chicks they were out with happy, did so easily. Hector didn't play those kinds of games, and that's why he'd made it clear to Charlee that from here on there'd be no guessing games.

He was so serious about getting this right he'd even responded to the text he got from Lisa last night, ending any interaction she might still have in mind—even just grabbing a burger, which she seemed to think was innocent. Any guy wanting to take Charlee out, even if it was for just a burger, would certainly grate Hector the wrong way. He'd cross that bridge if and when he ever had to and deal with it accordingly. In the meantime, he wasn't giving Charlee any reason to believe that he'd be okay with even that kind of *open* relationship.

Yesterday, Abel had totally wrecked Hector's plans. Hector had actually thrown a blanket and a small cooler with a four-pack of wine coolers in the back of his truck before picking Charlee up, something Drew had given him the heads up on via text. If he was going to get Charlee anything to drink, wine coolers were best and one or two tops. Hector hadn't been looking to get Charlee drunk or even doing anything with her beyond what they'd done so far, but he was shooting for romantic and relaxing. So he'd texted Drew beforehand to get a heads up. Unfortunately, the coolers never made it out of his truck.

Getting the inside scoop from Drew, however, was something that was going to stop. He was putting an end to the texts between them that would give him the upper hand with Charlee. It wasn't fair, and he'd been dead serious when he made it clear to Charlee that trust was something he thought could make or break this deal. He'd just wanted yesterday to be as perfect as possible, but that was it: no more sneaking around getting inside information he should really be getting straight from Charlee.

This was why that morning when he was tempted to text Drew to ask if she thought Charlee might freak out about meeting his mom this soon, he held off. He did however text her to thank her. He mentioned how he knew now how sneaky she was. Charlee told him she hadn't talked of moving back home in weeks, but, regardless, he'd never been so grateful to anyone in his life.

Drew's only response to him calling her sneaky was a winky face, and then she graciously offered to text him a list of all of Charlee's favorite things. She said it would make him the best boyfriend ever. As tempted as he was to take her up on that, he had to pass. It just didn't feel right. He said it already felt as if he cheated. From here on, it would be all him. He'd figure this out on his own one way or another.

Before dropping Charlee off the night before, he, of course, made arrangements to see her today. He'd always rolled his eyes at those guys who were so damn whipped on their girls that they had to be with them *all* the time. Well, he was certainly eating crow now because he hated to say goodbye to her last night and all morning he'd hardly been able to concentrate without thoughts of seeing her later that afternoon.

So what? He'd admit it now. He was crazy about her. It wasn't his fault no one had ever made him feel this way before. How was he supposed to know it'd be like this? He'd sooner swallow his pride now than be an idiot and pretend he didn't *need* to see her again already. If he didn't, he'd have to wait until tomorrow. Hell no. That wasn't happening. Last night confirmed it. He *was* whipped.

Only thing was he and Abel had screwed up that morning, speaking openly about Charlee while they thought their mom was in the shower. Abel had even asked if Hector was in love, and when Hector told him he hadn't known her long enough, his mother waltzed in the room, startling the hell out of both of them then made an announcement.

"Doña Benitez and I are barbequing tonight for Sunday dinner, and as you both know, I leave tomorrow to see your *abuelita* in Mexico." She turned to Hector with an overly sullen expression. "I know you boys don't watch the Spanish news much, but it's a very dangerous time to travel into Mexico right now."

"So why don't you wait?" Abel asked.

Sighing deeply, their mother shook her head and continued. "I just don't see a better time, and your *abuelita* is not getting any younger. I *have* to go." She turned back to Hector. "But *God forbid* something were to happen to me and I don't make it back—"

"Mom!" Hector hated when she was so melodramatic, and he already knew where she was going with this anyway.

"I'm just saying, *Mijo,* if I don't, this may be my last chance to meet at least one of my boy's *girlfriends.*" She lifted the famous Ayala eyebrow at Abel before turning back to Hector. "It's just a casual barbeque in the backyard. Would it kill you to invite her so I could meet her just once?"

Grumbling, Hector reached for the quick-talking short little woman that had the power to make him agree to almost anything and pulled her to him. "Are you gonna behave?"

She punched him playfully in the gut before putting her arm around his waist with a smile. "Of course *loco*! What do you think I'm gonna do?"

Hector took a deep breath and braced himself to tell Charlee. He agreed to invite her to the barbeque, but if Charlee were at all uncomfortable with it, he wasn't pushing it. This was *way* too soon.

Even Charlee's reaction to his invitation had him smiling from ear to ear again like he had all day yesterday. She was quiet for a moment when he first dropped it on her, and for a second there, he thought she might've hung up, but then she spoke. "I can make a chicken pasta salad."

He'd been so damn nervous about her thinking he and his mom were nuts. He wished now he'd asked her in person because he would've covered her in grateful kisses.

Charlee had insisted she could drive herself to his house so he wouldn't have to go back and forth to pick her up then drive her all the way back, but Hector wouldn't hear of it. Besides, he wanted to use the drive back to his house to warn her a little about his mom. He'd already cautioned his mom about Charlee not being Latina, and while she hadn't been thrilled, she promised to keep her thoughts about preferring Latina girls for her boys to herself.

"So my mom's a little on the . . ." He'd searched for the perfect word to describe his mom all the way to pick up Charlee, and now here she was in his truck on the way back, and he still couldn't come up with the right term. "I don't want to say manipulative because she doesn't even *have* to be." He wiggled his fingers in Charlee's hand. Maybe it'd be better if he just explained it. "You see it's always been just the three of us. My dad died when I was real young, and so basically my mom's had to be both mother and father to us. And she did a damn good job too. The thing is the woman knows whenever it comes to me and Abel, what she wants she gets. Here's where it gets tricky."

Charlee lifted her head from his shoulder and looked at him. "How?"

"Neither of us has ever brought a girl home. And she has these old-fashioned ideas about the kind of girls we should date." They came to a stop, and he turned to her, a little hesitant about going on, but he did. "She's always said we should stick with our own kind—our own culture." Charlee's eyes got noticeably wider. Even that made him smile, and he *had* to kiss her. "Don't worry. I've never bought into it, and neither has my brother, but since neither of us ever intended on bringing someone home—not anytime soon anyway, we didn't bother arguing." He kissed her again before stepping on the accelerator again. "She's been duly warned, I promise you."

"Was she mad?" Charlee asked.

"No," Hector laughed softly, squeezing her hand. "She's not the Hispanic Archie Bunker." Now Charlee laughed. "She just has all kinds of old-fashioned beliefs, rituals, and sayings. Like you don't ever even playfully pretend you're trying to stab someone like Abel and I did on occasion when we were kids because *se te mete el Diablo*."

"Huh?" Charlee stared at him.

Hector rolled his eyes with a smirk. "The devil will get in your hand and make you do it for real." Charlee's brows pinched. "Yeah, exactly," Hector said, nodding. "And she really believes it too. She had me and Abel believing since we were kids that if you hit your mom, *se te cae la mano*— your hand will fall off. I'm still not certain that's not entirely true. But she said it so convincingly neither one of us ever dared raise our hand to her."

Charlee nudged him. "She doesn't sound so bad. All parents have quirks."

"No, mine takes the cake," Hector insisted.

"Well, my mom believes you don't catch a cold from germs, rather from doing things like walking barefoot on the cold floor," Charlee countered, "or going out when it's cold just after you've showered."

"Yeah, well, when she does get a cold or the flu or so much as headache, does Seven-Up cure it all?"

Charlee laughed out loud now. "No, but lemon juice works too."

"Oh no," Hector said. "Lemon juice is for the cancer or for an open wound. Ask my mom. Can you believe she'd squeeze lemon fucking juice into our cuts and scrapes? As if we weren't in enough pain already."

He loved watching Charlee laugh, so he shared a little more. "And get this one. Bathing suits for kids are a gimmick. It's just the retailers' way of trying to make money. I can't even begin to tell you how many pictures she has of Abel and me in the summer, running through the sprinklers in our tighty whiteys."

Charlee held her hand to her chest, still laughing. "But did she ever dig a hole in the backyard and fill it with water for you to swim in?"

"Yuck," Hector said as he pulled into his driveway. "Okay, you got me there, but we do have a few pictures of Abel and me—once again in our tighty whiteys—frolicking in a storage tote or ice chest or anything we could turn into a pool because, according to my mom, they were just as good as those cheap plastic pools from Kmart."

Glad that Charlee didn't seem at all nervous about meeting his mom, he walked around his truck and met her by the front walkway to the tiny house he'd lived in his entire life and could hardly believe now he was moving away from.

Charlee looked positively adorable. Her long burgundy sweater, leggings, and boots weren't nearly as provocative as yesterday's jeans and tiny hoodie, but they were still enough to make Hector's heart race. "Ready?"

She nodded as he took the pasta dish from her then took her hand in his free one. "Smells good," he said, bringing the dish closer to his face.

"It's probably the only thing I know how make aside from the typical sandwich or generic stuff you stick in the oven or microwave."

"What is it?"

"Ranch chicken pasta," she said, crinkling her nose. "I got the recipe from one of those ladies passing out samples at the supermarket. It was so good, and when she explained how simple it was to make, I bought the stuff, went home, and voila!"

Realizing his friends and family were going to be around today and watching closely, Hector had to remind himself he couldn't be kissing her every time the mood struck him or he'd never take his lips off her. But damn it if he didn't feel like kissing her again, so he moved the dish aside and leaned into her against the porch wall just before they walked in. This kiss had to tide him over for a while, so he made it count, savoring her mouth deeply and sucking on her tongue and bottom lip. Suddenly imagining what it would be like to be *in* her, he got a little carried away, letting a moan escape.

The front door opened abruptly. "Down boy." Hector pulled away from Charlee and turned to a slightly amused-looking Abel at the door. "Mom's watching."

Hector glanced back at the window near the far side of the porch and winced, remembering they were visible from the kitchen. Turning back to Charlee, he saw she was already bright red. "Don't worry about it. If she saw the whole thing, she knows that was all me."

"Yeah, no shit." Abel took the dish from Hector and smiled at Charlee. "Hi, Charlee."

Charlee barely nodded, smiling through her redness. "Hi," she said softly.

Stepping back to let them in, Abel chuckled. "She's been waiting, dude, asking me all kinds of questions like just how serious you are, and then you put on that little show—nice."

Hector went straight to the kitchen to get it over with. The second they walked in, his mom gave him a scolding look, but it immediately disappeared when she turned to Charlee and brought her hands to her mouth, smiling. "*Ay, que linda!*" She held her arms open to her, and Charlee glanced at him cautiously before stepping forward and accepting his mother's overly zealous hug.

"This is Charlee, Mom." Hector said in an effort to end the suffocating hug. "Charlee, in case there was any doubt, that's my mom."

His mom pulled away to look at Charlee, and instantly, her hands were on Charlee's hair. "So pretty. No wonder this boy is acting so crazy. He does have manners. I promise you." She lifted that eyebrow at Hector again then brought her attention to the next most important thing about Charlee—her food. "What is this you brought?"

Abel caught Hector's attention and motioned for him to follow him out back. Hector shook his head. He didn't want to leave Charlee to fend for herself with his mom, but his mother noticed and waved Hector off. "Go on. She'll be fine in here with me." Charlee gave him a wide-eyed smile, but, otherwise, she seemed fine.

"I'll be back," he said in as reassuringly as he could.

He walked out, following Abel. Doña Benitez, the older lady that lived in the back house and her daughter and grandkids were already out there, setting up the serving table. He greeted them all as he followed Abel to the grill. "Dude, mom's gonna be all over your ass the moment she gets you alone."

"It was just a kiss," Hector rolled his eyes.

"Yeah, one that had you moaning." Abel laughed flipping over the *carne asada*.

If it were anyone else but his mom who'd seen, Hector might be laughing too. "Did *she* hear me?"

"I don't know, but I sure as hell did." Abel frowned when of the smaller pieces of meat fell in the grill. "Damn it," he adjusted the other pieces. "Listen, I'm supposed to be having that talk with you."

"*Again?*" Hector plopped down on the patio chair next to the grill. Now he could laugh. "What? Does she think this is my first time?"

Abel gave him that knowing look. "No, but she does have a point. You haven't been in any trouble or fights outside the ring in a long time. I saw you at the party the night of your fight. You had that ready-to-murder look on your face when she was dancing with that other guy. Don't even get me started on your flagrant broadcast to the entire gym that she was off limits. Are you sure you're ready to handle being this hung up on a girl?"

Hector frowned. "That was just Nestor, and, of course, I can handle it."

Abel turned to him, staring at him for a moment. "First of all, you *did* pick a nice one. I'll give you that. I never would've made you out to be into redheads, but she's beautiful, and that little body of hers," Abel whistled, flipping over the meat on the grill as he swayed his hips. "*Dayum!*"

The thought of Abel checking Charlee out so closely and what might be going through his head as he swayed those damn hips pissed Hector off. "Is there a point to this shit?" He squeezed the arm of his chair, glaring at his brother.

Instead of Abel smirking like Hector thought he would, his brother turned to him now, looking anything but amused. "My point is she's a head turner. Get used to it. You're gonna need to *handle* your reaction to it better than you have so far." Flipping the meat one last time, Abel closed the lid on the grill. He turned back to Hector, who was now feeling a little stupid that he'd walked right into that one. "You're not a minor anymore, little brother. Those fists of yours are lethal, but you can't go around unloading them like you always have in the past. The shit's real now. You can get your ass thrown in jail. And just now, doing what you did out there, knowing mom's just inside, already you're not thinking straight when you're with this girl."

"That's not true," Hector said, feeling annoyed that Abel would blame anything on Charlee. But he hated to admit Abel was right about one thing: Hector hadn't even slept with Charlee yet, and already he'd felt *ready to murder* for her more than once.

Abel shook his head. "Whatever, dude. Just the fact that you actually brought her home to mom speaks volumes about what this girl's doing to you already. You know me. I'm usually with you about mom worrying too much. But I gotta tell you this makes me nervous. You're a loose cannon as it is when you snap, and something tells me you'll snap for this girl in a heartbeat." Abel looked at him very seriously now. "I need you to promise me that you're gonna stop and think before reacting, no matter what the situation is. There's only so much I can do for you. You snap bad enough, no amount of money is gonna get you off."

Hector stared at him for a moment, thinking about that, then looked away. He *did* think before reacting. The night of the keg party he'd gone for that asshole's throat instead of using his fists. When he'd knocked the guy out for Walter, his only thoughts were to get him off Walter. He'd been in save mode—not attack mode. The night at the party, his thinking was different. He wanted nothing more than to hurt the guy—*bad*. If Hector had used his fists, he would've done some serious damage, and yet he had the presence of mind not to.

Standing when he saw Noah, Gio, and the gang arrive through the side gate, Hector was relieved he could end this conversation.

"Hey," Abel said before the guys got too close. Hector looked at him but didn't say anything. "Promise me."

He nodded, knowing full well that would be one tough promise to keep. "Yeah, all right."

Glad for the interruption, he walked over to meet the guys. He was glad they both brought their girls. Roni even brought her best friend, Nellie. "I thought you were bringing the baby." Hector asked Noah and Roni.

"My mom begged them to leave him with her," Gio explained. "She has my little cousins for the day, and they *love* helping her watch him."

Roni didn't seem thrilled. She even pouted. "I miss him already, but Noah said I could use the break."

"You could," Nellie said, taking a seat next to her around the patio table. "It's only for a few hours. You haven't had a drink with me in ages." She squeezed Roni's arm, teasing playfully. "Cut the cord every now and again."

"That's why Gio's mom is keeping him when we take that cruise," Noah said, taking the seat on the other side of Roni.

"Oh my God," Roni gasped, "don't remind me: a whole four days away from him. I don't know how I'll survive."

Noah rubbed her leg. "You'll be fine, babe. It'll be fun, and we'll be back before you know it."

"So is everyone in?" Gio turned to Nellie, who was the coordinator of all things 5th Street now, including trips.

"Everyone but Abel," she said, mouthing the words *thank you* to Hector when he handed her a cold beer then continued to pass the rest around.

Abel glanced back at her for a second before going back to his grilling. "I'm waiting on a call from my publicist to make sure I don't have anything lined up that week. I'll let you know."

"Just make it fast," Nellie said, taking a sip of her beer, "because the tickets are selling out."

Hector finished passing out the beers and started back to the house to get Charlee.

"Speaking of the cruise," Gio's fiancée, Bianca asked, "did you decide to invite that guy to the cruise after all?"

Slowing down, Hector glanced back at Abel for a reaction, his brother continued to grill, not even flinching.

"No," Nellie shook her head. "I'm still on the fence about him. I'm not sure I wanna be stuck on a *date* with him for four days. He might get the idea that I'm getting serious, and the only reason I even considered inviting him was so I won't be the third wheel to you guys all weekend."

Other than Abel reaching for his phone there was still no reaction from his brother. *Interesting.* Hector thought about it as he walked toward the back door. Like Hector, Abel had never been one for serious relationships, but Hector could've sworn he picked up on something from his brother ever since Nellie had been signed on as the gym's event coordinator. Maybe he'd been wrong.

His thoughts were switched over to Charlee the instant he heard her voice. Already, he could hardly wait to be near her again.

CHAPTER 25

The time Charlee got to spend alone with Carolina, Hector's mom, who insisted Charlee call her Caro, wasn't nearly as nerve-racking as Charlee had expected. She did ask a lot of questions about Charlee's family, her plans for the future, and, most awkwardly, her feelings for Hector. But all in all, things had gone well. Charlee had decided yesterday, when she agreed to no holding back or guessing games, she would be completely honest about her feelings. And since this would likely get back to him, she kept her response as true and uncomplicated as she could without sounding too sappy.

Trying to keep herself from blushing, she chewed the corner of her lip and smiled at Caro. "Your son is very sweet, and I'm very glad I met him. I like him a lot."

Apparently that wasn't enough for Caro. She stared at Charlee with a smirk so mischievous it made Charlee nervous. "What about love? Have you ever been in love, Charlee?"

"All right, Mom," Hector said, walking in the back door, once again saving Charlee when she'd needed him most. "I should've known better than to leave her with you so long."

"What?" Caro spun around to face him, her hand quickly on her hips. "I'm just making conversation."

"Yeah, yeah," He walked up to Charlee, immediately taking her hand in his, and kissed his mom on the forehead, almost as if to mollify her as he whisked Charlee away with him toward the back door. "That's enough alone time for you two. I have some more friends who want to meet her."

Charlee smiled at his mom with a look of regret that their conversation had been cut short, but that couldn't have been further from the truth. She'd never been so relieved in her life. If she was really going to stick to the being honest and upfront thing and Hector hadn't walked in at that moment, she may've had to admit the truth. With every kiss, every touch, every deep breath she was forced to take from just being near him, she was falling harder and more profoundly than she ever imagined was possible for Hector already.

This was something she wasn't ready to admit out loud yet. It was almost embarrassing, but the truth was they'd become official yesterday, and already he'd brought her to meet his mom today. The frightening speed in which this "relationship" was getting serious was coming from both sides. She'd have to keep that in mind as her wary heart feared her feelings for him were light-years ahead of where they should be.

"So did she grill you good?" Hector asked as they stepped out into the yard.

"It wasn't too bad." Charlee smiled then laughed at the astounded look on his face. "It *wasn't*." she insisted. "But your timing was, as usual, perfect."

He slowed down and peered at her now. "Really? You know you're still gonna have to answer that question eventually." He stopped, leaning in and kissing her softly. "Only *I'll* be the one doing the asking," lowering his voice to a whisper, he pulled her close to him, "because I really want to know."

"Get a room!"

Both Charlee and Hector turned to a smug-looking Gio as the rest of the gang laughed. Charlee glanced back at Hector, who wasn't laughing. "I usually use that one on him and Bianca." He smirked now. "I'm sure he's been dying for a chance to use it on me."

They started toward the patio table where all his friends sat except for Abel and Noah, who were over by the grill. Ironically, seeing the women with Gio at the table, knowing these were the people closest to Hector—the very ones she'd been reading about all this time online and now it appeared she may be joining their group—made her even more nervous than meeting his mom.

After meeting them all, Charlee sat and chatted with the girls who picked both her and Hector's brain about the U.S. chess team. They all seemed genuinely sweet and very curious about her relationship with Hector.

"Okay, you have to tell us how this happened, because there is no way Hector would be bringing a girl to meet his mom unless he was serious," Roni said, leaning on her arms against the table as soon as Hector walked away when the guys called him over to the grill.

"Yeah," Nellie sat back, taking a sip of her beer. "I wasn't aware either of the Ayala brothers *did* serious."

All three women stared at her. Roni and Bianca's eyes were full of anxious curiosity while Nellie seemed a little on the skeptical side.

As usual, hating to be the center of attention, Charlee felt her face warm. "Well, it was and it wasn't sudden." She had to smile at the confusion in their faces.

Explaining quickly and briefly how they'd known each other for over a month now and how things had been a bit complicated, she told them how she, too, hadn't thought he did the exclusive thing. "In fact, he sort of made that clear early on, and then, I don't know. He called me yesterday out of the blue and said he wanted to talk to me."

She gave them a very brief rundown of the agreement they'd come to yesterday then smiled. "And here we are."

"Well, good for you," Bianca said. "You stuck to your guns and forced him to give into things your way." She turned to Roni and Nellie. "For all his talk of never inviting any girls to a friendly gathering or even the Friday Night fights because they might get the wrong idea, I knew he'd give in eventually."

Charlee wasn't sure she liked the use of the word *forced*. Clearly, Hector had made up his own mind. She'd forced nothing on him. But she focused on Bianca's last statement now. Hector told her about the girl at the fight the night of the keg party, the girl he said had been the only other girl he'd ever even come close to having a relationship with. He'd been concerned that Charlee might not be over Danny—someone that as far as he knew she hadn't been in touch with in over a year. It never even occurred to her to ask if maybe he still had feelings for this girl. The fight he'd invited her to, after all, had only been a few weeks ago. And according to Bianca, unless he wasn't concerned about girls jumping to conclusions, he'd never invite any of them to even a fight. Not only had he invited this girl but he had her sit up front with him.

Pushing the thought aside, she concentrated on the conversation, glad that the curiosity had moved from Charlee and Hector to Nellie's love life.

A few hours later, Charlee said her goodbyes to everyone. The only one she hadn't said goodbye to was Abel, who was busy on the phone off to the side of the yard. He got off the phone just as Hector and Charlee had begun to walk off toward the side gate.

"I'm in," Abel announced, walking back toward the group.

"In what?" Hector asked what clearly everyone else was wondering since they were all looking at Abel curiously.

"The cruise," he held up his phone. "My publicist just okayed it. I'm good to go that week."

Hector laughed. "As if there were ever any doubt."

Charlee had no idea what Hector meant by that, but as funny as he thought that was, Abel didn't laugh. As usual, his expression was unreadable. Ignoring Hector's comment, he slipped his phone in his pocket. "You guys leaving?"

"Yep," Hector waved.

"Nice seeing you again, Charlee."

"It was nice to see you again too." Charlee responded, still baffled that she'd so easily and so quickly been accepted into this group of people.

Painless and uncomplicated was what Charlee had been shooting for at most when she decided to do this that morning. But meeting his friends and family so quickly and being completely unprepared had far exceeded her expectations. She hadn't even had Drew to help her plan her strategy to not screw this up, and she'd gotten through it. In fact, after all the curious questions from both his mother and the girls, Charlee had been able to relax and enjoy the rest of the barbeque. *And* her pasta salad had been a hit.

"Why are you smiling like that?" Hector asked as he climbed into his side of the truck.

She turned to him and lifted her empty salad bowl. "They liked my pasta."

Hector laughed, lifting her hand that was already entwined with his and kissed it. "*That's* what has you smiling so big?"

Charlee shrugged, unable to tone down the smile. "Well, that and everything else. I was *so* nervous about how this would go, and it turned out great. I really like your friends. They're so down to earth, and your mom is a sweetheart."

Pulling out of the driveway, he glanced at her pinching his brows. "You were nervous? I didn't pick up on that at all."

"I was a wreck, but I think I'm getting pretty good at disguising my lame fears."

"No," Hector shook his head adamantly. "Let's not start that. No disguising anything. Remember no guessing games. I suck at them."

She leaned her head against his shoulder, amazed at how quickly this felt so perfect. "Okay," she said, taking in a very gratifying deep breath.

Thoughts of the girl at the fight with him came to her again. But she'd since decided to leave well enough alone.

This day had gone too perfectly, and she didn't want to sour it up with that kind of talk. Besides, it wasn't as if she were worried about it. Bianca's comment about Hector not ever inviting any girls to even the fights at the gym had only made her curious as to why he'd invited this girl. Curious—not concerned. But she did make a mental note that if it did begin to bother her she wouldn't be letting anything stew, not with Hector being so adamant about his no guessing games rule. She actually liked the rule.

Her insides had begun to simmer as they got closer to her place. Knowing she had the house to herself for the entire night and as fast as things were moving already, she wasn't sure what to expect. As his hand caressed her thigh, her heart began that thumping that had started to become less severe the more comfortable she felt with him. But now here it was pounding away at her chest as he drove into the driveway of Drew's dad's home. Switching the ignition off, he turned to her and smiled. "My mom likes you."

"I like her," she smiled back, already feeling the comfort easing back by just looking into his smiling eyes, "and your brother. He's a bit more serious than you are, but he seemed sweet enough and very polite when he did talk to me."

Hector raised an eyebrow, running his fingers through a strand of her hair. "That reminds me. I still have a lot to catch up with. I don't even know if you have siblings."

She leaned into him and kissed him softly. "Well, if you're not in a hurry, you can come in, and I can tell you about myself."

The smile he already wore brightened even more. "I'm in *no* hurry at all."

"Good," she pulled away from him and grabbed her salad bowl. "Then come on in."

Talking she was good with. It's what might happen after that she was nervous about. But it was a good nervous: the kind that had her insides going crazy already.

They barely made it into the front room when they were already locked in each other's arms and Hector's tongue infiltrated every inch of her mouth. He pulled away, sucking in a very deep and dramatic breath. "I've been dying to do that all day."

Removing his arms that held her and taking her hand in his instead, he led her to Drew's dad's big fluffy recliner. "There's definitely more of that to come, but first we talk. It dawned on me when my mom started mentioning some of the things you two talked about today that she knows more about you now than I do." He sat down on the chair and pulled gently on her hand, patting his lap.

Feeling the excitement bubbling in her again, she sat down across his legs, and he promptly pulled her legs up so they'd hang off the side of the recliner. "You know there's plenty of room to sit in this house," she said, smiling.

He smiled then leaned in and kissed her neck softly. "I know, but then I couldn't do this." Feeling the shivers race down her body, she tried not to tremble, but it was impossible. "Okay," he said, rubbing his hand up and down the side of her thigh. "Let's do this. So how many siblings do you have?"

"One," she said, trying to relax and not have her body go into spasms every time his fingers grazed her neck while he played with her hair. "He's older than me and probably what I miss the most about not being home."

Hector stared at her, suddenly looking very serious. "Really? How old is he?"

"Twenty-five."

Sitting up, suddenly Hector stared at her, looking a little annoyed. "Shit. I don't even know how old *you* are. I'm assuming eighteen-nineteen since Walter said this is your first year in school."

She nodded. " Eighteen. You too, right?"

"Nineteen," he said, looking at her now as if he'd just thought of a bunch of other things he didn't know. "So that's a pretty big gap between you and your brother."

Nodding, she ran her finger across his brow. It was now something that made her feel at ease. She did so slowly, feeling the same way she did when she used to rub her mom's earlobe as a little girl. It was almost lulling. "Ryan is actually my step-brother, and I didn't even meet him until my mom married my step-dad when I was nine and he was fourteen. I only ever get to see him once in a while. His mother has always had full custody, so I only saw ever him every other week for a couple of days and then a little longer during the summer and the special holiday arrangements."

"But he's twenty-five now. You still only get to see him once in a while?"

The last twenty-four hours had been such a thundering storm of emotions, and Charlee had barely been able to sleep last night, thinking about everything that had happened yesterday. As she continued to run her fingers across his brow, she now felt as if she could easily fall asleep right there on Hector's lap. "He has Down Syndrome," she explained, "a severe form of it. So he's still in the care of his mom. As he got older, my step-dad petitioned less and less to have him over, so I got to see him even less, but I still miss him."

She didn't want the conversation getting so heavy, and she knew talking about her step-father could go there, so she kissed Hector before he could ask anymore. Sitting up a little, Hector let his head fall back against the chair, and this time Charlee did the devouring of his mouth. Running her fingers through his soft hair, she kissed him deeper and deeper until she could feel how undeniably aroused he'd become. Feeling him against her thigh, she was tempted to lower her hand and *really* feel. But her heart felt as terrified as it did excited.

Adjusting herself in his lap so that she could better angle herself and he could hold her even closer, Charlee was done talking. She had no deep dark secrets that needed to be aired out. Her life for the most part was vanilla compared to others. There was nothing about her that would have any effect on their relationship that couldn't wait until later, but her body didn't want to wait anymore for this.

When she pulled away to catch her breath after an especially long kiss, Hector moved so that her head fell back, and he cradled it on his arm. He kissed her neck then sucked for a moment, making her squirm. "You sure you wouldn't rather talk?" He murmured against her neck.

"Yes, I'm sure," she gasped as she felt him bite down just under her earlobe with a groan.

He worked his way up her jaw again and latched on to her mouth. His big hand moved up and down her thigh just over her leggings. She'd yearned for far too long to feel his hands on her, touching her in places she couldn't even say out loud. His hand moved up her inner thigh slowly as he sucked her tongue softly then a little more roughly. Creeping slowly, she felt his hand making its way up higher. Her body trembled as she burned for him to touch her *there*.

She arched her body as his hands reached that hot, aching place, and he stopped kissing her to look at her. Spreading her legs gently, his hand cupped her between her legs, and she wondered if her leggings were wet, because she knew damn well her panties had to be. "You a virgin, Charlotte?" She nodded, biting her lower lip, unable to refrain from continuing to tremble as he moved his hand and began to stroke her between her legs. Her leggings were so thin she was certain he could feel just how hot she was. "Well, then, we gotta take this slow."

Closing her eyes, she gulped, almost ashamed that she didn't want to take it slow. She needed him to do more, and as if he sensed it, he stopped stroking her up and down. Instead, he focused on the one place that had her body quivering all over and she turned her face into his shirt. "Don't hide your face, Charlee. I wanna see it." She turned her face up to him but let her head fall back, needing to spread her legs as he continued to stroke her in a circular motion right there, right where it was building too quickly, and she began squirming, tempted to hide her face in his shirt again so he wouldn't see her moan. "That's it," he leaned in and kissed her, biting her lower lip as the sensation began to erupt, making her gasp and moan a little louder. "Come, baby," he moved his arm when she began to moan into his shirt, grabbing a fistful of it.

Feeling how hard he was against her ass only heightened the explosion between her legs. She moaned again and again and squirmed uncontrollably as the waves of pleasure continued. Hector now sucked her neck gently. Charlee began to breathlessly plead for him to stop. She couldn't take it any longer. The sensation ran clear down to her curling toes as he softened the pressure but continued stroking lightly.

He kissed her, groaning against her lips. "*Damn*, that was hot." She lay back on his arm, and the waves of pleasure continued but began to weaken. Her heart still pounded as she lay there breathing hard with eyes closed. "When's the last time you felt that?" Hector whispered against her lips.

No way was she telling him. Purposely she kept her eyes closed and smiled. "I'm not telling you."

"What?" He poked her ribs, making her jerk sideways, and her eyes flew open. "Ah," he smiled wickedly, "you're ticklish."

He poked her again, and she jerked instantly, laughing. "Stop!" *Curse her ticklish ribs!*

"I will," he said, poking her other side now, and she laughed even more, trying to squirm out of his hold, "as soon as you tell me."

He tickled her again, and she was laughing so much now she could barely get the words out. "Okay, okay, a few days ago!"

Hector froze, staring at her. As her laughter slowly subsided, she noticed the rigid way he looked at her. She'd just admitted she was a virgin. Surely, he couldn't be thinking . . . and just a few days ago? She rolled her eyes, sitting up since she'd squirmed herself nearly off his lap. "It was D.I.Y."

With a pinch of his eyes, he looked and sounded almost annoyed now. "What the hell does that mean?"

"Think about it." She held his chin with one hand and kissed him. "Please, don't make me say it."

He thought about it, and slowly the glare turned into a smile so big she nearly blushed. "You can't ask for details," she said, already anticipating his next question.

In the next instant, she was laughing again as he poked her several times in her now-sensitive ribs. "Oh, can't I?"

"No fair!" she said, rolling off his lap onto the plush carpet.

She tried rolling away and making a run for it, but he came after her and pinned her down, placing his hands over hers against the carpet. He stared at her for a moment as her laughing calmed without saying anything. She stopped laughing completely and just stared at him silently before he said the very thing she was thinking of him. "*God*, you're beautiful."

They stared at each other for a few more silent moments until he brought his body down over hers and kissed her. The kiss was so tender and gentle it made her sigh. It wasn't at all like the feverish kisses they'd shared just earlier, but it held an intensity she'd only felt from him a few times. Extending the gentle kisses down her chin and onto her neck, he stopped at her ear. "I can hardly believe you're all mine," he whispered. She smiled, knowing her inner feminist was probably crossing her arms and tapping her foot on the ground. But Charlee couldn't help it. She loved the idea of being *his*.

Feeling how hard he was again or maybe *still,* she moved against it, wanting him to rub against her. She was so hot again she could hardly stand it. Obviously picking up on what she wanted, he began to sway his hips slowly, and if he didn't still have her hands pinned, she actually would have felt brave enough and the absolute need to touch him *there.*

Without warning, he stopped, and she could feel his pounding heart against her. "But you're a virgin, and . . ."

He didn't finish and she froze. Hearing the icy chill of the subtle yet shattering rejection brought back all the insecurities she'd managed to do away with and keep at bay in the past twenty-four hours. Now *she* was the one wondering what the hell *he* meant? The new girl she'd been in the last days being around him, the girl who'd actually begun to feel worthy of the affection Hector had given her, was suddenly gone. That girl might've had the guts to ask. Instead, she reverted to the old her and cowardly closed her eyes. Bracing herself, she waited silently for him to continue.

CHAPTER 26

Deliberating on how to explain this exactly, Hector struggled to come up with something that didn't sound ridiculous. Abel's words continued to rattle him. *Are you sure you're ready to handle being so hung up on a girl?* At the time, he had been. Hell, just a few minutes earlier he had been. He'd been fairly certain just from what little he knew about Charlee that he was dealing with a virgin. It hadn't felt so alarming until now.

Hector was sure he was ready to be with Charlee and only Charlee. But he'd had his share of experimenting with plenty of girls. Testing the waters—lots of waters. Charlee was only eighteen. Aside from that idiot she'd told him about, this was her first real experience. And this was literally happening overnight. How could she be sure he was the one this quickly? Because if this happened, he wanted to be damn sure he'd be the *only* one for her after tonight.

Abel was right. There'd be no way he could handle anything otherwise, and, suddenly, that scared the life out of him. Did people really fall in love, break up, and move on? His eyes slowly opened wider with the realization of where his mind had just gone. *Love?* No way.

Charlee pushed him off her suddenly, derailing his train of thought. He'd been so lost in thought she managed to push him aside and squirm out from under him.

"In what world is a virgin not good enough?" She asked as she stood up, crossing her arms in front of her. "Are you looking for someone more experienced? Less priggish?"

"Priggish?" he asked, getting up on his own feet quickly and noticed the hurt in her eyes now. "No! Whatever that means."

He had no idea what priggish meant, but whatever it did, he didn't like that it had those beautiful blue eyes looking so sad. Taking a step forward, she took a step back. "So then finish what you started saying," she said, lifting a very pretty but stubborn little chin. "Remember you're the one who said no guessing games."

Taking another step toward her, he stopped when she moved away from him again. "Okay, let's not do this," he said, pointing at the recliner. "Can we just sit and talk?"

"No!" She walked around the sofa and stood behind it, making it a barrier between them. "I will not sit on your lap again to talk about *this*. Just explain yourself."

She looked so damn cute when she was angry he had to smile. "All right, you don't have to sit on my lap. Just sit, please." He motioned at the sofa in front of her.

Considering it for a moment, she glanced down at the sofa, chewing the corner of her lip, then walked around and sat down cautiously. Hector took a few slow steps to the sofa, afraid that she might jump up and bolt. But she didn't, so he sat down.

He stared at her for a moment again, debating on how best to say this. "I don't know if I can handle this."

Her startled eyes stared at him. "You changed your mind?" Gulping hard, he reached for her hand, but she jerked it away, standing up. "Then go!"

The tears in her eyes had him on his feet instantly. "Charlee, it's not that I changed my mind. I swear it's just that..."

"Go!" She pointed to the front door. "You don't have to explain yourself. I don't mind *guessing*, Hector. Just leave."

He took her hand, and she tried pulling it away, but he held it tight. "Listen to me."

"No!" She was crying now, and it killed him, but he wouldn't let go of her hand even when she continued to try to free herself from him. "I don't even wanna hear it anymore. Just leave. I don't want you here!"

"Charlee," he tried, speaking calmly in order to calm her, but she was really crying now. "Listen to me, baby," he said as he backed her up to the wall, pressing his body against hers, trying to pin her down so he could talk to her—explain. But she kept squirming and fighting to get away from him. "I think I love you."

His words silenced her, and she stopped moving, staring at him as she continued to breathe harshly. He kissed the tears that continued to drip down the side of her cheek.

"I don't understand," she whispered, searching his eyes for answers.

Finally letting go of her hand, he cradled her face in his hands now. "I didn't even realize it until a few minutes ago," he wiped the corners of her wet eyes with his thumbs. "But I think I'm in love with you, Charlee, and if that's the case, I don't know if I can handle doing this and *you* changing *your* mind later."

She shook her head, her questioning eyes still searching his. "Why would I change my mind?"

"Sweetheart, you've never been with anyone else. How do you know for sure this is it for you?"

"I don't? Do *you*?"

He stared at her for a moment, feeling a little disappointed. Secretly he'd hoped she'd say she was, but her throwing it back in his face made him think. Was he?

"I don't know. All I know is if this happens—if we do this—I won't be able to handle it if you do."

She brought her hand up to his face and caressed it. For the first time since she'd become so upset, she smiled. "I think that's the chance everyone takes when they give into their hearts. I don't think I'd be able to handle it either if you changed your mind." She glanced away, giving way to that timid smile he *knew* he was in love with now. "I think we just got a little taste of how I'd handle it if you did." She kissed him softly, and he kissed her back, wrapping his arms around her waist. "I'd still be willing to chance it if you are."

Squeezing her even tighter, he buried his face in her neck, breathing her in. He loved the way she smelled, loved the way her small frame fit so perfectly against his body.

"I can promise you one thing," she whispered in his ear as she ran her hands through his hair. She had his attention, and he pulled away to look at her. He sensed a little hesitation before she spoke again, and there was a hint of insecurity in her eyes. "Unless I'm way off, and I have been in the past, unless you are this talented of an actor and the sincerity I'm feeling when you speak of your feelings for me—this trust that you've talked about taking so seriously isn't all real—then I promise you that can't imagine *anything* making me change my mind about you."

Seeing the insecurity in her eyes gave him a little hope that he wasn't alone in just how damn scared this made him. His brother may be older and wiser, but when it came to love, he was just as inexperienced as Hector. This wasn't something you just decided you were going to do. It was something that happened, and there was nothing in your power to stop it.

"I love you," he whispered, and she smiled, her big blue eyes immediately flooding with tears.

"This is crazy, but I love you too."

His heart pounded away with fear, excitement, and now exhilaration of knowing she was in love with him too. Picking her up like he had yesterday, he kissed her deeply. With both her arms and legs wrapped around him now, he started toward the sofa, but she pulled away and pointed. "My bedroom is that way."

God help him. This was really going to happen. *Screw the fear.* Hurrying toward her bedroom, he kissed her madly. He'd deal with his fears later. There was no choice now. Either he learned to handle what Abel thought and what Hector had begun to believe that he couldn't handle, or he walked away, and he wouldn't even consider that now.

Laying her down gently on the bed, he scooted onto it with her. Their lips never once parted even as he lifted his body over hers. Continuing to kiss her, he stopped every now and then to stare at her lips. He loved how red and swollen they were. The fact that he was responsible for how damn sexy they looked now drove him nuts.

Bringing her arms up above her head like he'd pinned her down earlier in the front room, he laced his fingers through hers, staring into her eyes. He leaned in and slowly began to kiss her freckles like he'd imagined doing when he first noticed them. He started on her forehead, kissing each freckle softly, and then he worked his way down her temple.

Rubbing himself against her leg, he wanted her to feel just how aroused doing just this made him. She squirmed in reaction to feeling him, and he began to sway his body very slowly against her like he'd begun to earlier but had stopped. Only now, he didn't stop, and she swayed with him, spreading her legs a bit. Knowing if he adjusted himself just slightly he could be rubbing up against the very spot that would drive them both crazy, he didn't. He wanted to— needed to—take this as slowly as possible. This may be the first time for her ever, but it was a first for him as well, and he wanted to savor every moment. Savoring it drowned out the enormous fear he'd begun to feel earlier about making *love* for the very first time, putting his heart out there as he never had before.

Working his way down the warm soft flesh of her face, he reminded himself, as he mentally was already beginning to claim each and every one of her beautiful freckles as his, that he could handle this. He kissed the freckles on her nose just under her eyes and around her delicate cheek bone, and then he worked his way down her jaw but couldn't help going back to bury his tongue in her red swollen mouth again. She kissed him back urgently, lifting her legs around his so his thigh rested now on the heat between her legs. Imagining burying himself in another red swollen part of her body had him squeezing his eyes shut now. He had to hold it together, or this might get embarrassing.

He began to ease her sweater up, and she sat up, helping him with it. She pulled it over her head and disposed of it quickly over the side of the bed. Awestruck, he stared at the milky white skin on her shoulders, chest, and flat stomach. There were so many more freckles for him to claim sprinkled all across her torso.

Starting just under her chin, he began kissing his way down. He kissed and sucked softly, down to the very edge of each shoulder. Pulling the straps of her bra down her shoulders, he brought it down until both of her beautifully pale breasts were completely exposed. Hector stared at them. They didn't get any more perfect than this—perfectly full, pure, untouched, and his mind once again went there—*all his.*

With his breathing accelerating, he focused on the coat of freckles sprinkled all over them. The coat was heavier around her cleavage and the only hint of color on her otherwise powdery white skin, aside from the very pale pink nipples that almost blended with the skin around them. He quickly latched onto one with his mouth, sucking softly then biting down gently. Hearing her soft panting and breathing grow even more frantic only made him suck harder.

Trying desperately to keep moving slowly was a challenge, especially now that her body trembled uncontrollably with every suck of her sweet nipples. He stopped for a second to pull off his shirt, needing to feel her flesh against his. She took that moment to undo her bra completely and took it off. Now she was completely naked from the waist up. He stared down, gulping hard. It took everything in him not to reach down and rip her pants off her. He wanted nothing more than to drive into her now—claim her. But *why* did the very thought still scare him so much?

Easing himself back down, his heart galloped away furiously.

"The heart is forever inexperienced," Charlee whispered, and Hector froze, staring at her.

"What did you say?"

She reached her hand up and touched his chest with her fingers. "Henry David Thoreau. There's something I didn't know about you, that you're into poetry, but I've also wondered for a long time what this was," she smiled timidly, biting her lower lip but continued touch his chest. "I even Googled your name and the word tattoo to see if I got a hit and nothing." Tracing the words with her fingers, she glanced at him then back at his chest. "What does that mean to you? And the broken heart." She lifted her eyes to him again, a bit confused, her own naked chest rising and falling from her still accelerated breathing. "Your heart's been broken?"

"Yes," he whispered, lowering himself onto her, "but not like you're thinking."

Jack's words couldn't have come at a better time. "The letters on the bottom are the initials of Jack, the late founder of 5th Street, and the only father figure Abel and I had since our dad died. I'm not big on poetry. It's just something he used to say to us a lot."

She nodded, her eyes full of understanding now. "I've read about Jack."

Hector rested his elbows and lower arms on either side of Charlee's face and kissed her softly, licking her lower lip, still so swollen and so red. Hearing Jack's words at this very moment was exactly what he needed. He'd said these very words to him and the guys often. Hector knew what it meant but didn't quite get it. It wasn't until he had to endure the loss of his good friend and mentor that he understood.

The loss of his own father had come at an early age, but Hector had still agonized over it. Losing Jack hadn't been any easier for him or Abel, nor had it been for Gio or Noah, who, like them, had also been through a loss of that magnitude. The heart didn't hurt any less because of their past experiences. Jack's words had come barreling down on him the days after his passing. That's why he chose to have those words forever be a part of him. So that he'd never forget that. Now here they were, reminding him of what he needed to focus on right now. Handling what he felt for Charlee would never get any easier. Nor would the exhilaration he felt being with her, kissing her, and making her his ever lessen. He may as well give into what his heart wanted now and start making her his so he could continue to do so over and over again.

Reaching down, he slipped his hand into her leggings as he continued to suck her soft lips. As he slipped his hand lower and she spread her legs for him, gasping against his lips, his heart took a flying leap when he felt the soft hair just above where his fingers were headed. She wasn't clean shaven like most of the girls he'd been with.

Smiling, he thought about how the less-experienced girls were the ones that obsessed less about these things, and this was just further proof of how inexperienced Charlee really was. He moved his fingers further down, skin to skin with the very hot place he'd only felt through her leggings earlier. And though he'd felt her pulsating through the fabric, it didn't compare at all to feeling the moisture on his fingers now.

He could hardly stand it anymore, plunging his tongue deep in her mouth, doing to her mouth what he wanted to be doing to her body already. He heard her boots drop, and he knew she'd kicked them off. She wanted it as much as he did.

While his fingers toyed with her soft, wet, pulsating folds, his other hand began to pull her leggings down. Charlee lifted her behind and helped him pulling her leggings along with her pink lacy panties down her legs. Hector had to move his hand away from her sweet wetness to pull everything completely off. He didn't think his heart could beat any harder until he looked down and saw her lying there completely naked now. Even though he'd just kissed and tasted many parts of her body, seeing her lying there like that, her freckles adorning every crevice of her delicately powdery white body, took his breath away.

As his eyes moved down her slowly, he froze, staring between her legs. He couldn't move his eyes away from the very neatly trimmed almost see-through perfectly heart-shaped patch of red hair. Finally he looked up at her. She lifted herself on her elbows and watched him now, her face slightly tinged with color. "You did that?"

She nodded that timid smile, relieving a tension he didn't even realize had built. "Last night."

Glancing back to it because he had to look at it again, he smiled now. "For me? But how'd you know . . ." He reached down to touch it, caressing the soft hair with his fingers.

"I didn't," she whispered, her breath catching at his touch. "It just felt good having a little secret all day and knowing if by chance we did get this far you might like it."

"I do," he said, slipping his finger down past the heart-shaped patch now and into her moist slit.

She gasped, spreading her legs, letting her head fall back. With his other hand, he began undoing his zipper, his body taut and ready for what was about to happen. Pulling the condom out of his wallet and ripping the package with his teeth, he sunk his finger in her, surprised at just how ready she was. As he slipped the condom on with one hand, he slipped another finger into her, keeping his eyes on her face, waiting for any signs of pain or discomfort. Charlee squirmed, arching her back as he rubbed his thumb exactly where he knew he'd make her moan. Bringing his leg over her body, he spread her beneath him.

Charlee lifted her hips. "Do it," her whispered pleas drove him insane. "I want you in me *now*."

He brought his arms down either side of her face again and kissed her hard. "I wanna be in you, baby."

"Then do it," she said, breathlessly wrapping her arms around her neck and lifting her face to kiss him just as frantically as he felt.

Hector had been with plenty of girls, but at the moment, he felt too dazed to remember if any of them had been virgins. For a virgin, Charlee hardly seemed nervous, or maybe it was his being such a wuss-ass that made her urgency feel that much bolder. Her legs were now spread as far apart as he needed, and he began working his way in her slowly, but there was no resistance as he'd imagined. She *was* tight, but looking at her face now as he entered her, he saw nothing but pleasure. "You okay?" he grunted as he forced himself to go slowly.

"Yes," she gasped, lifting her hips up, making him slip in deeper.

There was still no resistance or discomfort on her part, and now she wrapped her legs around him. *Fuck it.* He plunged deep into her with a groan, making her cry out. But they were cries of pleasure not pain. "Yes!" she said through her panting as he pumped her harder and harder. "Oh *yes!*"

Maybe she lied about being a virgin. At that moment, he didn't give a shit. He rammed in her hard, plunging his tongue in her mouth with the same force. Again and again, he thrust deeper and deeper as she panted and moaned in the pleasure of it.

Pulling her arms tighter around his neck, she lifted her hips as he thrust in her. Seeing her enjoy it so much confused him a bit but not enough to slow him down. "That feels *so* good, Hector." Her expression was anything but pained like he might've expected. Even her strained request just before she sunk her teeth into her bottom lip came as a complete surprise. "*Harder!*"

Blissfully, he obliged, but this was *not* how he'd imagined making love to Charlee the first time would be. He'd fully prepared himself to take things as slow as she needed him to, be as gentle as he had to be. But he had to admit fucking sweet little Charlee like this—like she begged him to—and feeling her claw her nails into his shoulders as she cried out was hot as shit.

Lifting himself so his arms weren't at either side of her and he was on his knees now, he slowed only because he didn't want it to end this soon. He wanted to rock into her like this forever. But she lifted her hips into him. "Don't stop!" she gasped. "Please don't stop!" Letting her head fall back again and seeing her closing her eyes, he could feel her body begin those familiar spasms he felt earlier. "Please don't *ever* stop."

Knowing how close they both were now, he grabbed her small waist with both hands and drove into her hard, making her cry out and moan at once. Her back arched in anticipation of what was building. She was so wet their bodies slapped loudly as he pounded into her, feeling his own climax building. Thrusting into her a few more times, he finally drove all the way in, feeling an explosion like none he'd ever felt.

Charlee's chest heaved up and down now as she squeezed her eyes shut, moaning in delight. Holding her by the waist up against him still, he gulped hard in an effort to catch his breath. He glanced down at the heart-shaped patch, now slickly wet and even brighter red, and smiled. "Maybe you could shave an H in the middle of it," he said.

He glanced up as she opened her eyes slowly, still breathing heavily. "Into what?"

Looking back down at it, he touched it, smiling even bigger then glanced back up at her. "The heart."

"Why?" She tilted her head with a smirk. "So that anyone who sees it knows it's yours?"

That wiped the smile right off his face. He moved his hand down from the back of her small waist and spanked her behind. "Not funny."

He didn't spank her very hard, but it was hard enough to make her yelp then laugh. "Ow!"

He stared at her wicked smile for a moment, and if he weren't mistaken, she liked that. Well, hot damn, he never would've guessed this is what his sex life with Charlee would be like. He collapsed onto her, instantly feeling aroused again, and devoured her equally eager mouth.

CHAPTER 27

Opening one eye slowly and then the other, memories of the night Charlee had had with Hector began warming her still-half-asleep body. She didn't even remember falling asleep, but she was surprised Hector still lay next to her. The light that crept in from the tiny crevices between the closed blinds meant only one thing: it was morning.

Hector held her still-naked body tightly against his own. She glanced at the clock and saw she had less than an hour to get ready and out of there if she was going to make it to class in time to make her presentation. If it weren't because she knew she'd startle Hector out of his sleep, she'd groan as loudly as she felt like groaning. Why today of all days did she absolutely have to be at school? Any other day she could've easily missed.

Slipping out from under his big arm, she got out of bed and threw on a t-shirt and shorts. She tiptoed out of the room and down the hall to the bathroom. He already knew about the class she couldn't miss today when she explained where Drew was last night and why Charlee hadn't gone with her. Curse the damn presentation. Her only consolation was that there would be more nights like last night. She'd make sure of it.

As she showered, she closed her eyes, breathing in deeply, remembering all the things she and Hector had done last night. She couldn't help smiling, feeling aroused at the very thought.

Once out of the shower, she brushed her teeth and stared in the mirror. Her breasts were covered with red spots—hickeys. She didn't remember him sucking that hard at all, but her skin was so fair he didn't have to suck hard at all to leave a mark. Looking down, she saw these love bites were everywhere, even on her inner thighs, and those were a bit darker. Feeling a surge of arousal remembering what he'd been doing between her legs, she took a deep breath.

After examining all the evidence of their amazing night, she tiptoed back to the room. He was still asleep. She stared at him for a moment. It hadn't been a dream. This was really happening. Her insides were doing that little victory dance again, and she couldn't help smiling. Hector was her boyfriend, her lover, but most thrilling and almost unbelievable—he said he was in love with her.

She didn't even realize she was staring ahead but at nothing in particular lost in thought, until she heard his voice. "Are you sore?"

He was up on his elbow now, looking at her a bit concerned. How was it that even first thing in the morning and a bit disheveled he was still so perfect? She shook her head, smiling. "No." She bit her bottom lip. "Are you?"

The corner of his lip lifted as he brought his legs over the side of the bed. "Not at all." He stretched, letting out a very satisfied groan. "But my body hasn't felt this content in," he paused, reaching for his boxer briefs on the floor then looked up at her, "ever."

Knowing she was now smiling silly, she glanced away, not wanting to be too obvious about how giddy everything about last night and this morning made her.

"I'll be back." He stood up and walked out of the room.

Snapping back into reality, Charlee cursed her damn presentation again as she sifted through her drawers for clean underwear. Hector was back in the room in minutes. It surprised Charlee that he didn't put on his clothes. Instead, he sat on the corner of the bed in his underwear silently. His eyes followed every move she made as she walked from one side of the room to the other, holding her towel together at her chest. Secretly enjoying how his eyes practically ate her up, she finally stopped and smiled. "What?"

"Nothing," he smirked. "I just like watching you." He shrugged then admitted. "Okay, I'm waiting for that towel to come off."

Biting her lower lip, her eyes traveled downward. Her heart sputtered at the sight of the massive erection pushing against his briefs that he did nothing to hide. Glancing back up, his eyes smoldered now, heating her insides instantly.

All right, maybe she couldn't miss her class, but she could be a little late. Her eyes raced over to the nightstand next to her bed. Among the several opened packets of condoms, she saw a sealed one. She walked over and picked it up then walked back to Hector and handed it to him. "Put it on."

She watched as he slid his briefs off then slipped the condom on. He began to make a move off the bed, but she placed her hand on his big shoulder. "No, stay there."

She dropped the towel and his eyes opened wide. Immediately, he reached for her, slipping his big arms around her waist. Running her fingers through his hair, she kissed him more passionately than she had planned to, sucking and savoring what she recognized as her mouthwash. She couldn't help it. Feeling his big, hard, naked body against hers again made her crazy. Already parts of her body were beginning to quiver. He pulled away from her mouth and took her breast in his mouth, running his hands all over her back. "*Damn*, Charlee," he said against her nipple before biting on it softly, making her cry out in pleasure.

As she brought her knee up on the bed, Hector grabbed her ass with both hands and squeezed hard. She gasped as she lifted her other knee onto the bed and straddled him. Hector squeezed her ass even harder as she slid onto him. The second she felt him going in, she slammed down, and wrapped her legs around his waist and her arms around his neck, loving how deeply she felt him this way. How many times had she fantasized about being completely wrapped around and literally a part of him like this?

It was as incredible as she'd imagined, and she swayed her hips in sync with his, lifting and slamming her back down on him. She spread even more, wanting him in as deep as possible. Every slide up and down on him rubbed that perfect spot, and she felt ready to come already. She moaned as she felt her climax building, and he began to slam her down onto him even harder. "Come, baby," he urged against her ear.

Holding on to him tightly, she began to come undone, crying out as a current of pleasure shot through her entire body. Groaning loudly, Hector slammed her down one last time with a harsh grunt, and his entire body went rigid.

With their hearts pounding at each other's chests, they held each other that way until their breathing began to ease. "You're gonna be late," he said against her neck without moving.

"I don't care," she responded also not moving an inch.

He laughed lightly then spanked her behind softly. It was much softer than he had last night, but it still made her smile. "You start that up, and I won't make it to class at all."

Now he pulled away and looked at her with a strange smile. "You really like that?"

She lifted an eyebrow, suddenly feeling a little self-conscious. "Maybe."

"No guessing games, Charlee," he warned. "How can you be into that if before last night you were a virgin?"

Seeing the suspicion in his eye, Charlee knew exactly what he must be thinking. She started to move off him, but he held her down. One hand held her waist and the other squeezed her behind again. "Look. I don't care if you weren't. I just wanna know why you thought you had to lie."

"I didn't lie."

"But . . ." He stared at her, and she knew what his eyes were saying.

Her behavior last night and today had been nothing like that of a naive and apprehensive virgin. Maybe she should've been less eager, but with him, that was impossible. Now she'd be forced to tell him something so incredibly embarrassing. Cupping his face with her hands, she kissed him. "Okay, no guessing games, but it's not something I can explain in just a few minutes. I'm already late."

He loosened his hold on her waist but squeezed her ass again. "Tonight we talk." With an evil smile, he added. "We were supposed to yesterday, until you took advantage of me. I feel so used."

She laughed, getting off him. "Poor guy." Smiling that evil little smile she got the feeling he liked a little too much, she bit her bottom lip. "I promise to behave tonight."

"Whoa, whoa, whoa!" He said quickly and pulling her by the hand toward him, "I didn't say all that."

Laughing, she kissed him again but assured him. "Okay, but tonight we will talk."

They both stood up, and for a moment, they both walked around her bedroom completely naked and it nearly dazed her. He disposed of the condom while she searched for the panties she'd held in her hand just prior to dropping everything and straddling him. How her life had suddenly changed so drastically in such a short span of time was still unbelievable to her.

***

Not surprisingly, Charlee spent her entire day, trying to concentrate on whatever she was doing to no avail. Her mind kept wandering, and she kept getting hot flashes. When she wasn't having thoughts that had her dampening her panties, she was struggling to calm her anxiety about the conversation she'd be having with him tonight.

What did come as an unpleasant surprise was how detached and indifferent Hector had behaved in the chess lab. While he did sit with her and pecked her softly one time, he was very reserved the rest of the time. She didn't expect him to be all over her, but the way he'd acted, even around his friends and family, she was sort of expecting him to be a little more affectionate. It felt almost as if he didn't want anyone to know about them.

She tried to not read too much into it. At first, she thought maybe he was just trying to be private about it. Maybe he was reserved about these kinds of things in public. Then she remembered the shameless little show he put on with those two whores in the parking lot just after the tournament and how he hadn't seemed to care at all if anyone saw him making out with not one but two girls.

Even after the lab as they walked with Walter and a few of the other guys to the parking lot, he hadn't even held her hand. It wasn't until they were in the privacy of his truck that he'd practically attacked her. If she weren't so instantly and incredibly turned on by it, she might've had the presence of mind to push him off her sooner. It took a while, but the more she thought about it, even as he sucked away at her tongue and lips, her lifelong battle with insecurity resurfaced, and she pulled off and slid away from him, quickly moving closer to the door.

He stared at her breathlessly, his brows furrowing immediately. "What's wrong?"

Trying desperately to squash any memories of Danny and how easily she'd been duped by him, she reminded herself this was completely different. Hector said he loved her and she believed him. He wasn't ashamed of her, and there was no damn reason for him to be. She wasn't that freak anymore.

Still overcome with emotion and unable to put into words what she was feeling, she reached for the door handle.

"Where you going?"

"I gotta go," was all she could manage to say, but he reached for her hand and held it.

"Wait. What's wrong? What did I do?" She tried opening the door and pulling her hand away, but he held it tight. "Charlee talk to me," he insisted, his voice as panicked as she felt. "This is why I said no guessing games. I suck at this. I'm totally lost here. Just tell me what I did."

She gave up trying to get out of the truck and let her head fall back against the seat and tried gulping back the enormous boulder lodged in her throat now. "You'll think I'm petty."

"No, I won't," he said, quickly bringing his arm around her waist and sliding her closer to him. "Tell me," he whispered in her ear.

That alone was enough to make her shiver even at a moment like this. Maybe she *was* a freak. She turned to face him. "It felt almost as if you were pretending nothing's happened between us again while there were people around. Then as soon as we were alone, it was okay to do," she touched his arm that held her close now, "this."

This time, he let his head fall back. "I *was* pretending nothing happened."

Her heart dropped, and she straightened out this time, successfully managing to pull away from him. "I knew it." She opened the door and rushed out, slamming it behind her.

Hector was immediately out of the truck too. "Charlee wait!" She saw him rush around to catch her just a few parking spaces away, jumping in front of her. The moment he was face to face with her and saw her tears, his face went hard. "Fuck! I knew I should've just told you."

"Told me what?" She searched his angry eyes. Her heart couldn't take any more. If it was anything like what she was thinking, she was flying home tonight and never looking back.

"I was pretending, but not around everyone, just Walter."

She stared at him, breathing hard as he wiped the tears from her face. "Walter?"

"Yes. He's the reason why I didn't try anything with you sooner." He spoke quickly and deliberately now. "He's why I asked you pretend nothing happened after that first kiss. He was totally into you, and I was supposed to be helping him impress you, but then I started falling for you. I tried my damnedest to fight it, but I couldn't. It wasn't until he told me he'd started seeing his grandfather's nurse that I asked him if he was okay with me asking you out."

He took a deep breath, pulling her to him, and wrapped his arms around her. She wrapped her arms around him, still processing everything he'd just said. He'd been helping Walter try to impress her? Walter was seeing Natalie now. But most importantly Hector wasn't ashamed of her?

Pulling away but still holding her hand, he continued. "That was Saturday. I called you as soon as I finished talking to him, but he'd asked me not to mention his being all into you. He said it was embarrassing, so I didn't think it was a big deal if I left that whole part out. Then tonight . . . It just felt weird. I know he's seeing someone else now, but realizing how quick I was to move in on the girl he'd been pining for all this time, I kind of felt like an asshole, so I thought I'd at least tone it down a little, maybe give it some time before I'm all over you in front of him." He shook his head, still wiping the corners of her eyes. "I'm sorry. I should've just told you all this Saturday." His expression went from deeply regretful to suddenly concerned. "But seriously, babe, why are you so quick to believe the worst? Did that sleazy first impression you had of me really stick that hard?"

"I never thought you were sleazy," she frowned. "I told you, you made the most unforgettable first impression on me. Remember?"

"Yeah, but then I went and made that shithead move, asking you to pretend that night never happened."

She nodded, glancing down. "I know, but I still never thought you were sleazy." She kept it to herself that she and Drew did think him a pig after seeing him with those girls, but who was she kidding? The very next time she saw him, she was ready to let him kiss her regardless.

"So why jump and think the worst so fast?" He peered at her. "Talk to me, Charlee. I told you I'd try my damnedest to get this right, and I'm going to, but you need to help me out here. I don't wanna have to worry you're going to run off every time you think the worst." He leaned his face sideways, looking into her eyes. "Tell me. What's it gonna take to get you to believe I'm not a sleaze and I do love you. I just make stupid mistakes sometimes, but I'd never purposely hurt you."

Charlee took a deep breath, feeling the enormous relief she'd felt a moment ago replaced with slow-boiling anxiety. "First of all, stop saying that. You're not a sleaze, and I never thought you were one, but," she glanced around then back at him, "you are right about one thing." He lifted his brow now, waiting. "I am too quick to jump and think the worst." She scoffed, shaking her head. "I was already having visions of jumping on a plane home tonight and never coming back."

"What?" He spit the word out staring at her.

She wasn't sure if he was more shocked at that or hurt, and, already, she regretted admitting it.

"Are you kidding me?" If it weren't for the hurt in his eyes, she'd think him furious. "Just like that you'd walk away?"

"It's what I was going to talk to you about tonight."

"Well then, talk."

"Right here?"

"Yes, right here, right now, because you just scared the crap outta me."

She shook her head, reaching out for his hand, and he took it. "I didn't mean to."

He touched her hair, his expression softening a bit, and stared deep in her eyes. "Okay, but you did. So tell me."

She wasn't sure where to start, and she sure as heck hadn't planned on having this conversation with him here in the middle of the school parking lot, but he seemed adamant. "It's long, Hector. It goes back to when I was a little girl."

He startled her by putting his arms around her suddenly and hugging her. The hug was a tight one, and she loved being in the warmth of his big arms. She gave into it completely, leaning her face against his chest. "I'm sorry I made you cry and think whatever it is you were thinking, okay?" She nodded without pulling away from his chest. "You forgive me?" She nodded again. "Are you in a hurry to be anywhere right now?"

She shook her head, smiling at how quick she'd gone from feeling mortified and hurt to utterly in love again.

"Good," he loosened his hold on her and pulled away. "Because that's twice that you've lost it on me and like that." He snapped his fingers. "And I need to know what the hell I'm doing wrong so that doesn't happen again, so start talking, and we'll go grab something to eat, but the whole time you talk. I have all the time in the world tonight, so I don't care how long it is."

She nodded in agreement. This was it. He'd either think her a pathetic freak or this would prove once in for all he really as wonderful as she suspected and she could finally trust that this wasn't too good to be true.

They started back to his truck. "I'm listening," he said.

Oh boy. It was now or never, so she may as well get it over with.

CHAPTER 28

"I've always been very awkward," Charlee began, "very shy, so bad that I had to be homeschooled because my socializing skills were non-existent."

They stopped just outside his truck, and she glanced up at him for a reaction, but at the moment, he reminded her of his brother because his expression gave nothing away.

"My mom coaxed me into trying to go to public school a few times, but each time it was disastrous."

"Why?"

"I haven't always looked this way. My hair isn't really straight either, it's super curly." He smiled. "But not like Roni's, okay? We're talking nappy curly. Add that to it being bright red with a face full of freckles and me being so incredibly shy that I'd turn bright red the moment any teachers called on me in class. I hated having all eyes on me, and I hated having to speak up, because every time I did, I'd flub my words. Once the kids caught on to how easily they could make me turn beet red, I was an easy target. I became their entertainment." He wasn't smiling anymore. Now she saw his jaw working. "None of the girls wanted to be friends with Charlee the Freak, and even though I had Drew, who had been my friend since we were babies, she couldn't always be there, so I begged my mom to take me out again and just let me be homeschooled."

Hector opened the door for her and she got in. As soon as he was in his side, he kissed her but then asked her to continue as he slipped the key in the ignition.

"Anyway, we tried it again in middle school, and, God, that was even worse. I didn't even last a week." Taking a very deep breath, she braced herself before getting the next part out. "There was a boy who lived up the street from me named Danny. I used to watch him from my window as he and his friends walked to school. He was one of the only popular kids who was actually nice to me, and by nice, I mean he didn't throw food at me or taunt me. He hung out with some of the kids that did, but he never joined them. And he even smiled at me a few times."

Sitting this close to Hector, she noticed his body go stiff, and he gripped the steering wheel a little tighter. "But he never stopped them from taunting you?"

She shook her head. "No, but silly me, just because he smiled at me, didn't actually do the taunting, and, of course, because he was popular and cute, I made him out to be some kind of prince. For years as I watched him go by my house to school, I daydreamed of him and harbored this massive crush on him."

He squeezed her leg, and she decided to spare him the details of all the doodling she did writing her and Danny's name all over her notebooks and journals. "By the time I was old enough to go to high school, I tried again freshman year, and that was another disaster. Looking back, I realize it was me being too weak to fight back or stand up for myself. But I was so shy it was paralyzing." She cleared her voice, realizing this is where the explanation about her behavior last night began. "As shy as I was, I was still your typical teenager with raging hormones. But as awkward as I was, I knew, or at least I believed very strongly, that I would probably never even be kissed much less experience anything more than just kissing. But as a young girl, I still daydreamed about it—a lot, especially every time I'd watch Danny walk by my house."

Again he squeezed her leg, and she straightened up a little, feeling her face warm by what she was about to say next. "Like any normal teenage girl," she turned to him, making sure he got this part, "because I'd been called a freak so often, I read up on it and looked it up on the internet. It was totally normal," she waited until he nodded. "I started doing things—touching myself."

He turned to her with a smirk.

"It's not funny," she said quickly.

"I'm not laughing," he responded just as quick. "I'm just visualizing it."

She nudged him, pressing her lips together. He's seen you naked. You've made love to him. You rode him this very morning, and any badass cowgirl would've been proud. You can tell him this.

"Anyway, as the years passed, I graduated from just touching to doing other things." She squeezed his leg now as he sat up, adjusting his pants. "Don't you dare ask for details. Just use your imagination. You'll probably be right."

He stared straight ahead, smiling, pulling into the parking lot of a charbroiled burger joint, parked, and then leaned against his door. "Okay, I guarantee you my imagination is going nuts right now, but, please, go on."

Charlee rolled her eyes, deciding not to further that part of her story until she had to. "So fast forward to senior year or rather the summer before I would've started my senior year in high school. The town I lived in was small, and everyone knew everyone else. I'd been labeled by all the kids as Charlee, the redheaded freak who couldn't even deal with high school. Drew refused to admit it, but I knew what everyone thought of me, and I had long ago accepted it. At that point it didn't matter. I hadn't planned on ever going back to that school anyway." She glanced down at his hand as he squeezed hers, hoping he wasn't pitying her. "Drew was doing everything she could to convince me to enroll for senior year, and let me tell you that girl can be persuasive."

He chuckled. "I don't know her too well, but she seems as though she can make a pretty good argument. I still have to thank her for convincing you to move out here."

Charlee smiled sideways, feeling bittersweet. "Danny had a hand in that decision too."

Hector's smile immediately went flat. "Fuck that. I ain't thanking him."

Soothing his suddenly tight upper thigh muscles with her hand, Charlee continued. "Now what I'm gonna share next stays strictly between you and me. It's something very personal about Drew." She paused until he nodded. "Right around that time, Drew's parents separated. It was sort of this big local scandal. Her dad was always gone like he is now, and her mom started having an affair with her brother's travel team baseball coach." Charlee shook her head, remembering how devastated Drew had been. "The coach was also married, and his son was also on the team. All the other parents were appalled because apparently the coach's wife was so very much involved with the team and well-liked that people took sides, and the team eventually fell apart. It was just a big mess. So only after having to see Drew go through all this did I begin to consider enrolling senior year. She said she needed me there for her. This happened during that summer, so she was dreading going back to school and have everyone talking about it."

He watched her intently, and now she had to tell him why she was ready to run the moment she suspected he wasn't being completely honest or that by chance he was secretly ashamed of her. "Since Danny lived up the street, we often ran into him at the local burger joint or convenience store up the street, and like he'd always been, he was nice to me: said hello, smiled, and was polite." Even though Drew had been right about Hector, Charlee still couldn't help roll her eyes having to explain the next part. "Drew's always said she has this sixth sense about certain things, and she started to insist she was picking up on something from Danny when he looked at me and smiled at me. Of course, I didn't buy it for a second. I was Charlee the Freak, and he was the popular good-looking jock in high school, but she insisted there was something about the way he looked at me. She said the same thing about you, by the way, when we first met you at the tournament."

Hector lifted an eyebrow. "Did she now?"

"Yep," Charlee nodded.

"And she picked up on the same thing from this guy?"

"Yes, but she was totally wrong about him. Only I've mentioned how persuasive she can be, right?" He smiled but it was strangely strained. "She kept insisting that every time we ran into him he stared at me a little too long or was a little too smiley or whatever. Finally, she asked him straight out when she ran into him at the library one day, and he said he thought I was cute and there was something special about me, so she gave him my number! Next thing you know he's texting me and calling me, and Drew's all full of herself." Charlee couldn't help laugh, but there was no humor in it. "I knew it! I called it! I knew he was into you and then . . ." She paused, unbelievably still feeling the hurt seep in. "After several long, very deep conversations with him where I really thought I began to feel a connection and he was so damn sweet, he asked me to a party."

She didn't even realize she'd fallen deep into her thoughts until he interrupted them.

"Charlee?" Glancing up at him, there was no missing how undeniably hard his expression had gone. "You said you're over this guy, right?"

"Yes," she nodded, but she was sure she wasn't convincing. She hadn't allowed herself to relive this in so long she was certain he saw the hurt she was feeling from scraping old wounds open and not understanding why it still hurt so bad.

"Are you sure?"

She stared straight ahead, nodding, realizing her eyes were now flooding quickly with tears and Hector wasn't buying it for a second, but she couldn't help it. After all this time, she still couldn't believe Danny had done that to her. He'd been so sincere, so sweet. He called her Tangerine, damn it, because it was the name of his sister's orange cat, which he always pretended to hate but secretly liked holding and petting when no one was around. That should've been clue number one: when no one else was around. He said it was because of her hair and the cat was orange and sweet, but she knew better now.

"Are you crying for this guy right now?" Hector straightened up so abruptly his elbow hit the horn, and he raised his voice just a notch, but Charlee caught the anger loud and clear. "Is that what I'm sitting here watching and listening to?" The anger changed suddenly, and there was suspicion now—severe suspicion. "Did you and him—"

"It was dog party, Hector. Ever heard of them? You were probably on the other end of them, not on mine: a party by his football friends where they compete to bring the worst date, and he invited *me*."

He stared at her, his hardened expression looking more confused now. "What?"

"I was the dog, the schmuck, the fucking freak! And guess what? He won." The tears were really coming now, and she hated that it still hurt this bad even after all this time. But she continued even through the tears. "He won for having the biggest, freakiest, schmuckiest date! That was why he befriended me. This was why he was so sweet and spent all that time with me on the phone. I was special all right, but not the way he made it sound. And I went out and bought a dress and did my hair and did all the things excited high-school girls do when they're invited to a party by the boy of their dreams." She wiped her face with both her hands, angry that she could still get so worked up over this. "For once I felt normal, like I actually belonged with the crowd my age. Drew swore she knew he liked me all along: that she'd seen it in his face, heard it in his voice when he talked to me and about me. But it was all a lie."

Hector shook his head, his face still full of disbelief. "How the fuck did you win?"

"Because he coaxed Charlee the Freak out of her cave and got her to come to a high-school party where everyone could laugh and watch me turn beet red at the drop of dime. The worst thing was I didn't even know. I was actually proud that I'd gone through with it, and it wasn't until he took me home and refused to kiss me because he said he didn't deserve to that I knew something was wrong. Drew was there before he even left."

"How did you find out?" he asked, wiping more of her tears away.

"Drew," she said simply. "It was all over Facebook already, and she was there to warn me. She told me not to look, that I didn't want to. But I had to. Danny had been so sweet and so sincere the entire time I talked to him that I just couldn't believe he'd do that to me." She stared at the floor, a bit calmer now, but the memories she'd worked so hard to let go of all came flooding back so vividly. "They'd tagged me and him in all these congratulatory pictures of dogs in dresses and tiaras. It was mostly the guys from the party, but there were a lot from other random people in my neighborhood."

"Did he ever apologize or explain himself?" Hector cupped her hand in his, caressing it.

She shook her head. "I shut down my Facebook page and blocked him from being able to text me or call me. He did relay a message through Drew not too long after to say he was sorry, but I cut Drew short. I didn't even wanna hear his explanation. What more was there to say? The rules were simple: bring the most pathetic freak you can think of, and he chose me."

Taking a deep breath and glad that the tears were over, she decided she was done with this subject. She actually preferred to go back and talk about the more uncomfortable side of her being a freak now than this. "So as you can imagine after that, there was no way I was enrolling in school for senior year. Drew didn't even try to convince me anymore. She knew it wasn't happening after that. And the very idea that I'd ever show my face at any parties or anywhere in that town to socialize was completely buried. Drew dropped that as well. I was afraid to run into Danny, so I hardly left the house after that. I was certain that I was doomed to be a lonely hermit forever." She bit her lip and glanced at him quickly then looked away. "But I still had urges, strong ones now, and I really began to feel like the freak everyone made me out to be because I was doing it more often."

She wouldn't look at him now. How could she admit the next part?

"Charlee, babe," he said, kissing her hand. "I know it's embarrassing for you to admit, but not only are sexual urges normal sex in general is huge. Let me assure you, you are not the only one with urges. It's what marketing and advertisers bank on. They use sex to sell everything because that's how powerful it is. It goes all the way back. Why do you think all those famous sculptors who are hailed most for their tastefully artistic sculptures happen to be the ones who sculpted naked people? Artistic my ass, it's the sex appeal that everyone is drawn to. As freaky as it may've made you feel or think you were, it's perfectly normal."

She didn't want to argue, but he didn't know the half of it, and she had to explain last night. The look in his eye earlier when he thought she was crying because she might not be over Danny was telling of what he still might be wondering about her behavior last night. "I bought toys, Hector. At seventeen, I ordered stuff on the internet all on my own. No one encouraged me or told me about these toys. I looked them up all by myself, bought prepaid credit cards, and I purchased sex toys—more than one."

He seemed stunned for a moment but then regrouped looking almost relieved, not disgusted, and nodded. "And there you go. The adult toy and porn industry—huge. And why is that? Because sex sells. And why does it sell so much? Because it feels damn good. You're far from being alone on this, Charlee." Suddenly his face soured. "I just found out a few months ago my mom went to some party with her girlfriends and my aunts." He shuddered, pretending to gag with his hand at his neck. "She told us it was a sort of Tupperware party with margaritas and shit, and Abel and I found the flyer a few days later. It was an adult toy party. My mom!" He shook his head, looking absolutely disgusted. "As much as it makes my skin crawl, it's normal for everyone to be in touch with that side of themselves."

Amazingly, Charlee actually felt better now. She was even smiling and felt on the verge of laughing. "Well, it's why I was the way I was last night. I may never have been with any guy, and you are the very first person to touch me that way, but I had experienced certain things most virgins haven't, and I just assumed I was probably the only freak on the planet had done that to themselves."

"Are you kidding me?" Hector laughed. "Every guy in the history of man has been going at it long before they get any real action. And seriously? You really think you're the only girl who's done this?"

She shrugged, still unable to believe she'd actually told someone about this, and not just someone, Hector. He pulled her to him and kissed her forehead. "I don't think you're a freak at all, not like you're thinking anyway, but I do like that you're *freaky*." He slid his hand up her thigh, making her breath catch suddenly. "In fact, up until I brought my mom into the conversation and totally killed it, I don't remember ever being so damn turned on just listening to someone talk."

He kissed the side of her face, moving down her jaw. "In my defense," she said, feeling the shivers already from his soft kisses moving down her neck. As much as she wanted him to keep going, she needed to explain and make this very clear. "Until I moved out here, I really believed I'd never have a boyfriend and, therefore, no sexual encounters or pleasure aside from . . ."

"I get it, Charlee. I do," he assured her, pulling away to look at her, and lifted an eyebrow. "So what changed when you moved out here?"

She smiled softly. "That was the whole point of moving so far. So I could start over. Drew wanted to move away from her mom and the ongoing scandal, because after her parents separated, her brother's coach ended up leaving his wife for her mom. They're now engaged, and we both knew as long as I lived in that small town I'd continue to be the anti-social hermit I'd become, forever. So she convinced me to straighten my hair, get a new wardrobe, do my makeup so that my freckles weren't so blinding—"

"I like your freckles." Hector said very seriously.

"I know," she smiled. "That's why I'm not covering them anymore. My point is Drew is very good about getting things together once she has a plan." Hector nodded, smiling now. "So she convinced me to agree that once we were out here with this new transformation and fresh start because no one knew anything about me, I'd be open-minded about socializing."

He went in for her neck again, his tongue making her tremble. Moving his hand between her legs now, he bit down on her neck. "Are you really hungry right now?" he asked against her neck.

"Not for food," she said with a smile.

"You think Drew's home already?"

"Doesn't matter." Her breath caught as he licked then sucked just below her ear. "My bedroom door locks."

Pulling away from her suddenly, he stared at her. "You serious? She won't mind?"

"Nope," she smiled, feeling wickedly aroused already. "Knowing her, she'll be thrilled that I'm finally acting like a normal college girl."

Sticking the key in the ignition immediately, he turned on the truck and backed it up. Brimming with an unexpected feeling of inner tranquility, Charlee hadn't realized how good it would feel to finally tell someone her deepest secret. She was also glad to tell him about the incident in her life that that nearly broke her. She didn't think it possible, but having everything out in the open like this with Hector might make for even better sex. Squeezing his inner thigh and making him squirm, she leaned against his shoulder, the anticipation already intensifying.

CHAPTER 29

The rest of the week, Hector had to help with the move to the new house. He actually went a few days without seeing Charlee. Thursday was one of them. The one day he got out of moving duties early so he could surprise her at the chess lab when he'd already told her he wouldn't be there, he got a text from her just as he hurried through the campus.

> Since you weren't going to be there anyway, I decided to skip the lab today. Drew and I are shopping for some last minute things I need for this weekend's trip. I hate that we didn't get to see each other today, but I can hardly wait to spend the entire weekend with you. ;)

Stopping in his tracks as he finished reading her text, he nearly growled from the disappointment of it. His dumb ass should've just told her he was coming. He nearly spun around ready to head back to finish helping the guys with the move when he looked up and froze. Ross was lurking around the physics building, looking a little too suspicious for Hector's liking. Maybe his trip down here hadn't been a waste after all.

Starting toward him, he didn't miss the moment Ross saw him coming. Instantly, he stopped leaning against the railing on the staircase—the one Charlee would've walked up to get to chess lab.

With a little skip in his feet, Ross began rushing off in the opposite direction. "Don't make me chase you, asshole," Hector called out behind him, already picking up his own pace, "because I will."

With his adrenaline pumping at full speed, Hector was already having visions of chasing this guy down, tackling him on his ass and beating the living shit out of him. He didn't even care if it got him kicked off the chess team. One way or another, he'd get this creeper out of Charlee's life.

He calmed when he saw Ross slow down then stop all together. Abel's words came to him. *This shit's real now. You can get your ass thrown in jail.* Only because of this Hector didn't slam Ross up against a wall or even grab him by the shirt like he really wanted to. But he did walk up to him with a purpose and got in his face.

"You here looking for *my* girl again?"

Seeing the stunned look on Ross face only enraged Hector further, making him clench his fists. The guy shouldn't be so surprised. He'd seen Hector kiss her.

"I just wanted to—"

"Ask if you still have a chance?" Hector cut him off, his insides getting hotter by the second. "You don't." He gnashed his teeth. Remembering that this was the same guy who once wondered if Charlee was red *everywhere* made it even harder for Hector to hold back.

"I just want to apologize—"

Hector grabbed him by the shirt now. He was done listening to his bullshit. "You already have. She told me you did. Now you have a second to tell me why you're really here before I beat your creepy stalker ass into tomorrow."

"Okay, okay," Ross spoke quickly now. "I know she didn't buy my apology, so I just wanted to explain to her how that first day I met her that wasn't me. I was high and I'm not usually like that. Before that day, I'd never seen her once, and it seems like after that I saw her *everywhere*. It was driving me crazy. I hated that she still seemed so freaked out whenever I tried to talk to her. I wanted her to understand. I'm not a bad guy like she thinks."

Incredibly, this annoyed Hector even more. "Nah," he shook his head, "you *are* a bad guy. You don't get a second chance, not with *my* girl. And let me tell you something else. If I see your ass creeping around or I find out you're still trying to *explain* your stupid shit to her, I'm coming after you. Stay. The. *Fuck.* Away. From. Her. You hear me? You see her, you look the other way." Hector squeezed Ross's shirt even harder, nearly picking him off the floor. "This is the only warning you get." The second Ross nodded in understanding, Hector let him go. "Now go!"

Hector wanted him out of his face before he changed his mind about letting him off with just a warning. Not a bad guy his ass! He knew he promised both Charlee and Abel he'd be cool, but if that wasn't warning enough, the idiot deserved anything Hector did to him if he even thought about still coming around Charlee.

***

Friday hadn't come fast enough. Hector was now on at the airport ready to board a plane and spend the entire weekend with Charlee.

He took the moment she went to use the ladies' room as they waited to board to finally talk to Walter again about her. The guy had made some major progress on his weight loss, and from the looks of it seemed Natalie had dropped a few pounds herself as well. Hector hadn't been back to the old folk's home with Walter in a few weeks, but Natalie had dropped Walter off at the airport tonight, and while their goodbye kiss was awkward at best, Hector was fairly certain this was a huge step for Walter. "So I take it you and Natalie are getting serious."

Walter smiled sheepishly and nodded. "I guess. She's met my parents from all the times she's been around them at the hospital and having to talk to them when they asked her if she was interested in being my gramps' exclusive nurse. Now she's talking about me meeting her mom and grandma."

Hector smirked at Walter's uneasy expression. "That's good, right? You don't wanna meet them?"

Walter shrugged. "She's told me about them, and from what I gather, they're both hard asses. Not sure I'm ready for the inquisition."

Hector laughed now, for a second, the thought of Charlee's parents coming to mind. He'd gotten to know her a little better in the last few days, but she'd still told him very little about her family.

"You'll be all right," he assured Walter then decided to just put it out there. Walter had already witnessed them together at the lab, and since that first day when she'd been so upset about his lack of affection in public, Hector hadn't held back after that. "Charlee met my mom."

As expected, Walter seemed surprised. "Already?"

"Shit, first day," Hector laughed, leaning his elbows on his knees and put his hands together. Hector explained about his mom overhearing him and Abel and how she'd be gone the next day and as usual got her way

"I was worried too and it went fine. You should be too. Whatever you do, don't blow it by refusing. If she wants you to, just take one for the team and get it over with. You're going to have to eventually anyway."

Walter agreed with a shrug then smirked. "So you're serious, too, then? No more threesomes or juggling more than one hot babe at a time."

Hector sat up, glancing in Charlee's direction as she walked out of the ladies' room and walked toward them. "Nope, only one hot babe for me now."

"That's kind of hard to believe," Walter said also looking in Charlee's direction. "But since this is Charlee we're talking about, I can see how she'd make even a player like you wanna settle down."

"Well, she has," Hector said quickly. "Now shut up with the player talk."

Walter laughed just as Charlee reached them. "What's so funny?" she asked, smiling.

"Nothing, he's just being stupid," Hector gave Walter, who was still chuckling, a look. "C'mere." He reached out for her and sat her on his lap.

He could hardly wait for this weekend to start. Even though they'd booked two separate rooms for them, that wasn't happening, though they planned to make the most of both beds.

Once on the plane, Charlee snuggled up next to Hector. All three of them sat in the same row with Charlee in between him and Walter. Hector rubbed her leg openly. Any consideration for Walter's feelings was long gone. Walter had Natalie, and Charlee's feelings came first now. It still bothered him that, even for a minute, she'd think him capable of being as shady as that asshole that had done her so wrong. Though the fact that he and this guy did have something in common made him sick. They'd both stood idly by and watched without speaking up as their idiot friends picked on a weaker kid.

Hector pushed the thought aside and tried to focus on something more pleasant—Charlee's libido. As much as he wanted to reassure her that what she'd shared with him about her rabid sexual appetite was nothing compared to some of the real freaks he'd been with or heard the guys at the gym talk about, he wasn't going there. Being open and honest was one thing. Sharing about past conquests was quite another. Even if Charlee had ex-boyfriends or experiences with other guys, he had no desire to hear about the details. Just hearing about her feelings for Danny had been grating enough. He was certain she didn't need to hear the details of his previous relations with girls, even if they would make her see she wasn't nearly as freaky as she thought she was.

Still, she was just freaky enough to make him one happy guy. He didn't think it could get any better than this. He now had a girlfriend that craved sex just as much as he did.

Their flight was a late one and over five hours. Normally Hector would've been dreading such a long flight. He was used to the short ones to Vegas and Big Bear and into Hermosillo where his grandmother lived, but five hours sitting next to Charlee, after not having seen her yesterday, sounded like heaven now.

This entire week had been crazy. Between things moving so fast with him and Charlee and then moving all week, he hadn't really had a chance to think about it. It dawned on him now that he could finally put some thought into this trip. "Aren't we going to be close to your hometown?"

She leaned her head against his shoulder and nodded. "Less than an hour."

"Are you gonna try and get together with your mom or anything?" Without looking up or even answering, she simply shook her head. "Why not?"

"She's working all weekend," she said then yawned. "Twelve-hour shifts and then sleeping. Besides I don't think I'll have time."

That seemed odd. Here Charlee had mentioned she hadn't been back once since she'd moved out here, and now she'd be less than an hour from home, and she didn't want to stop in and visit? Frowning, he figured she wasn't anxious to revisit all the shit she'd been through or to run into any of those assholes in her small town that labeled her a freak. Squeezing his hand into a fist, he kissed the top of her head.

She didn't say anything else for a while, and when he looked down he saw she'd dozed off. He must've dozed off soon after that, because the next thing he knew, he woke up to the usual erection he always woke to, only this time Charlee's hand was wrapped around it, stroking him under a towel she'd thrown over him.

With her free hand, she covered his mouth as his eyes flew open, and she smiled that wicked smile that turned him on so much. For a moment, he considered protesting but instead let his head fall back as the pleasure of it was just too much. He did glance over at Walter, who was fast asleep next to Charlee. Charlee lifted her finger to her mouth with that same smile that drove him nuts and continued to stroke him. Okay, maybe she was a little freaky, but he certainly wasn't going to complain.

The cabin lights were all off and it was dim enough, but he wasn't sure how he'd get through this without making a sound. Already he was beginning to squirm, feeling the buildup. Not able to stand it, he brought his hand around the back of Charlee's neck and kissed her long and hard then froze when he thought he felt Walter move.

Looking over Charlee's shoulder, he could see Walter was still fast asleep. Charlee hadn't even flinched, continuing to stroke him until his toes were practically curling. He was too close now, and he didn't want to make a mess. "Do you have tissue?" he whispered, panicking because he could already tell this was going to be a messier than usual.

"Use the towel," she whispered in his ear, and as if he needed her to, she sped up the stroking.

Clasping the towel around himself, he held in the groan he wanted so badly to let out as he came epically in the towel. He squeezed his eyes shut, pushing his head back into the back of his seat, feeling any strength in his legs drain completely. Charlee leaned her head against his chest as her finger grazed the tip of the very tender area then pulled her hand out from under the towel.

Hector opened his eyes and smiled at her, his heart pounding so hard he was sure she could hear it and gave her the most pleading look he could. He couldn't take her touching it again even for another second. With that smile that was going to be the death of him, she brought the finger to her lips and licked it clean.

Immediately, he squeezed his eyes shut again, and she fell into his chest, muffling her giggling. "Shhh," he urged, putting his free arm around her.

Walter shifted in his seat but didn't wake. "Did I mention today how much I love you?" he whispered in her ear. Charlee nodded but didn't pull away from his chest.

"Well, let me just say it again," he whispered even lower this time. "I love my freaky little girlfriend."

Charlee giggled even louder this time, and he hugged her harder, muffling her laughter. Hector should've been trying to figure out how to clean the mess up as fast as possible before Walter woke. Instead, all he could think of was he had entire weekend of this to look forward to.

~*~

Arriving at their hotel at nearly three in the morning last night should've meant they'd be too exhausted for any funny business, but apparently not having slept together for over two days, Hector had a lot of making up for lost time planned. They'd been up for hours last night and were now paying the price. The meeting was purposely scheduled at ten to accommodate travelers like them who arrived so late by giving them some extra sleep time. Unfortunately, even early that morning as they both began to stir, they'd put their extra sleep time to better use.

Charlee couldn't help smiling, thinking of their night last night even as she yawned; it was completely worth the exhaustion as far as she was concerned. The speaker's monotonous tone as he explained this weekend's workshops didn't help either. She couldn't help but giggle when Hector was startled out of nearly dozing off when they introduced him to everyone as the newest member of the team.

The surprised expressions on everyone when he stood as he was asked and said a few things about himself, his love of the game, and how he felt about being on the team, didn't surprise her. Though catching the way two of the girls eyed him then whispered something to one another smiling silly wiped the smile off Charlee's face.

None of them had been aware this was going to be a workshop with scheduled tournaments between the team members. Hector had been scheduled early that afternoon while hers wasn't until later, which meant they'd be separated most of the day. The only good thing about it was that Charlee was now having visions of heading back to their room and taking a much needed nap while poor Hector had to go straight to his tournament.

Halfway through the briefing, Charlee's phone buzzed. She clicked on the envelope, holding it under the table so she wouldn't be caught reading her texts. It was from Gwen—her mom.

> I know you said you might not have time to visit, but I just wanted you to know Ted is not here this weekend. I'd love to see you if you get a chance, honey. I could even meet you somewhere if you'd prefer.

Her step-dad Ted was the reason Charlee hadn't made any effort to plan something with Gwen this weekend. Gwen had obviously read through her excuses about the visit being a busy one. Charlee was still angry at Ted because of the way he'd all but abandoned her step-brother Ryan.

Charlee really missed Gwen, and now that she'd be free of both chess and Hector for the morning, maybe meeting her for lunch wasn't such a bad idea.

> I'm free for lunch, but I don't have a car. Can you come here?

She glanced up as Hector took his seat again and looked at her curiously. Just then her phone buzzed again.

> Yes!!! =) I'll leave now and should be there by noon. <3

Feeling bad now that she'd even considered blowing Gwen off, when obviously she was anxious to see her, she texted her back with her hotel information and then reminded Gwen how much she'd missed her and loved her. Bad daughter.

When the briefing was over, Charlee walked Hector to the convention room where he was expected to be at A.S.A.P and explained to him about her change in plans.

"That was her texting me. We're gonna meet for lunch. She'll pick me up around noon, and then I gotta be back here later for my tournament."

Hector frowned, playing with her hair. "I guess I won't see you until tonight."

"Yeah, but it looks like tomorrow we get to sleep in again." She smiled, biting her lower lip.

He leaned in and licked her lower lip. "I vote we stay in tonight and order room service."

Her body was still spent from the night and morning they'd had, but already it came alive just thinking about getting back to the room with him.

She'd fallen asleep in the room when her phone pinged loudly. Charlee had purposely set the ringtone to loud because she had a feeling she'd doze off waiting for Gwen to arrive. Sitting up, she read the text from her. She was downstairs, waiting for her.

Surprised that she actually felt a little choked up when she saw her, Charlee hugged Gwen tightly. Gwen pulled away to look at her, her own eyes a bit watery. "Oh, honey, you look so good. I've always loved your curly hair, but this looks so pretty too."

Charlee smiled, nodding. Her full transformation hadn't been made until she'd moved out to California, so Gwen hadn't been privy to fully the new and improved Charlee until now.

They ate lunch at the restaurant right there in the hotel. The entire time their conversation had been pleasant enough with Charlee catching her mom up on everything about school and the chess thing. Her mom was noticeably surprised to hear about Hector.

Charlee showed Gwen the picture on her phone's screen saver. Charlee and Hector had taken a ton of cutesy pictures with both their phones of the two of them kissing and hugging, but she especially liked this one she'd taken accidently before either them were ready to pose. She'd been holding the camera up above them and didn't even realize she's snapped the picture of them staring into each other's eyes. It was the same one he chose to use as his own background picture for his phone.

"Very cute," Gwen said smiling as she stared at the photo. "So when do I get to meet him?"

"Not this weekend," Charlee took her phone as Gwen handed it back.

Explaining quickly, Charlee tried changing the subject. She knew it was as easy as bringing her mom back to the hotel and having them meet quickly, but it would be a fast hello and goodbye in the lobby, and Charlee wanted their meeting to be a little longer.

Moving on to other things, their conversation had already veered on the tense side when Gwen told her about Ted making more of an effort to see her step-brother, Ryan. Was that supposed to impress Charlee that the man was making an "effort" to spend time with his son, when nothing or no one was stopping him except himself?

But nothing brought the conversation to a faster screeching halt than Gwen's sudden and very blunt account. "I ran into Danny this week at the Chili House."

Charlee stared at Gwen, not sure why she felt the need share this with her now. Then Gwen reached into the paper bag she'd walked in with and pulled out an envelope with Charlee's name written on it.

"When I ran into him, I mentioned you would be in town this weekend and that I was keeping my fingers crossed I'd get to see you." She held the envelope out to Charlee. "He came by last night and asked me to please give this to you if I saw you."

Staring at the envelope, Charlee gulped hard, refusing to reach out for it. "I don't want it."

"Charlee, honey, he said he still feels terrible and that he really needs you to read this. I saw it in his eyes. He really is sorry. I haven't read it, but I think maybe if you could understand why things happened the way they did it might give you some closure."

"I have closure." Charlee said almost through her teeth. "I've had it since I left, and I do even more now that I have Hector. I don't need to relive that part of my life again."

She really didn't, especially not after having just relived the whole damn thing just this past week when she told Hector about it. She was so over it now. The last thing she needed was to hear why Danny had chosen her to invite to that party. She knew why. He'd be a sure win if he brought the freak. But she wasn't that person anymore. Even with all her faults and weaknesses, Hector loved her unconditionally. That's all she needed.

"I really think—"

"I said no."

Gwen lifted her hands in the air. "Okay, okay." she conceded. "Have it your way." Slipping the envelope back in the bag, her mom pulled out what looked like a scrap book instead. "I haven't had the heart to change anything in your bedroom since you left. But I did go through some of the old poems and photos you had on your corkboard, and I put this together for you." She smiled, handing the scrapbook over to Charlee.

This Charlee took happily. She opened it to the first page to a picture of her and her late nana—the woman responsible for introducing Charlee to the world of chess. Immediately, she felt overwhelmed with emotion.

"I was gonna say," Gwen said as Charlee glanced up at her and saw that her eyes were just as dampened with tears as Charlee's felt. "You might wanna wait until you're home to go through that. You're gonna need a box of tissues and a little privacy. I know I did as I put it together."

Deciding her mom was right, she glanced back at the photo one last time before closing the scrap book. With no room for it on the table, Gwen placed it back in the bag until they were done with lunch.

She walked her mom back to her car and hugged her tight. "Will you be home for Thanksgiving?"

Charlee shook her head. She'd warned her mother when she left she may not come back for a very long time. And even though she'd been ready to run home more than once, it was only to hide away from the entire world in her room like a hermit again, not because it was a place she yearned to return to. For now, she'd keep the thought to herself, but Charlee had no desire to step foot in the town of Heron's Nest ever again unless she wasn't forced to. "But maybe you could come out to California," Charlee offered, "if not for Thanksgiving maybe Christmas. You can meet Hector then."

Her mom smiled, understanding, and handed Charlee the bag with the scrapbook. They said their final goodbyes, and Charlee walked away with a strange lump in her throat. Knowing she'd be seeing Hector soon, she forced herself to snap out of her weird mood.

The rest of the weekend was as amazing as she imagined it would be. Their night and the next morning were as passionate as always. They did finally sleep soundly for a several hours Saturday night, and it was probably the best night's sleep Charlee had ever had.

Sunday afternoon, when they were packing up their things, Charlee pulled the scrapbook out. "What's that?" Hector looked at it curiously.

"A scrap book Gwen made me." He looked at her strangely. "My mom," she explained. "She was a single teen mom when I was born and still lived at home. We lived with my grandparents for the first eight years of my life. Everyone around me addressed her by her name, so I did too, and no one ever corrected me." Charlee turned back to the scrapbook. "Anyway, she said I should wait 'til I'm home with a box of tissues and some privacy to look through it. But I think I'll be okay," she sat on the bed.

"You want some privacy? I can go check us out while you look through it."

Shaking her head quickly, she patted the bed. "No, I've no secrets, and there's nothing in my past I'm hiding from you. Besides," she smiled as he sat down next to her, "I doubt she'd put anything bad in here."

"You sure? There might be some naked baby pictures in there." He smirked.

Charlee couldn't help laughing, even as she opened it to the same page that had choked her up yesterday. "I doubt there's any part of my body you haven't already seen or touched."

"Or kissed," he said, leaning in, and nibbled her ear, making her giggle even more. "Is that you?" He stopped nibbling and focused on the photo of her and her nana.

Nearly cringing at her nappy hair and big toothless smile, she nodded. She wouldn't say it because it was in the past and she was over it, but, geez, no wonder the neighborhood kids thought her such an oddball. She was only five, and already she was holding up the king from her very first win against her grandmother. Looking back now, her grandmother had probably gone easy on her, but Charlee remembered that while all the other kids were out playing tag or dressing up and having tea parties with their stuffed animals, Charlee spent her days studying her homeschool materials then trying to figure out how to master the game of chess.

"See what I mean by me being a little odd?" she said.

"You were a kid, Charlee. We were all a little odd at that age. I lost my front teeth around that age too. Is that your grandma?"

"Yep," she smiled. "Her uncle was a grandmaster, and she was one of the very first women to make the U.S. chess team. She taught me everything I know."

He smiled, staring at the picture a little closer. "Nice."

They flipped through the pages as she explained every poem or ticket stub her mom had included, but then she froze when she turned the page and saw the envelope from Danny. Staring at it, her heart thudded when Hector picked it up. He flipped it over. "It's sealed," he said.

"Yeah, um, Gwen said she wrote me a letter." Taking it from him as he handed it to her, her hand nearly shook. "I think I'll read this one in private. She can get pretty sappy."

Sticking it in her jeans pocket, she continued to look through the scrapbook with Hector though she could barely concentrate now. She didn't think Gwen had done it on purpose. Charlee had watched her as she'd placed the envelope back in the same bag. It was an honest mistake. Obviously, even Charlee hadn't thought twice about it when she took the bag from Gwen. She too had forgotten about the envelope being in there still.

As tempted as she was to just rip it up and throw it away, she was suddenly overwhelmed with curiosity. Curiosity killed the cat. Her grandmother's words suddenly sprang in her head. It's what she'd say every time she caught Charlee staring out the window at the neighbor kids playing jump rope. Any thoughts of getting the nerve up to go out there and play with them were squashed. The only neighbor kid she ever played with was Drew, Gwen's best friend's rambunctious platinum blond daughter.

Gwen and Drew's mom had gotten knocked up the same year. The only difference was Drew's dad stuck around and eventually married her mom. Luckily for Charlee, Drew's parents couldn't afford to live on their own, so they continued to live next door for years. Then when Drew's grandparents passed, her parents inherited the house and stayed there for good. That is until they divorced.

Going against her better judgment, Charlee left the envelope in her pocket. She'd let it simmer there for a little and decide what to do with it later.

As the day passed, the contents of her front pocket weighed heavier and heavier. What could Danny possibly have to say now that would make a difference? Why would he want to rehash something that was long over? It made no sense. While her head said she should just dump the envelope in one of the airport trash cans and be done with it, a part of her needed to know why he did it. Drew had been so sure his feelings for her were sincere. The conversations they'd shared as she sat in her closet on the phone with him for hours felt so real. Maybe Gwen was right. Maybe having some closure would finally let her leave it behind her once and for all.

Their flight was another late one, but at least with the time difference, they wouldn't arrive too late in California. Hector dozed off, and as tempted as she was to pull out the letter and just read it already, she couldn't chance Hector waking and possibly seeing who it was really from.

Unable to stand it anymore, she got up and headed for the bathroom. She'd read it and rip it up and be done with it. She didn't expect there'd be anything new that she and Drew hadn't already discussed in length, but, still, it was burning a hole in her pocket, and she had to know now.

After locking the bathroom door, she pulled the envelope out, ripped the side off, pulling the sheet of paper out, and braced herself.

CHAPTER 30

Charlee,

I've wanted for so long to apologize from the bottom of my heart for all the hurt that my actions caused you. If it hadn't been because I knew how close you were to Drew when she insisted you'd understand once she explained, I would have never agreed to go forward with it. It's unfortunate the way things went down, but we really had no choice. I swear to you like I did to Drew back then, I didn't know they were going to do everything they did on Facebook. I didn't realize how cruel they'd be about it. For the longest time, not a day went by that I didn't think about it. Before you left, Drew promised me you were over it. And even though she said I shouldn't ever contact you, that it would only bring back the ugly memories, I just had to. I really, REALLY needed to apologize to you personally, even if it is in the form of a letter. I want you to know that I meant it when I said you were special. I meant everything I said to you back then. I truly hope you have moved on and can someday forgive me.

Danny

Charlee had gone numb the moment she read Drew's name. There was no way, *no way*, this could be true. She crushed the letter in her hand. How dare he try to put this off on Drew, the one person besides Gwen and her grandmother she'd always trusted with her life? Drew was the best friend anybody could ask for, and she'd been just as devastated about this as Charlee had been. She even cried with her for days. For Danny to throw this on her—Drew insisted he go through with it? Horse shit!

As livid as she felt, she was glad now that she'd read it. Now she could accept what a worthless piece of shit Danny really was. He was still trying to feed her the crap about thinking she was special and meaning everything he'd said so sincerely back then. Did he really expect her to believe that when in the very same letter he accused Drew of being in on the whole thing—the worst thing that Charlee had ever had to live through?

Even as she walked back to her seat with the letter now crushed in her pocket, she felt a bit numb. She knew this was impossible. Drew would never do something like that to her. Charlee couldn't even think of an instance in which they'd have no choice but to go through with it.

She racked her memory now, thinking back to how it all had happened to begin with, and her stomach dropped a bit, remembering how Drew was the one who had encouraged her to accept the invitation that she'd already turned down. As much as she liked Danny, she was so excruciatingly shy she couldn't even imagine going to a regular party with him. But Drew was the one who insisted she go. Charlee had finally agreed but said she would only go if he asked again. There was no way she was bringing it up again, and secretly she hoped he wouldn't—that maybe he'd already asked somebody else. Then the very next day, he brought it up again.

With her heart starting to thump, she shook her head as she reached her row of seats. It was just a coincidence. There was no way in hell Drew would do something like that to her. No way, and she was done even entertaining the very idea.

They landed at LAX just before 9:00 p.m., but since their bodies were on Eastern Time, they were all still exhausted. Natalie picked up Walter while Abel and Drew picked up Hector and Charlee. As much as she hated saying goodbye to Hector, she could hardly wait to get to her bed. She was so exhausted.

She told Drew all about her weekend and even gave her some of the specifics of how she'd finally got to live out some of the hot fantasies she'd had of Hector. Drew giggled incessantly when Charlee told her about the way she'd woken Hector up on their flight there.

"Does not surprise me in the least that he's so damn hot in bed," Drew said as she pulled into a gas station. "I'm not gonna lie to you, Charlee, and this was before you two got together. So like we've always fantasized about the same guys in the past, and I wasn't breaking any girlfriend code or anything, but I'm just gonna admit it," she said as she parked and pulled the hand brake up. "I had a few pretty steamy fantasies of my own that involved Hector." She shrugged, opening her door. "You're one lucky girl. Your man is hot."

Charlee sat there as her friend walked around the car and swiped her credit card at the pump. Normally, this wouldn't have bothered her in the least, but given the crumpled letter in her pocket and the roller coaster of emotions she'd felt ever since she read it, her mind was still a bit dazed. Thoughts of Drew fantasizing about Hector continued to linger annoyingly for a few more minutes until Drew's phone ringing loudly startled her out of them.

"Is that my phone?" Drew asked from where she stood, pumping gas in her car.

"Yes," Charlee yelled out.

"Answer it if it's my dad. He's actually home tonight, and I told him to text me if he wanted me to pick something up for him on the way home. But he always calls instead."

Charlee glanced back at the screen on Drew's phone. Sure enough, Daddy flashed across it as it rang again. She picked up and answered. "Hi, Mr. Morris, this is Charlee. Drew is pumping gas right now."

"Hi, Charlee," he responded cheerfully. "I trust Drew was on time? She was worried she might not be."

"She was right there waiting when I came down the escalators." She smiled; already any negative thoughts of Drew were fading fast.

He told her what he wanted from KFC, and Charlee assured him she'd relay the message. When she hung up, she noticed the picture on Drew's screen and smiled. It was one Drew took just after they arrived at the airport this past summer. They both smiled big as Drew held up the phone in front of them and took it. Drew said the photo would represent their "new beginning."

Drew had taken a lot of pictures that day and in the ones that followed. That felt like a lifetime ago now, and Charlee searched her phone for more photos. Hitting something that popped up Drew's text message log, she froze when she saw Hector's name near the top. Was it possible that Drew knew another Hector? Not likely. Charlee would've heard about him already. But Drew would've mentioned it to Charlee if they'd ever texted. She hit his name and was certain now this had to be another Hector. There were way too many messages between them for Drew not to have mentioned this.

Feeling a little underhanded and guilty that she would suspect anything of not just Drew but Hector as well because he hadn't mentioned anything either, she glanced back to see where Drew was. She appeared to be wrapping it up, so Charlee scrolled up quickly and read a few of the exchanges.

Drew: Are you sure?

Hector: . . . Tempting. Very, VERY tempting but as much as I'd love take you up on that offer, I'm gonna have to pass on any of that from here on. It just feels wrong now.

Drew: Okay, but just so you know the offer stands indefinitely. Charlee can be . . . complicated. So just remember I'm your go-to girl, and I'm only a text away. ;)

The driver's side door opened, and Charlee set the phone down immediately, the blood thrumming against her ears loudly.

"So does he want me to get him anything?"

"Yes," Charlee said at the moment, unable to remember what her dad had asked for. "Uh," Drew started the car but didn't pull out. She stared at Charlee, waiting. "A chicken sandwich," Charlee finally said.

Whatever they talked about on their way to KFC and then back to Drew's house was a blur now. All Charlee could think of were the texts. There had to be an explanation. So why not just ask her? She couldn't. The fear that this might be what it actually sounded like was paralyzing. It just couldn't be true, but why hadn't either of them mentioned that they texted each other? Certainly Charlee would mention to Hector if she was texting with any of his friends, especially if his friends were making her very tempting offers that felt wrong. And what did he mean he needed to pass on them from here on? The offer stands indefinitely. What the hell was she offering him? His go-to girl?

Charlee rushed straight toward her room as soon as they got to the house.

"Aren't you gonna eat?" Drew asked.

"I need to unpack first," she said as she blew past Drew, the anger and feelings of betrayal mounting.

There was a knock on the door. "You okay?" Drew called from the other side.

"I'm fine," Drew said, reaching for the crumpled letter in her pocket.

"*Okay* . . ." Drew said, obviously picking up on Charlee's not so fine tone. "I'll be in the dining room with my dad if you wanna join us. You should before your sandwich gets cold."

Charlee couldn't even respond now that she reread the letter from Danny. If this were really true, if Drew were capable of doing this, tempting Hector with who knows what and telling him Charlee was complicated, then maybe she did know about the dog party beforehand.

Her mind raced now as she paced in her room. Could Hector have really done something with Drew, even if it now felt wrong and had turned Drew's offer down? She remembered his interest in Drew before he showed any in

Charlee. Her head buzzed with so many things coming to her now.

The day after the keg party, Charlee had gone back to bed, and Drew was gone when she woke. Then Drew had acted so weirdly when she got home, and Charlee had asked her where she'd been. Unable to take it anymore, she rushed out of her room, stopping only when she saw Drew's phone on the table in the front room. She picked it up and opened the text message log and clicked on Hector's name. She scrolled randomly, reading the first exchange it stopped on.

> **Drew: I can't believe you've never noticed. She so pathetically obvious about how lovesick she is!**
>
> **Hector: Yeah, well, kill me I hadn't. Maybe my mind being so preoccupied with another girl had something to do with it.**

"Are you . . ." Charlee looked up at Drew, who stood by the dining room entrance staring at Charlee holding her phone.

Hot tears blurred Charlee's vision now. Drew had been the number one advocate all her life for trying to convince Charlee she wasn't pathetic. Her using the word in describing her, and to Hector of all people, hurt more than her not telling her about the texts.

"Did you know about the dog party before I went to it?" Her words were a strained whisper. She could hardly believe she was saying them.

Drew's expression fell, and Charlee knew right then it was true. "Who told you?"

A numbing chill ran down her spine. This couldn't be possible. "Danny did. Is it true?"

She shook her head, but Drew's words said otherwise. "I couldn't tell you, Charlee."

Feeling as if her heart had just been ripped out of her chest, Charlee sucked in her breath but couldn't hold back the emotion any longer. "You knew?" Drew's own lip quivered now. There was no denying Charlee's worst nightmare. Drew had done the unthinkable and joined the bullies against her. "You knew and you let me go?" She raised her now-sobbing voice. "*Encouraged* me to when you knew I didn't even want to in the first place!"

Drew's dad came to the dining room doorway, looking very concerned.

"I wanted to tell you," Drew took a few steps toward her. "But I couldn't."

"Why? How could you let me go? How could you do that me?" The pain was so profound Charlee could barely breathe between sobs now.

Drew turned to face her dad then Charlee again. "I just couldn't. It wasn't supposed to turn out that way. You know I'd never hurt you like that, Charlee."

"But you did! You knowingly let me do something that you knew would humiliate me. You pushed me to do it!" She sobbed, unable to understand how she could be so wrong about Drew. Then she gasped and looked back down at Drew's phone in her hand. "You and Hector text?"

Drew's eyes became a little wider. "I didn't tell you because I thought you'd be mad."

"You think!" Charlee dropped the phone onto the sofa and spun around.

The mortification that possibly Drew had told Hector about the dog party and maybe he too knew that Drew had been in on it sunk in.

"Charlee, please let me explain," Drew hurried into her room behind her.

Charlee grabbed her still-packed carryon, her purse, and her keys and rushed out past Drew. "I'll send for the rest of my things."

"Don't go, Charlee. Please!" Drew sobbed. "I'm begging you. I'm *so* sorry."

Ignoring Drew's pleas, Charlee walked out of the room and stalked through the front room.

"It's late, Charlee," Drew's dad insisted now also. "Maybe you should wait until tomorrow morning if you really wanna leave."

"I'll be fine, Mr. Morris," she managed to say before walking out.

She wanted to thank him for his hospitality, thank him for allowing her to stay there rent-free all this time, but she couldn't. Her throat was so swollen it hurt. Saying the few words she had said alone was a struggle. Drew followed her all the way out, continuing to plead and apologize over and over.

Throwing her suitcase in the backseat of the car, she glanced back at Drew, who was now on her knees on her front lawn while her dad stood over her with one hand on her shoulder. "I love you, Charlee," she continued to sob.

Never, not in a million years, would Charlee be able to understand how Drew of all people could do this to her.

~*~

The continued buzzing woke Hector. Frowning, he glanced at his nightstand as his phone finally stopped buzzing. He laid his head back and began to close his eyes when the buzzing began again. Grumbling, he reached for it. It took a moment for his eyes to focus enough to read the name on the screen, but he sat up instantly when he saw it was Drew calling him.

"Hello?" he answered, hoping nothing was wrong.

Drew said something he couldn't understand through her sobs, but his heart was already racing. Something was definitely wrong. "What?"

"Is she with you?"

"Charlee? No? She's not with you?" Hector pulled his legs off to the side of his bed.

"She left about an hour ago. She was upset." Hector heard Drew take a deep breath and clear her throat in an attempt to speak more clearly. "I figured it would take a while to get to your place since I'm assuming that's where she's going unless she's headed straight to the airport."

"The airport?" Hector gripped his phone. "Why would she go to the airport? What's she upset about?"

"I couldn't tell her, Hector. I know she probably thinks I'm the worst person in the world, but I couldn't, and it killed me to not be able to, but I swear if I had known how things were going to turn out I would've never encouraged her to go to that party."

Hector stood up, bringing his hand to his confused head as he shook it. "What party? What are you talking about?"

"The dog party last year. She said she told you."

The puzzle came together suddenly, but he still didn't understand what Drew was saying exactly. "Yeah, she told me about it. So back up. What happened now?"

"She found out I knew it was one of those parties before she went and didn't tell her."

Everything Hector was trying to put together in his head stopped at once. "You knew?"

"Yes, but I couldn't tell her—"

"You fucking knew they were setting her up, and you still let her go?"

"I couldn't explain to her because my dad was here. I wouldn't have even cared if he found out about the picture I texted an old boyfriend of my tits, Hector. But I didn't want him to hear the rest."

The anger was already too overwhelming, and she was still saying things that made no sense to him. "What are you talking about? What does that have to do with you not telling your best friend she was being set up?" Thoughts of Charlee being out there right now possibly on a plane back home inundated him. He rushed to the window, hoping he'd see her car out there.

"Danny came to me and confessed about the party. He said he only asked Charlee because word had gotten around that he was talking to her and he was being pressured to invite her to it. He said he only had because he knew how shy she was and was certain she would turn him down, which she did."

Hector started out of his bedroom toward the front door. He hadn't seen Charlee's car from his window, but maybe he would if he walked outside. This shit was getting more confusing by the second. "I don't get it. She turned him down? So how she'd end up there anyway?"

"I convinced her to go."

Feeling even more disgusted with Drew, he understood completely now why Charlee would be so upset. He stopped at the top of his porch steps. "Why? Why would you do that?" Then it suddenly hit him. "How did she find all this out now?"

Drew was quiet for a moment then finally spoke again. "I don't know. All she said was Danny told her, so I'm assuming she saw him in Maryland this weekend."

Hector stopped once again at the bottom of the stairs and thought about that. Charlee had only mentioned meeting up with her mom on Saturday for lunch. She didn't say anything about seeing the asshole. He did remember thinking she seemed a little weird on the flight home and when they said goodbye tonight, but he'd assumed she was just as exhausted as he was.

"Hector, she didn't give me a chance to explain," she said, her voice cracking once again. "And I know it was awful of me, but I had no choice."

"What do you mean you had no choice? Of course you did. You know what?" he said ready to hang up on her ass. "I don't even wanna hear your bullshit reasons. What you did was *fucked up,* and I don't blame her for leaving. I don't care that you're feeling like shit right now either. You should be." Slammed with another realization, he stopped where this thought was going, his mind rewinding back to a few things that infuriated him even further. "Was this why you said you had to do this for Charlee as much as yourself?"

"Yes," she whispered.

"You selfish little bitch." The words flew out without thought. "So after you literally helped set up your best friend, the one you claim to care so much about and who deserves to be happy, you watched her fall apart, saw what it did to her, and then you brought her out here and took credit for making everything better. So you could feel better about *yourself?*"

"I do care for her!" She yelled. "What I did could not be helped. I feel terrible about it, yes, and does it help me feel better to see her happy? Yes! Because she *does* deserve to be. And you will listen to my reasons, damn it. You are no angel either. You know all about feeling guilty and wanting desperately to make up for it."

Hector didn't say anything, but he continued to listen to her, partly because she was right: he wasn't without his own faults, but mostly because she was hysterical now and he figured he may as well let her finish. But there was no way she'd let her lump them in the same category. He wouldn't even help set up someone he didn't know well much less one of his closest friends.

She was just about done with her explanation when his other line clicked and he saw it was Charlee. His heart jumped to his throat with excitement, but at the same time with the dread of hearing her cry. Because if Drew was hysterical about this, he knew Charlee must be too.

"That's her on the other line," he said quickly. "I gotta go."

"Call me back," was all he heard as he clicked to the other line.

"Charlee!" he said, bracing himself to hear her sob.

The last thing he expected was to hear a dude on the other end and the resounding words he said loudly. "You're an asshole. You know that? And I don't care if you are a badass boxer. If you were in front of me right now, I'd still take a fucking swing at you!"

CHAPTER 31

"Walter?"

"You suck!" Since the day Walter had thrown his own backpack at the fence after getting his ass kicked in front of Charlee, Hector hadn't heard him this wound up. "How could you do that to her, man? If I'd known this is what you were up to, getting your jollies by doing two best friends, I would've never agreed that I was okay with you asking her out."

"Whoa, whoa—" Hector tried to interrupt, but Walter kept on.

"Charlee's not like one of those skanky whores you're used to dating, okay? She's a nice girl, and she doesn't deserve for some asshole stud like you to come along and trample on her—"

"Dude! What the hell are you talking about? I didn't trample anything! Everything's cool with Charlee and me."

"Oh, you call banging her best friend behind her back cool?"

"What!"

"If everything is so cool with you two, why is your girlfriend passed out on my bed right now after crying herself to sleep?"

Hector spun around, already on his way up his porch steps. "She's in your bed right now?"

"Yes. She said she didn't know where else to go, but she did say she's driving home tomorrow. You know how long that's gonna take her? All because not even Charlee was enough for you."

Hector rushed through his house and into his room. Holding his phone between his shoulder and his ear, he pulled off his shorts and pulled on a pair of jeans. "She is enough for me, Walter. I don't know where she got the idea that I'm doing anything with Drew."

He sat down and pulled on some socks, wondering if maybe Charlee was too embarrassed to admit to Walter why she was really so upset.

"It's not an idea. She read the texts between you and Drew. That's proof, so don't try to worm your way out of this one, asshole."

Read the texts? Hector stood up after slipping on his shoes. "Okay, first of all, you really need to stop calling me that," he said, more annoyed now than ever. The fact that Charlee was in another guy's bed right now was already annoying as shit, even if was Walter's. "Second, I have no clue what texts she's talking about."

He sort of did, but he wasn't going to tell Walter about his and Drew's combined effort to help set Walter and Natalie up so he'd be free to go after Charlee. He slipped a white t-shirt on that was too damn tight, but he didn't have time to look for another one.

Walter let out an exasperated breath. "Hector, the jig is up. She read a text where you told Drew it was very tempting to continue doing what you two had been doing but it didn't feel right anymore."

Hector froze in place. "*Shit!*"

"Yeah, shit," Walter agreed, disgustedly. "I can't believe you. Is it really that difficult to keep it in your—"

"She didn't read the whole thing?" Hector grabbed his keys, glad Abel was out *taking care of business* again tonight and his mom was still in Mexico; otherwise, they might try to stop Hector from leaving.

"She said she didn't get a chance to read all the texts, but what she did read was enough. And she said she wouldn't put anything past her ex-best friend anymore. Said she's not the person she thought she was and she doesn't trust her at all. She's even dropping out of both chess teams. Says she wouldn't be able to stand being around you. Talk about screwing with someone's life for your own selfish reasons."

Hector rushed out the front door, trying not to panic too much. He stopped for a second to lock the door. "It's not what she's thinking. She'd know this if she'd have read the whole text. And she's not dropping out of anything. Give me your address, and I'll explain to her when I get there."

"You're coming here now?"

"Yeah," Hector rushed around his truck.

"No! She'll be mad that I told you where she was. Plus she doesn't wanna see you right now, and I don't think—"

"Listen to me, Walter," Hector spoke very firmly now as he climbed in behind the wheel of his truck. He'd been patient enough with Walter. While he appreciated Walter's concern over Charlee, there was no fucking way he was letting her leave or drop out of any teams, especially now that he knew why Drew had done what she'd done. He only prayed now that Charlee would agree Drew really hadn't had a choice and stay. "I have the texts. You can read them when I get there if you want, but nothing is going on between me and Drew, and nothing ever has. I'm in love with Charlee. I meant it when I said I was done with other girls. Now would you please give me your *gadamn* address so I can explain all this to her."

Walter told him he'd text it to him, and after waiting for what seemed like an eternity, Hector began to wonder if the jackass had changed his mind. Just when he was getting ready to call him back and tell him off, the text with the address came through.

Taking what felt like the deepest breath he'd ever taken, Hector skidded out of his driveway, ready to do or say whatever he had to make Charlee stay.

~*~

Feeling the familiar soft kiss against her temple and her hair being caressed, Charlee smiled. Then her eyes flew open, and she sat up suddenly, whacking her head against someone else's. "Ow!" They both said at the same time.

She massaged the spot on her head, realizing it was Hector whose head hers had just collided with. He sat there on the edge of the bed, his fingers at his own temple wearing a very pained expression. As nice as it was to see him first thing when she opened her eyes, reality hit and she began kneeing him until he toppled off the bed.

"Why are you here?" she demanded, sitting up on the edge of the bed now. "How did you know I was here?"

She turned to a remorseful-looking Walter and let her shoulder drop in utter disgust. "Isn't there *anyone* I can trust anymore?"

"You can trust me," Hector said, standing up.

Refraining from giving into the urge to kick him, she glared at him. "Really?"

"Yes, babe." Hector held his hands up in front of him. "Look, I know what you're thinking, but you have it all wrong. There are a few things I do need to come clean about, but none are as bad as what you're imagining." Charlee stood up ready to bolt. If she had to get a room for the night, she was prepared to, but she wasn't about to stand here and listen to him *come clean*. She already knew enough. "Please, Charlee, I have proof that I didn't do anything with Drew."

"Oh, and what is that? You're going to bring her in here to attest to that? Are you both gonna stand here and tell me that neither of you are as bad as all those bastards that made my life miserable? Because I know the truth about her now and about you, Hector!" She cried. "Walter told me every bit of it!"

The stunned look on his face made the hurt in her heart even deeper because he didn't deny it. She'd still hung on to the hope that maybe it wasn't true. Maybe Walter had misinterpreted things. Maybe Hector wasn't just like Danny.

But, no, she could see the truth in his guilty eyes. He was *just* like him, only worse. At least Danny didn't think he'd deserved to kiss Charlee after the party.

Seeing Hector's Adam's apple move as he gulped hard, she tried not to fall apart completely. "I've apologized to Walter, Charlee." He turned to Walter his face pale now and full of regret. "Did you tell her that too?"

Walter nodded. "I did and that you weren't the one actually harassing me, just your friends."

When Walter had mentioned this earlier, she felt sorry for him. Just as she'd been so quick to glorify Danny's noble behavior because he hadn't actually thrown food at her like the other kids, Walter gave into the obvious man crush he had on Hector and overlooked that he allowed his friends to treat him that way—ostracize him until he dropped out of school. Now it pissed her off.

"Oh well, take a bow, Mr. Ayala," she said, her words dripping with venom now. "I guess that makes you better than them. But don't talk to me about proof, Hector, because if you think I'm going to believe a word Drew says—"

"You don't have to! I can show you the texts."

"I've seen the texts!" She tried walking by him.

"Charlee, it's true," Walter said. "He showed me. You didn't read the whole thing, but it's really not what you're thinking."

Pathetically, Charlee felt a glimmer of hope that maybe, at the very least, this part was explainable. She turned to Hector, her chest now heaving. She was so worked up.

"I can explain it," Hector said, the remorse still so heavy in his eyes that it scared her. "I can't take back what happened in high school with Walter, but I swear to you I tried to make up for it. I nearly sacrificed the best thing that's ever happened to me just so I could make up for it. And that's *you*, Charlee."

Charlee turned to Walter, wondering why he hadn't told her this, but he looked just as lost as she felt.

"Have a seat please and I'll explain," Hector said then turned to Walter. "You too. I have something I need to come clean to you about also."

Confused, Charlee and Walter exchanged glances then took a seat on Walter's bed. Suddenly, Hector seemed nervous, and that made her nervous again. Did she even want to hear this?

To her surprised, he addressed Walter first. "Walter, I think I've been in love with Charlee since the night of the speed tournament. I tried to fight it. I really did." Charlee, whose weak heart was already swelling, stared at him, trying not to give in so easily. He turned back to her now. "I felt so guilty about the shit my friends had done to Walter in high school I just couldn't justify going after the girl he was so infatuated with."

"Dude," Walter said, squirming in his seat.

"It's okay, man." Hector assured him. "She already knows, but only because I had to tell her." Feeling the need to, Charlee smiled at Walter, and he glanced away quickly, obviously embarrassed. "Anyway," Hector continued, his attention back on Charlee now. "That's why the texts between Drew and me started. Your friend really does have a sixth sense. She was right about me, and she was also right about Danny."

The smile completely vanished as Charlee stared at him, confused now. "She came to 5th Street the day after the keg party." He smiled a little crooked. "She called me an asshole. She said she knew I had feelings for you but was under the impression that I just didn't want to commit to one girl." Now he turned to Walter and explained the whole Operation-get-Nat-and-Walt-together scheme.

"You and Drew planned that?" Charlee asked, surprised it never occurred to her that her scheming friend had had a hand in that.

"Yeah," Hector winced. "But that's a good thing, right, Walt? Things turned out beautifully."

Walter smiled, nodding, so Hector turned back to Charlee and explained the texts. "She was offering to text me a list of your favorite things, but it didn't feel right to continue being sneaky when I didn't have to anymore. But there was never anything inappropriate about our texts. I can show you them, and you could read them all from the very first to the very last."

Relief sunk in, and she could already tell her heart would be willing to overlook his past mistakes about not standing up for Walter. Walter seemed to be okay with it, and Hector did make a great effort to make it up to him and do right by Walter by staying away from Charlee for so long. She could certainly attest to that. He did try to keep things between them from happening for *too* long. Sadly, it didn't change the fact that Drew had still betrayed her in such a horrific way.

"Are we good?" Hector asked, looking very worried still. "I think I covered it all, but tell me if you need anything else clarified."

She stood up now, anxious to hug him and so incredibly happy that at least *he* hadn't betrayed her. Immediately his arms were around her, and even though they'd just spend the entire weekend together, it felt as if she hadn't been in his arms in so long. He kissed her softly, and after the kisses they'd shared all weekend, she got the distinct feeling he was holding back, but she didn't blame him. They were standing in Walter's room, and he was sitting there watching them.

"But now I have a question for you," he said as he pulled away. The worried expression was back. "Did you go see Danny when we were in Maryland?"

"No." She shook her head immediately but braced herself to tell him the truth. "That letter I said was from Gwen," she paused, waiting for him to nod. "That was from him. Gwen ran into him last week, and she mentioned I'd be in town and was hoping to get together with me. So the night before, he brought it to her and asked her to give it to me. She brought it to our lunch, and the only reason I didn't tell you it was from him was because, at the time, I wasn't planning on even reading it, so I didn't think it mattered."

Charlee paused once again because the emotion of knowing what Drew had done overwhelmed her again. Before she could continue, he pulled her to him again and kissed her head. "I know that had to be a blow, babe."

She shook her head. "I didn't even believe it at first. I thought for sure Danny was lying, and then she admitted it." Charlee glanced away, wiping the tears that had once again begun.

"Charlee, please don't be mad at me, okay?"

Not liking the sound of that, her brows furrowed, and she stared at him. "What?"

"Drew is outside." She pulled away from him. "Listen to me, baby," he said, reaching for her and holding her to him. "She explained it to me, and trust me, I felt ready to spit when she first told me about what she'd done too. But after hearing her explain why, I think, maybe, you'll understand."

She shook her head. "There's *nothing* that could excuse what she did."

Hector bobbed his head from side to side. "Well, maybe not, but I think you should at least hear her out. If I really didn't think you'd understand, I would've told her to go to hell instead of where she could find you. But it's up to you."

Suddenly choked up, Charlee wanted nothing more than there to be a good reason for what Drew did, not just so she could forgive her, but so that her heart wouldn't hurt so much. It literally ached, mourning the loss of her best friend.

Visions of Drew on her knees, sobbing on her front lawn came to her now. If that wasn't genuine regret, she didn't know what was. She nodded and followed Hector outside. Drew stood across the street, leaning against her car. She straightened out when she saw Charlee.

"I'll wait here to give you your privacy if you want, but if you prefer, I can go with you too," Hector said, squeezing her hand. "Up to you."

She smiled, feeling a little shaky already but decided she needed to do this alone. "I'll be okay by myself."

Drew started toward her when she saw Charlee coming to her, and they met at the curb. Drew's face was a mess, and Charlee hated that she already felt like hugging her. For a moment, she didn't even care why Drew had done it. She could see it in her friend's sorrowful eyes she regretted it immensely, and that's all that mattered.

"They had a picture of me," Drew began her voice so broken it choked Charlee up instantly, and she brought her hand to her mouth in an effort to not break down too. "The one I'd sent of my breasts to that asshole Greg I'd gone out with. Apparently, he'd forwarded to someone who was threatening to go viral with it. When you turned Danny down the first time, he came to me to confess about the party and asking you to it, but only because he knew you'd say no. He didn't want to do it. They were pressuring him. They told him to ask me to try and convince you, and if I didn't, the picture would go viral."

Charlee nodded. She understood why Drew felt she *had* to. It made total sense. She'd be applying for college the very next year. That could've ruined her.

"I told them to fuck themselves and I didn't give a shit about the picture." She shrugged. "There were more scandalous things out there than a girl flashing her boobs. I'd live. Danny was really happy. He thought for sure I'd agree to convince you."

Charlee stared at her confused now. "But you did."

Drew nodded. "He went back and told them what I'd said, and few days later, he came to me again." She scrunched her face up and looked away. "You remember what was going on around that time with my mom and my brother's coach, right? My dad was already so devastated." She shook her head. "Well, my idiot mother and that fucking coach taped themselves having sex. Someone got a hold of that too, and they were threatening put a like-mother-like-daughter video together, alternating my stupid tit's picture with her video and going viral with that. They sent me a snippet of the disgusting video, and there was no way I could let my dad to see it or be publicly humiliated that way.

"Danny assured me that it was an inside-joke thing and that you would never even know it. He said all the girls at these parties never knew about it, and they kept it on the down low so the next year when it happened again no one would know. It's the only reason I agreed to do it." Her face suddenly crumbled again. "I wanted to die when they did what they did on Facebook," she cried. "I swear I wanted to kill all of them. I went to Danny's house and physically attacked him, but he swore to me he didn't know they were going to do that. I didn't believe him, until there was this huge brawl at school, and I found out it was Danny and his closest friends against some of the bigger assholes behind the whole Facebook thing. It really divided the whole," she lifted her fingers to do an air quote, "popular crowd at school after that. I wanted to tell you so many times, but I just couldn't. You were so devastated. I was terrified you wouldn't understand. And earlier when you confronted me about it, I couldn't tell you because my dad was there. I just—"

Charlee hugged her, and Drew cried openly now against her shoulder. She'd heard enough. As hurt as she'd been just hours ago, she now felt for Drew and all she must've been going through herself that entire last year. "I love you, Drew, and I understand why you did it now."

Drew squeezed her tight. "Please tell me you're not going back home."

Charlee smiled, feeling an enormous and complete relief come over her now. For several horrifying hours there, she really believed she'd lost her best friend and her first love all at once.

"No, I'm not going home. Are you kidding? And give up our new beginning? Not a chance."

They both glanced back at Hector, who stood at Walter's stairs. His muscles were bulging a little through his tight t-shirt, and he was smiling at them now. "You'd be nuts to walk away from that hot thing too. He really is a dream, Charlee, and not just because of his looks. He truly cares about you."

Charlee mouthed the word, "I love you," and Hector mouthed them back.

"He is," Charlee sighed deeply, feeling completely drained but more content than she ever had in her life. "He really is."

EPILOGUE

A four-day cruise was exactly what Hector and Charlee needed after the grueling Junior World Olympiad. As a team, they came in second, which was excellent because they hadn't even been expected to place in the top three. The Ukraine had been favored all along to take it all, and they did. But the U.S. pulled a major upset against Hungary, and now Hector and Charlee could celebrate in style.

Charlee had actually taken first in one of the longer tournaments. It was very impressive. Hector had been so proud of her he'd skyped Sam, even though it was about four a.m. in Florida to say, "In your face!" when she beat out the contender Sam was so sure would take it.

The cruise was nice; although, they were sharing a cabin with Abel. So they had to get really creative and sneaky about any alone time in bed. As freaky as Charlee thought she was, doing anything with Abel in just the other bed in the cramped cabin was not going to fly. Not to mention Abel had warned Hector before they even boarded he didn't want to be walking in on anything or waking up to anything that would make things awkward for the rest of the cruise. He'd actually told Hector to keep it in his pants for the weekend. *That* wasn't happening, not with the incredibly romantic sunsets, dinners, and general atmosphere of the cruise. So far their creativity had come up short.

They were up on the top deck now, looking out into the moonlight. They'd be docking in Ensenada in just a few hours. They really should be in bed already. It was late, but Charlee had insisted on going up there to take a look at the stars. It was such a clear night you could see them twinkling as far as forever.

Hector stood behind Charlee, hugging her as she leaned against the rail, looking out into the ocean. "I don't think I've ever been so content in my life," she said, taking a deep breath and leaning her head back into his chest.

She echoed his sentiments exactly. Although he wouldn't ruin such a romantic moment by mentioning what would make this moment even more perfect, he did glance around to make sure no one else was up there with them. The top deck was completely abandoned, and it was well after 2 a.m., so he didn't expect anyone else joining them anytime soon. He kissed her lower chin, and she tilted her head in reaction, granting him further access to her neck.

"Happy anniversary," he whispered.

Her body suddenly went stiff. "Anniversary?"

He smiled, kissing her neck again, a little smug that he had one up on her. He knew coming into this new world of being in a relationship that this is the kind of stuff girls usually kept track of, not the guys, and he had a feeling he'd suck at it since he was so bad at remembering birthdays even. Though he had to admit it was Roni and the other girls who teased him just before the cruise about actually being with the same girl for months now that had made him check a calendar out of curiosity. The weekend just before they moved into their new house—the day he'd gone and picked her up and they made it official after eating grilled cheese sandwiches from a truck was exactly six months ago today.

She turned around to face him, looking a little worried. "Yep," he said, kissing her nose. "Today is six months since we made this official."

Her eyes brightened now. "You're keeping track?"

Though she smiled, she sounded as if she felt a little guilty, so he let her off the hook. "Not so much," he pulled her closer. "Roni and the girls brought it up just before the cruise, and I had to look it up. But six months, huh? Feels like just yesterday that I couldn't keep my eyes off you at that tournament."

"And you couldn't keep your hands off those two girls," she teased with a smirk, though there was a hint of distaste in her eyes.

So many times Hector had wanted to explain to her that nothing had ever happened between them except for the kisses they shared in the parking lot that night, but he never thought it a good idea to bring up. He'd just as soon let her forget about that and had since decided to never revisit it. How the hell was that coming up now, on this most romantic of nights on a cruise ship, in the middle of their anniversary talk?

Charlee spun herself around slowly in his arms to face the ocean again. "I know you think I did, but I didn't actually ever do more than what you saw in that parking lot with them." She didn't say anything, and he was almost glad she wasn't facing him now. "I told you about Sam getting in a wreck just before he moved, right?"

He filled her in on how it had happened that very day and he'd had to cut his night short as soon as he turned on his phone and got the news.

"But you would've otherwise, right?" Without giving him a chance to answer, she added. "I take it with the amount experience you have with those types of girls you've done a lot of crazy things in the past." Just when Hector thought the conversation might be taking a turn into the uncomfortable, she moved her ass against him, rubbing him in just the right place, instantly arousing him. "Ever done it out in the open where you just might get caught?"

The second it hit him what she might be suggesting, the tension he'd begun to feel bubbled over into smoldering need. Bringing his hand down to the bottom of her adorable one piece shorts suit, he ran his hand up her bare thigh and leaned in to her ear. "Not out in the open . . ." he whispered. "Like here."

Feeling her tremble, he brought his hand all the way up her thigh and around to feel her bare behind. His heart sped up when he realized she wore nothing underneath. He'd been around her all day, saw the jumpsuit she'd chosen to wear, the one he'd at first mistaken for a very short sundress because the shorts were so loose, and not once had it crossed his mind that maybe she'd worn it for a reason. "Did you have something in mind today with this outfit and no panties?" Unable to stand it anymore, he squeezed her ass.

She giggled in spite of the tense reaction her body had to his question. "Maybe."

With a near growl, he sucked her neck, bringing his hand around the front and between her legs. She gasped but still spread her legs for him. Hearing her made him even crazier, and he rubbed what was now fully erect and throbbing against his shorts on her behind.

His perfectly freaky little girlfriend swayed her hips, driving him even more insane. Glancing around again to make absolutely sure there was no one around, he moved quickly, pulling a condom out of his wallet and himself out of his shorts. Amazed at the easy access the loose and stretchable fabric of her shorts provided, he effortlessly bent her over then slid right in.

Glancing around again, he could hardly believe they were doing this. If they got caught and he got arrested or something—he wasn't sure what the penalty for this would be. His mother would have his head on a platter, not to mention the *guerita* she now adored would be flung from the pedestal she now sat atop. But this felt so damn good, and the added eroticism of doing this in public place only added to the excitement. There was no way he was stopping now.

He plunged in and out, pulling her by the waist so he could get in as deep as possible. Shushing Charlee because her panting and moans began to get a little loud, he had to smile at what a fucking lucky guy he was. He was certain he knew plenty of girls who'd be up for something like this, but he knew it'd never be as good as with Charlee. This wasn't just about what he was feeling physically.

Helping any girl to live out her wildest dreams, and this no doubt had been one of Charlee's, would be a dream in itself. But doing so with the girl you were utterly in love with, well, there was just no explaining how that felt on an emotional level, especially given Charlee's past, fragile self-image. He loved that she said no one would ever make her feel as he did. And, damn it, he'd make sure no one ever got the chance to.

She was *his*.

He pumped her harder.

All his.

He slammed in again.

Now and forever.

And again with a groan as she spread even more for him.

Normally when they did it this way in private he'd bring his fingers around front to give Charlee the added pleasure of playing with her as he fucked her, but there was no time for that now. As good as this felt and as dazed as it made him feel, he still had enough presence of mind to worry that someone might walk up the steps to the deck any moment now.

Seeing Charlee take the initiative and use her own fingers for her added pleasure only furthered his excitement, and he knew he'd be a goner way sooner than he anticipated. Feeling her body tremble and hearing her soft moaning, knowing she was nearly there, was all it took. He drove into her one last time with a groan, clenching his teeth and squeezing his eyes shut in reaction to his massive and heart-pounding release.

Unable to stay in her and enjoy it for a while as he normally would, he had to pull out and clean up. Taking the few steps it took to the trash can, he could feel his legs were like noodles now. Any strength he had earlier had completely drained from them. He turned back to Charlee, who leaned against the railing, still catching her breath.

Walking up behind her, he wrapped his arms around her delicate little waist and rested his chin on her shoulder, staring out into the ocean. "Did you plan this since this morning?"

She didn't answer, so he glanced at her face, and she was smiling. "You did, didn't you?" He squeezed her tighter.

"Actually," she smiled even bigger, "Drew and I went out in search of this outfit weeks ago."

He pulled away, his mouth falling open, and she giggled. Charlee had told him that, after the truth came out about Drew knowing about the party, the two had made a vow to never be afraid to tell each other *anything*. Charlee said if she would have known going to the party was going to help Drew keep that video from going viral she would've agreed to go in a heartbeat. So if Drew hadn't been afraid to tell Charlee in the first place, it would've saved them both much heartache. But Hector wasn't aware Charlee was telling her *everything*—even her fantasies.

She turned to him and cupped his face with her hands. "I just said I was looking for something with easy access, but I didn't tell her exactly what I had in mind. *That* I save for only you."

He pulled her to him, loving the way that sounded. "Only me?"

She smiled, kissing him softly. "Yep, *only* you—forever."

A NOTE TO MY WONDERFUL READERS

To all my wonderful readers, I hope you enjoyed reading Hector and Charlee's story. Please take a moment to leave a review on Amazon.

The first two books in the <u>5th Street</u> series, <u>Noah</u> and <u>Gio</u>, are also available.

Next in this series: <u>Abel</u>

If you haven't already read them, please check out the books in my first series, <u>*The Moreno Brothers,*</u> *which are* available now!

<u>Forever Mine</u>—Angel and Sarah's story

<u>Always Been Mine</u>—Alex and Valerie's story

<u>Sweet Sofie</u>—Sofia and Eric's story

<u>Romero</u>—Romero and Izzy's story

<u>Making You Mine</u>—Sal and Grace's story with a bonus Angel and Sarah short story.

My latest is the Fate Series.

Fate is a spinoff series of my first series, The Moreno Brothers. For those of you who are familiar with my books, there will be more in the *Fate* series, including other characters from the MB series whose stories need to be told because we never got to find out what happened to them. Stay tuned and visit my blog for more information on this.

<u>Fate</u>

ACKNOWLEDGMENTS

As always, thanks to my wonderful husband and kids who have now become well accustomed to the "the rules" when I'm working. And I appreciate that you understand why it's necessary for me to work such late hours sometimes. You can't just turn off my muse. He's funny that way. I love you all for being so patient and understanding.

To George—thank you so much for your extensive knowledge of the world of chess. I never realized there was a whole other world out there. Thank you for allowing me to pick your brain and for putting up with all my endless questions. My head was spinning at times from your highly enlightening responses, but I am eternally grateful that I had a real person walking me through this rather than me having to look it all up on my own. Cheers!

To my critique partner and good friend, New York Times best-selling author Abbi Glines—I'm blessed to have a superstar author like you reading my work and giving me feedback. And the biggest perk is I get to read all your stuff before it's out too! Don't be hatin', everyone. ;)

To my beta readers, Dawn Winter, Judy DeVries, and Emily Lamphear, you're all just an amazing group of women, and I feel so blessed to have found you. Aside from always being floored at how quickly you all read the MS and just as quickly have a full report back to me, you have all slowly become very special to me. I really don't know what I'd do without you guys! I look forward to working with you on all my other projects!

To my one-stop superhero beta reader/editor/formatter and listener to all my whiny rants/vents and obsessive worrying Theresa (Eagle Eyes) Wegand! You have truly been God sent, and I'm so, so glad I found you. Your work is impeccable, and I can't say enough about it. Thank you so much!

A special shout out to "my girls," my very special group of authors who without you I think I'd be insane by now. You really are the only ones who truly *truly* "get it." Thank you for the support, love, and *always* being there, ready to say the perfect thing when I need to hear it most. I love you!

And, of course, my incredibly awesome readers! Thank you so much for your continued support, emails, messages, and comments, which always seem to come at the most perfect time, making me smile and sometimes even tear up. I love you guys, and I can't wait to get the next one out to you!!

About the Author

Elizabeth Reyes was born and raised in southern California and still lives there with her husband of almost nineteen years, her two teens, her Great Dane named Dexter, and one big fat cat named Tyson.

She spends eighty percent of time in front of her computer, writing and keeping up with all the social media, and loves it. She says that there is nothing better than doing what you absolutely love for a living, and she eats, sleeps, and breathes these stories, which are constantly begging to be written.

Representation: Jane Dystel of Dystel & Goderich now handles all questions regarding subsidiary rights for any of Ms. Reyes' work. Please direct inquiries regarding foreign translation and film rights availability to her.

For more information on her upcoming projects and to connect with her (She loves hearing from you all!), here are a few places you can find her:

Blog: authorelizabethreyes.blogspot.com

Facebook fan page:
http://www.facebook.com/pages/Elizabeth-Reyes/278724885527554

Twitter: @AuthorElizabeth

Email EliReyesbooks@yahoo.com

Add her books to your Good Reads shelf
She enjoys hearing your feedback and looks forward to reading your reviews and comments on her website and fan page!

Printed in Great Britain
by Amazon